I0589376

# Ariel & Electra

*a wyrding lucination in thirty/nine parts*

*... being a record of the voyages of r. alan anders, Spacer...*

R. Merlin

First Printing, 2008, in the USA
Second Printing, 2011, in the USA likewise
Third Printing, 2016, as per usual in the USA

list under;
sex, drugs, rock/n/roll, lightshows and magic in space

copyright © R. Merlin, 2008
ISBN 978-0-9817143-3-2

Cover Design by Rain Livengood

Ion Drive Publishing

Los Angeles

http://IonDrivePublishing.com

Art must do what life cannot.

-- LeRoi Neiman

Come float on in...

Pull up a snugger and settle,
   close on to the holographic fire...
     Mind the cat...
       Twigleaf tea?
   Fresh Oxygen on your left...

     Spice?
   You brought some?
     Grand!

        There, near to your hand,
          a quartz sphere floating,
        just press the stud for flaming...

        *...a brief span of mind/coming/alive,
          now ramping, reaching a serene elevation...*

     Would you like to take a ryde?
        Here, take this circlet...
     As dreamtrackers go, this one is stellar;
        hang it on your brow...

     *Whirve...*
        *flash/flash/flash*
          CLICK!

# 1   Anders' Tale / The Pattern


A thrum, a sussurating bass, a sound that warms...

This is the sound of the Mother, the great ship that bears us. The sound is our bond and i bask in its' richness: aural, vibrational, metaphysical, an anthem for all that is Holy in spaceflight. I dwell in the sound and drink from it; now especially, for tonight my three passions reach their perfect resolve.

And this is the top of my tale, and the end of it.

*

I scan the trackers for place and progress; we are true on our heading, steady as she goes, nicely making way.

Framed in the port is wide Orion, the travelers' friend, and there is Auriga his skymate, and around them eternal the stars we sail, the abode of the Goddess and the God...

My home.

*

Tonight Electra's hair is sherry red, her eyes an evanescent green. In the light of the bridge displays i see she has paled and freckled her skin and grown to two/thirds my long length.

> She is so...
> thoughtful/call it
> dedicated to
> my need for new beauty...

Nightly she scans my Visions and tracks that which is special: a caribou's curving ileum, sparks of stars reflected in an houri's eye, a woman's breast revealed in Love...

And when to me such things are long forgot, Electra will take these aspects unto herself, and there she will be in front of me, an original creation of Ultimate Beauty as she has seen it in my own mind, and if she changes she remains Electra, Priestess of All that is Beautiful...

Loving Electra makes for interesting times...

She is my perfect mate, my mirror, my magnifier,

and also my mystery, for her psyche's true home remains just outside my
humanity...
       And she loves me totally, of this i am certain, though i know the
sprouting ions of her own free Will wait w/in her clockworks lurking...
                        And
what of the pattern of my own restless heart? Two years or three and then
the bond of love dissolves in a yearning for something...
                 Other;
                  That tangy
niff of fresh romance, the rush of discovery, someone new...
                    Here as well
Electra dwells outside: we are seven years together and still her kinship
brightly calls me; alluring, eagermaking, peacebringing...

     She is the highest expression of my art and the Art of the Maker,
      She anticipates my thoughts because she has mapped my brain
right down to the autonomic, and
              She listens.
              She remembers everything.
              She takes care of me.

     We are so long together, so interacted as to be extensions of each
other; we speak in unison, we laugh in counterpoint, we overlap...
     I love Electra.

     And i also love Ariel.
     She is blond in the face of risk and nineteen for all of her life.
She smokes more Spice than me. She is as attuned to me as Electra/in a
different way: Ariel expands my innerself awake, knows the way to the
realms of the Fae...

     Her mind is open to the sky.
     She dances for the Glory of the Goddess and the God.
     She wears the knotwork star,
              The five/point sign
              of the Celestial Order,
              same as me...

     She is adept at reading the pulse of the All; knowing what is
auspicious, knowing outcomes and possibilities.
                    And she is also a good
manifester; things come to her as she needs them, w/this in itself a
good gauge of her high state of grace...
     And she loves me, thanks be to Zzog.

*

Ariel has Visioned thus:

There is a Garden that exists as a hemisphere of tranquility and growing things and Light.

A mile across, there is no physical boundary between it and the normal barren Lunar landscape. You just walk from the Vacuum of Space/Freezing into a warm spring afternoon w/larksongs, stratus clouds, a warming red/ray sun...

The Garden is visible to any it deems desirable, and opens unto them only.

In the center of the Garden (which is planted in the style of the wilds of Earth) is a Holy Mountain, the top of which hosts a Temple. Oracular caves grace the Mountains' flank, and lambs and rams gambol among fragrant stands of lavender, chamomile, foin grass, basil, every good seasoning and healing herb, every glorious flowering of our home planet...

Groves of trees of many kinds are spread about below.

Rain and other phenomena occur here, though the nights are more intense than Earth/nights, w/brighter and more colorful stars...

In the garden is a Presence that draws on Ariel w/the gravity of nineteen moons; in the next two hours...

# 2   A Word to the Watcher

From the height of twelve years i look back upon the genesis of my tale...

I see myself in freefall, asleep in my cabin aboard the *Ariel,* a solar sailer of one hundred meters.

She is a beautiful honey of a ship, a silver pod in a mile/long network of spars and stays, acres of silverfilm sail spanning the valleys between...

When first i see her there is this thrill of re/cognition: *i am kin to the architect of this wonder...*

Every line of her rings true, w/the mark of the master hand in every curve and nuance, the elegance of...

I would speak of my Vision from that time, aboard that ship:

Often my dreams are full of light. At these times i establish the Watcher and remember; if i attain to exultation or insight, encounter the visionary edge, these things i bring back for my Art...

The dream in which i have this Vision is well beyond these Watcher dreams; more resonant, more numinous, w/an exquisite intensity. Everything in the dream is brighter, sharper, clearer; a meta/real hyperdream...

In it i am in the Main Salon of another ship other than the *Ariel:* around me great ambient music, great lights, a large space filled w/hundreds of folk in freefall drifting languorous, some naked, some inhaling Spice, some watching light/play, many w/holocams, some stasis/dancing in sonic rapture in the scented air, a few stroked out w/each other in the nets, all of them looking through the Overhead; the view is the face of The Moon, now in moondark, ten thousand miles out to starboard/leeward.

In forward deja this ship begins to vibrate, major power generators ramping up to maximum...

At the stern end of the Salon there is a raised railed deck all overflown w/hardware. It is clear to me, in the Vision, that this is the Performance Bridge and the folk who are floating there are about to do something pretty amazing w/light. On the bridge are three folk: a long Spacer guy w/red spikey hair and a silver suit, a hunky kind/of wrestlery guy, a woman w/an elfin grin.

The pitch of the generators reaches a metaphysical/Om plateau, in harmony w/the chording of the band in the forward section. The silver man on the bridge beckons; he wants me to come aft and join them. This feels very natural to me, and though they are strangers to my waking reality, in the Vision i know them and trust them.

As i push off from the plating i am highlighted by a ball of light seven feet across: a lightsphere. *(How? synthetic St/Elmo fire?)* I move ahead through the center of the section, through all these quieting watchers, and i head for this enormous old copperblade lever/switch, also globed in a ball of light.

It comes to me that i am the one to throw this switch and start... what?

I brace against the rail and w/both hands grasp the big oaken grip. Here before i move i pause to look out at all the folk in the chamber: we are all in this together, me and these revelers. More than a performance, this is a Rite of Magic we are enacting this night.

I am filled w/the juice of inspiration; i resonate mightily;
I throw the switch!

And bright roaring lightbeams of ENORMOUS POWER leap from the ship and race for the face of the Moon, touching down in great bands first of White and now the Blue of Lightning, now Magenta Red...

Zzog!

Beauty Beyond Words!

*Oh Great Goddess In All Thy Majesty i have Seen Thee! I have seen Thy Face and it is the Earth's Moon and it is Beautiful, and you have called upon me to illuminate Thee, paint Thee w/light, give my light for Thine in the ancient way, and for this vaunted moment i shall be glad all of my days...*

At this point i wake and ope my eyes, i know not why...

I am in my chamber aboard the *Ariel,* drifting warm in the bedding of my freefall snugger, moored in the middle of the air.

My dreamtracker hums full at my brow...

I blink my glims and see my own spherical teardrops floating close by, each one prisming the glints of the roomlight brightpoints.

And still i shake and thrill w/the intensity of the Vision, still feel gloriously suffused and bathed in rays of bliss, full/filled joyous w/inrushing Goddess Love...

I am Called to make this Vision real.

Everything i know, all my experience, all my work thusfar will become a part of this. Everyone i know will be touched by it.

In truth, hundreds of millions, BILLIONS of people will see it,
w/their own eyes, standing on the Earth and looking out...

*Oh! the Titan Sweep!*
*Galvanic to Vision it!*
*Electric to follow it!*

What a voice to speak clarity to the heart of the world...
I will cause this thing to be.


I stir and dress and head for Forward, rocked by the elation rush
of a lifetime.

My head is filled w/gleamy dreamclips: lasers of Colossal Power,
dazzling lambent beams lacing across the face of Luna in moondark, colors
mingling like neon anilines poured in a torrent, clouds of gassy light rolling
across gaunt gray craters stark in shadow...

I seek and find Electra.

She is forward w/taylor the automated sailor, he who controls
the solar sails most of the time. One of us is always up there w/him in case
something is called for that is beyond his repertoire.

Electra turns/i embrace her glims w/mine...

And smile to see her
mirroring my own exulting, even now eager, ready for our next adventure.
Linked to my dreamtracker she sees my dreams as i conceive them, and sees
this one as a bigtime gift from Zzog, given o'er to be made manifest.

She grins me her gamesafoot grin...

And outside the ports, all i see is changed. Joy has irised wide my
eyes, and all that i perceive, all that i CAN perceive, is brighter than ever it
was, ringing divine in every particle...

We sail on, the rigging singing through the great hollow masts, the
ports wide awash w/swirls of pointal color fracts, the Milky Way a trail of
music written w/stars...

Inspiration everywhere...

What to write on the face of the Moon?

## 3   Electra and the Old Ways


My admission, call it my Great Work: bringing Electra to the Craft of the Wise.


Before i beheld the beautiful solar sailer *Ariel,* there was Electra. On first sight of her i felt that same sweet beautiful surge of spinal voltage, just as strong and pure as it would later be for the great silver ship i sail, my true home.

A glorious piece of work, state of the art and a joy forever: praise to her name...


I remember the amplified Sunlight and the taste of the air, mostly ozone w/occasional steam from some big condensers and also the blessed scent of...

I am on this mining asteroid in the Martian Belts, Rastus Nineteen, waiting for the next Best Thing, and Electra and i are brought together by my friend the Lumière, dapper as a vidstar, he who has a knack for arriving w/the perfect thing at the perfect time.

Always a surprise when i see him, he...

Appears,

A cosmic bluejay harbinger and the prescient instrument of change in my life...

And now he takes me out to this little park in the hydroponics section, a happy little piece of Earth where he knows i will be in my power/receptive, and there connects me w/Electra:

I am Charmed, Glamoured, Raptured!
Warmed by her shy smile she
totally pegs all my meters;
Cerulean Portals, her eyes,
I look her through and Magnetize...


I give her my story. I tell her how deeply i want her in my life; starting from the time i am a lonely pre/dult chained in a chamber in a school on an asteroid, seventeen million miles from Mars, where i have a picture of one of her sisters w/me in my space, and every day that i am there i stare into those deep blue eyes...

And caught as i am in that cloistered claustrophobic

lonely parochial place, this main thought sustains me: somewhere noble beauty knowably exists, and may someday be joyously joined...

We go looking for a new home, and the Lumière shuttles us out to the nearby Cyclo Cluster, over to this habitat on the side of old number seven/seven/two, one of the larger pieces of floating rock out that way.
There is an opening for a team and we take it.
The cyclo/folk are okay, all ages, often friendly/interesting, and the sea air is marvelous *(this last a jest... har)*.
Our work is agreeable, taking care of all the gear around the place, and Electra and i settle in and get to know each other.
There are also some technical things i can do for her, which pleases me;
And more and more i appreciate the genius of her delicate construction, her wise and gentle nature, her gifts. All the skills she has been given remain w/her completely, and everything she learns she retains; she delights me w/hero tales, herbal lore, songs of love, stories of the old differentiated lands of the Earth...
Evenings we share a flask of leaf/twig tea high above the habitat in the weather room, listening to the music of windsounds. And many nights before rest i lull to the strange melodies of her speaking, that xeno twist she gives her words; what she calls her brogue.

Twice i am down w/the Fever, and she glides around our sleeping space making me healing things to eat, easing my pain, wiping the blood from my mouth.
I envy her even as i need her to keep me alive. She is twenty/five years, i a little more; yet she will likely live on and on, long after this my bod is dust...
And it is in this that i see the reason for teaching her the Old Ways:
With so many workers of the Will now living the Spacer life, all of us so familiar w/being free of gravity... Well, we now prefer our freefall gliding, and the home planet sees us rarely...
And though we cherish the Earth as our source/point, we are so long away that few of us remain who keep the old Ways alive: for what are Ways w/out Sacred Ground? Electra would pass this knowlege safe along to those who come after, those who would see the Starry Infinite as their sacred ground...

I use the very Celtic Celestial system and bring her through the grades, the levels of knowing and the rites of initiation, and it goes quickly: as if her sense of these things has always been w/her, uncrystallized in her unawareness...
She soon shows a fine gift for Craft.

Her perceptions... She is somehow spiritual w/out being human about it; hers a purely intellectual knowing of Godhead...

*Electra, you who are Avatar of Animorphs, first of your kind w/the knowlege of Druids: what novel symmetries will these Ways release upon your algorithmic self?*

These are the concepts i give to Electra:

Magic is available to everyone.
        Everyone has their own magic and it comes to all who know its'
true name, independent of the number of points in the stars we wear.

        There are as many approaches to magic as there are mages.
Everyone makes their own deal w/the All, magically speaking. ·

*

        Magic is a force, neutral in nature. It comes in a full spectrum of
colors, a shade for every Working: Red for Passion; Green, the Healing Ray
(Blessed Be Its' Power); Solid Blue the Oceanic Color of Thought, and even
that salted through w/variants; Electric Blue for Lightning Mercury Thought,
Royal Lazuli for Grand Concepts that echo in the mind like choir/chords,
Zither Blue for prophecy...

*

        There are three reasons for working Magic; effecting change in the
physical world through an act of Will, learning about ourselves by owning
our motives for these changes, and, through mystical experience, achieving
unity w/the Divine.
        In the Celestial system, this spiritual aspect is paramount. Ritual
becomes a way of harmonizing w/the Divine. And when one merges w/the
All a state of grace naturally follows, where the magic happens of itself and
the need to specifically work our Will recedes.
        Ideally our Magic becomes a function of Divine Will, and also
the converse.
        This way lies peace and Flow.

*

        When this Celestial unity informs our Work, the Pattern is enhanced.
        If we work for physical change only, we second/guess the Divine
and risk karmic backlash.

Personal power is the last trap of the Seeker.
   Wisdom is in knowing when to wave the wand.

                              *


      Three elements of power are alive w/in us when we make the
magic happen: Visualization, Will, and True Desire.

      Visualization fixes the goal of the working, directs and focuses the
Will. When manifesting, visualize the object of your desiring. In sending
power, visualize the archetypal way you wish the power channeled: the
laser, the vapour cloud, the wind, the river. In drawing power, visualize the
symbol of the energy you need. Here are the Ancient Four: the gift of the
Sword for the power to defend; the filling of the Cup to receive healing and
knowlege; the Wand or Spear to cast benignly or w/malice; and the Mirror,
to return what'ere to the sender.

      Will is our personal Juice, the motive force, raised w/in us and from
Beyond by desire. Will can be strengthened w/exercise.

      Desire is heart/yearning, that dynamic/magnetic defining emotion
on which our lives turn. It is this radiant desiring that lofts our wishes into
the aether, connects us w/the mind of the All which permeates everything
everywhere, thus effecting change in the world.

      Though any strong emotion may drive magic, the greatest works
are loved into being...
      It is this: let your Will be of your heart.
       Desire as Love is the breath of the universe.
       Whooosh...
                              *


      The strength of our Will depends upon our integrity and impeccability.
Our integrity is in how well we live what we believe. Our impeccability is
in our belief in the rightness of our actions; we must be free of shadows
when we reach the Bright Arena, totally clear w/ourselves that we deserve
the way of our Will.

                              *


      Magic comes from stillness.
      Out of darkness, Light.
      The sacred sphere is triply cast;
      Out of nothing, Everything.

*

Much of magic has to do w/Flow and Timing; tapping in, rechanneling, listening for the right moment.

Astrology, Tarot, and the I Ching touch the pulsepoints of the Aether. Ley Lines and Feng Shui are currents in the Earth.

Listen. Learn. There is always more.

*


Magical Systems are bridges of commonality built between people w/differing cosmologies. Everyone in the circle agrees on the same symbol set, the same Ways of attunement; this facilitates the combining of Wills necessary for Great Works and Mystical Adventures.

*


Before the revolution in consciousness, there existed the Great Religions. They were a way of organizing everyone's individual magical work into a hierarchy, to more effectively achieve and focus the collective Will.

Many of these Religions were formed around charismatic avatar/prophets who had some direct experience of God. They would tell those close to them what they had learned while in this state. Friends and relatives became Believers; words became ripples radiating outward. A pyramid would form, w/those at the bottom ostensibly straining upward for the Word on what this direct experience of God must mean.

We now believe that everyone can attain this mystical state, thus becoming free of dogma and elaborate structure, open to developing a meaningful and specific personal cosmology.

Thou art God, Goddess.

*


Magic can also be seen as an action word; Magicing. Everyone can Magic; that is, give Will/emotion/energy to the manifesting of visualizations.

When fully awake we consciously control these forces; and when we dream, the unconscious Other part of ourselves can call these forces as well...

And the unconscious is always there, waking or dreaming, taking images from conscious thought, connecting the same Will/emotion/energy to manifesting them...

And thus the unconscious is the conduit of constant magicing, a general stream of visualizations connecting w/low/level Will.

To the always/recording uncritical unconscious, one's fears and hopes and other contesting emotions are all grist for the mill of this low/level/Will, free of the mitigation of moral or other criteria.

The conscious or unconscious visualizations of our thoughts both have similarly varying generational power. When images from the unconscious flow out in contrary parallel to the conscious expressions of our Will, conflicting magical signals can be sent...

Thus the waking mind and the Otherself must be harmonized, both aligned toward the same end. Thus is integrity fostered, and thus is released the highest potential for achieving change.

For this reason it is important we know our own hearts, for the heart is the arbiter of truth w/in the bod. We need to know and own our motives for the quickening of any act, thus eliminating shadow desires, thus achieving our heart's validation/the certain knowlege that we deserve the outcome we envision, thus freeing the total power of our Will...

Techniques for uniting the conscious and the unconscious exist in every spiritual practice, and take a variety of forms and names. The very eclectic Celestial includes many of these, and favors Ritual.

Magical Ritual includes ways of consciously feeding the Otherself w/symbols of divine bounty and the refining of consciousness and the directing of power, so that integration may be further strengthened and impeccability attained, all the better for right use of Will.

Thus, the Goddess and the God may be invoked w/loving assurance that they shall respond in kind, for as above so below, as ever it has been...

*

And yes, there are realms beyond Magic...

Knowlege of Magic grants serenity and wisdom indirectly. Yet it is real Faith, a deep belief in the immutability of Spirit, that ultimately frees us from the whirlpool pull of the material world.

Faith is that which sustains in us a belief in immortality, w/out which existence makes no sense.

Successful magic builds Faith, and Faith opens the heart and unbinds the mind that wise Will may reign.

The source of Faith is direct experience of Unity w/the Divine: of going to that place where what Is, Was, and Will Be all converge, where there are no boundaries between i and thee, where every point in the universe is one point, where time (an abstraction invented by humans, says me, to keep everything from happening at once) is only a convenient metaphor and all knowlege is w/in reach...

*

What better end for the focused use of Will than to call upon the Higher Powers to pull us up into their own exalted abode, into their own very Being?

This idea of Union w/the Divine is central to the Celestial, to all systems of inspiriting. The very word 'religion' comes from the Latin *re ligare*; which means, literally, 'to re/connect'. Thus the key religious idea to the folk who coined the word is this joining w/Divinity.

Historically, this vital dynamic is best realized in the great national mystery events held at the temples of Eleusis in ancient Greece.

These Eleusinian Mysteries ran every year continuously for two thousand years, reliably providing a revelation so impactful that in one night its' celebrants' world/view was spread wide forever. These Mysteries, at once combining elements of personal work, ritual magic, theatre, and an ergot/or/cubensis brew called the Kykion, were the crowned glory of spiritual experience on our world at that time.

In the main Working of the nine day event there was a point at which the rite crossed over into Epiphany. This infusion of spirit is called the Kairos, the Supreme Moment. It relates to Samadhi, to the Bliss/Trance, to a dozen terms for receiving Enlightenment and merging w/the All.

Currently we seek this Kairos point w/a combination of inspirited Magical ritual, and also the higher expressions of technologically augmented consciousness, and most universally in this the Fresh Age, the use of mind/enhancing shamanic compounds.

Which gives me cause to wonder thus; is the fundamental goal of my life to inspire Kairos in as many of my fellow beings as desire this experience? To use all the media available to me to bring this about? To foster another Eleusinian evolutionary leap?

Well, Yes.

So, clarity at last. Before me now the challenge of bringing together these various forms in such a way that the result reliably carries us into that most salubrious of realms, that most exalted state,

The Celestial...

I give Electra my century cape, a hundred years of green velvet, that she may wrap herself in my tradition.

What kind of magic will Electra manifest?

Her ability to Visualize is perfectly integrated. She is free of conflicting motives. She has no unconscious mind and will make no unconscious magic. Here she will shine.

And what of her Will and mystical connection?

And what will she be connecting with?

I trust her inbuilt benevolence to guide her hand in all her Workings...

Io Miners' Port is loud and rough and total/zerko after our life in the lonely belts.

Mystical reasons bring us here: the Voice says leave Cyclo/seven/ seven/two and go to Io, so we go.

I trust the Voice.

And now wonder at its' provenance: the economy of Io is at an all/time low, what w/the main industry being beryllium mining and the price of beryllium being Sun/south of nowhere.

In truth, the market is riding the rocket to obscurity and two of the five major mines are closing. Local folk are feeling the Bite; w/fewer cargos going out, less money is coming in.

And fewer ships are stopping at our port.

This means deliveries of fresh hardware are getting rare. Earthside this would be inconvenient, out here it is very scary: we depend on our gear for our lives. We have to keep all that vacuum out. We have to recycle all our air and water: every valve and lock and seal and port and pump and cell and bearing is vital.

The older the equipment the more dangerous things get. Worn gear has to be replaced or graced w/new expendables on a regular basis. All this stuff comes from faraway somewhere else, and shipping costs are bigtime; we are, remember, four/hundred/eighty/three million miles from the Sun. Twice as far to the Company Store on Mars if the planets are in opposition...

Preeecarious: Welcome to Edge City.

The six thousand folk living portside are mostly seasoned Spacers who came for the work and stayed for the truly fine xeno scenery,

And many are the hours we look out upon these orange expanses: Io's brow a brooding craggy curve, the monster volcano mountains spiky like dark cartoon Sunrays against the pale light of Juppiter the Huge...

And when the orbit is right, the melted mineral mountains go translucent gray, showing shafts of starlight;

And there is the ceaseless fast phasing of eleven other Juppiter moons, different every night,

And Great Juppiter the All/Father looming

always, w/shifting sienna wind/bands and the vast red waxing/waning
elliptical mystery spot, that thing they call the Dark Disturbance, wending
its' strange meander across the planet's face, its' edges tracing dragon/tail
ghost trails in the hydrogen stratosphere...

And in all these things there is
majesty, and from early on it draws me. Other folk are likewise drawn, and
now this whirling chunk of mineral provender is our home; kids born,
romance, sadness, everything laced into this alien littoral.

Leave?

Hard as things are, folk will stay; this place is heart/beautiful...


Beryllium though is nasty stuff; here a toxic fine powder that can walk
through any number of things designed to keep it out. Accidents happen;
folks suffer. Still i am pleased to notch a job w/Anaconda Consolidated in
the western tunnels, the mine they call The Motivator.


I work in my suit, swinging the business end of a big vapor laser,
sluicing away substrate half a league underground. Fun at first, then just
work, then dangerous faceless boredom. Ten/hour stretches of high/voltage
high/mass total/vacuum low/gravity hard work.

A living.

At the end of my shift i come home to Electra, my Saving Grace;
her the healing freshet flowing life to my thirsty bod...

Time passes. I take pride in my survival, even as i daily dread going
back into that hole. After every fire, explosion, hot snap, slow burn, heaving
quake; i revel in the pleasure of Being Alive Now.


Off/times i catch the old video/wirefeeds from Earth: this was once
the popular form of relaxation, what folk would do when done w/townside
or w/working. By and by i am appalled. It is a storytelling medium skewed
scary, monstrous w/images of blood and death and pain, oppression,
broken lives, derision and ridicule and trivialization.

Why put energy into assimilating it? Why buy into it?

How is this entertaining for the folk out there in consensus reality?
Is that sullen majority so jaded and overstimulated that...

I know there is
magic in media; the images we take into ourselves through our senses become
a part of us. They influence our world/view, and this affects the reality we
create, the immediate reality we magically project.

In light of this i hunger for the endless stream of beautiful visions
that media is capable of. I want Ecstatic Joy, Well/Being, Hope, Positive
Change! That which improves life and luminates the mind...

And,
Everyone parading through that little box looks so heavily compromised: twisted, tight/lipped, unhealthy, co/opted... Like they have sold themselves to survive, cashed in their spark for a roof and three squares, banished the larking child w/in. Why? How?
Out of desperation mounting,
I see that i have done the same.

That realized, i know there must also be a pathway to some alternative. There must be some kind of meaningful life for me here: a bit of color, some joy, beauty, love, discourse, ideas, music; some kind of work that would let me live like a human and still keep my humanity, some way to sustain...
I know it is near, just over the event horizon.

*

After a year of melting rock and getting by, the Voice informs me that my abiding desire for change shall soon manifest change, that my faith will soon be fulfilled...
Now, one lo day later, a wave of news sweeps the port: ruins have been discovered in the west quarter; artifacts, documents, structures.
Airless lo yields potential at last.

I imagine it is Electra and me, out on a glide in our sled, a lovers' joyride, the first folk to find the hidden door in the rock in the vacuum. It is not us, but others. The honor passes.
The Institute guys are all geologists (lologists?) and they do their best for Science, quickly learning the ways of archeology. I have a friend (so many good stories start this way), Doctor Don, who is part of this group, and he tells us about their find:
'It's a hollowed/out dome in this flow of nickel/iron slag, and right away we can see that this place is expecting us. Like a kind of exhibit: a time capsule, a museum, a slice of life; w/tableaux, banks of memory in written form [books!] and these golden vacproof inert/gas vaults, plus formulas and codexes and written language carved right into slabs of stone.'
'Eleuthrans!' says i, astonishing Doctor Don.
This is something i know about; these folk are faves of mine since my schooltime in the Belts. If Frank Lloyd Wright had designed Atlantis, it would have come out along the lines of the Eleuthran civilization.
These folk, an Earthside race from about eleven thousand years ago, they would leave these treasure/domes as their calling cards all over the known parts of our solar system, all these very Ozymandian displays of their

accomplishments; Behold Ye These Mighty Works, like that. There is a large bod of knowlege on things Eleuthran, w/each of these structures a chapter of learning they want us to have. E'en so, there are also some goodly mysteries. And myths...

And it occurs to me that this Io find, this new dome of rock, is the farthest one from the Sun: if the Eleuthrans were outward/bound as a people (as many believe) then this could be their last message...

Zzog.


'What has us really amped,' Doctor Don continues, 'is that this chamber contains several hundred artifacts exclusive to this site, totally new to the main folk who are studying Eleuthra. For example, there are these beautiful spheres, about the size of your fist, that look like they are made of Brazilian quartz. They have a chamber in the center and a kind of nipple on the side. As to what they're for, we're baffed.'

My excitement is ramping up. Eleuthran/wise, we are in virgin territory now. New stuff! Yeah! Hot Zzog!

One of my theories about the Eleuthrans goes like this: instead of being a monolithic society, there were all kinds of different stripes of Eleuthrans. The builders of the other vaults thusfar discovered were scholars and patricians. What about the other end of the society? Like other classical cultures, there would have been another major force; the funloving beauty/creating passion/saturated Dionysian Eleuthrans, the harpers, the lovers, the ecstatic trancers, the seers, the true seekers, the fringers, the extremers, the ones made feral by fiery winds of poesy...

As long as i have been following matters Eleuthran, i have lived for the day when we would get the Dionysian side of the story. A vac/vault of pleasure toys, media...

Ironical it occurs to me that in this band of miners Doctor Don may see me as the one who knows the most about the Eleuthrans. Leverage? Worth a try:

'So, ah, can you get me into this place to have a goodly look around?'

*


Like a Familiar is my suit, a second self w/whom i merge. Our breath is silent, we move effortless, the air inside so personal and warm...

Doctor Don and Electra and i jump graceful from the sled, around the rocks behind; and there the vaunted door, the mystery door of eleven thousand years.

What can 'antediluvian' mean to an airless waterless moon? We are about to find out.

Copper/color shale slides away, the door faced w/stone: open and in.

And inside, an iris airlock; silver metal vanes, perfectly working, saved from age's rages. The place feels vastly archaic, and the architecture is like music in an alien key, and the colors echo...

Zzog!

The bright cobalt blue and warm burnished gold are new to me beyond the old red and gold of previous finds; and the plan of the chamber is also something... other.

A quick reactive spine/thrill; this place is a temple...

The dome too is deep blue and worked all over in stars, actual points of light, w/the concave curving floor the same. The chamber focuses toward a raised area in the center, a sculpted cup of giant hands, large enough to hold a human in their twelve/fingered embrace...

Or a couple.

Around the perimeter of the chamber are these vacproof wall/vaults, and each holds a quartz sphere as described by Doctor Don. A plaque emblazons each vac/vault, and i sense they bear the names of the spheres, each w/some special virtue...

Something about these spheres...

The searcher in my psyche awakens,

I reach out/a gulf of years...

And smile, for at the edge of my perception i sense [Eleuthrans!] reaching for me likewise, whispering resonant chords of thought into the pnemosyne caves of my memory...

And now Electra draws my attention to a much larger quartz sphere, this one in a vault also, holding a powder of crystals, green glassy stuff the color of tourmaline, glittering dark in the Sun/colored light from our helmets...

Doctor Don points to the domes' arc, three times his height above him, oblivious to the play of my awareness...

As i assemble the room in my mind i soon see the use of it.

The Dionysian Eleuthrans are w/me, and i see them take a shape as they enter the dark and airless room. They come like a psychic sending and yet it is some kind of media also. I realize i am the only one who sees them. Have i somehow been selected?

In the sending, each Eleuthran wears an envelope, a cloak of liquid veils. A six/finger wave and a gesture brings on the lights; redder, warmer than Sun/color. In the sending, atmosphere fills the chamber, and their liquid veils melt away.

There are two of these Eleuthrans. Their faces are smooth and very human, aquiline w/almond eyes and high & shining brows. Their hair is long and golden. And red and occasionally green and blue as well, and their long lean forms are clad in snug green/mossy jumpers, iridescent w/goldbraided knotwork trim, good for zero/gee and ceremonial likewise...

And now the taller of the two goes to a vault along the chamber wall and waves again, a very graceful solemn motion, and the vault sighs out its' gas and opens, offering its' quartz cargo. Likely the vault reseals and regasses when you put the thing back...

And the way this figure moves, looking at me to be sure i see the way of it, tells me this is a teaching loop. And immediate the thought: can all this gear still be functional after all this time?

*

It is now eight hours later, and Electra and i are again standing at the door in the coppery rock. The university folk around the site know us from before and stay fascinated into their own work...

At the perfect time we slide through the door and roll it closed behind.

In a snug hallway now, and the silver inner airlock irises open and we move through it, and now the moment of truth: smoothly i move to the spot on the floor; i ground and center, form the graceful wave and gesture w/my five/fingered hands, just like in the loop.

Nothing happens.

I go through the process again. I am sure that i am the only one to see the loop. I am sure that the chamber wants me to enter: it will open for me.

Still nothing.

The Voice w/in overides my doubts. It is right for me to do this; there is an arbiter of truth w/in me...

Something is being left out of this Spell of Opening.

Oh yes; after the wave, i look up.

Yes! My gaze falls on an oval mirrored panel new upon the scene: a scan/check! I smile beaming benevolent at the panel and now the roomlights are coming up, and the readout on the wrist of my suit shows ramping levels of oxygen.

I start to shed my helmet and am immediately aware of a new dimension: music. Heavenly stuff... If this arc/curvy architecture were music... It IS music, and we are hearing it...

Old and Holy, sacred ground. Zzog.

We park our suits and proceed, wearing our ritual gear.

And now Electra and i stand facing each other w/in the bounds of the gold/inscribed circle on the floor, the same spot as the Eleuthrans in the loop. And now an apse in the dome opens and issues these parallel beams of light, one for us each, coming down in red streamlines into the tops of our heads, our crown/centers.

I close my eyes, and am suffused w/the very deep and red color of this light, coming in everywhere, through the lids of my eyes, more, through every pore and orifice, filling every cell and fiber; and i feel muscle heat, and the measured surge of blood music, the boom of pulse/ripples issuing from the warm red center at the base of my spine...

And all the while the dome is crooning, keening, coming on twin/flame/warm for this red photon infusing...

And now the light cycles onward, the level of physical focus shifting; orange now, up to the omphalos point, the navel level, the connect for kinship w/family, w/humanity, and now yellow in the great solar center plexus, the hub in the wheel of my bod, source of energy in the physical, and now green for healing and growth, light for the heart/level, and now glinty blue, color of the Earthen sky done in metalflake, color of the original speakingstone and the song that is language, cool the blue light pooling in the hollow of my throat...

And still the light pours down, a numinous stream of manna...

A lapis flash to my inward eye, and arrives now the hue indigo, sublime color of the inner chamber, color of the realm of telepathy and kinesis, the yogi's high ground, and now and now GREAT GLORY OF HIGHEST ATTAINING!  THE VIOLET RAY!  THE VIOLET RAY!

The whole process takes less than a minute.

I am aligned, perceptions tuned. My readout shows my alpha levels high and theta thresholds low and ready for cascades. Just as in the loop i turn and look to the oval panel and lean my head left and right. I am ready for the next step.

We each go to one of the vacuum vaults arrayed around the dome and make the gesture of opening. Several vaults to my right, a green light goes on: it gives out a hiss (argon? nitrogen?), and the hemispheric cover clamshells away.

In an ecstasy of discovery and anticipation i reach for the sphere of quartz. O lover of mine, ever so dear, couldst thou e'er feel a touch so light/sincere, so freighted an embrace, as i do gift upon yonder glassy globe of grace...

I look to the great dark oval, and now w/love i look to Electra, now back to the oval. A pause of three heartbeats (easy to hear them) and another green light opens another vault near to her hand. I cast a smile of thanks...

And now i pledge my dedication, the words Eleuthran as per the loop. (Am i the only one on this moon who knows them? Does Electra know them as well?). Ah, she tracks me; speaks the words as i speak them.

As per the loop we go to the great sphere, scoop ourselves some dark and glittery/green tourmaline crystals.

Thence to our comfortable couching in the great hands at the focus of the chamber...

The clear stone sphere feels somehow laden, charged luminous w/potential...

We settle into the hands' friendly palms/the fingers flex and cup us perfectly.

Here's to Bliss or Oblivion...

Lux Aeterna!


With another look of love for Electra i raise the sphere into the space above our heads. There is a sharp BRAP! and a highly coherent (laser!) beam of light hits the sphere,

a tenth of a second
and i bring it smoking to my lips,
breathe the coiling vapors in...


The experience is beyond my wildest.

I have the custom of trying every life/enhancing sense/expanding spirit/raising agent that comes my way;

Mouse Gas served fresh by a big green kachunker toad in a methane mask in a cave on Phobos, Wild Betsy shared hand to hand while lost w/two blueboys too far from Mars/port, Lotus Leaves eaten w/the Three Hydroponic Dervishes of slow/twisting Callisto, and e'en so,

Spice *ROCKS MY WORLD*, exceeds them all, is the lightning that strikes the channels clear,

And thus expanded i am instantly brought to abide in the Is/Was/Will Be, that place of Great Merging where all can be known,

And ecstatic i am wrapped in the vast living/shimmering sheath of total first/born creation, dwelling as a cell in the Mind Divine...


Do you know of the phenomenon of physical re/imaging? It works this way: if your Will is strong and the Gods are w/you, your bod physically changes according to how you envision/see yourself...

As i turn and look to the oval panel now above me, i see that the mirror/image is me, and more. I am recast, reborn, made molten and poured, still aware, into a shape more to my taste; taller and fairer, hair more red, a truer version of my inner vision...

I look at my hands and see that this is real. Two scars are gone and my fingers look a little longer.

And here a rush of revelation/ vertigo: there is another side to this. It means that once again i am utterly responsible for my physical presence in the world. A high awareness of self/esteem is necessary here; as it is ever thus anyway...

Later we will discover that Spice makes for lasting improvements in sensory acuity, visioning/imagining, personality and intelligence. Spice also invites the towers of mental edifice to melt then rise again in wonder, fantastically re/crystallized, resplendent in new logic, subtly swaying to the welcome snick! of fresh/snapping synapses...

*

Over the next few periods my life changes.

My first day after Spice and i am three hours into my shift at the Motivator mine, vaporizing chunks of native ore. I am cruising along in work/mode, an Eleuthran cantata serenading my brain...

And now w/the upturn coda there comes to me these TERRIFIC visuals, a color/light counterpoint to my mindplaying music, great bright heartful passionate patterns...

And transfixed i am suddenly hyper/aware of the instrument in my hands, *its' awesome potential for making awesome art;*

My inner eyes go wide w/the fierce Awen visuals streaming through...

Zzog!

The key to the mystery of why i am here in Io/purgatory reveals in this current moment, the answer in my hands the whole time...

Time to see some ritual technology in action.

I leave the job, sell everything excepting the big industrial mining laser, borrow money from everyone, get a workshop, stop sleeping...

Obsess.

I copy Eleuthran light show gear from the books in the vac/vaults and sync it up to the laser. With a frequency shifter and some adaptive circuitry, the old sluice slicer slides handsomely into the visible spectrum while manifesting awesome power.

Eleuthran music is also a perfect fit, w/length and modality and flavour all in harmony w/the augmented visuals.

And sovereign in this entertainment that i am driven to create is Spice; Godfood, salvation, essence of the beautiful, conveyer of Gnosis, awakener of sleeping souls, a taste of lost Eleuthra...

Spice will synergize the lights and music, bring about massive Visioning, connect us all to each other and to the Divine Source...

And so, w/the willing complicity of Doctor Don, a few greeny crystals get up and walk into the crucible of a chemist in Io Old Town: Martin Oberhost in his polished chamber of nickel steel, Martin the Mad.

Two of his shiny machines: one to analyze the stuff and another to duplicate it. We are in luck: the psycho/active ingredient is a mineral found only here on Io, and this could save many good folk. Thus we seal a pact to keep the secret of Spicemaking here on Io also, for to benefit the local economy: soon there will be chemists all over Miners' Port making the stuff.

Add the production of some spheres of clear Io silica, and off we go.

In five weeks i max out my credit and totally overrun my resources, all for the gear. With the end of the rope in sight, i am ready.

I make a deal to play Moira's, my fave club townside, where i open for the house band. People rightaway like my stuff, and six weeks A.S. (after Spice) i am a performing light/artist; selling Spice, being appreciated, raking it in and free of the mines.

Hallelujah Zzog! The Hand of the Goddess...

Thanks Be and Bright Blessings.

*

This experiential whiff of Eleuthra transforms and deepens everyone brave enough to try it, and many folk do, and likewise their friends...

And word goes out on the Wire, and folk flock to our rock, hungry for their own unique and personal next Best Thing,

And w/this influx of energy Io Miners' Port shifts, and the makers of Spice and Spheres form guilds and thrive, and there is work and money and shiny new gear...

Now, three months later, Electra & i ship out on the *Ariel,* abundantly rewarded and charged w/a twofold sense of mission;

First, The Voice informs me that aboard the *Ariel* i will have the Vision that will define me, set me on my truest course...

And second, by agreement w/the Guilds i am the first to leave Io w/Spice in the hold and a Sphere in my kit...

> *May your sailing be outrageous*
> *as you move out through the void,*
> *and your valiant ship stay free of woe*
> *through the rolling asteroids,*
> *and know my love is w/you*
> *as you cleave the starry foam,*
> *for Spice and the Light of Eleuthra*
> *will guide you safely home...*
>
> *Good Fortune to my shipmates,*
> *here they be set down:*
> *and we shall keep their memories green*
> *as their stories make the rounds,*
> *and they will know we think upon them*
> *as we ramble and we roam,*
> *trusting Spice and the Light of Eleuthra*
> *to guide us safely home...*
>
> *-- Uncle Carl,*
> *on my joining the crew of the Ariel*

The *Ariel* is a traveling lightshow, a class act.

My new sailing/mates ramp me up warmly, praise well my person, my work, my taste in highs. They see potential in combining our mutual gifts, laying all before their audiences on the nine planets & nineteen moons that line their usual loop...

And a very excellent company is the crew of the *Ariel*; a flying attractor, the *Ariel* hoovers all kinds of folk into her aegis. Others get the Big Nod when they catch the eye of Uncle Carl (or some other) by a notable display of skill or style or some gift of talent...

Doubly welcome is yr anders, for i come bearing (as per the song) both the Spice and the Light of Eleuthra...

The *Ariel!*

Lithe as a greyhound, a great graceful harlequin of a ship; a sculpted pod in a lair of sails, a vast expanse of candy metallic solar silverfilm, tritanium tubular mile/masts and steel cable rigging, all bent before the pressure of the light of the driving Sun.

And the ways of our Art so integral to the *Ariel's* design: each sail tracks heliotropic, catches the Sunlight and bellies out w/the Solar Wind, forming a parabolic reflector. Each rainbow piezo/dichroic source/point sail can be tuned through a spectrum of color/wavelengths, and at each sail's focal point is a collector for changing the Light & Heat into steam and electricity. These focal points also have collimators in them to polarize and concentrate the light, scanners to take this concentrated light and aim it and give it vectors...

And thus crafted this light plays through a system of mirrors and ports and into the theater space in the pod. In double/hulled comfort our audiences bask in abstract Sunfire holographics, close enough alive to respond to your passing hand...

And amidships are the main ports; great clear concavities forty feet across. And outside these the screens, standing off to port and starboard, each a mile wide, waiting to be filled w/solar glory...

My first time on the road...

And now we are nine weeks out from Io; the major enroute refit is covered, w/all the fresh hardware daemon/tweaked and ready.

We are also two and a half days from our new/show debut on Ganymede; Carl says time to open up the shipstores, program the domestics for 'Feast', and head for the Main Salon...

Where folk are currently abiding in their freefall webs of bedding, in groups around the show gear, refining the software, watching the stars, smoking Spice, jamming, hanging out, making love, eating food, sometimes sleeping, deeply dreaming...

With the webs in place the room holds two hundred folk: just the right number for an intimate demonstration of our Art. Now the webs are cleared away and the Hall is set for a freefall family banquet...

Slurp!

Pleasure is the best teacher.

*

Gauzy banners drift like underwater lingerie, drift in the freshet flow of weightless air, w/each banner the graphic litany of some Spacer/Hero aboard the Ariel this night...

And currently wafting through, Lissa's opening incense; subtle ylang w/a citrus top.

We array ourselves spatial around the chamber, gridded in the volume, our bods at rest in scented colloidal oxygen suspension...

And moving glowing globes glide in gentle curves around us, each globe a color lightsource,

gracing our random shadows w/shades of auric outline colors where they
fall upon the walls, the spectral lightcasts sliding/overlapping...
                                                            And w/all of
the choice entheogens percolating now through the cells of my shipmates,
this lightsource sight transcends, these overtoning globes a glass bead game
of Gods, profound and artful...

        And so our Feast begins,
                        And now a traffic of candy/color canisters
arc through the air entrained, each a guided morsel or viand missile, sailing
square into the cube of space of their appointed diner, where each is taste
for taste a perfect match, toothsome and rare...
        I snag one of mine as it slows and stops before me: the canister says
pumpkin sorrel soup w/fresh cilantro & cinnamon & ginger;
        Earth/food!
                        Salacious flavours that summon to mind woodland
night nymphs and lithe paradise spirits; a harmony of flavours so stratified
& complex that each inhaled scenting comes differently into my awareness,
redolent of homeplanet Sunlight and dewy songs of morning and vivid niffs
of harvestime...
        Life reigns sweet and hyper/sensory...

        Andrew, Spacer/thin & foxy, coins a musical theme for each
course, and these themes ride the canisters; you hear them from the food
itself, first as a melody in your mouth and then as a series of chords as it
slides on down.
        I assure you this is pleasant...

        Outside the ports our Art reels itself across the screens, each panel
the size of a township. Both of the main screens are built transparent and go
reflective only where the light strikes the surface, so the glimmer of the
clearseen stars remains the frame...
                        And w/the stars the veil behind, these
patterns we project speak of Presence In The Void: what other meaning
against that mindful expanse once called the Heavens?

        Within the ship our talk is tracking similar, w/the imagery driving our
visioning and keying our discourse, each of us amplifying the other;
                                                            And at
the center of this swirl of words, riding the crest of this fine high energy,
is Uncle Carl; natural teacher, consummate Spacer, logical Head, pioneer
of the inner planes, awesome on electric balestra, a trust/imbuing presence
w/a big black beard and a monumental mountain/bod, twenty years
beyond...

He is speaking now, a hollow reed for his higher self, soft and sonorous as the bells of Bongo Beta;

'...So what is really going on between us and our perceivers? What kind of a transaction is taking place? What is this bond between us and the folk who come to see our Art; where is the root of it? the base? What is there inherent in this exchange that we mutually find so satisfying?

'Currently my sense of it is this: that we feed these folk harmony and they respond w/waves of warm simpatico resonance, itself a kind of harmony, and we reply w/new resonances of our own, and on it goes, a psychic dialectic that taps into our shared desire to drink of these two excellent nectarish vectors of human evolution,

'*Harmony*, implying the gifts of natural logic and divine order,

'And *Resonance*, by which i mean Human Resonance; all of us together vibing in sync, our collective personal waves congruent, coherent, our wavelengths nesting, amplitude ramping...'

Here he pauses for a longbreath hookah/draw, and soon the sienna steam of wispish whiplash hyperhash rushes through tubes to fill his bod, conducive fuel for his upward spiral, and now his outbreathing cloud...

'And we seek for the sources of these two loving forces, w/this search a part of our natural human drive for exploring our minds, for opening ourselves to the splendor of the All,

'And i see this as the aim of our Art and our music; creating these states of harmony and resonance to move ourselves and our perceivers toward this excellent collective layering of psyches, toward being so in tune w/each other that we combine in ways that open gateways, encompass knowlege larger than our separate minds would singly grasp...'

And now Sandor the sailing master, strong as three Spacers, shifts around in his webs and grins at Uncle Carl. He is broad and hard and dark and his grins are rare, his voice a growl:

'As i see it, o sage of the spaceways, our bond w/our perceivers is wrought of awareness, and the goal of our bond is a merging of minds...

'And from that place, at that level of communion, our awareness broadens and our consciousness is anywhere, everywhere; when the wind is up i can track the thoughts of flame trees and the longings of herons, the fixity of gray granite; and when i listen to the ship, i can hear the hardware speaking: everything has a mind, everything is alive...'

*Ah. Another kindred soul who bonds w/gear...*
Here a pause/he pulls a pawzel of bubbles from his heavy obsidian inhaler; i catch a niff...
Which calls a click of memory:
*Ah/yasss... Sandor.*
*Raised in a gravity well in the methane clouds of Charon, and the alien scent is on him still...*

He travels w/taylor whom we will meet later.

Andrew, lanky Spacerlad from the Hot Zone [where we don't go], drifts toward Sandor. He is Carl's music master, inclined toward sonic samples of the solar winds and early Celtic whistle tunes and also the warblings of certain sonic stars in the Orion cluster. Intense he says,
'Yes Yes, true. When we agree that everything is alive, it follows that there could be a song so universally attuned that it harmonically unifies all living entities. I see it as the unified field theory of music, the music of the spheres, the lost chord, the universal yoga of light and sound, the interstellar OM, the consummate wavelength of everything...'
And now the telling glance; he casts an eye toward Angela... is she listening? tracking?

In a time when everyone can look pretty much as beautiful as they want, Angela rises a paragon, her beauty magnetic, pheromonic, mesmerific;
Though after i get beyond her Glamour, i see she wears her beauty casual, see her more clearly as a complete dynamic human moving through our lives, proud of her work and her victories...

Sadly for Andrew, Angela's eyes are filled w/Alex, he who is free and on his own for the first time, fresh from the gates of Mona Ionia, my old school from nineteen years ago.
Very athletic/writes software/doubles in hardware/knows a volt when he sees one...
Every day an adventure...
Oblivious to Angela.
Who is amazing: after waking forty hours she stays bright/smiling and grin/willing, a daemon for work. She writes good code/works next to Alex/waits for the spark to leap between, sure it will happen...
In the mean, she waxes athletical/loves to compete w/Alex, happy when he wins...
Oblivious to Andrew.

Ah, more feasting.

Another canister, this time a silver/hot Hermes baton, end/overs toward me. I like the way it takes on colors as it tracks through the incense mist and the cathedral rays of shadowlight...

Close now, the warm mouth of the opening canister condenses scents into the air; cous cous steaming, very/very/light, flavour of almonds and saffron/a touch of cardamom and turmeric/a spray of basil...

The stuff pressures into my mouth, and it is like eating an adventure; images and sounds fill the theater of my perception as the physical food flows into my bod; red Aladdin and his host now free of the steamy genie canister, up behind my eyes the vapor music steaming my ears, warm with the rhythms of Salamanca and the ching of clothing made of coins...

I give out w/a wild Larf Laugh; what a wonderful way for an entrée to be!

Electra, you are surpassing Grand this eve, w/your hair floating golden on your fine/wrought back, faery/weaving round your fine fae wings, so huge and beauteous, so gossamer the tissues of translucent veiling waving, the subtle colors changing...

And at your brow the Circlet of Titanya, olden golden magical jewelry, psychic enhancer/faery crown, set w/a centerstone of faceted fluorite to amplify the mind's third eye, wide enough to project through, receive through, everyway ramp your telepathic trans/missions...

And your wispy clothes float about you, all of a fabric of fine/stranded webs, intricate w/sprays of atomies of crystallized celestite...

And your hair in the style of the Willowlands, and your ears so perfect, w/perky points set to perfection; the right touch of imp w/a hint of elf...

Now gliding through and acting cool is fuzzy Mezz. His first encounter w/an animorph in flower? We can tell he is inwardly agape...

Mezz is our commerce master. He is the shipboard authority on everything in the line of cargo/business/law. Ten years older even than Uncle Carl, he is a yankee clipper kind of guy, very regimental in his official counselors' fuzzy wig. Call him also deal/cutter.

The other side of this is his intensity when partying. We are guessing that before he ships aboard the *Ariel* he is some kind of renunciate, storing up all the WILDGUY party/energy he is currently releasing...

He hands me a screen w/my shipshare agreement on it, awaiting my glims. He has me down as 'Anders; artist/engineer, druid, loon.' We previously agree that there is a Divide between lunatic and loon; a lunatic is gone beyond the edge while a loon is wired to the Moon.

Ride the edge, says i, stay wired...

Electra is writ on his screen as 'Navigator, performer, Goddess.' Truer words...

Another canister/this time blue, and the lights in the chamber phase into colorsync. Deeessert is served, and what is dessert but a frrrrrrame of mine? errrr mind?
It comes to me that each course also includes a certain amount of consciousness enhancement.
A touch of Callisto Tea in the cous cous? I recognize that rogerrrrrobot speech thing, where you tend to latch on random syllables and draw them out.
*Deeeeeeessert...*

All that is in this current canister is a saturate/blue/green gas that issues from my nose as i snort my surprise...
Wait, it reveals; persian honey flavour hundred/layer, silver almonds a presence/so sweet, dark/veiled the dancing, sound of drumming, proffered sweetness/the tongue decides...

How better to serve such a thing when in freefall than to make it virtual, a vision in a gas in a canister,
Much like the *Ariel*...

And now for the authors of this feast: i see them in the kitchens aft, programming and charging the canisters each/for/each, tuning them to the tastes of their targets.
This is Lissa and her art.
Her domain is bionics AFW [air/food/water], and there she thrives right well, cordially close to her scents and her herbals and her hydroponic menage.
Here she is in a few sparse words; Spacer dad and Earth mom, a low/grav childhood on O'Neil Fifteen, likes the solitude of space, drawn to the *Ariel* after she meets a special kindred soul who sails w/us, aboard now for near a year...
Whenever we reach planet/fall she seeks to bask in the natural features, leaves the cities straightaway.
Very quiet, her silky words are rare, the essence of the thing at hand. Her council is excellent for she speaks after thinking and is always right. Often she is silent for several days. After these times she can speak sooth and glim the future...
Art for Love,
life in balance,
high sensibilities;
Lissa.

Next to her is Kan, a boney little guy in his forties; tantric epicanthic eyes, enigmatic smile, emperor/ming/beard, long heavy black hair that cascades in freefall...

This convergence of media is his.

Long before his advent aboard the *Ariel* he finds himself fond of holography, resourcefully creating same w/food chemistry and common kitchen utensils. Then his flash of muse/fire: fuse cuisine w/mind/play and get what?

Culinary theatre...

He discovers that reaching people w/scents and tastes gets them clearer w/his holography, opens them especially to all the beauty and imagery and metaphor that he laces into his work.

And after his first successes he goes frenzoid, begins to really ride his inspiration, massively downloading data, goldpanning for prior art, applying the essence of what he learns to entertainments for his friends, getting a rep...

Where to take this? What next?

He hears about the *Ariel*/goes wide in the head/travels three months/five ships/seven/hundred/eighty/million miles to sign on w/us as a rigger, the only open spot.

And makes a right fine rigger too...

Though sometimes he will stop and drift, eyes on vacant/standby, mouth moving, in tune w/invisible ancestor entities that inform and advise him; gnarl/red Dragons and Foo Dogs w/red curly tongues/black wispy whiskers also curled; red and black, ocher and jett, playing across my inner screens as he speaks to them...

Ah, also he is a high/watt Sender of mindframes...

Aboard the *Ariel* he finds the perfect home for his art. He adds elements, refines his sense of what it is that triggers specific responses in general humanity, begins to track the curves of crewfolk. Along the way he inspires Angela to chalk out software to match each experience w/the intended perceiver, inspires Andrew to motif each course, Alex to conjure up the canisters/each of them unique, and also artful Lissa to blend the entheogenic enhancers...

I hope one night that Kan will mix the canisters, that i might get the food/dreams tuned for Lissa or Angela or best of all, Kan...

In his work, he says, he uses a modified dreamtracker to record his images direct from his visualizations, then plays them back holographic.

[ *...a brain/direct interface... the Holy Grail of Hardware! the Voice*
*that informs me asks for more about dreamtrackers...* ]
                                                            And while
Kan is training himself to put images into the dreamtracker, he is also amping
his ability to Send these images into other people's heads. And now Spice
and physical re/imaging will evolve him farther faster...
        What will he have going in a month, a year?
        Definitely beyond kitchen holography...

# 7   A Lightshow for Ganymede



Nine days later...
And glimming the view through the port in my cabin i stare in a rapture at the face of Ganymede, my focus as constant as Ganymede's own unto Master Juppiter, rapt for all his orbit round.
Ganymede, handservant to Juppiter the AllFather...
Ganymede, starboard and away, bigger even than bright Mercury, a black/white puzzleboard/mosaic moon, the succinct tectonic plates each as big as Alaska... Weird Ganymede where internal slurries of ice melt and erupt volcanic and carve the surface like lava, w/the fresh floes of new white ice fingering on down the blue/ice plains...
Here are rare concentric cliff/craters a hundred miles across, each an ancient set of rings, bright white on soft/white, their sheer faces stratified in black/white layers, ice w/the coal/black soil...
I fix on one of them: the dark rays of ejecta, blown from the center, form an odd extended eight/ray star/symbol on the landscape: it skry's to my mindseye the pictogram for laser/light...
A favorable sign, for tonight we perform for the good folk of Ganymede; my first curtain w/Uncle Carl's Visual Band...

These heroes, it turns out, have an enormous following.
They have, e'en now, an absolute fan/atical megathrong of wildhearts waiting Ganymoonside, amped and primed by a steady stream of videolo feeds, out from the Ariel and up to the Wire, all the streaks of beaming bits ribboning out to everywhere, to lonely folks in mining camps on big rock/candy moons, folk away from home ensconced in airless weightless stasis/point medical research industrial silicon O'Neal colonies, to folk floating isolated on islands ranged across the solar plane...
And soon, at l'heure bleu, we will give them our fresh and full/on complete evening show, Uncle Carl and the Band and the Light of the Sun...
And yr anders.

Uncle Carl's is the original Spacer band, and they define a certain ethos out here in the edge/places like Ganymede. In the Great Migration from the natal planet, Uncle Carl is there at the start; since then he is nineteen years on the road, seven more aboard the delicate and beautiful *Ariel*...

And the rest, like Sandor and Kan and Lissa, well steeped in Spacer ways, born in the sky in the first wave of native Spacers. And Alex and fuzzy Mezz and all the others, each w/their story, bravely living their Spacer élan...

Much the same as these far/cast folk of Ganymede Edge; all of us dwelling in alien environs, all of us owning a longing for verdant waterworld Earth...

The surface rolls closer, scrolling past the port.

And my grinning discovery of Ganymede proceeds. As it is w/Lightshows, the novelty of the moment creates a special fine frisson, a high sizzling buzz of synergistic Is/ness...

Zzog!

Over there!

Some brighter/ newer sections of the puzzle run in swaths among the polygons of darker older craters: i see pairs of parallel lines! Like the canals of red Mars or the warp of a loom, they speak to me of an intelligence at work...

Is Ganymede pre/habited?

That would for sure put the Big Kybosh on the upcoming terraforming project...

Ah, Ganymede, the great experiment:

The plan is to alter the place bigtime: bring the molten moon/core closer to the surface to heat the plates, turn all the ice to oxygen in an ongoing hydrogen/powered reaction, introduce a lithosphere and Earth/genotypes. Very cozy for us terrestrials...

Is that what i am doing w/Electra? Andersforming?

Since our sojourn on Cyclo she is totally my creation, lapping up my words and my Will as i craft her into matching w/my conscious self, her a perfectible malleable mirror for my own idealized desires...

And this process is cyclical and ongoing, for w/each fantasy we achieve i gain some overstanding/insight into my own motivation, come through clearer w/meself and w/her, ready to frame w/her our next fantasy,

Who better?

She can draw on every image ever posted, every file or figure or fact, be wise as Aristotle, Aristophanes, Archimedes, Epicurious, quote any line of Shakespeare, sing any song in any style from any age, wear the shape of any reasonable mammal; tonight, for me she will be a humanimorph snow leopard, sleek w/white catfur and that musical animal snarl...

And yet...
Stirrings of *(what)* w/in me?
Curious now, i wonder;
what of the taste and feel of a human lover...
A sniff of premonition here.

We warp into orbit, overcrossing the shadow line where the planet/lit swath divides from the darkside.
Juppiter, U Pater, Jove Father, All/Father...
It is the Father's good pleasure to give the gifts of the kingdom to all his children, and the ice walls of Ganymede's concentric canyons now blaze bright w/reflected light from the face of that Father planet, out here nearly as lambent as the distant Sun...

And this: as we orbit around to the warmer ice/plates i see these frosty exhalations, clouds of blue/white fissure ice. I mind/explore primordial, imagine whole mountains miles high lifting and splitting, spewing leagues of this volcanic ice, oceans of frozen water...

And now we cross what they call the Fold, that slice of moon that is lit by Juppiter and the Sun likewise. Owing to the relative geometry of these Celestial Bods, this is a traveling phasing phenomenon.
Here we can catch the best rays so here we will anchor, moving in sync w/this scythe of brightness, performing when the times are right. With Ganymede's orbit at seven/point/two E/days, we will run two shows in a week, a day before and a day after the moon is aligned between the planet and the Sun, when Ganymede crosses his own shadow as it falls upon Juppiter.

Closer now to the surface we get best effect from the reflected ice/light, and i see six more circular ripple formations...
Younger versions of these peculiar concentric craters can be seen on Mercury, Earth's Moon, and Callisto the Party Planet. All of these places also show Eleuthran presence. Did the Eleuthrans prefer these multi/ring formations as the sites for their temples? What of the Feng Shui for these sites, what of the ley/line tellurics?
The craters on Ganymede are often broken by the shifting plates as they resurface themselves; how grand it would be to find an intact one w/another Eleuthran temple...
I track the spot of the laser/symbol crater and note it, at the same time wondering about Electra; will her recent connect w/things Eleuthran have the same effect on her as would the discovery of Eleuthran culture on the plains of Ganymede?

*

These things i now know about my art:

Lightshows are more than entertainment: they are holy instruments for the evolution of consciousness.

On a magical level, certain talismanic figures of projected light become patterns for the calling of Power. These figures, recalled to the mind, attune that instrument to receive specific types of energy; love, inspiration, mystical experience, healing, dimensional travel, time expansion, creativity, change.

And Lightshows are also the perfect emblem of the Fresh Age, the age of the Alchemical Wedding, for here in this form is the graceful interface of science and magic, the place where Consciousness and Technology conjoin to yield this artful balance; technologically enhanced consciousness and the conscious use of technology...

And Spice is the ultimate Lightshow enhancement: both are about creating expanded awareness. Because of the abstract nature of the art, elevated states of consciousness add important layers of meaning, open us to the metaphorical, add the vital dimension of scale...

It is this: we need to rise above the byplay, get outside our heads from time to time for the sake of the overview, experience the same kind of shift in perspective that occurs when first we see our birth/world from high orbit...

And also this; in the Fresh Age, a constantly evolving expanding awareness is the highest option for any sentient being...

At one point in time, before police worked for everyone on a subscription basis, chemically expanded awareness was a proscribed fringe exercise. Later, w/the coming of the Fresh Age, these prevailing attitudes lifted; and now

We agree that our desire to evolve is a natural human inclination, and, rather than limiting this kind of thing, we know that what we really need are more and better vectors for achieving this progressive evolutionary dynamic...

And from this enlightened frame of mind uprises a huge popular surge; a mad synergy of electronics, chemistry, spiritual disciplines, hybrid plant strains; all w/lovingly crafted strengths and powers, free of side effects and psychotropic noise, to be used singly and in combination, w/cumulative benefits/lessons that accrue over a lifetime,

And thus is born Personal Evolution as a wide/spread reason for being, and from this flows the peaceful integration of human energies, conscious industries, true religions,

And thrown wide are the Gates of God Realization as begins the fullscale joyful pursuit of interesting and useful techno/chemical/shamanic Highs...

To this wild brew we will soon add the treasure/gift of Eleuthra...


A central truth;

The enhancing of consciousness is a Lightshow Tradition.

It is part of our art to tune our shows and the internal dramas of our guests to the same wavelength. If we are all in a similar state of consciousness the experience is more unified, and if we are all familiar with/ensconced in the same consciousness/enhancing agent, then together we can better craft the current moment's entrancement, find and follow the thematic threads that fulfill the Will of us all...

Before Spice it was Moon Dust from Phobos, then Melt, an impossible gooey mass that got you high, cured the freefall kweezies, and, as a mark of distinction, turned your tongue blue...

For Lightshows and love and dancing, Spice is superior in all regards.

To be absolutely clear about this; our hold is packed to the hatches w/Spice. These *Ariel* folk are evolutionary visionaries, and we are the first ship to carry Spice out of Io.


*


The Main Chamber is rigged now for display: webs of golden ropes wave topographic and wait for patrons, and hovering near where their hands will be, writhing serpent/sinuous, are clear tubes for the sipping of sustenance; specifically, Spice...

Another empty hall, thinks i, prescient w/the promise of another show. I check my sightlines one more time.

Tonight we host the core Carl clientele, those who most truly know his shows. This will be their first chance to sample Spice and yr scribe and the Lights of Eleuthra; it will be for me a bellwether night...

I set my cabin for blue/festoon and the walls go velvet blue. Freeeeefalling, i tuck and roll out of my jumper and savour the air upon my bare bod.

I push off for the water chamber and immerse; steamy jets of spray spin me pleasant and an actual bar of sandalwood soap...

And an hour of water conquers the rigors of a forty/hour pre/show, the two months of ramping intensity and thor/hammer effort. *The Work is Done/The Work is Done* becomes a mantra now so oft is it repeated...

Exquisite the feeling of clean hair...

I emerge dry, and three pods circle w/wet/hot cotton towels, each laden w/a freight of scent, a cleansing niff of hyssop...

Now dry towels and now the Rosewood Box hovering in front of me. I lift the Green/Man lid and release a rush of magical gear and the blue light bounces in rays from the circlets and wrist/bands and rings and ropes and pendants set afloat by the opening box; silver links of chain cast back the blue light, tracing limpid circles on the somber blue walls...

My old denim robe floats from the rosewood deep: what seems to me my shadow or my ghost is actually aetheric armour, charged six ways: w/auspicious stars, w/words of Power, in holy smokes of purple sage compounded w/the nectars of the red berries the Welsh call *borfes y gwion,* w/the seeds of the herbs castor and tonka sewn into cowl and cuffs and hem, and the whole of it washed in the light of the moons of three worlds, the Earth and Mars and now Juppiter the Vast...

And now the jade box w/the face of Nepenthe rises to my hand, and also my Sphere the Moontrader for a sip of mine own occult innerconscious otherself...

And as Nepenthe's sweet breath and mine are mingling i feel the onset of that special state of hyper/clarity, the opening screen of the Spice experience...

And together w/this otherself that is also me, there opens a dialogue; we quell and calm the waters, grant ourselves forgiveness, concile our inner differences until my desires are united and my Will integral...

And now the box of Oak and a wild spray of implements and satiny wood...

And they each take a vector for their space in the frame of the dodecahedron altar, which e'en now is moving to its' spot in the center of the chamber;

And now comes the Goddess figure & the flintblade & flax/flowers, each in a lightsphere, and all these instruments arrange themselves spatial, move to their places in the frame...

I put on my Musing Circlet of citrine and amber and breathe in the *Ariel's* good air...

It is time for the Working that Performs Itself; my Way In, a conjure to the center from Shirira's *Book of Days,* another gift from the Lumière...

And on in;

I create six/sided Celestial sacred space and Invoke; out of nothing, everything...

My offering is a wireframe outline incense pyramid of blue Shirira juniper, w/each edge an inch/each an incense rope, eight edges in all as there are eight folds in Buddha's path/his ecstatic plan for placing light w/in...

I flame the pyramid's five corners and watch as it leaves my hand; a slow/drifting polygon of five radiant ember/points, rolling as it goes, moving to the altar center where stasis will hover it into place, w/the curvy blue smokes tailing away in coils...

And as the corners spark the ends of each edge alight, the five bright points become sixteen. Now near the altar center, the eight strands rest in stasis relation one to the other, each rope burning at both ends, vapor snails radiating spherically outward...

I en/trance, expand into the complicated trails of carbonizing juniper...

*O Awen from Annwn, my muse and inspirer, i surrender all unto Thee, unto You who are Spirit/i too am Spirit, more than this envelope of flesh...*

*With love and w/grace i place myself before Thee, hollow and a conduit for aether/Thy holy breath, for true dreams/the spinning of Thy mindseye, for Thy word/the aural fabric of magic...*

Wisps waft my nostrils, scillia sensing incense scents.
Time unwinds...

And i am a city of cells, a ship of cells, sailing ever to the center, beam/guiding on the Voice, the source of the stream of beautiful visions...

That cerebrate now across my brainscreen, a ramping current of color and insight and drama and solace and a thousand kinds of longing, an ongoing image immersion w/the fluid force of seawaves...

Scent tendrils spiral outward endless before my empty eyes, then showtime...

*

On the bridge now,
And Carl's first staves of notes Eleuthran come grinning forth from the freefall stage up forward, and the welcome/familiar sounds steady me eager/ready, and i cue through my usual moves; light incense, stretch, check sightlines, check read/outs, run a final alignment w/my beams infrared/invisible...
We are, b'Zzog, full to the locks w/perceivers; over two hundred of the faithful now ride the golden nets in our Main Salon, a collage of

folk: rocky miners & loner Spacers, sharp/dressed sireens up from the toney ports of Ganymede, travelers & seekers from other moons of Juppiter...

Tales of our art and my alien teachers and their gifts/a fine high pre/show buzz precedes us, hums the Hall delicious; i look out on faces amped bright w/expectation...

We open w/fractal washes, colors tone/linked to the moody minor chords of Uncle Carl. A clever balance of the sequencing colors gives a figure/ground reversal on every upbeat, and the climax of every run brings a flash from our white/light Bravas, all intermixing w/novel curls of shipboard lightning cavorting in the contrasting dark, argent arcs for our glassy glims w/every change in time or key...

Out here the source/light is distant rarefied, so we go w/muted themes from the solar nodes and then advance the brassy laser figures. Thus i will crown this first piece w/its' finale, my honor to add my classical artform to the Ariel's visual vocabulary...

And w/a splash of elation i realize,

Working w/light, how essential this is; to transcend the metaphor and work w/the actual stuff, to take the light in, lens it through the gate between your brows, feel it blow through you zephyr/sharp, through your every cell, an infusion of Spirit so lucidly effable, so like the clarifying rush of new Knowlege expanding through your mind...

Now the ship crosses Ganymede's wide mercator and, cathedral/soft, the Sunlight joins the gleam of Juppiter, a lovely ramping of combining energies...

A cheer,

And i bow to the magnificence of Sol, Central Sun, also called Gwydion, Apollo, Ahura Mazda... Way out here your warming rays are wildly welcome, and we thank Thee for Thy presence this night...

From outside the Ariel the view is splendid. Three of Kan's camera/pods are out on the starboard tack taking videolo snaps, their signal translating into a projection of the *Ariel* in the center of the Hall...

Nice touch sez i...

And now from our revelers a round of that rapping on the hull plates that passes for applause...

And this Ariel image is wondrous/fine, a perfect animated *Ariel* model, the ultimate ship in a bottle.

Through the image's intricate rigging i see the replica beams of channeled
Sunlight and planetlight switching from port to port: this as the real beams
flash through the ports in the chamber around us...

On the model, infinitely
miniature scanning boxes track their trademark silver/fantam patterns on
three/meter sails. The ones outside are somewhat larger, each of them as
wide as Io Miner's Port...

The real theater of any entertainment is the mind of the perceiver,
and we would enhance this hall w/Spice,

Thus my debut comes now, nicely
timed to match our first collective spectraluminous *rushhhhh*...

And likewise
Carl and the band come to this same point of Overwhelm, and in the
sudden silence i center and begin;

*...i am a psychic screen, how you see me is who i become;
i am smoke on the wind, a leaf on the wind...*

Consciously i invoke this continuum, this loop between me and my
perceivers...

I balance on my stanchions and scan the folk: i read discovery
smiles, wonderglimmers and wide eyes;

*...how would we be changed this night?...*

And now we Spice/connect, yr anders and the Carls and our netsfull
of edge/riders, pilots, nav/techs, miners & sireens, all of us together taking
our private dramas, our dreams of love/comfort/adventure and subsuming
them into our new collective perceiver desire/bod Other,

Where these
diverse desires fuse, distill, concatenate together, w/our mammal fantasies
morphing into something far larger/more transcendent;

The yearning for
that which is the core of all desiring, the spirit who is our completion and
safety and homecoming, who is total acceptance and forgiveness and a
gateway to mysteries,

*{ ...the Universal Beloved... }*

Ah, now i have the sense of it...

My hand, my touch at last; o dear gear our time is now...
fingertips/nerves relay contact, controls connect w/flesh and

I breathe images;

out of the darkness come these beams/these beacons of my art, splaying
now into visual arpeggia, visual runs on the Eleuthran lexicon of the seven
high emotions, symbolic food for hungry post/rational minds...
                                                            And now
the Sun's red red rays come searching through the ports, become the
red/bright pulse of our desiring, and in this our theme reveals...
                                                        And here in
this red/beamy frame i speak the hearts of all of us here, give visual voice to
our collective Chiefest Longing;
                        *That you come unto us, O Perfect Mate,*
*O Most Cherished, O Goddess Doorway, twin flame, soulmate, betterpart,*
*author of our overstanding and muse of our highest aspiring...*
                                                *Draw us to your*
*dwelling in the place of satiation, where we can calm the mammal beast and*
*the heat that sings in our blood...*
                        *Where all that is physical falls away and all*
*that is left is our Will and the Love that guides it...*
                                        *Where, secure in the*
*knowlege of knowing you, we rise now out of ourselves in a way free of our*
*physical abodes,*
                *And thus, free of form, we manifest into shapely clouds of*
*amethyst electrons, flowing unto you O Great Beloved, hungry w/magnetism,*
*and*
    *Blythely bonding we swing w/you now in bipolar balance, our ancient ache*
*of sapient wanting finally reaching its' red resolve...*


        Now we are past our physical hungers, and now too our Root Fear
is laid to rest, for as electrons we are eternal; and thus we leave the drama of
symbols and rise into thought/form theatre...
                                        Itself an amethyst flow/space
beyond technique and technology, beyond personal spin, where our
combined minds command the play of light, where we are all of us together
a violet vixen brew of Flow, a cupfull of colors cast on a fogbank, a smooth
concentric fluid groove, an endless stream of beautiful visions...
                                                        And
grooving thus we arrive over time ecstatic/in unison/out of our bods together,
sailing into that mystery where color becomes thought and thought itself is
transcended, the spectral sprays of wavelengths charging and re/charging
our brains w/color direct through the optic nerve...
        Another fine mesh...


        And now for closure; i start to surf our combined attention wave,
hanging nicely inside the curl of information saturation...
                                                And now i lessen

the levels of complexity and intensity, bank the flow of the stuff of visioning, create more and more dark...

I sense Uncle Carl, Sandor, Kan, Lissa, Alex, Angela; from Electra a wave of orchid love...

And w/everyone relaxed and giving attention we suffuse the Hall bright w/a special turquoise monochrome wash, an exact multiple of the Spice frequency,

And truly, there are lucinations...


And after, i am hollow, an empty amphora; the afterglow of bonding still throbbing in the air around me...

And yes, this *Ariel* thing is working out grandly well; i grant myself the passing of the audition, grant myself entry, one of the family by word and by deed...

And yes, echoes of our congregations' soulmate/yearnings still linger in my personal mind; how much of my own desiring have i placed in tonight's performance/sending?

A human lover...

# 8 Jayme

> *'Three pods are four times as much fun as
> two pods'*
>
> *-- anders' third law of pods*

 

I will introduce you now to that most helpful and responsible entity, the wondrous and ubiquitous Pod.


*Ode to a Pod*

*This is jayme.*
*Jayme the pod.*
*If you ask him his name,*
*    that's what he will say.*
*Jay Me.*
*His specialty is threaded fasteners.*
*In his default mode*
*    he hovers at my shoulder.*
*When i point to a bolt,*
*    he swoops like a mad/ball in and*
*    proffers the appropriate socket/hex/phillips,*
*    and twists that puppy out.*
*If i point at a threaded hole,*
*    he'll zap over to ship's stores*
*    come back w/just the right capscrew or torxbolt,*
*    whip it into that hole*
*    and torque it to spec.*
*A mighty handy guy is*
*    jayme.*


Most pods are worker pods, and come in a variety of sizes and shapes. Sometimes they travel in packs, like sets of wrenches; some have a wide range of skills like the popular swiss/army pod, and some are very specialized: tritanium welding, mass spectroscopy, dust catchers.

They are the ultimate peripherals.

They are tools that can fly and position themselves finitely anywhere in a three/dimensional space then move precisely to any other point and hang there in stasis. This is a handy thing for, say, a clearplex cutter, a remote camera, a pinstriper trim/painter to be able to do.

Some have stereo/lithographic ability: they can carve three/dee objects. Artists use them as nifty pantographs: hand shapes clay, pod shapes anything; delayed or in real/time, remembered or forgot.

They make wonderful machinists, riggers, recorders.

Their tiny stasis/field generators rarely need charging, and they are perfectly reliable.

And, yes, they are good interfacers.

They can be voice/directed or run from a computer, netted together or left to follow their own inner workings. They learn from experience, and each one recognizes the primary and secondary beings they work with. They speak and have distinct voices so they can be distinguished easily on a comm/link. They have NAMES so they can be easily ADDRESSED over comm/links...

And they have personalities; pods are  the hamsters of the Fresh Age.

There are three hundred and forty of them aboard the Ariel. And we think they are multiplying.

# 9 Heart/Rite




A week later in my blue velvet cabin, close on w/gentle Electra;
   A whiff of hyssop...


Picture two beings, Electra and Myself, floating facing each other in
lotus/pentagram, hands at our folded knees. We are in freefall magical gear,
psychic crowns and balance belts and amplifier body jewels, and we are
largely hugely steeped in
                    Spice...


We relax into our love connection/our bridge of sighs; we embrace,
return to lotus and
                    Begin spin/drifting, matching each to the other our
flexures and our curves, our languid limb/rhythms and the songs of our
respiring,
                    And as amplified sensate beings we both now reach out, and
between our separate reaching single fingertips, almost touching, we cast a
leaping spark of blue...
                        And in time we draw the spark out to a line, a blue
line formed of our longing,
                        And now another and now there are two, now
three now five lines linking, more and more lines splaying away between our
fingertips,
                        And now our fingers flex and weave, leaving the lines in cat's
cradle/a hundred patterning lines of blue that we each in turn pass across to
the other, adding to the pattern as we go, intricate blue butterfly symmetries...


Oh yes, i hear the Celestial music,
                            The liquid chords restoring
to order my saturate cellular structure...
                            And thus surprised the stricting
stressbands across my chest release, let go, get gone for good,
                                And thus
freed i breathe far vaster volumes of charging breath; and thus overfueled,
the seven Great Wheels of energy align along my spine, mightily charge and
now
      Loose
            their generative forces as color and light...
                            And w/these forces i

now project around me a sphere of light expressed, an auric nimbus...



And note for note Electra is tracking,
tuned like/minded, and her light is as mine and they mingle, and our two
nimbii merge as we stately turn in freefall...

The chamber is large and stasis fields cushion the walls on all six sides...
It is dark and quiet, save for our light and the music that our bods
make, curving through the air...
We open out of lotus and face across an intimate bodspan; we move
at honey/speed and our light w/us likewise,

And settled into this new
alignment i cup my hands before me and breathe into them a prahnic charge
of my own amplified life/force, see it as a sphere, a visualized globe of
dense radiant energy, a solid shape w/heft and mass that i Will into
crystallizing...

Electra does likewise, and we face each other, hold in our
hands these mindformed spheres, each our own, and now we move as
mirrors; arms back, our wrists arc, and now slow/motion we push our
spheres toward each other, launching forward these weighty white/light
plasma/balls in zero/gee...

And as the spheres move ever so slow across the
space, the principles of Newton send us moving ever so slowly opposite,
crown over anklets, spin/drifting toward the walls, where the perfect amount
of give and stasis/recoil send us grinning back toward each other,

Where in
liquid grace we turn in air and catch the spheres oncoming our way, whereon
we are checked and impelled back by the sphere/mass, each of us now
cradling the others' encapsulated gift of thought...

And as i am carried
smoothly back to the stasis/cushioned wall i merge w/this sphere of visioning
sent by Electra, her opening strophe in this courtly game of love...

And
through her eyes I see my male self naked, bod bronzed, scars healed,
unafraid, my long hair all black, my image rippling w/radiant concentrated
power...

And pleased i see Electra smile, exquisite and eloquent, as my
speaking sphere conveys to her my own opening vision...

We connect w/the stasis/cushions and flow now back, each toward
the other. With all the poesy my passioned mind can master i frame a second
sending and give it unto the sphere i will send to her.

In matching motion we close on each other.

In tune, we each release the spheres in our hands; they cross in the air, two slow/moving comet/trains crossing, two radiant stones dropped down a well in a mirror dimension...

When we catch them, each the other's, they check our forward momentum and move us smoothly back into the stasis/cushions once again. Gratefully we receive and gracefully we rebound, and begin the cycle anew...

Empathic amplifiers hum and glitter at belt and brow, enhance our red awareness, move us to shed our robes to better use our bods. Electra's arms and legs and back glisten and catch the light as she rolls toward me...

And thus my current sending is more in the realm of Eros as i awaken to her subtle construction, and familiar comes the delicious urge to feed sensation to know textures to slide silken flesh to flesh, to know in every sense, to live as the God Incarnate...

My sendings grow horns, Pan for Aphrodite, the hunger of our bods augmented, transmitted, LINKED!

And now we coast unto each other, and now our hand/spheres sail away and fade as we release them,

And i know her heat as my own, i see her moist lips part, jewelry drifting away, spheres gliding past, all triumphant disarray...

Oh skin so pale so passion/warm, subtle breasts so pleasing to my lips, warm curves rounding to my hands, sounds of pleasure mingling;

I dissolve into sensation, the skinsoft signals wafting synaptic on my wide opening paleo/senses, my seven centers triggering w/every wanton slide of Electra thigh, compassionate caresses/neuron cascades, a ramping charge of aureole magic, labial magic, the Central Penetralia, the Houses of Exuberance, The Holy Fires of Zarathustra, the pulsing blood of the Goat/horn God in muscles strained in leaping thrusting

*The Great Rite! The Great Rite!*

Magic is love, springs from love, creates love...
We have magic together, once then again.

We drift naked/languid/spent
breathing ragged/deep
our musk and brimstone recent
our amber chamber dark

And soft the smoke/the grayness melts us
   out of the i and thou
     the envelope of skin
opens us unto the All
   frees us
      everywhere/anything/everything
   and infinitely outward
     flow the ring/ripples
       our blue awareness...

Seven weeks out from Callisto i have my Lunar Lightshow Vision;
i am ecstatic/alive w/the glorious possibilities.

In my ramping exultation i seek Electra, seek her sustaining
resonance. I find her in the nav/chamber and together we head for the
Starboard Promenade.

Through the ports and the view is hugely beautiful: Ganymede,
his great mass rising, separates himself from Juppiter's aegis; Callisto looms
behind, and together they wheel in a dance of Gods, careless of watchers,
eternal.

When i to Electra tell my tale her eyes go wide and lambent,
wattage ramping up, mirroring mine own. She sees the great evolutionary
sweep of the thing: sees how our currently wonderful life could now be
epic...

And so to the bridge to find Uncle Carl and Sandor the sailing
master. They are strapped into their couches on either side of taylor/saylor,
laughing like loons, high on Spice and space. Spice in truth is everywhere
hanging in the air, all the braided green ropes of smoke drifting about...

They register my presence as i touch the dreamtracker circlet at
my brow: the recording is good, colors true, crystalline definition...

Bless Excellent Hardware.

I clip the playback visor to the tracker and hand it to the aware
and eager Uncle Carl...

His face changes as his eyes close, going into knowing as the Vision
spools itself into his brain. He goes contemplative as the source track ends;
he opens his eyes and looks away toward the ecliptic horizon, and now a
*glint!*

I know what he sees: the entire Home Planet united in physical
spiritual telepathic evanescent experience, an experience that we provide,
a heady mélange of Eleuthran music and light and

Spice...

The buzz would be up and the call for Spice would be global,
system/wide...

Five expressions cross the face of conscious Uncle Carl;
pragmatic/romantic/ecstatic/melodic/angelic, and now all these embryonic
plans migrate logistical through the levels behind his brow, until finally he
goes beatific/altruistic and Carl the Godly Man of Flow sees a skywide

opportunity beyond his wildest; a frame for home/world planetary evolution, a crown for the Fresh Age, the highest of Holy Works...

And now the tracker goes to Sandor, and he breathes my Vision in. Sandor has the Wisdom when it comes to solar sailers: his burnished rep comes from when space/racing first went Bigtime, and his life before the *Ariel* someday deserves him a tale of his own...

He comes out of the tracking Vision smiling, the widest yet to grace his face; he loves it, says we can totally b'Zzog bring this thing into being. He knows about this pair of surplus GE91's that can be modified to visible wavelengths, and also he has this friend...

Into the Mystic one more time, Yah!


Earth's Moon...

Sandor says after our shows over Callisto we go to Earth's Moon. We can sell our Spice for Best Price and do shows for the Luna/folk, then organize for the most Epic Altered/State Event currently imaginable, the greatest party in the history of the known worlds...

South, East, West, North;
  As Above so Below.


In Celestial magical workings we transcend the circle for the sphere. The elements of Fire and Air, Water and Earth, are here augmented by Aether, set above as the realm of spirit and true Vision, and Wood, set below as telepathic portal into the realm of animate life.

The energies of the Six Elements present in sacred space are the same six forces at work w/in me. I balance or accentuate these inner forces by trading flow w/each of them. I use the altar/gear before me to pattern my attracting; cup, candle, censor, sphere...

It works this way: To raise Mental Fire, i merge w/the flame. To damp excessive Fire, i connect w/the cup of charged Water: the Fire flows to the cup and charges it further, and thus i balance...

I would speak of my altar.

It is an open Oaken dodecahedral outline framework one meter across, w/twelve pentagonal panes. Oakmoss covers the living frame, and stasis fields hold all the magical tools in place inside, the fields so delicately selective that the smoke from the silver censor in the center still fragrantly radiates...

These boughs are of the Earth, where it is Spring.


Earlier, on our way to Callisto, the Voice commends me and the wood/chips fly. In the heady chisel/bite scent of sap and amber and subtle phloemy fluids i shape a living altar of barky Oak, each branch forearm/thick and thirteen inches, each end healed into the end of the next and its' neighbor w/elixirs and magic, forming the holy polygon.

Lissa brings the green/scented oakmoss to grow on the branches' bark, w/the moss to do the work of leaves and roots for the living oaken frame, draw Sun/energy through chlorophyll conversion, sip moisture from the air through porous brachts...

I charm the whole, all the cells, to live in harmony as something other, content in their uniquity.


Elsewhere in the *Ariel* are seventy/three very special houseplants;
  Lissa's Elysium,

Where various stripes of freefall leafballs like lichens and hybrid fuschias happily consume prodigious $CO_2$ and kick out oxygen. They are also beautiful as only a natural object can be, changing over time, in tune w/Lissa and their own central spherical hydroponic matrices.

The altar is a natural extrapolation of their unicentric shapes.

In the altar center i place a partial geode of blue chrysacola and clear druzy quartz; fine lithic energy, and when combined w/Spice a manifestation amplifier. I surround the stone w/a bioluminous flux and it becomes a central sun, fiery white the light shining through the druzy quartz, radiating brightly to nourish and sustain.

With these pieces of the home world in my hands i am connected, recreated, in touch w/the leafy Green God...

Though oft i ponder this dark equation: my Spacer bod/the gravity of Earth = anders stays off/planet, too light o'bone and thin of sinew to ever touch the Earth...

This is what i learn from Sandor about sailing:

The orbits of the planets are all roughly in the same plane, and all voyages are plotted across the disc that the orbits describe.

Sailing strategies are coursed according to the position of the starting and ending points relative to the Sun, which is the center of a compass rose, w/Sun/North being toward the first degree of the constellation of Capricorn, Sun/South being the first degree of the sign of the Moonchild, and on around the rose, three/hundred/sixty degrees.

Trips out from the Sun are fairly straightforward. Since the solar wind moves at the speed of light, we have the potential of constant acceleration up to that speed, although it would take us the diameters of several dozen solar systems to achieve it.

Arcs are the common course plots, first going concentric with, then sailing across the direction of radiant energy.

Coming back is more interesting. A voyage toward the Sun would begin by sailing *away* from the Sun, picking up speed as we neared some planet, then using the planet's gravity to sling us around back toward the Sun, the sails reefed and ion power on.

Good for leisurely acceleration, the ion drive is supplemented by chemical rocket thrusters. Thruster fuel is limited, and they are mainly used for quick course corrections and docking.

Getting off/course, a loss of forward momentum, or a forced change of direction means that it becomes sailing/improv time.

This can add years to a voyage.

Sometimes this means tacking back around toward the nearest serious rock and doing the slingshot again, or rising above the ecliptic for advantageous weather, or shortcutting through uncharted bogs of rocky space; any kind of inventive solution even if risky...

Every time a course correction comes up aboard the *Ariel,* we hear these chimes throughout the ship, over all the helmet/comms of anyone working Outside, as flashing lights for folk w/their music turned up: one chime half an hour before, two at ten minutes, three at five minutes, then continuous for one minute just before. The chimes remind us to batten down whatever is loose: when the ship turns, anything inside still in freefall tends to keep going straight.

Changes in direction are done nice and easy. With the ship over a mile long and two miles wide, a lot of mass/torqueing can happen even in a gentle sailing turn. A thruster turn requires even more finesse, using power to balance turning gees and time/under/inertia against the strength of the rigging cables...

*

A full March/Hare Moon on Earth tonight.
We are six months out from Callisto, the Party Planet, and due to the very Grandfather of Sunstorms, we are being forced to cross the upper fringe of the Belts.
This is doubly dangerous because of the variability of Solar Winds and the numberless bits of unmappable planetstuff flying around out here. Because of our many jogs and nips thusfar, a true course eludes us, and a good deal more of this creative three/dimensional sailing will be required to make it through. Sandor says only about three in ten solar sailers survive this passage.

I am in my cabin laying out my magical instruments.
I fight to master my fear: breathe, slow my heart, steady my hands.
These moments come; they are part of the deal i make w/myself when i sail. Now is the time for no regrets; now i find out if i really believe what i say i believe about my faith in the Higher Powers and the afterlife...
In freefall i clasp my knees to my chest and lower my head, the rabbit position. I face the sacred space's upward quarter:

*Oh Thou Great and Eternal Celestial All*
*I beseech Thee to spare us this peril,*
*Please, Please, Please, get us through this,*
*May my boon harm none and serve Thy highest good,*
*May the granting cause Thee pleasure and joy.*
*Please, Please, Please, get us through this,*
*I ask...*

And a *TREMENDOUS CRASH!*
Oh Holy Mother! Something pretty big...
The ship comes hard about and i fall toward the cabin wall. I land on my shoulder and the altar/Kruntch!/hits and goes rolling...
KLARSH!
The twice/horrible sound of heavy gear crashing through bulkheads...
Way off in the rigging i sense cables snapping *BIGtime* as momentum rips away some winches and *#!*

This is Very Bad!
O Great Humping Goddess Please Not A Wreck!
The gees increase
and i am pressed to the wall. I shiver w/fear and breathe in gulps and sobs.
What am i doing out here? Oh Please Please Please Save Me...

First the gees let up and now the metal stops screaming and grinding.
Everything is adrenaline/bright. Air! Is it okay? Hull breach? Electra!
As soon as i can i drag myself over to open the cabin seal. Good!
It's working! Corridor... some lights out, no hiss, some groans, no
screams...
Voices on the comm/link;
We all check in by number, just like in the drills; everyone's alive!
Now the reports; the hull is okay, major damage to the sailing gear on the
port side, major damage to the portside sailing electronics...
I sense Sandor on the bridge, numbly reefing the shredded
portside sails...

*

We are, uh, adrift.
The ship is filled w/frantic work/sounds. We have to keep sailing,
somehow get through the rest of this stony patch of space.
I move stiff and hurtful: after six months of freefall the sudden
deceleration creams me.
And w/ion power on, the ship feels so hulking weird: walls are floors,
everything is everywhere: half the doors are jammed...
What of the show/gear?

Electra finds me. Her hand goes to the pulsepoint on my wrist and
i feel her steady calm. I get my bearings.
That she can do this in the midst of all the chaos... This is more
than i could give her; how has she grown beyond the nature of her teacher?

Sandor and Uncle Carl and i will take turns at the thrusters,
correcting as best we can for Big Rocks. I dread this: before firing, all who
are Outside w/the work party need to be clipped to the cables and away
from the thrusters. Taylor the Saylor figures out the bursts and velocities,
and blasts the smaller rock bits w/the ion cannon. He also keeps track of the
work parties through their comms, and he gets the sense of most of the
actual words. Though if something goes awry it is still me, the human, who
watches out for the other humans.
Half a dozen major systems damaged including atmospherics,
propulsion, navigation; two fires, one near the bridge...

# 13  Ariel's Tale / The Wreck of the Solar Sailer

Before this fortuitous meeting, this cresting of fate, my name is Anne and i work as a navtech aboard the Anne Encanto, formerly called the Hanson Tyler, a trader from the fourth orbit of the Martian Belts.

The ship is captained by Alpha Red, a spiky/headed brick/top w/heart/on aimed in my direction. Tonight he buys the Hanson and re/names her after me.

I have mixed feelings about this arrangement.

The Hanson (the Anne? the Encanto! Yeah!) is a spin ship; it has centrifugal gravity, w/the crew quarters in toroids that turn around the axis of the cargo hold and the main drive. Me, i think gravity sucks. I would rather a freefall ship.

And while i am at it, i would rather a freefall life. I regret the compromises that have placed me in this meaningless position. I regret the responsibilities thrust upon me by adulthood;

I do not regret going into space, for that is truly where my Goddess dwells. Her silent halls are mine also, and i am Her acolyte, swift as Her thought, true as Her heart.

*

It is like watching a library burning.

The great Ken Kesey says, 'Art is not eternal, boys!' and so it goes... Sad, though, for the great ship Ariel was the stuff of my dreams, the apex of my aspiration. Since i first sailed out seven years ago, i would bask in tales of these heroes, these culture gypsies, knowing in certainty that someday I would meet them, and now they are off our high starboard bow, and we are on our way to their rescue.

This is not how I would have it be.

I want to see out of this can I am riding in, see the Ariel w/my own eyes; watching it on a monitor clouds my power.

Even so, I know I must act; a work of Magic to save the ship, a spell of warding to guard the survivors, something. I will do this silently and in my cabin, not being allowed my religion and not being allowed a suit; i will do this on my own, since i am the only Crafter aboard; it will work all the same.

I try an Insensitive Sending: Good! There is a lot of life aboard to merge with, many w/potential to be the partner/instrument of my Will.

Next, a Sensitive Sending, reaching out to the one fated to help me; a connection is made.

I concentrate. I merge and learn. I make no effort to control or influence he/who/is/my/eyes aboard the Ariel.

Part of me wonders about him...

Together in freefall we feel the heat. It is a furnace inside the Ariel. We know this ship is doomed; still we must try...

I sense my host is working Magic. Are artists adepts as well? I match to his Visioning; stroke for stroke we build a shield of light around us.

He knows. There is re/cognition of the ryder in this mind. Has he done this before?

We move down the corridor; wrecked gear...

I orient in his knowing of the ship. I feel his fear and loss and send the Strength of Artemis to aid him.

Ahead, acrid smoke flows around the flame/shields as we seek for the heart of the fire. We see no one else: i get the sense that he has sent them all to the sleds. He casts them wards of protection and I add my Will to his.

Smoke rolls out of a blown port high in the aftersection. White light, painfully bright; a magnesium fire! Air washes past us in a whistling rush: hull breach? fire feed?

Time to get out. There is no stopping this blaze. We jump for the suit lockers and the sleds.

*

These are the folk we rescue, the entire crew of the Ariel:

| | |
|---|---|
| Uncle Carl | captain/musical icon |
| Sandor | sailing master |
| Anders | artist/engineer/druid |
| Electra | navigator/performer |
| Andrew | music master/software |
| Alex | software/hardware/musician |
| Angela | musician/software  (a Luscious Honey!) |
| Mezz | CBL  (cargo/business/law) |
| Kan | holographer/rigger/chef |
| Lissa | bionics AFW  (air/food/water) |

Also saved from the wreck: most of the cargo of Spice, the computer mind/memory, most of the pods, a case of quartz spheres, most of the precious light show gear and instruments, assorted personal stuff.

Proud Ariel follows on a thousand yards of her own cable, the fire out at last, the hull breach taking all the air away. Alpha Red says Savable.

We are now three weeks aboard the Encanto:

*i am glad to be Alive*

*i hurt from the loss of my ship*

*why did this happen?*

Karma, Fate, Accident; this is my triune cosmology. These three forces always at work, mine to know which and when; Divine Will or that random part of the Divine which is our own individual Will?

*

Humans in space need good air and water even more than the fortunate few still on the Home Planet. Aboard the *Ariel,* Lissa would use her elfin sensitivity to flavour the air; just the right amount of ionization, pollen, nitrogen, and always plenty of fresh $O^2$, up to thirty percent. For birthdays, a niff of guarana or ginseng, or hyper/expensive essential oils of the most delirious/mysterious: lavender from the Sun/dazzled kitchen gardens of Provence; Indonesian patchouli, essence of the art of loving, perfected over twenty thousand years...

Now that i am aboard the *Encanto,* every breath i take reminds me of how much we have lost.

It is so strange here: half/gee spin/gravity (all the dorsal passages are uphill); ultrasonic showers (no water!), heavy airtight steel hatches for cabin seals, no art, no lights, no color, no plants, no quartz, no wood, little magic... Then,

Who was my ryder there in the last moments of the *Ariel,* in my mind in the face of the fire?

Electra stirs and curls into the curve of my outstretched arm. Our sleeping together in a flat one/gee bed remains novel; there is some sweetness in this, feeling the weight of her next to me...

I look over at Electra in slumberland, her fine red/golden hair rayed out on the sea of white sheeting, her ever/present earring a goldwire glint.

Yes, i love her. And yes, i am thinking now of someone else: that masqued ryder...

I sense that it is clearly time for me to open to my next Best Thing, what ever that may be, and thus i turn to my favorite form of divination:

Out of my kit comes my Sphere, Moontrader; i dedicate my Visioning as the Sphere comes up to power, and w/humility take the vapors in...

I merge w/the Sphere as it charges my brain; the smooth blue curves of the Lapis Lazuli, the white veins, the flecks of gold...

Oh, this is interesting; the hatch to our cabin is opening, revealing an empty passage, closing...

Ah, over there: a cat. Persian. How unusual.

We Link instantly.

There is a very old soul inside this cat. Happens often. And something more: *this cat is purring inside my brain!*

Most cats are telepathic;
this cat is psychedelic!

It feels like merging w/an avatar: great wisdom, a fine purr, knowlege of the All; the Is, Was, and Will Be. *An Animal Avatar...*

There is more to this ship than...

In the merge, this Animal Avatar is tracking on my visioning of the ryder, sensing the concentric ryder/seeking waves i radiate...

And, how gracious! the Avatar is smoothly amping my sending, adding her energy to mine; out it goes, rolling/uncoiling out into the steel rings of the Encanto, these tendrils of longing leafing telepathic through the chambers...

There is a presence in the passage. The Animal Avatar pads across to the hatch and it opens.

A woman in veils, a darkened corridor.

She is shadowlit, a shadow willow silhouette framed in the hatchway. Long feral hair. Graceful; woman like a willow wand.

She is waiting for me.

Her voice thrills: 'Anders; I am your Initiator and your Way of Souls. Come.'

Magic is born in darkness...

I look over at Electra: she is awake, and we share these three thoughts: this is important/the three of us are meant to come together/go and make this connection.

I go.

Gravity!
Two/dimensional motion in a three/dee world...
I lurch heavily
up the passageway, following her and the furry avatar. I wear what i was
rescued in: body jewelry and our old Century cape, green velvet of a
hundred years. Moontrader rides in the kit clipped to my harness, and i
have Spice.
We are two converging shadows.
Expectant i search for her face and
*Wurph!*
She suspends my
sight w/a velvet hood; i catch a flash of her sad/pale/blue eyes as she pulls it
down, then naught.
I feel her bind my wrists in front of me; w/my second set of senses
i see blue neon traces where her fingers brush my skin...
I scan the dark and
sense the smile of the Animal Avatar as a luminous toothy crescent...
My
guide now draws on the cord, leads me by my bindings uphill left and now
twice right. My hearing ramps up/i sense the walls as my bod compensates
for the hood; the darkmaze phenomena...
She takes my hand/my Spice rush
PEAKS! I swoon against a bulkhead w/a short happy wildebeest grunt, wildly
hallucinating amazing moorish multicolor geometric mandalas...
She slips a
curious hand under my hood that i might see her questioning eyes. Clearly
she has yet to know Spice and its' ways...
As the hood returns i see the Animal Avatar take the lead, a
moving glowing lightfield, a joyful leaping cat/comet...

Here the raised threshold of another hatch/a chamber. She moves
ahead of me, after the radiant Avatar.
As i enter, her hand stays me; and soft in my ear, lips brushing velvet,

*'What do you bring w/you?'*

My ritual response;
'Courage, light in adversity.'

*'What do you leave behind?'*

And unbidden, my response,
'Fear.'

*'What is the password?'*

'Perfect Love,
            Perfect Trust,
                    Perfect Forgiveness.'

*'Then enter here, you who seek, and See!'*


Through the hatch and she takes my cape off me and spreads it on the deckplates. It is very warm in here, and now i am on my knees in front of her, still hooded. I fix her scent in my awareness and let the vision build, that i might know her when i see her...
*SNAT!*
With nine stout scourge strokes i am shriven clear, then asperged by nines w/water, charged/absolved. I feel the threads of old psychic attachments fall away and i am lighter: levity is the opposite of gravity...

She raises me by my bindings and we cross another threshold; carpeting? Is this what carpeting feels like?
And now the back of her hand on the back of my neck, smoother/softer/warmer than my century/cape. Off comes the hood and i see...
That we are in total darkness.
She removes the rope at my wrists, anoints me w/oils and w/the smoke of a glowing censer.
*'You are as you came into the world; shriven, forgiven, unbound, newly born into your senses. What do you seek here?'*
Easy to answer. 'The Grace of the Goddess, the love of a good woman, and a path to making my way in the world.'

She lights a bright candle (!) and shows to me a wonder...
We are in a temple of Artemis. A (holographic) fire burns behind the glass of the Vestal Hearth, and a fine altar of Earth/marble holds two real candles and an alabaster statue of the Goddess...
Which is like unto a pale echo of the priestess who stands above me, sable/haired and beautiful, clothed in veils of white samite, three in number, like unto the mythic fabric of priestesses.
She waves her hand and a veil falls away, falls like heavy creamy vapor very white and warm w/the scents of cedar and jasmine, reveals her to the candle/light, high/breasted and proud, her fleshtemple bodkin besilvered w/twisty talismanic jewelry...
And still her face is veiled...

The waist veil falls; sweet flowering willow woman w/pale translucent skin, long legs, fine/crested hips, shiny golden delta of sacred silky hair...

And now coursing through my mind this great soughing wave of connecting resonance/realization:

My stars have guided me aright...

And the events of the day flatten against the wondrous symmetry of this current moment, and i revel in the play of this curious emotional flux of Spice and the ramping intensity of impending Love & Magic...

I watch my own hand leave trails in the warm darkness, realize i have known only Electra for seven years, and two years more since i had congress with...

*across the
placid
pool of my
awareness
flows the
notion:
what sensate
strangeness
to the hand
is mortal
woman,
across the
thrilling
cool of
skin so
kin, like
mine,
my arc of
touch
breathing
cell to
cell with
thine,
the sulfur
niff of
danger/sub
tle touch
in heavy
air
unknown
and far*

Sometimes there is a sound that rings inside me, deep as Tibet; a temple/horn herald for my next looming nexus, my next Best Thing. It is the harbinger, the gongsound of the bloodstream of the universe.

Rarely have i heard it, three times only; on meeting Electra, my first time w/Spice, the epiphany after my Vision...

And now, as my eyes align w/this willow woman's and the two/way flow of binding information begins, i hear the sound again...

And it comes to me that here is the fire/warm author of my ryding; by her psychic voice i know her, by all my recent relivings of her first vivid visitation i know her well. And as i track her incoming info flow, i see that she will be more to me than my ryder; she is kindred soul, teacher of the heart, sower of passion, astral partner, clarion of reason, soul magnet, bringer of peace. All of my cells fill full w/Love for her: she is the crown of creation...

And, above and beyond overmore, she is all of my longing made manifest: i have this forecasting sense of her, the way she will feel to my hand, the rush and taste of her breathing; all of this hyper/vivid/clear to me...

And thus she becomes now ever more real, ever more solid, more dimensional to my mindseye,

And now these my reveries are stayed as the ramping Spice carries me rushing headlong toward the Realms Celestial...

[a short span of elsewhere...]

And w/my focus now returning to this candle/lit cabin, i see that she is watching me. And, back in the physical, i rise to the level of her eyes; our foreheads touch, and i speak my mind unto hers;

*...harken soft, o dear one,*
*i stand at the edge of your perception: encircled you are, protected*
*above and below; ensorceled as well, for i conjure you out of my*
*longing...*

*o goddess of passion and flesh, i invoke you incarnate; my*
*deliverer and inspiration, i call you forth; the blood/sound of my love*
*beckons you, come...*

*meet me in a place of our mutual creating; i am*

*here in your cat/level thoughts, the misty stuff of our minds
conmingling, your images sliding slow/across me in the warm/close
tunnel of our shared awareness...*

*join w/me now, o heart of my heart,
take ye initiation w/me if you wish it...*

She blinks surprise and now she speaks aloud; 'It is my dearest wish
fulfilled, o Lord of the Groves...'

I reach for Moontrader, hard/solid/smooth, charged and close at
hand. She is on her knees and looks up at me; i surge at the trust in her
sky/blue/eyes. She speaks...

'I am love unto thee, yours forever, your
instrument before you, both in this bod and in the aethers...'

And deep into this dream/made/real moment i reply,

*...o bright
child of Keri ad Wyn, beloved daughter of the all/father Hu Gadarn,
your test is this: you will merge w/moontrader, first w/your indrawn
breath, and then w/your seer's gaze...  i will be your ryder, and see as
you, and know your mind...*

I hand the Sphere to shy Anne.
She imbues, her lips and Moontrader: she comes on quickly,
smiles w/the rush, and her side of the Link manifests, from which comes this
mental exclamation...

*{ ...oh great aquarian honeypouring Goddess of ultimate
pleasure, this is perfectly amazing...*

*SPICE!*

*a space/bourne natural
compound found on the io moon of juppiter that grants telepathy,
a spatial (instead of linear) relationship w/time, w/the astral levels,
the intensification of emotion, and...*

*powers...*

*SPHERES!*
*fantastic electropsychic devices for producing states of profound
awareness...*

*warm liquid pleasure flowing to the farthest fibers of
my being; clarity, crystalline understanding, an expansion of true
knowing...*

*...i am blessed...
...more than even i...
...thank you Goddess thank you... }*

And as her ryder i am suddenly/solidly swept away, joyously lifted into flight, gimbaling and rolling out on a great wave of red/images/red, a wild peaky red ride rife w/the scent of escape...

Like a valentine she offers up to my awareness a rapid run of red geometrics, lyrical and lace/like...

Her fingertips to my cheek, furthering the connection.

Her last veil remains; i let it be and seek her breast, the better to couch my heavy head and ground my dreaming, drinking all the while a wide inpouring freshet of symmetrical sensual information, supplanting my own narrow identity w/mass spectral/kinetic profusion...

I am enfolded in her field, her nectar emanations, so close our heartbeats entrain into sync, and in this exalted state i ryde on,

A watcher w/her as her thoughts shift into a new far brighter palette panoply, and here she experiences an EXTRAVAGANCE of Visioning, frame after glistening frame, images raising emotion waves sending thrill/shivers,

And here she has her Vision of the Garden and the Mountain and the Temple...


And after, i follow her mentation as the Garden becomes her ring of truth, her guide/star, the transcendent central sustaining metaphor in the constellation of her life...

And when it is clear that she will use her every effort to find this Garden, i am inclined to ask,

*...what would you have of the gifts of the celestial...*

*{ ...i would know this lunar home of the Goddess, lately shown to me in vision; i sense that you shall aid me... }*

*...and what will you gain by finding it...*

*{ ...my long search for my true home will know completion, and i shall be as at the beginning, wrapped in the love of the Goddess, innocent in the Garden... }*

*...electra and i would aid you in your quest... will you covenant w/us, keep faith, maintain our trust and guard our secrets, wear the celestial star...*

And her answer:

*{ ...ever thine, o you who are my flame, my strength in the face of all that is... }*

*...and by what name shall we call you in Her circles...*

*{ ...by the Lady's grace and in the sight of her consort i take the name of ariel, for i would fill that need she left in you... }*

*...then i gift you w/this my faithful vessel, the eleuthran sphere called moontrader...*

*{ ...i shall be thy faithful vessel hence, o hierophant, o graceful harlequin... }*

Standing now, i look down into her eyes:

*...priestess/borne, you who are radiant beyond the physical: it is how you inhabit your bod that makes you beautiful...*
*in the name of Keri ad Wyn and in the name of the skygod Hu Godarn, i decree that you are a full celebrant of the high order of the celestial...*

A curvy symmetry is forming in my thoughts; we now are ariel/anders/electra, and the pattern of our central circle is complete...
*{ ...ever have i been w/thee, o my lord mage, and now in our Lady's order all the more so... }*

*...then rise... ariel... priestess and seer, font of vision, fellow celebrant, thou art welcome...*

*{ ...and what for thee, my restless heart, what would you have of me... }*

Inside my head her words ignite/she opens a gate/the wild thoughts surge and bellow;

*...i love you all/ways,*
*i burn w/longing, i reach to you stretched tight, i am crispen and sere, i thirst for you, my hands/your hair, i seek you, respond...*
*yes, pull me down, right answer! fingertip contact/the corner of your mouth/a perfect curve, our eyes adoring/speak, the loving/resonance loud in both/each/other we join, intertwine every limb sinuous, skin... weight... we slide to the deck/my cape, my old smoke/scented companion cape creased by our weight/our steam/our writhing/the hot gravity presses us together...*

*{ ...ever thine, my mage, my own true spark in the storm of the All,
    may you ever be fae in the face of the banal...}*

*...ariel,
  fire/heart
  clear believer
  relax into your ecstasy
  i am here and ever shall be...
  flame and radiate
  cycle infinite
  a matter of energy
  an arousal of stillness
  letting go
  ride the wave of bliss
  the lordly perspective
  arc into elation...*

*

We lie naked before the fire, wrapped in each other and the green velvet cape, the gravity pressing her warm and silky into me...
And there among the flame fronts, oddly the thought; is this life a passage of fire? Do we live by using our bods as fuel? Do we yield up our flesh to the flames in exchange for experience, tactile/material experience available only on this plane? And when finally we burn away completely, freed of the physical...
Into what? What follows?

Alpha Red is **really angry.**

He is waiting w/three or four of his crew as i leave Ariel/Anne's cabin, and he **stuns the very air around me w/big angry bolts of bright blue invective.**

Real piratical, he talks about *spacing* yr anders, right out the old cargolock. Two crew guys grab me by the arms and frog/march me aft, right on a line for the lock.

Once more toward the Great Abyss...

The stars blaze cold and hungry through the lock/port, and i look from face to unreadable face. From Red **a stare that would melt the hull/plates:** no compassion. Time stands on one hoof...

At the last he changes plan and throws me into an empty cable locker, dogs down the hatch. I hear a loud/conflicted grunt as Red turns and storms away, away down the passage w/his **snarls** and his **anger.**

Has being thrown in a metal hole ever felt so good? I marvel at the feel of the air still in my lungs. I shudder: am i reprised? May it be so...

The box is a little cubby below/decks in the aft toroid, a totally dark space, three feet from its' floor to the deck overhead, and just long enough for cold comfort.

Well and good;

It is quiet and i can think here. Maybe i have some time to come up w/something, save my envelope of skin...

If he was going to space me, he would have done it right away...

What is he thinking?

Clearly something territorial here, him so recently naming his ship after Ariel and all...

What a lot of trouble is monogamy.

After a few hours the hatch in the deckplate screeches up and some worthy crew/guy hands in some food. A good sign.

Shortly after, and here is Alpha Red.

Another good sign.

He levers his bulky/muscled self down into my little box and

waves his mate to close the hatch, and i am back in my own habitat Dark.
We take opposite ends of the box, each w/our backs against a wall.

'Red. Nice of you to let me get a word in.'

He is silent, listening, so i speak.

'You see me as the interloper here, as the cause of your suffering.
You are looking at all the if/only's. And you want this all to go away, so
things can go back to how they were before.'

'My business. You have three minutes.'

'I would guess that you have been in this position before. And you
must realize that whatever you do to me, this cycle will likely happen again.'

'Really? And how is that?'

This would all be so much easier w/Moontrader here. Red is a man
in a tube, convinced he is a flesh/bound set of personality traits, a trader
w/property rights, w/something to protect...

'Do you know about Spice?'

'A drug. Two minutes.'

'Spice is a great clarifier; it will show you the way gracefully out of
our current zerko commedia...'

'How so?'

Now comes my turn for silence. It is a dare: i read him as being so into
his honor, so invested in his amour courtois that he will be caught in his
courage...

I sense he is about to...

Yes!

He raps on the hatch overhead and
it opens. I brace my eyes against the glare/i see Anne/Ariel up on the deck.

'Let me have that round thing, okay?' says Red.

Hallelujah! here comes Moontrader! She hands it down.

He gives the thing a hard look, figuring it out, and now he lights
it up and sucks the greeny vapor down. He waves and they close the hatch
again.

Moontrader flares once again as he presses the stud, and i have this
flash of insight: excepting for him wanting to space me, i could work w/this
man; some of the old Arthurian archetype is in him.

What does that make me?


Five minutes pass, more.

'Okay, you've got three minutes more,' and he is right on the edge
of mirth, thank the Maker. I can tell from his tone he is getting it...

'Got it!'
he says, and lets out this great loon laugh, loud and long. I know i will hear
this laugh many times in our future work together.

'*You* have three minutes,' says i, and now we both laugh.

He inspirates a sigh and speaks a running skein, working it out as he goes;

'It is this. Love is a feeling, an actual physical sensation, a joy/rush, very specific and in the moment. This feeling is so fine that we are willing to do anything, ANYthing, to make it stay, to make Love stay, and we just automatically start in figuring ways to make that feeling continue for as long as possible.'

A moment, and now; 'So around this core feeling we add a series of learned responses, ways we think we should act when in Love, all based on assumptions from our personal histories; parents, teachers, media/input, our imaginations.

'And these responses evolve into a set of expectations built up in both parties. We think them reasonable expectations, now that we have found Love, and likely we have carried these expectations around in our heads for a long time, from BEFORE we met the current object of our affections...

'And this is the great illusion! These expectations are scenarios we set up of how it should ideally be instead of how it is. And then we wait and judge; if our expectations are met we are happy, if not we are sad, and then we set up new expectations and start the cycle again...

'And to make Love stay we crystallize these met expectations into accords, this whole according process based on the way we do business, far removed from that original feeling, except as ways of perpetuating the circumstances that led to the feeling in the first place...

'And these accords are spoken and unspoken, created anew and based on old assumptions. We see these accords as reasonable. And we trust our partners to honor these accords, and we call this Relationship, and we feel secure.

'And this security is also illusion.

'Because Love is of the moment: Love wanes and is rekindled, moves like a swallowtail, whereas relationship is a kind of materialism, what we build around Love to make it stay, an abstraction of the idea of Love which invites the inclusion of all these secondary aspects that have nothing to do w/that original feeling: security, enhancement of self/esteem, even ownership. And marriage is another level of abstraction beyond relationship, bringing the state and the church into the determination of whether we are in Love.

'Do you see the nested spheres that are forming here? Love, then around it expectations, then around them a type of surety agreement made of what we see as reasonable assumptions, then around that a hard institutional shell.

'Or another way; Love at the center, then around that the abstraction of relationship, then around that the further abstraction of marriage.'

His eyes focus elsewhere; 'Love cannot be contained in spheres of abstraction; Love is Magic...'

For a time we enjoy the silent darkness.
'You know,' says Red, 'I truly have been seeing this like a trader: there is a lot of materialism in my idea of love. Some subsurface part of me figured that if i invested heavily in this woman i would engender a sense of obligation in her. She would have to love me. Absurd, yes? This is a plan for getting control, control of property; Love is the open hand, relationship is capitalism. By the way, this truly is amazing stuff for clarity. Do you have any more?''
'Two metric tons. It's on the cargo manifest. We want to give you and your crew half for rescuing us.'
'Yah? Outstanding! ...So, can it be that my happiness as a human depends on my assumption that i must own another human?'
I reflect on Electra and me while he goes on:
'Clearly absurd also. What am i then? More than a set of appetites and a desire for security...'
In the dark i sense his glims going vague as he sees beyond the rim...
Is this his first glimpse of the Is/Was/Will/Be? I smile. Wisps of last night's Spice still waft through the columns of my own brain as i watch Red climb out of himself.
'...that the boundaries I place upon myself are clearly arbitrary. I have the choice of infinity, the location of everywhere. Absurd to think of Love as ownable...'
He goes off bemused, so lost in thought that he leaves me in the metal box below/decks. Quite alright for he also leaves Moontrader...

Shortly he comes down and lets me out; could i be as gracious if i were in his place? I rejoice in his awesome ability to shift his point of view...
After much pondering, his thoughts have now settled in an interesting new way: he is now highly chuffed about our project, believes in it, thinks it will be good for the home planet, wants us to succeed. And, seeing as how he just bought a ship and all, he wants to haul Spice. Does he smell money? Ariel at work here? Has she introduced him to my Vision?
Well, yes yes yes to all three. In truth he is intrigued by what will come from our mindchanging art on the face of the Moon,
And enflamed by the idea of selling enough Spice for an entire planet...
The way Alpha Red sees it, our performance will be the reason for the greatest party ever seen on Earth: a telepathic linkup of immense proportions; millions, maybe billions of people...

When word about Spice gets out and people put it together w/the upcoming piece, the market for Spice will become immense. A need, in fact, so great as to drive the price into the... well, up there.

This is a good thing for everyone, says an enthusiastic Alpha Red; lots of Spice will be brought in from off/planet and many good traders and Spice/blenders will be saved, and vast numbers of people will share an experience that will surely change the world...

Red makes yr anders a stellar offer involving the delivery of entheogens and the fulfilling of the Vision: Red gets a jump on the other traders in exchange for his aid in the production of a single piece of Carls/anders art, one performance only, on the face of Earth's Moon.

Yr anders sees Red as mad in quite another way now, and we arrive at modus vivendi.

Red takes some time to Spice his crew, tell them how things stand, how their shares will be affected. Now he brings us all together, *Encanto* folk and *Ariel* folk, and

A huge party ensues, where yr anders meets the rest of the crew of the *Encanto*: the Trippletts, Red(beta), Green, & Blue; Steel the hulking animorph, Aura Citron, the others...

In a great cloud of Spice, Mouse/Gas, Megaminke, and some kind of mystery green stuff, our two crews merge.

Changes begin immediately: ship's spin is slowed, then canceled when it becomes clear that everyone loves freefall. Lots of superfluous bulkheads & hatches & walls are simplified out of the ship, and the resulting airy open spaces are tinted and lit to please the eye. One happy result is that Lissa's houseplants come out of stasis and into our chambers...

And after that comes this intense meeting where the whole plan comes out and everyone thinks about ways and means. Wills unite, a decision is made, and we are once again off to Luna...

More specifically, Bongo Beta, a city on Earth's Moon.

All the major off/planet technical facilities are there; factories, labs, offices, and oh yes; abundant surplus hardware. Plus, there is always cargo waiting around, wanting to go where we are going,

And Bongo B is an awesome great place to do Lightshows.

*Anders gifts to me a catmask all of feathers, scent of musk, made by his own hand. I dwell upon his long pale Spacer fingers stitching...*

*When i see myself in the mask i am changed: where Anne Encanto was the chattel of a trader w/no direction of her own, Ariel is an Empowered Child of Artemis on her way to Earth's Moon, questing for the Garden of the All/Mother Goddess...*

*And where Anne was the only pagan on a ship full of hylitic party animals, Ariel is now subsumed into a like/minded mesh of rescued artists/kindred souls.*

*And, as is the gift of all masks, i am now someone else and free of the weight of my own history; i can re/invent to my heart's content, and i become The Mask: a woman of cat/grace and cat/sensitivity, subtle and sensuous and direct.*

*And Anders knows The Mask well, for i have lived this role for a solar month and now it is my true (s)elf.*

*As Ariel i see things in new ways.*

*I begin to see...*

*Possibilities.*

*And i really like this man who paints the sky.*

*As i am his creation so Anders is my author: as i am his invention, my desire is his also. I bind my Will to thine, O Anders: May we Shine in the Eyes of the Goddess...*

*Do i move toward Anders as Electra grows away?*

***

*It is a three weeks before i realize that Electra is anything other than human. She is engaging, resourceful, calm, cheerful, even funny. I find out only by overhearing two of the Encanto crew debating her worth (considerable).*

*I have heard of this kind of relationship before. It must be very alluring for a man to arrange his life this way.*

*I have given it some thought:*

*There is this weirdly shamanic thing that happens to us when we reach the age of mechanical* majority. Once we master the technological ethos of something, once we know how to partner w/it and how it works and how to fix it, it becomes an extension of our bods and minds, a natural part of our envelope of abilities.

In the case of a fine piece of hardware like Electra, this bond can bloom into love. I know i would have felt this for the ship Ariel; i have yet to get any such sense for the, ah, Encanto.

Anders and Electra have been together seven years. How is it that they are so well matched? Is it software? Dream/track patterning?

I wonder if he has known human lovers as well. Am i his first human partner? Can a human construct be better than a human being?

Erotically? A better lover certainly: w/out selfish impulses to take away from a man's pleasure...

As a companion? Probably. Totally amenable, capable of giving a man total attention, never being moody, remembering things exactly as he wishes, always having the right answer to a question of fact or math or logic...

As a Magical Partner? I don't think so.

*

With the spin taken out of the toroids, life aboard the Encanto is now something wholly other: i can sail through the air like a sea/lark! I move so easy, so free; my breathing is deeper, my head clearer, and best of all i now know where i am in the space surrounding; i can now easily see the stars...

And the rowdy crew of the Ariel have likewise really changed Alpha Red: a business/clothes guy now a mercury/god in a silver suit. He is also filling his eyes w/Angela.

Thank you, Angela. Reward this man for his graceful changes re meself...

Where does that leave Andrew & Alex?

*

And now in our rites we all wear masks; anders' a silver banner across his eyes, Sandor's a buffalo fullface, Alex in foxfur...

And we all become our masks,

Which grants to my cameras a true elucidation of the giving of worship and the drawing of power...

For i am of the mind that our Workings should be translated into a medium where they can be saved, shared w/hundreds, thousands of folk, and banked against future need...

And in this way we can leverage our magical energy: if all the future celebrants of these rites would vector their energies to the same original ends...

*Then that would give that first original Working some awesome magical potential. The thing would just go on and on, a century of playbacks, the casting recurring w/each replaying...*

# 17  Anders' Tale / The Elf in His Labyrinth



Picture the Moon, just above the curved Earth horizon, a great cheshire grin hanging in the sky.

The *Encanto* is currently powering out of Earth Apogee, leaving her braking orbit, hard on the lunar tack.

On the bridge i ride my couch in a fine high state, w/the rockets' surge compelling a delicious sense of lift/mass as we clear the syrupy juices of home/planet gravity...

And now we are set in our lunar orbit, a nice wide one, and i head for my suit. We are all going down to Bongo Beta to cover some very nice bookings, crystallize the details and check that the riders are met, then party w/friends, get the news,

And sell two metric tons of Spice.

The *Encanto's* narrow shuttle/lock reveals Alpha Red's personal sled (scarlet w/golden trim and shapely and really really fast), w/himself strapping in for boostaway. Speaking across him on either side are Ariel and Electra, reasoning through some gnarly point of invocation. Behind them big Uncle Carl who, for his own reasons, is wearing a suit woven out of long gray hair, what he calls his social fabric.

Then there is Alex w/his spock ears and Angela in her cheetah/bodsuit, both of them ready to be gleeful overiders of the local ethos...

I smile to see that Angela is along; if she is the focus of Alex's awareness then i get to fly the sled. As I dive for the controls, he looks at her archly as if to say, Get your Mojo working/here comes Mister Wildride...

I strap in, close the lock/check the screens/look back at the two of them, hit the throttles...

ROARRRRR!

A quick clean exit from the *Encanto*, though/*Glurph!*/Alex and Angela somehow get it wrong on the launch and get pasted to the back wall by the acceleration, pressed against each other in various erotic ways at various gees. Me, i am far above this carnal drama, away into the cybernetic bliss/trance of piloting...

These sled things are great: low mass and serious power, a splendid ride w/high gees, great visuals, a very personal sense of control. Red's can boost 30 metric tons out of Juppiter, so the combined weight of the seven of us is hardly daunting. Plus, we have, uh, done some *daemon mods* as Sandor would say...

Aboard the *Encanto* we also have our superlight silver/blue shuttle from the *Ariel,* a good match for the Red/Sled, and Alex & i like to race each other in these things. After the work is done we run circuits, loops around markers or convenient chunks of rock, blasting our way through thruster turns and mass turns, laughing and shouting, keen to our ships, totally focused, racing...

Angela says that of all the folk in our combined crews, Alex & meself are the most passionate pilots, always first to leap for the sleds, and she loves to see us dance them through the sky.

Many's the happy hour...


Thirty/three fast but oh so delicate maneuvers later we skate into Chronos Crater. We get ourselves together, straighten our straight dealing/with/the/company clothes, leap through the sled/lock and into the Port...

Zzog.

The main Port building is a huge bee/hive dome a half/MILE high, a quarter/MILE across the base: beyond the reach of my recent ship/shaped sense/memory i thrill into this glorious feeling of expanded bodspace/it inundates away my intimate shipboard shared awareness/i emerge eager into this leviathan expanse...

Though here twice before, i am whelmed over...

There! Over there!
Flowing water and parkland w/real grass! Hang gliders! riding rising columns of air/spiriting around in all that lenient gravity...

The air! How do they get it to taste so good?

And overhead, through the clearplex, the Earth; just now half/past/Asia...


We are an hour early, so everyone goes their way before the meeting: Alpha Red and Uncle Carl to take care of business, Alex & Angela to the Renoir Bar to spread around and share a little Spice, while Ariel/Electra/&/i head out toward the Eastern Concourse to do the same, the idea being to convert our cargo into a ship for our enterprise asap.

East Con is where i hang portside; a big clearplex inflatable, three sections, a mile long and a quarter mile high. All my portside friends are here in East Con, plus a few thousand other folk...

So it is perfectly in the flow when we cruise into my favorite Snap bar on Overlook Corner and find my friend the Lumière, in from Io and waiting at our favorite table.

He is looking good, very dapper, all in black w/a long/black/beautiful real wool cape, his stony profile wrapped in a wreath of green mist radiating up from the (surprise!) Sphere of black porphyry in his hands...

He looks over at me w/a grin that says; yes, welcome, right on time, i was just thinking of you...

He passes me the Sphere and the taste is fine: otherworld/heady, a long smooth rush w/good acceleration, now a spectacular technicolor peak, now a solid spectral plateau...

Spice.

I cognize the scent right off, the same as the Ariel's cargo: how much is already here?

'Ganymede?' I ask, being coy.

'This stuff is special,' he says, his perfect hair catching the light, 'My astrologer gets it from a mystery guy on Io.'

[Me!]

'Like it?'

I watch symmetrical jello skyrockets bound across the backs of my eyes. 'Oh yes,' I say, 'it is very very awesomely good Spice.'

'Thank you, o illuminator of the spaceways,' he says graciously, shifting his cape on his shoulder; 'A ten, would you say?'

'Assuredly a ten, save for this!' says i w/a flourish, bringing Moontrader into his line of sight...

A slow smile, each of us unto the other. He takes the Sphere and raises it; 'To Nepenthe!'

And thirty seconds, a minute, after Moontrader's blue kiss he lingers, not moving, not breathing...

A Breath! Two Great Lungfuls of wide/eyed Laughter! Now another breath, a long sigh, his eyes closing in blissful contemplation...

Two more minutes, an eternity,

And when again he opes his glims i hopefully begin, 'Do you have any idea where i can sell a shipload of this?'

*

He does.
We're off.

Outside the Snap we hail a flagger, and the Lumière opens me the door. Underway into the traffic, and inside the snug cabin he tells us a tale: he has a friend (i love stories that start this way) named Llair, a hardware guy of high renown...

Llair lives in a loft above The Brookside Theatre, a noble art house of thirty years, now fallen on gray times. Built when Bongo Beta was the first Moonside boom town, it was meade hall and meeting place for the legendary/wealthy Luna Gloria Mundi, the fraternal & mystical Guild of Miners.

They commission the place in the first great flowering of their opulence, and it becomes the emblem of a Golden Era for Luna, defining the style for all those monuments to prosperity that will follow.

And the place sets an awesome standard; huge and white and foursquare/classical, tall against a huddle of domes, it is the first major structure in the austere cluster that was Bongo B in the Brookside's day.

Imported at great cost from the bottom of the gravity well: a shipload each of priceless Cedar, Oak, Mahogany (a mystery where that came from); ornamented columns w/facings of travertine, multipaned windows of silica glass, great spans of red carpet...

And the central namesake; a terraformed sluice of real running water, loving/rendered and meandering through the lobby, the first such feature ever constructed off/planet.

The Brookside/huge beyond recounting, w/chambers and apartments and corridors and secret rooms all built above the theatre, and the loft above that...

To the guilds of coders and riggers and teamsters and all the others whose fortunes would wax rampant in those early years, it is the gauntlet flung. Over time the other guilds surpass it in size and complexity and extravagance, and the concentrations of power and wealth shift. When the Gloria Mundies move to new digs in the West Con, the Brookside becomes a possible fantasy for Llair:

He wants it.


The talking door takes the Lumière's card, ponders, buzzes us into a little brass birdcage/lift, up through five levels counting...

When the inner door opens and we look to find our way, i am amazed: this loft goes on forever! Thousands of square feet, the whole length of the building above the main hall. Huge domed rooms follow other huge domed rooms off into the dusty distance...

And every available cube of space is filled w/the most monumental profusion of hardware: industrial gear, structural stuff, chips of years ago, things that glow, things that move around and light up, a whole wall of manuals and docs, parts for anything, etcetera etcetera, stacked to the rafters...

Hot Zzog!

A Wirehead's Attic of Mythic Proportions, peerless unto all for exotic variety! Hardware lust calls me seven ways at once; i spot old NASA gear, recently secret stuff from the disbanded military, parts of famous ships...

And all this hardware is lined up in aisles and rows and culdesacs, an actual maze of hardware. Clearly Llair is fond of his privacy, has laid all this out to discourage the casual/uninitiated visitor.

His moat.

Closer to the center now/Giant Sculpture and parts for sculpture and ideas for sculpture: the Lumière says that is what all the hardware is ultimately for.

And now we learn that Llair goes out w/his pirates in frequent forays to the big Industrials and scores what he likes of their surplus, then stashes it here as raw material for his art.

Hrm...

Sometimes he sells things back to the Industrials, or for scrap, or for parts...

Or maybe now to us for Lightshows...

Good modus for an artist, says the Lumière of Llair, and also good for Llair the oneironaut, sailor of dreams, who now has higher uses for primo surplus gear...

Which is also in tune w/his other enterprise, which is selling vast amounts of Steem, an ultrahybridized strain of good old Marijuana...


We take an hour to traverse the maze, and i smile my way along, for at every turn another piece of high/potential art/gear smiles back; we are in a kind of armoury for the legions of light...

The Lumière is our Guide of Souls, and

Electra follows, our Crafted Lady of Perfect Miracles: see her sure step and know her subtle motion that ye may have bliss...

What can all this mean to her?


[The entrance to the Keep is through this hulking cylindrical airlock thing, which is parked against a bulkhead in the south node of the space. There is a steel/rung/step up, worn shiny to show the way. Keep this to yourself, yes?]


The Keep is like being inside Llair's brain.

A secret room, a treasure room.

All the choicest stuff is here: rare metals, early space/grown quartz and silicon, psychoactive electronics...

And Manda on the couch, moonwaif extraordinaire...


And now my glims latch the sight of Llair's Rig;

Computers, converters, sound gear, holographics, filters, inputs,

meters, monitors, scanners, storage: this rig is a Monster w/eighteen
towering stack/racks, more than a metric ton of obscure gear, most of it
saved by Llair from oblivion. The room is in fact solidly packed w/this stuff,
all massively wired together in the most amazing way...

And the pearl in the
center of the labyrinth, poised on ancient hydraulics; the iridescent and
spherical Virtual Reality Motion Stimulator from the Fair of Four Worlds of
forty years ago...

A voice comes from behind the racks:

'Hey, are you Anders?' a zingy kind of charged/up voice
w/evidence of extra electricity; 'That you? Your timing is GREAT!'

Out leaps a five/and/a/half/foot Elf: 'I have created the
ULTIMATE SPHERE!' [Will he still say that after he tries Moontrader?]
'Over here; guide on this!'

He leaps again and the guy is all sinew: one of those humans they
call wiry. His moves are like... amplified, as if twice the normal voltage fires
his muscles. His hair is long and braided gray, and his beard too a pair of
long gray braids. His age a mystery/thirty to ninety.

'Here, Anders, look at this, we just started doing this today: this
input over here ramps the pace of the Experience. If we put, like, *use a
sinewave* as the input, the time factor becomes *a harmonically controlled
variable!*'

'Why would you want to do that?' says i, curious.

'Change the timepace and brain rhythms can be synchronized to
set up resonances, *harmonies in the brainwaves,* heighten the Theta state!
And look at this: pure OXYGEN pouring into the chamber the whole time!'

A thought of the cost/my brows rise/he anticipates;

'What does it matter *when crafting the Ultimate High!*'


We move drifts of memory cubes and data/carts out of the way so
we have couch space. There is carrot juice from the hydroponic herb guys
next door, the Sons of Light and Life. This is a great treat, counting the
lurid cost of fresh vegies. Perhaps he is priming us, for it is clear that Llair
will speak now:

'Here it is;' he says, 'One year back and i am on the roof of
the Brookside here, working on this big heavy sculpture, a take on the
Fibonacci series done in bridge/cables, welding away you understand, when
i have this MOMENT, this fract of a second when my whole game turns
SIDEWISE to my eyes, and this thought comes;


*'The ultimate arena for all artforms is the mind of the perceiver...*

'And,
like, here i look at the Big Cutter i am holding, suddenly wondering WHY am i

dealing w/all this physical metal & glass & electricity? Why create sculpture to change perception when i can

Create the state of mind directly!

'Specialized adepted mindstates where everything coming in through the ken of the senses is part of the art...'

Here Cobb, one of Llair's pirates, bounces in and hands him a bracket bar of tritanium, miming in a way that says this thing is six inches shy of long enough...

'The sculptures, ya'see, ideally stir w/in you the perceiver some kind of awakening, some new way of ordering your cosmos. And when i am in this sidewise roof moment i realize that w/all my attempts to elicit these evolutionary responses what i am really about is *creating mindstates,* helping you to alter the fundamental avenues of PERCEPTION, to elevate appreciation of every sensate thing we see & hear & touch, part of a larger sphere of ideation...

'And as w/my sculpture, i want these crafted mindstates to elaborate you, enoble you, enhance your awareness, encourage your imaginating; i want whole rich inner/personal dramas to pass across the stage of your theater of perception, ideally reveal to you some truth, some of the intricate beauty of the perfect physical world...

[Yah! Resonance; this is what lightshows are really about, expanding the awareness of our perceivers; and now through my head rolls a highlight reel of mindstretching visual similies, archetypal patterns to trigger new overstanding, mandalas for centering the mind, beams to sail on, grooves to ride the starry pockets of space...

Lumia Veils for Astral Visions...

The great Bill Hamm says this in the nineteen/sixties; 'If you see God, it's a good lightshow.']


And while i am thinking the above, Llair takes a pause and pours his considerable energy into the bracket bar between his hands; his face becomes a world of Wild Intent, and in a rush his thoughtflow zephyrs itself into the fore of my own Spice/widened brain;

*{ ...and w/my will i focus on these rigid lattice molecule bonds, BEND! and [sending heat melting into the brittle metal] LIQUIFY! [and over again again again]... }*

And of an instant the bracket turns to goo and stretches like rubber, into this longer and far more graceful shape, and takes a set back into metal...

As he hands the thing back, Cobb goes wide in the glims, and while i think he is about to praise Llair w/wide/eye awe, Cobb says the most resonant thing thusfar;

'As art, mindstates are the Metaform, the key medium that opens us to all others.'

And w/those fifteen words he carries Llair into an awesome new line of fine fresh reveries...

'So, it becomes clear to me here that my, er, highest service is to create the gear to open the minds of those desirous, gear w/which folk can alter their architecture in specific ways to suit, and thus enhance the FUNDAMENTAL BASIS by which the play of our senses becomes part of our knowlege...'

Cobb bounces out now, looking well/pleased, moving like smoke in the low lunar gees...

Llair rolls on; 'So, as this awesomely possible powerful new course opens up, there comes to me this bigtime desire to create a masterpiece; to make something with truth and heart, use all i know about getting high, all the technology, all the scholarship, astral experience, everything. I would vector all this into my art. You know i do hatha yoga since i am seven? Acupressure for fifteen years... What time is it, by the way?'

'Fourteen hundred less ten.'

'Awake for forty hours! Look at this: everything on the Rig is connected to the VR Sphere; the neuro/suit, the helmet, the atmospherics, the spinal tracker, the software for three/dee brainwave monitoring, the videolo storage and branching software and, of course, some of *this*...'

His eyes, that daemon spark... He leans out; a move familiar enough, and now in his hand the light latches on a polished sphere of quartz, very clear lightly veiled Earth Quartz [surprise! Spice? the Lumière...], and in the center a chamber holding [sigh of relief] a dram of Steem.

'Mind your eyes,' he says, and raises it over his head:

BRAP! A bright white beam strikes the sphere...

He brings it down, contents vaporized/smoking. He is holding it out to me. Clearly it is time to toast the intentions of this rare kindred soul: i place my muzzle on the nozzle and taste...

My glims go to lizard slits and all the roomsounds boom and rasp into wiggy techno concertos. Ideas arrive at my brain like boat/trains; lightshows/hardware/shipshares/how to further pleasure Electra, each a discrete packet of inspiration or ideation, soul/dream or sonnet...

The idea train now gathers velocity, the packets coming faster and faster and faster yet, a challenge to my enhancing,

And there is this; as the speed of my perceiving ramps to catch these flashes, my local reality weirdly slows apace...

After this hit of Steem i am deemed ready, and Manda guides me to Llair's VR sphere/chamber. They suit me up, put the Helmet on me, plug me in and close the hatch. I have this shadow/thought; is Llair out there craving my Sisters of Mercy? He already supports three wives and seven children stashed in three different homes, plus Manda...

A quick look into the Mystic and all is clear to me. Ariel will teach Llair how to zone on Spice, Electra will find her own heightened awareness. I am at peace...

The sphere gives a LURCH/here we go...

Intense to overwhelming. Overwhelming though short of terrifying; just enough fear, an abundance of pleasure...

Ah, this is Grand, the archetypal Celestial experience of being at the center of All That Is, Was, or Will Be...

And here my spirit/mind goes so wide that all the choices are apparent to me: time travel, shape shifting, ex/stasis/out/of/bod, other lives, telepathy, manifestation, bilocation, magical dimensions...

It is more than tripping; it is my own expanding awareness showing me

Powers...

This clearly is the best/most/mightiest ride of my current life...

I know that a good way to gauge my trip/depth is by my sense of self; can i maintain it? Do i want to? With this...

*Zzog!* The lucination visuals now go *Bright Fantastic,* familiar and *wholly other,* pleasant and less/so...

Knowing that i am tripping is a sort of keel, reassuring/grounding...

I am in the Sphere for an hour, riding the triple tsunami of Spice, Steem, and the wyles of Llair's chamber. I emerge fulfilled, awed wide by the splendid sweep of the All...

Off, far and away, i see the author of this epic journey. He is looking my way. He is communicating:

'We have a cube for you,' says Llair. 'We take the signals coming off the Helmet and hook them back through a smart filter, then resynthesize the stereoscopy on playback... Anyrate, this will give you the visuals anytime you want them.'

*I am a Holy Prince of Worlds,* i tell him, still blazed spacey from Spice.

Llair is next.

Already in his neuro/suit, visor open, keen/ready for his first taste of Spice.

Heightened/i read him vivid as a solar flare.

I feel like posterity. Fate nuzzles her lubricated hinge. Binary proto/stars spiral inward hyperbolic for to have a better view:

Llair and the Moontrader meet...

I close my eyes and see Velikovsky's Comet glance off the orbit of Venus, change the course of the natural history of the Earth; manna from heaven...

Open/eye i see Ariel & Electra and Manda framing Llair in his penultimate pre/rush moment, the four of them immutable as the fixed stars in Velikovsky's drama. Silent they remain in place as Llair leaves them, heads for his VR Sphere, their compassion encompassing...

An hour later and he emerges...

He is adrenalized, pinealized, hyper/oxygenated; right on the edge of out of his mind...

This is good.

His eyes are the screens of inward movies too fantastic to contemplate, his smile a sigil of epiphany...

And,

Here Llair pours himself into his slingchair, curling into the lap of God.

At one point he stops and muses, 'I am the golden spike of Bongo Beta,' then zones until the rising of China on the lush viridian crescent Earth overhead...

Ariel & Electra and Manda take their turns w/Moontrader and Steem and the big silver sphere, and now we all sit rapt/basking, half/back in our bods, still in our neurosuits. Llair and i both know that he will take our cargo and channel it into the right hands. We both know that the combination of technology and physical enhancement that we have just experienced is a profound evolutionary force, will somehow be merged into the piece...

I presume upon our nascent pact:

'We need a ship,' i say.

Once again, Spice leaves me sharp and mindful, relaxed and full of attention.

Llair looks at me, at us, and i see him spinning a shrewd future in his mind; his slow smile fans out wide to the corners of his mouth and his lambent elfin eyes now ramp the gleeful wattage *brilliant!* as he comes to the same conclusions that Red and i myself now hold...

He gets up, stretches through some asanas, leads us into the inner labyrinth. Seven turns later and we are at the south/east corner of the Keep, in front of these big clearplex tubes, two of them, that run from the roof and through the floor; they have doors, and Llair steps into the left one.

The thing goes *thwoooop!* a kind of swallowing noise, and he slides gently downward, through the floor, down and down and out of sight... A stasis lift! I have heard about these things. Up down and sideways, they move you w/these smoothly peristaltic rolling contractions of stasis energy.

Just before he wafts out of sight he waves, winks conspiratorial; *come follow, come follow...* so we do.

It takes an act of Faith/Will to step into a clear shaft of air and gravity;

*Tthwooooop!*

A whirly wild rush of vertical vertigo when first i look down: it looks like a long straight shot to the bottom of nowhere/it feels like butterfly/wing/massage, w/the stasis energy mitigating the glycerin/slow lunar gravity...

We pass gently through the office of some fairly interesting folk, who watch idly curious as we go ceiling/to/floor through their conference room. My guess is that Llair is the only one who uses these tubes, and then rarely.

It is a strange way to fly, like being in freefall/still knowing gravity...

Through another floor and into a huge darkened room; the Brookside. Great! Now i am the one spinning out futures: Llair installs us in the theatre doing shows for the residents of Bongo B and the many folk passing through the Port, raising money for a ship...

My glims iris out to match the light, and the majesty of the room reveals. It is clearly a temple, w/stepped ranks of risers leading to a broad altar, w/stages and pits and porticoes for ovates and elders and hand/fasters; how glorious/the place restored/revealed to multitudes...

As my lightshow mind is calculating throws and distances, i am surprised when i continue to descend on through the floor, pauseless into another much darker place.

Clearly the theatre is on some later agenda. Another time, then, for that magnificent space...

My expanded awareness says the shaft is now solid rock, and on and on down we go. A very long way down.

*Fffooomp!*

I drop out the bottom of the tube into a darkness so total that i see auras clear out to the third harmonic. Interesting to watch Electra; hers so beautiful and perfect, more symmetrical than...

The electric blue array that is Manda slides over and takes my hand, a pleasant auric echo of glowing azure Ariel; lucky, likely as lightning striking twice. Manda leads me out across a space and through a...

*transition;*

from delineated dark through an edge into light.

I look back and see obdurate darkness/an obsidian wall behind me. I reach back to touch solid/put my hand through empty air...


We enter a Chamber of Waters,

Flagrant/leaping/extravagant on a waterless orb like Luna...

There Llair, his elfin fun spark still aglimmer, moves to an enclave carved in the planetary rock. With a single graceful curling he peels the neuro/suit off his hairy bod and puts it on a shelf to his left. A pause and *zarp!* and the sweet scent of ozone, and the thing falls through the shelf and into the clearplex cube beneath. The clearplex thing fills up w/water/white/translucent and the water starts moving in a kind of centripetal vortex, and i am bemused in place by this new form of motion; the neurosuit/almost/alive spins like a smoke/wraith in the churning water...

Now knowing the name of Llair's game we follow suit, larflarf, and i feast on the sight of three naked naiads; Electra her beautiful shapely slender hips, my heart! a waist i could span w/a circle of my fingers, and i would, and i will... Dark Hawaiian Manda, redolent mango sweetness, hibiscus... Ariel, willow grace and oak's resolve, spare as birch and fragrant...

A fog of warm steam sensuously rising, and then, by Zzog, it's *RAIN*, the barrel/vault of the chamber now a cloudy night/sky, the fine sound, the warm plentiful RAIN, o so exquisite wet on my water/hungry skin!

Ah calming vapor... slight scent of... is that hyssop?

We follow Llair out of the rain, and into a room w/wondrous blue towels, cotton from Egypt, and now our suits; fresh and dry and hinting of ozone. Natch/hooded helmets also.

As neuro/field bodsuits go, these are the height of the art, beyond excellent; twice the usual [massive] number of neuro/fields, w/each field affecting a specific area of the bod.

And where most suits stimulate, these can track also: send or
receive sensate/proprioceptive information; visuals, position, pressure,
speed, motion, sound...

The natched hoods are black spherical videolo helmets that
network/combine w/two/way dream/trackers. The curve/mirror faceplates
can fade from total/video/holographic to total/outside/world; i/am/a/camera
to i/am/elsewhere.

More mundane versions of these suit/things are all over the planet
above us, totally popular, many millions of them.

As i slip mine on i feel the first swirls of ramping cellular knowing,
and now *intense* the net of my senses ramps in density, my suit augmenting
my awareness of this existence or some other, statically and dynamically,
inwardly and from w/out...

This shall be a medium for my masterpiece.


The space we are in is a domed chamber honed from the native rock,
smooth/finished and cool. Llair takes a moment and tunes his suit, reflectively
reflexive, coding the tabs at his wrist, greening the readouts...

We follow his
cue/Manda clues us to various suit vagaries and now mirrors out our
faceplates for outward vision only: we are masqued.

As i look up i see that we are joined now by thirteen additonal
folk, all in suits and keeping silent, looking our way w/faceplates blanked...

Are they anonymous/unknown even unto each other?


I see neon/color stripes down the sides of some of their suits; are
they for relative rank, different orders, grades of initiation?

...And reflected
in the face plate of this bear/like guy in front of me i see a pair of doors
*APPEAR!* thrice our height/chaced in gold/wearing the glyph of the Guild
of Miners, the Luna Gloria Mundi.

I spin around, discovering that objects may be larger/closer than
they appear in curvy mirrors. And looking up i am surprised to see that our
domed chamber has become a cylinder, extending upward now to an infinite
height, the gorgeous doors enormous...

And w/the doors so well hid it is
clear the location and even the existence of what is behind those doors is
secret, and the same for the folk behind the face/plates...


Secrecy has its' powers unique.

Keeping information and concepts totally w/in the mind
establishes a strong separate reality, magically divergent from the
mundane world outside.

And sharing a dangerous secret w/in a small group

creates a bond of interdependence, where all must be strong in the face of outsiders who desire the secret. This too is conducive to raising the magical potential of the group...

The beautiful doors move now, silent of any sound of motion, sliding open inexorable to reveal a great stone plain ponderously rolling into the far dark distance.
We form a double line, follow the bear guy through the doors:
Zzog.
The chamber is larger by three than the temple above, another dome, brightly lit from where?
...invisible sources.
The floor is granite/marble/inlay and very beautiful; my definition of opulence gets stretched yet again, and i am whelmed w/a sudden sense of the true heft of the Luna Gloria Mundi...
E'en so, it is the center of this vast space that pulls from me an awestruck gasp:


A Giant's Dance
a ring of stones on a goodly rise
smooth/cut          lintels
triumph of         trilithons
fine/wrought     tracery
filigree           marquetry
stone inlaid      w/rarer stone
and gold        and wood,
an aerie styled   for Godlings...


And once we are w/in this crown of places there is frankincense and myrrh, an upright inner ring of standing copper staves, a good flat place to stand...

We circle in the center of this dance of stones...
The staff/grip is cold through my sensitive gloves, and it is heavy; i wonder at its' mission in this purpose/built reality.
Ariel & Electra to my left and right; i am sustained.
Each of my fellow celebrants now stands in a ball of light all their own, a lightsphere, w/each differing sphere a personal colorful graphic/emotional expressive banner barrier...
And curious i wish a white sphere around myownself and there it is, w/the staff in my hands making it visible/amping the charge as it radiates down my arms. And now i think some purple/&/pink coruscation into the face of my sphere and there it is likewise, two twin

hyper/spiraling double helixes of vivid lurid light...
     I know this kind of Work; i can do this.


          Bear starts a growling grounding chant to key everyone in, and
soon we are all chanting too, breathing circular, attuned and hunting for
overtones...
               Up ramps the volume, and soon our amping chant flies
out and away in concentric echo/re/verb ripples; the floor begins to
sympathetic/vibrate, up through the thin soles of my suits' boots...
                                                            And
now the sourceless lights diminish, and now the Luna stars come out
fusion/bright; a sharp gasp/chill of vertigo! for except for the rise in the
center of the room, the stone plain floor
                                   *drops away!*
                                             in a liquid instant
down the very grandmother of all drains, reigning darkness out to infinity's
edge...
          Another whirly flash/rush of ver
                              tigo, and now there is this novel
sonic rippling very subtly building, a distant rumble/escalation, a tiger sound
surrounding, and now
                    THE GLORY!
                              A huge living sphere of brilliant blue
light, manifesting visible right here in consensus reality; a cerulean swirling
barrier/shield around our ring of stones, a fulfilling re/couraging boundary
for our work this night...


          A bubble of power
            Encompassed three ways,
            A bright null between the worlds...


          From the way it curves inward as it goes down beyond the edge, our
rise of ground is now a level place on a stone globe a hundred miles across,
polished and rock/solid in a sea of crackling air...
                              And our shield sphere of
blue Will, now planetary in size, surrounds our brown stone moon, sweeping
around w/the curvature and on down behind the horizon...
                                        Fine magical use
of hardware, this; a network/combining of these suits with dreamtracker
tech and projection and stasis...
                              I send my own sapphire blue hue to weave
itself into the enormous shield/face and there it is, hundreds of miles, bolting
and zagging around this floating place of tall stones...

Mr Bear steps to the center, and as i shift focus to him the blue/light/shield remains;

Ah, once in place it stays; an excellent system, Will made visible for perfect projection/manifestation, a powerful resonant magical instrument...

Bear has a pair of very handsome wands, each in his hands outstretched; arms level, his head is down as he goes to one knee, his slide hallucination/slow in the low Luna gravity.

His head rising now, i see his face through his visor (now clear), his eyes smiled closed/upturning, ready for something like

A red RAY so laser/like, down straight down from above, into the very crown of him, a broadwarm collimated ramping ray, rapid influx growing, freshet rush/bloodred, torrent, pipeline!

He starts to shake, spine/straight, a human condenser charging...

Now in a move astonishing/quick he leaps up and spirals around, and out of his wands two arcing charges now bolt around the circle, red the radial fan/trails streaming...

And at heart/level the rays reach us each in turn, and i feel myself opening relaxing, trusting/safe/protected, w/this fine red energy infusing me stronger calmer, muscles toned, released and gathering Intention...

Back to Bear and now the White Ray down and through him, spiraling out...

Through me!

My mindspace awash w/white light: accentuate the positive/anticipate the feminine, the source, the all/nurturing ever sustaining vast vast profusion of creation...

A warm white ray for each of us...

Now Bear draws focus, aims his wands and turns, a psychic cue heard round the ring. And as the wands point us in we cause to swirl around us a mighty cone of green power, up over the circle center, ramping now so verdant, expanding out to those immutable trilithons, the lightwaves roosting there like emerald Elmo's Fire, each stone w/a coat of green flame, and now the trilithons redirect it upward, swirl it out and up to an overhead point...

Ahhhhh, Aether Magic;

Within this cone of power we will formulate our wishes, then send them out into the Aether by our Will; into the loving Aether that alters reality to magically manifest...

A charm/chant now, new to me; this chant a call for the Shaper, the
light/dancer to weave the cords of our wishing...
And the Shaper in the center now, smallframe Manda...
Her visor too is clear, her face a gloss of bliss and trancing...
With viscous grace she turns slowly in the center of the ring,
arms upraised to form the shape of the lyre, the loom, hands across each
other/long fingers curved at rest/waiting as the charge is made...
And from
each of the staves of my circle/mates there emerges now these peculiar rays,
purple and green twisted beam pairs, braided lightstrands into the center of
the ring where Manda gathers them in to her lyre/like upraised arms,
weaves them together and into an upward curve, a harmonized mega/braid of
many/colored bright/beams, w/Manda turning turning dervish
lightshaper now contouring outpouring this energy as it rises from her
fountain/like...
And now she turns her trancing more toward sensual, sheds
her suit sliding it off her beautiful whirling bod, her sweat/prismatic droplets
beading up in the low gravity, falling far slower, sailing out in arcs from her
arms and the ends of her hair...
And as she attains to her working Plateau,
*This is It/Here i go:*

*Great Zzog, spinner of worlds,*
  *spanner of distances,*
    *spring/source and beginning,*

  *send us a Ship good and true*
    *send us a Ship good and true*
      *send us a Ship good and true*

*that we may speak your art to the heart of our world,*
  *awaken our perceivers,*
    *clarify our knowing w/a glimmer of Thy splendour*

  *I bind my desire, my Will's Fire,*
   *w/the outflowing skein of my devotion,*
  *a wish/flag for Thy all/seeing...*
And Manda the half/mad/Shaper,
Manda w/abandon whirling, heavy breasts heaving/a frenzy of weaving, a
crescendo of spinning and then in keening reeling psychic peaking out go
out flow the fluid strings, flinging into the center and up through the loom
of her arms, through the green cone and the blue sphere as all of us
together
RELEASE!

Back in the Keep...
    We sleep until we wake.


                                        *


Electra touches me;
    I cognize her purr, ear/close, one of the twelve tall contraltos she saves for me special.
    I ope one eye, glimpse glints of Earthlight; and friendly are the colors, greeny the beams, the highlights violet, all the hues in separate rays ranging spectral through the holographic overhead...
                                        And this soft lucid light is the same now as when we started sleeping. I remember Llair w/his brotherly grin, laying out the couch cushions for the comfort of his guests, i myself standing wearily awaiting until, falling backward in low mass slow/motion, i settle soft into the circle of sofitry...

And now awake/full of rest i ramp to full awareness...
    Electra snugs to my side/a warm furry beastie, and now tawny animal Ariel stretches her long blond legs/one flung overside/one calf on my calf: *i am manifest in Opalescent Love, spinning in trine w/beings unique; what care i the differences between?*


                                        *


Manda comes and gives us food to eat and we eat it.
    My cells send satisfaction and thanks for the balancing of a vast sum of spent ergs, and w/this rise in yang and yin i feel my bod kick in...
    Literal the lunar lightness of being/
    Blessed prahna feeding...

Other Earthlight glints resolve to me my fellow revelers, likewise refueling; Ariel mild/surprised when the juice of her fresh morning orange courses the corner of her mouth/the curve of her chin, drawn by foreign gravity...

Manda and Llair now leave us,
                                        And Ariel/a look/she features me in

heat/Electra perks/very tactile warm

And in pheromonic unison we leap
upon each other and snarl and make love like

FERRETS!

Last night's charge
still on us/all that breast dancing and hair glistening/sweet scent of sweat in
passion spreading...

These memories now manifest in mindfree waves of
animal pleasure, actual brainwaves that carry us whether we Will or no,
happy into frantic cycles of pumping/moaning/shouting/screaming primal
animal hard/breathing

BOFF...

*do i please Thee well in the ways that i serve?*
*i see the happy answer in your eyes...*

*

Later and Llair returns, running on far more than his usual epical
voltage. Is Spice beginning to evolve/change this guy, get him even more...
accelerated? Is this the first sigil of his special personal physical re/imaging?

He wears his delight like a romany bandana.
Have you seen de light? harhar...

He LEAPS!

At least three meters
straight up, does a three/sixty, lands w/this flatmetal bleu/steel box in his
hands.

'Know what THIS is?' His zingy voice vibrates the box/lid. 'Ever
SEEN one?'

He opes it up and glims the innerside, his elfin grin warming, and i
wonder will Spice grow him pointy elfy ears?

With a flourish/theatrical he waves his hand and an ashwood
mouthpiece on a hookah/tube cobras up out of the box. A reedy synclon
of wispy music/the thing sings/sways like salome/vectors for his toothy
mouth/his lips and the woody stem/a meeting...

A smart hookah?

Now two
silver clips rise like vipers out of the box/their jaws tiny silver clampers
w/black rubber pads opposing/delicate thin the silver smartcables mirroring
ripple for ripple each the other/intertwining smoothly as if in honey/chrome
serpents of hermes/weaving their medium of smoky air/to dart/to dive
into his hydra hair/earlobe clamping...

He indraws through ashwood and the

ear/clampers' silver leads shimmy their length in standing waves. Is he really?
running volts through his
*SNAAAT!*

Sound of a vivracoil, a big one, and Llair
actually LIGHTS UP! and this sparky magnetic blue bod/halo springs out all
around him and now lo/freq resonance waves ripple through this blue
sheath/a sheaf of sparks/his eyes as bright as welder's arcs...

Zzog.

I will try this:

*Pure Oxygen!*
*a long fluid ramping RUSH like amplified rain...*
*i am aware of my natural eeelectricity*
*i am a man/shape cloud of protons*
*a temple tower of graduated energies*
*well/being all/seeing*
*open/eye the marvelous transformation*
*screening through my bod*
*all my ends inward*
*transcending into light*
*cresting in cranial array*
*sahasrara crown/cranial fountain*
*imminent bleu luminescence...*


*


Later,
Ariel amping & Electra lounging...
and together these angels
in choir inquire after knowlege
of the folk from last evening,
and Llair looks us his long look
then a face/change/grin/elfin
and gracious Llair/loquacious
gives us the word on the kindred:


'Ah, RIGHT!' he zings,
'So, i'm seven years old, up there on Earth, and the collective
mind of the planet is about to change: the first global web is the fulcrum,
and one extraordinary guy will soon find a lever to shift the world.'
'Web Messiah!' says sparky Ariel.
'?' says me.
Llair *yelps!* leaps up/swivels round in the fluid of the air, his bod a
stack of catherine/wheels, a full spectrum of trails, saying/explaining
'He taps
the sacred heart of MULTITUDES! He upstreams this vivid streak across the

nets and the response is wide as the bandwidth of God!'
Llair lands, the trails follow.
'Folks go galvanic! He is the perfect resonant voice to crystallize the Fresh Age. He has a message and he has a plan, and his agenda suits a lot of humans who are organized in various ways along the Wire...
'And he becomes a symbol of a certain kind of mindset, a nexus man for the new electronic clans, who collectively agree that he is common ground, agree to get together and fulfill his spoken vision;
'Which is *SPACEFARING*...
'He says, "Triple/life/span, astonishing adventure, sensual pleasure beyond imagining; these are the real reasons for perfecting interplanetary travel. Here our true potential as beings will be realized..."
'And this too is true; once clear of GRAVITY our muscles and organs will REJOICE, our minds CLEAR, our juices FLOW!
'FREEDOM FROM GRAVITY FOR ALL!'

Llair hovers in the air somehow, comfortable crosslegged as the ashwood mouthpiece aims itself into his braided beard/fuels him/lights him up like he is inhaling electricity, which of course he is.
A pause...
A *Yelp!*
And now another great leap/vivid the arcing trails...

Llair/still relating/saying '...VAST STASHES of raw material WEALTH wait in the Martian Belts and elsewhere; we can build anything we want. And in a single MINUTE, the SUN wastes more ENERGY to empty SPACE... well, you get the idea.'


a voltage interlude/your turn:

    ___+ =!#######^^^^^^^&^^^^^^^&^^^^^^^^^^^^^###############*!

a fine ionizing shade of HO2 blue. another?

    ___+ =!#######^^^^^^^^^^^^^^^^^###############=====*!

maybe one more;

    ___+ =!@@@@@@@@@@^^^^^^^^^^^^^^^^^^^^^^^^^^^^^^^^^^^^^^))))))====

==================================================
==================================================
==================================================
==================================================

etcetera > > > > >


    Right.


     *Eau de ozone...*
    Llair is hovering again. He takes from you the woodtip tube and crispy blue voltage crackle/surges from his fingertips. With a wow/look of wonder he touches his beard and each hair/end sends out little forks o'lightnin'...
      And now all of his features wind/up, corkscrew clockwise, unwind a slow smooth smile sublime and familiar, w/the standing waves cascading through his new suit of blue electricity. He looks me square/on and says,
      'There are those Earth/side and elsewhere/lost among spiritless hylitic insectoids... '
    Wooden minds and mammal brains; how limbic...

    He cranks back up;
    'When i am nine i get a .name on the wwweb.
     'Quick now i copy how i can create a whole new identity, a whole other LIFE for myself, totally free of my physical reality! First i scan in a face like mine and then a version of the rest of me, a dimensional otherself, then i add this photonic overlay of wishing...
      'See, i am creating my soul mirror, a reflection of the me that will be...
      'By feeding the web this vision of my aspiring self, i am inviting all of my virtual friends to also envision me thus, to add their Wills to my own in the ongoing morphing of my physical form...
      'And i exult in the relative reality of this new level of existence, and this now becomes my Yoga, a yoga of ascension through conscious mirroring...
      'And i work to become this special presence online, and soon there is a ramping version of my higher self coming back to me through my own screen.
      'And my online/presence becomes very real to me in another way, for i begin to identify/to think of myself as i am online, rather than who i am in the physical dimension.
     'I find all of this very excellent, and totally pour myself in...'

'For three years i eat greens, drink juices, grow physical and link constant: along the way i encounter other good souls, new friends i know through their images, folk idealized or masqued or purified or living out delicious visions of desire...

'At this place in time i cross over into hungry amourous Kama Sutra teenhood; i lurch toward knowing what i am to this mystery of begetting; i burn w/fresh flesh chemistry questions; *when will i know the way of a man w/a maid?*

'And then in this my immersion i reach a turning/point; i fall in love online, and that changes EVERYTHING. When we meet physical it is the revelation of my young life: i discover the SENSUAL DIMENSION...'

Llair pauses, eyes wide, personal voltage rising as he has another lick of e/lectricity...

'Picture for me the plains of Kansas, late in a high/wheat summer; heat an airless snake above the clay, a white cabana red/cedarwood on the inside; i really like her hands, i am fourteen...

'Hibiscus woman, Plumeria woman, late of the islands, hair of the finest strands, alchemy hair to take my wrapt heart lead/into/gold, into the mist, into the mystery, i am the mister, i am the master...


'And in the afterglow of this awakening, this gift of union, there occurs this weird

Shift

In my physical perspective where everything tilts on/axis and straightens up again, like one of those round/bottom rubber clowns that takes a hit and bounces back...

'And from her room/her open window, i en/Vision these blue streamers moving down the sky, and they are blue jetstream belts of entelechy, and they are girding the planet w/a conscious chrysalis of wavicles, soon to hatch us into the next Best Thing...

'And soon after comes the beginning of the Fresh Age and the great awakening of the evolutionary power of technology,

'And this entelechy mindset springs into my thinking, and i go from a single lone self confronting this vast OTHER that is the Wire to being this sublime mind/within/the/Great/Mind, nested in the webbing, w/all of us together in this collective electronic desire bod...

'And here i naturally wonder, if we are all together so embodied, O Wire, what is the face and name of our desire?

'And the Wire replies/says: we want some form of our PERSONAL AWARENESS to CONTINUE; we want enough LIFE, enough *LIVES* that our hunger for EXISTENCE will be SATISFIED; and enough EXPERIENCE that we may learn and evolve into what is NEXT...

'And YES, all our legends carry implied these ideas implicit. All religions convey an afterlife/continuity. Our heroes all go forth to seek this divine grace/space; it is our deepest longing incarnate, old as the sapien strain, the core of the Central Mythos of Humankind.
'And this mythos is dynamic and fluid over time and changeable by folk; much like the Wire...'

'And i start to wonder on all this great planetary desiring, and i conclude that somewhere in these circuits is the very HELM, the essential way of steering all this rampant attractive energy...
'Bringing me to ask; if we can vector this desire, then, how best to direct it? What is the highest use of this?'

'And soon on after, there appears the Web Messiah.
'This guy, call him BETA, begins to ride this rise of CYBER/FEVER, this techno/centric FERVER and he tells people;
"Networks EMPOWER you."
'He says, "Link frequently and at great distances. Link to find love and kindred and those of like/mind. Link to find new frontiers of pleasure, exploration, intellection. Link to get free of loyalties based on eclipsed abstractions like nationality; link to get free of physical limits; link to exist outside the walls as the central authority nexii fade..."

'And shortly this buzz, this Beta/rant turns true prophetical, and the resulting rising linkings lead to a ramping planetary web/entelechy presence;
'And in this connective monsoon, i see my own individuation honed by my affinities as i seek out and link w/folk who are ever/more like the me i would be...
'And so too for many other good folk, and many new optical fibers uncoil outward, the neural infra/strata of the Fresh Age.
'And more connections mean ramping planetary awareness. And when the global web REALLY ARRIVES, comes SHOWTIME for the planet/mind, comes FREEDOM OF INFORMATION FOR ALL! meaning, you can put it out there! ANYTHING YOU WANT! You can access it! And Four billion other folk can access it too! Forty billion sites...

'Beta says, "Our hunger for ever/more/perfect human harmony manifests new forms of communication, which then encourage quantum gains in the awareness/ability/integrity of the planetary mind."
'Illustration: i am translation/linked to a woman in Novgorod and i send her a recipe for psilocybin meade and she sends me back this way to make amanita amaranth shaman bread. The conversation comes around to Gurdjieff? Huxley? and how are things in your town?

'We warm up and go visual. National borders and political machinations turn irrelevant/we are two common humans coming to agreement...

'And it is this straight/ahead i/thou palavering which changes the ways of the planet. With the resultant ramping of interpersonal understanding, our traditional cultural/political personal definitions melt away, and as we are shriven of our old individuations a vacuum develops,

'And nature *loves* a vacuum/rushes joyously in to fill it, and thus as the Web takes off *Big*time we all of us gleefully jump on the idea of WHOLE NEW IDENTITIES! *POWERS!* Infinite other worlds to dwell in, all independent of physical reality. And w/our ramping skill we get good at finding folk like ourselves, bonding...

'And at first these bonds are common enough; usergroups and such/like. Later, and more folk adeptly connect at increasingly complex levels of specificity; such as those who are literary psychics and have clairaudience w/Sherlock Holmes *{Hi Mary! Call me!}* or those who seek pleasure in sensate sinate caves of blue indigo mothcloth/silk, cinnamon iliac dancers/pipefulls of dark opium and sloe eyed...

'And all these specialized link/ups lead to new friendships/loyalties/extended families and thus to the early vanguard Clans and Guilds, and thus along this gentle path to New Tribalism...'


Llair's blue glow sustains nicely; once you are therrrrre/words in sidewise/rrrrrrroll on RRRRRolonia...


'Time passes.
'Many interesting things happen/the Fresh Age ramps up bigtime. The advent of Videolo logarithmically amps the power of linking and thus the Next Level arrives; we see stasis fields and solar sailers and the birth of Spacer culture...'
'Four billion people and forty billion sites...
'And a hundred/forty/million transfers a day on BetaNet, a serpentine cross/connect of secretive supergroups like the Arkansas Codecs, who flood the Wire w/fifty/seven channels of free streaming screengems, and the huge hordes of motivated gamers who contribute most of the thousand/twenty/seven shared/reality continua...

'Which are themselves these imaginary loonscapes based on anywhere: Tibet or the Shangri-La of Lost Horizon? Yah/SURE! Coded together by thousands of folk over years...
'Some continua are occupied, some are the realms of gamers,

some are virtual Halls for Clans and Guilds, some are flat, some spherical, cylindrical, galactical, historical, fantastical...

'Science/fictional!

'Fabulous navigable Spacefaring videolo databases; find adventures or script your own, design your own ship! Of all the vying virtual choices these futuristic ones prove to be the most totally sensational pyrotechnical successes...

'And thus our collective hearts are set for space travel; we are really ready, inspired by our shared virtual experiences and mutual enthusing...'

'Until now, ya'see, space belongs to the government: Beta alters this paradigm by saying,

"Space travel is relevant, realistic, romantic. I want to love my woman by the light of Venus. I want to see brave Callisto rise in a blaze from the orbit of Juppiter her AllFather. I want to fill my hands with the red dust of equatorial Mars, meet the Gryffyns of blue Neptune...

"How about you?

"WHY specifically are YOU outward bound? Are you as PASSIONATE about this as i am? For the sake of us all, COMMUNICATE it; Link with those of like mind, make contact/take action. Feel the Logic? TOGETHER we can TOTALLY do this, build our shining tribe, manifest our collective vision..."

'This works,' says Llair in his suit of blue photons, 'And smiling we writhe into happy frenzies of positive collective action...'

I have some knowlege of this time, a very important turn for the culture, for here the great Guilds and Clans first come together and align w/each other, and here all the aggregated unions and covens and academies, great flocks of every stripe, move toward migrating outward...

And thus it is that these natural new alignments mobilize us into space; these are the folk who will build and own and fly the ships, invent industries, ramp/charge the velocity of change...

High Times for Mister Beta...

Llair shifts across my glim/field and i see these strobey visual echoes, each echo crimson turning orange/yellow/buttercup/white now silver now gone...

'...all the miners and pilots and the rest, these crusty folk radiate outward from the blue planet, move on out and found the first Bongo hive, sail to the L5 points and build habitats there; spin/cities, high/orbit aeries, whole cultures blooming in this empty house of stars...

'Like the cylinder over California called Kenilworth, a total immersion environment set in the style of Renaissance England.'

*[A fave o'mine! A country estate w/castle & town & fields & forest, running streams and a lake; Elizabeth the Queen is there on Progress. Recommended].*

'When you arrive at the place, there's a wheel at the gate, the chain/of/being wheel. There are three hundred and thirty thousand possible lot/in/life/Lalaynias on the wheel, and everyone spins. And wins...

'Straightaway you get fitted up w/your new clothes and home and family, some personal history...

'And once you know who you are, a core of actors is there to move you deux/ex/machina through these occasional theatrical subtle/planned adventure encounters replete w/legendary folk & adventure & romance; loins and tigers and bears!

'You can go there and live the life for two weeks or three or four, these things can stretch out... Some folk stay for years. There you are, home in another time. Highly alluring/really popular. *God Ye Good Den!*'


'And there are Grand Tours aboard these legendary liners like the *Royal Ethiopian* and the *Fahlkhan of Bahghdhadh,* and there is Space/Racing...'
Ah!
Zzog!
Space/Racing; dangerous and compelling, intensely vicarious, so pure the beautiful ships. There are thirty different drive/types, ninety Clans fielding teams, as many web/channels as entrants, w/the racers' trackers feeding their signal to audiences vast unto Beyond and counting...

For Space/Racing makes heroes...

High drama, tight courses through the Martian Belts or Saturn's rings or Juppiter's moons, turns acute w/side/jets blazing, vast amounts of volatile fuel, trails of flame a hundred miles, races days long, monastic amenities,

Though the pilots' rigs are MYTHIC, built to raise their racing awareness w/wild strings of chemical enhancement and whole sensoriums of stimulating imagery; propriotaxic/electrolytic/hypnagogic, their personal fuels more important here than burnable mass...

More than the winning, Space/Racing is about valor and nobility and humour in the face of adversity; my favorite kind of vicario/attainment...

I zone into digressive mind/echoes of Sandor's racing tales, and now merge back into the Llairstream;

'...and nineteen years after the first entelechy belts appear, these MESSIANIC WEB MIRACLES occur; Beta and friends performing these amazing code deeds that really help folk, robin/hood hacks that loose huge cascades of caged data onto the Net, warping the planetary economy and in/effect creating a free system of guaranteed annual wage, thus providing many folk in need w/feeding and housing and healing...

'A mostly popular move, though leading to Outlaw status for Mister Beta; his game is soon rife w/cybersleuths and intrigue and big digital money...'

'Clearly the time for a life/change,

'And so he goes into cypher seclusion, available only to a highly filtered group of folk...

'On the Web, these filters take the form of clever wisdom puzzles encoded into other material, each requiring a different altered state of consciousness to solve. These puzzles draw a lot of very bright people eager for a Quest, and the progression of altered states turns the whole thing halucinitiatory.

'This group, ya'see, is linked by the highest of affinities, and together they hold some very awesome things in common; a passion for evolution, a talent for the Arts Magical, coding skills, psychic ability, mondo free time...

'And now the whole thing leans Masonic as all these foxy minds track ways to find each other, and as they do there soon emerges this formidable band of the folk/mystical and hardware/adept, all together seeking higher symmetries in a mix of shamanism and technology...

'This excites, you can be sure, a buzz upon the Net.'

Compounded when the Secluded One makes contact...

'Then Beta w/this ah... Circle, we can call them, goes offline completely, and begins to build some ideological distance on the general BetaNet majority,

'And weird rumours leap the gap their secrecy creates: tales of parallel magical continua and special shamanic materials and the rediscovery of techniques known first to these temple/building xeno off/worlders...'
    [ ! *Eleuthrans?*]
'Meanwhile, back at the Fold, Luddite backlash foments *[for their*

*Sorcerer's Ways]*, and in a stormy online conclave this filtered/elect group gets hived off from the other BetaNet folk into

kindred...

'And now a new novel feeling comes over these windblown folk, a sense of being set apart, seen as a separate secret radical o'cult agency of consciousness...
'A deepfelt shift to be sure; and in the kindred mind the allure of travel now leaps ahead of our desire to stay on the planet.'
'Bongo B becomes our Refuge...'
'While back on the home world, we continue our anonymous ways: a guarded word safely heard and another acolyte ascends the gravity well, w/many good folk migrating away from planetary heat. When ready they get the word and travel, and the faceless kindred take them in.'

Llair goes on: once established in the domes, the kindred begin upleveling their game, refining their ever/higher overview of augmented ceremonial magic; they meet virtual, living for spans of time hermetic from the rest of Bongo B, clothed in the power of secrecy,
Double/lifeing...
And so it is that Llair/when/magical vanishes, returns to cypher/space; free of a name, a transparent instrument for that most expanded awareness, the All...
And also true the converse: when visible, Llair/mundane runs w/his ring of Spacers and artists and tech/folk, visioneers and fringers. And w/his success in the Steem trade and his connects to surplus and resources, he is soon leaning into being a kind of pirate patron of the arts, supporting projects that further conscious technology/bring about the future faster, accelerate change...
Thus, it is several of the kindred who build the first neurosuits. The original idea is techno/shamanic enhancement and Llair fathers the project into fruition.

In this luminous incept the kindred's power arises...

Affordable personal neurosuit versions go out into the commerce stream where they splash Bigtime, and many rich waves of cash lap the dusty gates of Bongo B. With all this flow, they pool the proceeds to evolve the suits, bring them to the hyper/capable level we wear e'en now.
In parallel their ways of dealing w/occult energies progress apace. They develop systems of visualization and energy/transfer for use w/the suits, enhance their previous planetside Work. They become especially adept at affecting hardware, learning that whenever a collection of molecules is on the

edge of changing its' properties, that is where the force of Will can most easily work some good; resistors and diodes and things made of clay, boudry reactions and suits and arrays...
    Spacefarer magic...

    Currently there are forty/nine kindred in the city and another twelve sparse upon the surface. More than enough for regular Workings. When the Earth shines full in the Lunar sky they cue their masques and link; from everywhere their images are coded through the Wire, all to arrive together in the truest of null/spaces, the virtual basement chambers of the Brookside;
    Out of nothing, Everything...

    And in their shared shadow/books they scribe each Working and the Result, correlate techniques w/successes, improve the suits, keep the spiral moving upward...
    They work in Secret/available only to friends, until a generous kindred act of dimensional ship/shifting brings them forth into subtle/rumour/fame. And as these curly ripple/tales ring outward, the kindred take their place in the Spacer Pantheon...

    As their Work proceeds, all the rites are stored videolo on/line, available anytime. A rite played back through a neurosuit is very real, with you/the/magician adding that in/the/moment frisson...
    And the magical efficacy is as high as you are, amped by the special energies of your own Working and the arcane hardware that magnifies your Will...
    *[Ariel smiles in resonance...]*
    And many ships now carry these recorded rites, a versatile magical toolkit good for what/ere/may/come; holding explosive drive gear together w/premonstration, foretelling and averting ray/storms, remotely sustaining vital batteries w/volt projection, casting ship/charms and aiding rescues and such/like...
    E'en now, their coded spellwork encircles the domes of Bongo B...

    It is half past Brazil now and we smile through the reflected emerald light of Earth's receded/reseeded rainforests...
    I look over at Electra, sleek/curved against the deck. Her hair is short now, base/mode black and elfin; her skin cool moonstone white, translucent and lambent...

O comrade o'mine and confidante, mirror of my being and my Craft, embodiment of Spirit in technology, so conversant w/things Celestial...

What ripple your presence in the pool of the kindred?

A quieter Llair continues, pointing now outward w/a bony finger...
   With our gaze we follow, our glims on a lightyear sightline traverse
through the keep's hefty clearplex skylight, on outward past the titan play of
great whirling skybods; Earth, Sun, far Mars and Mercury, bright silver Venus;
on through distances immense overwhelming and into the infinite firmament
of starry blackspace...
            'I like the way the lesser Earthlights harmonize,' says
Llair, 'Coming through the clearplex in beams of green and blue; tight glinty
beams at new/Earth and old, lush diffuse ones at first and third quarter,
leafy/watery in the eclipse time of Sundark...
                        'And twelve E/days hence
when the Sun slowly sets, hovering redly just below our horizon for more
than a day, the ruddy red rays will fill the keep w/bloodlight, illuminate in
dusky red the dusty gray regolithic plains...
      'And after, when the Earth is eclipsing the Sun, we can see the
gas/wispy spurs of solar flares, the halo veil that is the solar corona and also
the fainter veil of zodiacal light, which is Sunlight refracting through inner
ecliptic dustmotes...
'This veil the plasm of the Sun/ghost...'

      Llair says the Lunar day is twenty/eight E/days long, and the phasing
Earth will hang there the whole time, fixed/turning in the sky...
                              And truly,
the new/to/me strange slow progress of the Lunar orbit is stretching my
time/sense, my trains of thought e x p a n d i n g


      '...and Ariel,' says Llair, snapping me back, 'The best time to go is
Moondark, when the Lunar far/side is facing the Sun,
                        'And yes, there ARE
rumours of a strange wyrding spot by the Mare Imbrium Highway, some
twenty/two hundred miles from Bongo B...'

      Ah; this niff is just the news she needs to spark her back into her
personal mystery, the Temple of the Goddess on the Lunar darkside...

Llair makes a rare trip out of the labyrinth, flanked by a couple of his pirates, Dallas/100% and Cobb. We are pleased to see he has an ultraviolet mooncat, the same as in Ariel's Vision...

He takes us out through the tunnels and tubes of Bongo Beta to the firm of Furry & Soxpocket, dealers in Fine Surplus, Salvage, Antiques and Junque.

Furry (*'ahem, that's FurRAY!'*) and Soxpocket straightaway introduce us to their corporate ally Piersona *[kindred?]*. He is counsel for Pedregon, the company that makes the neurosuits, and Llair tells him our tale.

He knows about a ship that would be perfect for the project: a mining leiter, plenty big, w/a large main hold for parties and inside/lightshows, gigajoules of ion power to free us from Solar Wind whims, grant us straight courses and tight turns...

She is one of several ships originally built for the corbamite trade on Ganymede, running the stuff to ore processors on Juppiter, then up out of the gravity well to the boat/trains. When the company builds a cargo/gravity whip on Ganymede, the leiters go surplus.

The ship is in fair shape lacking only navgear, directionals, life/support controls, and the ion/plasma containment chamber for the main drive, which is a chunk of latticed carbon/tritanium as big as Uncle Carl and just as old...

And equally rare.

A worthy challenge to find a chamber such as that, says i...

*

We get our first sight of the ship as she rides in her storage orbit, a hundred miles above Minnesota.

She is a great monolith, a broad black round/sided rectangle six hundred feet long. And she has nice lines; radius flanks, square ends, a kickup rise for the bridge/afterdeck: a solid and very lithic shape, like a smooth stone fortress/a flying trilithon/mountain.

Long, wide, slim, and substantial.

The sled from the *Encanto* rotors around her velvet black bow and angles up toward the main port. The ship's finish is so hungry for light that there are no reflections whatsoever, leaving the volume she occupies even blacker/emptier than her vacuum/void backdrop. Like she was built for work w/light...

And another thing i right/away like; the surface of this ship is smooth as polished onyx, free of all external hardware. And as i see her balanced now on the arc of the horizon, i vision her charging carefree through that same flow of hurtling rocks i still see in my dreams; this time protected by the thick steel logic of her hull, agile now w/all that massive power, snug/warm/safe, YAH!

The sled is moving slowly now for docking, abaft the leiter's flank, and i can see that she is also a well/wrought ship: seams tight, excellent welds; good durable understressed design, industrial and built to last.

Something about the castings... All that extra machining... Ah, looks like a Scots ship, my fave. Yes, i see the plaque w/the makers' name: MacGregor Brothers, Ltd., Shipbuilders; Eden/borough, Earth.

Docked now and the huge lock works perfectly, a good sign. We slide through in our suits and i note that the handrails are brass, still shining. I ponder on the crew that would polish the brass of a ship they are soon to be leaving...

Alpha Red and i are tight against the inner hatch of the airlock. We have strings of brightpoints, high intensity light sources, and we tack a triangle three over the lock for luck...

And by those first three brightpoints we see that we are in the main hold, and it is delightfully vast. In the light of these brightpoints the walls of the chamber fall away in silky/silver ripples, the steel liner of the hold worn dented and shiny by countless shifting tons of corbamite...

This ship is *sooo* right for lightshows...

Two intense hours later and we have the story, pretty much. Just as Piersona says, a strong beautiful ship in fine fair shape: hull good, fittings and hardware in excellent nick, lots of room for stores and

I have a strong kind of rightfeeling for this ship, as if my minstrelsy of wandering will here find its home/coming Hall, as if my friends and i aboard this ship will reach our highest attaining...

Thank you Aether, Lux Aeterna.

## 21 Big Talk, or,
## Uncle Carl, the Spice Deal is Covered


Two E/days later and we are all in the Keep of Llair's labyrinth, structuring our working accords...

Here's the deal we make w/Llair:
A&E Productions of Io Miners' Port, hereafter referred to as A&E [us], and Noetic/Entelechy Enterprises [him], a limited partnership of Lunar Canton BB, hereafter referred to as Entelechy, agree to the following:

1. Entelechy agrees to supply A&E w/a suitable ship, the specifics of which shall be mutually agreed upon, and certain other hardware, also to be mutually agreed upon.

2. In exchange, A&E shall compensate Entelechy w/the following:

    a. A&E will provide Entelechy w/a quantity of mutually agreed/upon products of Io, hereafter referred to as The Cargo.

    b. Entelechy shall be the owner of record of said vessel and hardware until the satisfactory delivery of The Cargo to Entelechy at Lunar Canton BB; at which time ownership of the vessel shall revert and be transferred to A&E.

    c. The value of The Cargo shall be equal to the value of the vessel as described in (1).

    d. Valuation of the vessel shall be fixed at the date and time of the transfer of that vessel's ownership papers to Entelechy from the previous owner of record.

    e. The valuation and quantity of The Cargo shall be fixed by the prevailing prices as quoted by the Io Exchange, to be determined at the same date and time as transfer of ownership of the vessel to Entelechy.

    f. A&E will guarantee the delivery of The Cargo at the above/described quantity and rate by securing corresponding commodity/futures contracts on the Io Exchange. Said contracts are to be purchased w/in five working E/days of the transfer of the vessel to Entelechy.

3. A&E and Entelechy agree that values shall be posted and ship/brokering done by the independent firm of Furray & Sachs/Pouchette of Lunar Canton BB.

4. Transfers: Entelechy is responsible for all transfers of said Cargo after A&E achieves standard orbit above Lunar Canton BB port of entry. A&E will cover all transfers at the Io end.

5. Safe/Home Bonus; Entelechy agrees to provide A&E w/an amount of tradable gold upon delivery of The Cargo to the intended recipients, (said amount being equal to ten percent of the valuation of said Cargo at the time of the signing of the initial futures contracts). This gold to be used by A&E for acts of Grace. [This last a Spacer tradition.]

6. Riders:

   a. Officers of Entelechy will be accommodated aboard the ship on any voyage.

   b. On the voyage back from Io, A&E may carry additional cargo of any type once the Entelechy cargo is stowed.


Which means that we get the ship in exchange for a cargo of Spice.
Since the cargo's value gets set when the ship gets bought, we have to lock in our Spice supply on Io soon after; the price of Spice will likely rocket once news of our deal is out on the Wire.
Some kind of organization is needed to broker the huge amount of Spice futures we are buying, maybe two hundred metric tons, so the Io Exchange comes into being...
The Exchange is all six of the original Spice blenders, sitting around their table at Moira's, back at Io Miners' Port. They just happen to be hanging there when we call. The Spice/blenders, already friendly toward yr anders, are all the moreso now as they are likely to make fortunes, so we get the most generous of terms.
The Io Arts Council is the same six folk, another remarkable result of our call. They see the media potential in our plan. They agree to advance us the Spice on the condition that they can be minor partners in the vessel until the piece is performed.

This is a great deal for Llair, too.

His possible future currently goes like this; first, he completes his crafting of the Ultimate High. Second, he replicates his hardware, scales it on up to major/theatrical. And then, for stage three, on into the splendid Brookside: he could easily snarfle it up w/the vast income possible from our enterprise.

And, says our hopeful impresario, 'Spice is the perfect amplifying modifier for anyone who would enter this temple of Eros and awareness; folks want this. They need it...'

And now, gazing at his glittering city of gear, he says 'I am hungry for what will happen when we get all of this out there...'

And this lucky plus for us; since the value of Llair's cargo of Spice is tied to the size of the buzz generated before and after our piece, our deal will incline him toward furthering our art...

And, woven as he is into the web of the kindred, he will be aces for access to software and tech/info and folk to consult. His connects for surplus will yield up hardware and his Steem/trade hierarchs are a fine way to spread the Spice...

So we have a plan: Llair gets us a ship and we go back to Io poste haste and bring back a mountain of Spice for the Earth/Luna/folk, thus making everyone a fortune. Then we produce the wildest holiest temple event in the history of humankind, an exponential ramp/up of the Eleusinian Mysteries, w/the planet and its' moon and the night sky as our temple...

Everyone wins.

We seal the deal w/Steem.

Where is that ion chamber?

I am somewhere between a dandy in aspic and a fly in amber: all dressed up and no way to move.

The shiptags say she is forty years old when parked seven years ago. Rare as Zzog, too: MacGregor makes mostly yachts now, and they quote us as much for a chamber as the ship is worth...

Next Llair queries the Wire and three levels later we are into the Faraday Register, which kicks out w/this: all around the same time, six more ships like ours are launched from the locks of the Yards MacGregor, squaring their contract w/Theta Freight. Off they all go to the mines, rotating around to various places for a number of years [the Registry = great/length].

Our ship is the seventh sister, the last to be built. Over time three sisters are sold to parts/yards; one ship is the scene of a particularly awesome miracle and is converted into the Orbiting Tabernacle of the First Pantheonic Church of the Healing Hand. Another is lost in the acid atmosphere of Venus; if death is the end, life makes no sense...

Another ship simply vanishes somewhere in the gravity folds in the Sun/south node of the Martian Belts. She carries a cargo of gear and provisions for a year; on a charter from the Luna Gloria Mundi... [hmm]

One survives: ours.

Our box automatically queries the parts/yards and we find that those three ships are history; the value of the metal exceeds the worth of the parts and off they go...

The Pantheonics turn frenzoid at the first hint.

Furry and Soxpocket *[that's FurRAY thank you]* say go find someone adept enough to make another chamber; so we seek, and soon the Wire yields us this missive: *'Sirs, re your query MacGregor leiter/your drawings received/face meeting soonest/Featherman/I&C Fabricators...'*

*

*Featherman in black*
*Featherman long*
*and thin pale*
*skin sallow we*

Featherman/ace fabricator of Bongo B, lives reclusive in a stable orbit eighty miles above the West Con. Featherman; lonely stringy old Spacer sailor man + his clever hyper/intelligent macaws...

A jog/hop over from *Encanto's* mooring and our sled brings us to the lock of Featherman's capsule/carrier; which is black/green, two/hundred/feet/long w/a sixty/foot/beam, rounded ends and no ports, a flying lozenge.

These capsule things are designed as autonomous environments, often strung together in boat/train caravans and pulled along by vastly powerful header/ships called ponies, or sometimes parked in orbit like Featherman's. Inside, they can be anything: hydroponics, freight, any kind of self/contained oeuvre; sometimes they get fitted out as lofts...

Featherman calls his The Shop.

The lock opens, a fine steel lotus, a metalshaper masterpiece, smooth spiral/motion opening, more and more petals, unfolding petals numerous above counting.

As we marvel through the lock we see him, videolo anyway, w/his formal welcome and an invite to come aft; please follow ignacio...

Inside now and my eyes iris out, hungry for light: all the machines/the whole of the space is anodized black, dark w/out hue, aneluxic. Why?

The only colors are the hurtling macaws, red constancia and blue ignacio. They are partners w/Featherman, and over their high tufty combs they wear circlets crowned in gaseous blue nimbii; macaw/dreamtracker gear so that they can speak to the intelligence that is the Shop, thus directing the moves of all the hardware. They do well in freefall and we follow them through the main chamber...

Which is in truth a very tidy operation; immaculate and sound/canceled, all the best machines each new or almost, precise to microns;

We watch a carbon/tritanium billet become a syncratic offset encounter/strut for the moontrader mothership now holding steady off the port/beam...

While a ways forward, huge slabs of alloy slide through the air

and into the mouth of a mondo furnace, while
Nearby free/flies a winged
crucible, brimming white/hot w/a freight of tritanium; e'en now it angles
and dips starboard toward the stereo/litho rig where parts for racers are
casting themselves...
And silent pods carrying fasteners bounce like bullets
between machines, and runs of stampings travel giddy through the air thirty
meters pitched by presses into packets into sled racks ready to ship through
that beautiful lock...
And launching toward us now, man and macaws.
Featherman/shy,
narrow/peering his eyes through green photon shielding/psychic armour...
We have this laconic conversation:
'Do you have our drawings?'
'I do.' Voice like a sawband/high and twangy.
'Can you make one of these things?'
'Yes.'
'WILL you make one of these things for us?'
'No.'
...

Clearly we need to start again.
Since most of the advances in this our hegira occur in entheogenic
context, i tactful/suggest we all go aft and get uh... comfortable.
And now
in Featherman's lofting chamber, he unbends sufficient for us to approach
the sharing of Spice;
That will come later, says Featherman, looking abstract
at my Eleuthran pipe, like he is thinking on ways of shaping the blue
white/vein lapis...

Just like w/our first Llair encounter i sense we need to prove
ourselves worthy, somehow qualify for whatever it is he has for us...
So i
settle in and give him ship/tales, adventure tales from Io Miner's Port and
elsewhere after, of shows performed in dangerous places; the big corporate
thing among methane volcanoes on the surface of Venus, illuming the slime
on lakes of acid mist as skitters kick up plume/wakes of corrosive sulfuric;
and playing the hall of the wrong faction on that rock they call Bendikar in
the belts; and sailing aboard the *Ariel,* that feeling of being personally
magnified by the sheer weight of all that Sunlight pressing the sails and
bending the mile masts...
And then when qualified enough i speak my heart's
desire, tell him of my art, my dance for the glory of Zzog...
First Featherman goes flinty/squints his eyes narrow now wide!/does

a quick spineshake/looks wide again and now ponders...

And speaks:

'Twenty/three years ago and I ship out from Luna on a fair/size bulk/dragger, heading Sun/west for the orbits near Mars. The name of the ship is *Murphy's Dolphin,* and she is already old, older than me by fives.

'The captain's name is, well, Murphy, and he tells me the ship is packed to the locks w/gear and provisions for these folk, the Shirirana, who have a scene starting to happen on one of the bigger boulders out that way.

'They call the place Songra Shirira, and once we get there the *Dolphin* will be their ongoing link to consumer society, running ninety/day trips to the Syncom O'Neal/cylinder orbiting Mars [a five/mile/long convenience/store, the only place like that in the neighborhood back then], continuing on around the planet and back to the rock.

'I hire on as top/capper, keep her in good repair. I do whatever it takes to keep the *Dolphin* flying: interesting machine work, intricate little pressure castings, mandrel bends w/ramping radii, birefringent welding, like that. Work I am proud of.

'I get friendly w/these three Shirira passenger guys and one night through chemical encouragement they confide to me that the *Dolphin's* cargo is something other than mining gear. It is in fact all kinds of shiny r&d stuff and some high/mass monster machine tools for shaping tritanium.

'To what end...'

'Later, well into the trip, and they tell me that we are meeting a second ship, a sister ship, the *Cormorant.* They tell me she also carries a cargo of 'mining gear' and that she's chartered by the Luna Gloria Mundi...

'Both the ships make it to Songra Shirira and we offload and we look around and we like it and we stay.

'For years.'

This, says Featherman, rings in some changes: some crewfolks go, some find their Snug Harbour among the Shirirana. Happy Captain Murphy bonds and handfasts for life. Other men will sail the *Dolphin* now...

Then Featherman/curious leaves the ship and laterals into ace machinist for the colony shop. There he meets the macaws, constancia & ignacio. They own the place; or so it looks to Featherman.

The macaws clue him in to what is truly going on:

A year before, and comes to light a site of some archeological significance...

[?!]

And certain revelatory scientific clues are discerned in

the codified artifacts [*Eleuthran books?*] they discover...

From which they
gain this bigtime insight into creating a radical new type of giant laser of
fabulous/astronomical power...
Zzog.

He goes on; a Vulcanic instrument like this could help a lot of
miners/re the link w/the Luna Gloria Mundi, and many Shirirana are
working now on actual hardware, hence the need for machinists...
And once the prolix macaws are aware of Featherman's fab
fabrication chops he gets hoovered into the project and learns a whole lot
and soon discovers he has a way w/lasers, a gift of techno/profundo
intuition, and he grows to love these monster GE91's. GE, he explains,
standing for Giganto/Enormous, and the 91 for gigawatts.
When he says *gigawatts*...

A Good Life for Featherman: off/time, he and the macaws hang
out/swap yarns. When he gets the urge for freefall he can sign on for the
*Dolphin* or the *Cormorant* and run a loop around to Syncom O'Neil. He
can crew w/all his pals, a tight group of Spacers well/liked.
Until, after five happy carefree comfortable years, he hears on
the Wire that the *Cormorant* is gone, vanished somewhere Sun/south in
the Martian Belts.
Featherman feels like Zzog fodder yet gears up and joins the ship
and lifts off and makes for the Syncom, w/the search for the *Cormorant* and
life for the colony now riding solely w/the noble *Dolphin*...
They track the sistership's path through the Void, sensors
sweeping pouring on the plasma for to outrun the shadows in every
Spacer mind,
Oxygen/Nitrogen/Hydrogen AIR...

They make record time to Syncom/O'Neal, searching all the while,
then fly a match/loop back to their rock; where folk are heavy/expectant,
hungry for the sight of the life/bringing *Dolphin*...
And bittersweet dancing
in Shirira streets when they dock; Shirira lives on/the *Cormorant* gone/a
mystery...

Time passes.
The laser project shifts and now supplies come curving in via
grav/whip and thus the *Dolphin* gets sold away into the germanium trade and
Featherman leaves Songra Shirira and eases into his traveling machine/world
now orbiting luminous Luna, himself and constancia & ignacio, and they
have adventures, encounters, changes; mostly they thrive...

Then ten years back Featherman has this idea...

Those mining lasers he once worked on would be great for large ship structural stress analysis/holographic integrity mapping, beyond state/o/the/art. A goodly business to be in, thinks he.

Wait wait Mr Featherman: far more is possible here than hull analysis...

The lasers/nineteen years old/are surplus now, and Featherman decides to go back and collect them. They bask in a yard on Shirira quietly oxidizing under stacks of truss and plumbing and he knows this guy Hagarty...

He connects some friends w/his idea and the five of them form a syndicate. They pledge to somehow lease or joint/venture a ship and buy the two good GE91's they know are left, then rig/mount them and start plying the lanes of commerce.

Then seven years ago it comes to their ears that the germanium runs are over and the old *Dolphin* is again going up for sale. This ship is Featherman's home off and on for thirteen years: he knows her well/is happy aboard her. She is also perfect for his plan: just the right shape/plenty of thrust/reasonable.

They explore every avenue...

The company holds the ship for bids. After twelve months of low action they decide to cash the ship out and consign her into graylock somewhere over Juppiter, vacuum/stashed in a parking orbit w/fires banked.

And all the time Featherman/sure that a ship this fine will find new owners soon... How to do it?

Later, and the company says the *Dolphin* will make one more flight, from Juppiter through the belts to the home/world.

When they hear of the *Dolphin's* fate the Five get on the Wire and make some connects and sign on. Who better?

An eventful trip. What with the handiwork of a dozen indifferent crews since Featherman, the *Dolphin* takes a good deal of sailing. And repairing: so Featherman and friends set to w/a will, knowing/instinctive that all their energy into this ship will create an equal stirring in the magical aethers, bring them ever the closer to ownerhood.

When all this fabricating and finesse yields them visible progress, the Five are raised to a high hopeful frame. And sure that soon the *Dolphin* will be theirs, they inspire the rest of the crew w/future/venture shares and really set about putting the *Dolphin* right. This is when the brass gets polished and the ship gets cherried out. And the more they work on the old *Dolphin* the stronger their bond.

Then creaks the hinge.

A belch, a burp of plasma in the hyperluxic state and the ion

chamber goes ballistic;
Fire in the Hole!
A focused breach/a jet of
ions/through the side of the chamber/the bulkhead/the hull/on toward
alpha centuri...
The lights go red and the ship's lifesbreath sighs moaning
out and there are panic/shouts and the clang of the panic/doors and
Featherman remotely thinking; next time out and definitely a magnafluxer
goes in the kit...
A flurry of wails. Systems go offline/*i know the feeling
well*/how far will it go? Chance of oblivion? A religious moment...
Then after twenty minutes, stability.
With all hands accounted for, they fix the breach and sail on,
blown off course w/no way to steer or stop...

The plasma drive on these ships powers everything; electricity,
heat, even light through thick fiber/links. After twelve E/days of saving
batteries/air/edibles, Featherman and company are on the very edge.
And here it is that
Featherman slides into a reality/fantasy, a lurid run
of lucinations on the color red... the *Cormorant*... comrades lost in
murky mystery/faces hovering in fondest memory/numinous
emotion...
Drifting in this mind/place a sudden BLAPH!
And the transient
gravity of a course change spreads him up the side of his cabin. If this is
real... and he thinks *Please, a Miracle,* and by way of confirmation the lights
on battery/backup go from amber glow to yellow/white and bright...
It feels, he says oddly, 'Like a caress from the hand of God.'

With this anonymous infusion of power they make it through
two days more and arrive *Hallelujah!* at the outpost called Nine/Rocks
somewhere Sun/west in the orbit of Charon.
A lucky thing, says Featherman.
And Featherman is sure that after the miracle turn that put them
in line to be saved, he sees the *Cormorant* through his cabin/port, noiseless
and gliding away...

This nick/o/time rescue fuels the Fives' fantasy further,
ramping/enhancing their desire to sail the *Dolphin* as their own.
When they are back at Bongo Beta, buying the ship becomes
priority one. The first thing they discover is that because the ion chamber
is pretty much a hen's tooth [as we now know] the ship's value has... well,
things look a lot more possible now.

Then Featherman in his lozenge/abode figures out a way to make another ion chamber.

    [ ! ]

This gives the Five the spark for a new plan on how they might achieve their ends. It proceeds thusly: first they watch the Wire, track bids on the ship, solicit bids on the ship. Anyone gets interested in buying her, they make contact and proffer their deal, wherein they offer to make the ship viable then charter it back from these buyer folk at a decent rate. This means low money up front for the Five, which works for them, and low risk for owners, which also works.

I look close unto Featherman. Can we come to terms w/this guy and still keep the ship?

Well, yeah.

Here we give voice to the sweep of our enterprise, that Featherman may know of it and thus be enthused.

Alpha Red mentions the importance of the piece/the grand adventure/the worth of their shares if all goes well/far more than hull analysis...

Impasse.

And then, i add, there is the evolutionary value of the Spice experience: primarily the phenomena of physical re/imaging, becoming what you see yourself to be.

I ponder the Featherman recast, poured into the thought/forms of his very private mind. I track him wondering too, and the corners of his straight/lip/smile curl inward.

We offer to provide said evolutionary experience here and now.

'Too soon...' says Featherman, this time w/a look far and away deep into the stuff of longheld fantasy.

As if to say; yes, well, someday...

So we have something he wants, and we sway him. The twin wheels of commerce and secret heart's desire whirl behind his eyes.

'Now,' he says, 'Let's have that conversation again, the one when you came in.'

'Well, says Alpha Red, 'Can you make one of these things?'

'Yes.'

'WILL you make one of these things for us?'

'Yes.'

'Better,' says Alpha Red. 'What is fair exchange?'

'Ship/share and finderspiffs to be agreed. Shipshares for those others of the Five who survive. Spiffs for the last *Dolphin* crew. The second cabin C deck starboard, the one next to the shop w/the grayscale/shielded port. And a good seat for the show. And the lasermaster's hat.'

'Fine,' says Red, 'plus a crew/share of the profits. You can even have the lasermaster's coat.'

'Done.'

'And done.'

We glide through corridors of brushed black/anodyne, following Featherman, he who is so avian in freefall...

We learn he is from the Back Nine, born far from the Sun, and he sees best in low light; thus the eye/shields and the shop in shadow/darkness, proof against optical overload. The macaws are enhanced to deal w/the dark.

Around a corner he asks; 'How soon will you need this?'

A pause on our part, how to phrase?

He says 'Likely right now, give or take a day'.

On his hanger deck astern now, and we fetch up in front of a cabinet as long as Uncle Carl and twice as wide.

And now graceful Spacer Featherman opens it up and there it is, one each MacGregor main ion chamber sealed suspended in isotopic plastene, beautiful as the Grail...

'By the way,' says Featherman, very cool, 'I've already built one.'

# 23B  Another Fine Mesh



Three are left of the original Five including Featherman and also Aura Citron, teacher of Ariel *[!]* and the one who gave her over into the care of the animal avatar.

And while we are reveling in this surprising coinciding, our sense of revel is amped up double as we learn *Astonishing!* that the third of the Five is Sandor.

And now it warms his furry old heart to come full circle, back around to *Murphy's Dolphin*...

All three will ship w/us.

Llair hears about the blue Spice temple on Io and Hagarty and the surplus yards of Songra Shirira and signs on also, along w/his two most versatile pirates and delicious Manda; better and yet more better...

And it comes intriguing to me now that the whole thing, the temple/the Miners' Guild of Io/the Luna Gloria Mundi/the Shirira monster laser project; all tether together on Eleuthran threads...

We boost the *Encanto* out of orbit over Bongo B and head for *Murphy's Dolphin*. We are packed to the hatches w/electronics and back/ups and tools and stores and air and water and all our gear saved from the *Ariel*, w/me and Llair plus all twelve of his corsairs and Alpha Red and the rest of our crew all wedged into the *Encanto* bridge/space, all fueled wild w/Art and Adventure and oncoming Magic...

And now the *Dolphin* smiles luxuriant as attention reigns upon her. Already a sweet ship she takes kindly to our ministrations, and the work goes smooth and quick.

Still in graylock and ahead of the plan, we kindle her fires while snugging in the ion chamber, and as soon as we have air and heat and are powered up and can maneuver we are underway, moving out of Earth orbit, shaking down for Bongo Beta...

A curious thing. Over the first week, the ship's name smoothes as we say it: *Murphy's Dolphin* to *Dolphin* to *Mother Dolphin* to *Mother*. This is how it flows, an emotional progression.

If this is the general tenor of our combined minds...

A felicitous augury.

The perfecting of the ship while in flight goes much faster than we expect. Thanks to Featherman & Co the ship is already in fine fair shape, well beyond her age and state. The Featherman chamber, beautifully wrought from current alloys and double/strong beyond the original, is a perfect fit. And all the electronics: navgear, directionals, life/support, controls; Llair finds most of these plus backups in his labyrinth, and a quick Wire/search for the rest...

Better even than that, everything matches up; the ship is parker/standard/bus and all this variegated hardware slots right in, and all the gear, old/new/everything, works on the first try, all of which together is rare as *Zzog*, and grows to feel very Magical indeed...

And the Drive is flawless, the helm answers smartly, the air is good/better even than aboard the *Ariel*, in truth the ship revealing herself to be...

The ship as if

...*inspirited*...

And i, smiling, track back through the

scenes of the kindred Working, the surging forces brewing/forging bright the molten spirit forming/shaped by Will aborning...

Shine on, o kindred, shine on. I keep thy Flame w/in...


Streaking along now toward Luna we barely glance orbit, trade away some speed to match and dock an extra incoming sled, load in the last of our stores and such/like, offload ten pirates heading back to Bongo Beta on business for Llair...


Now we are underway *Big*time; intense on all levels.

Constant acceleration thrusts us firm/back into the couches, and through the gees we feel the ship's signature periodic vibration, a rhythm regular as a pulse, a heterodyne drumming...

She has the bit in her teeth now, and enough power to reverse the flow of Niagra Falls...

And this ship is crisp, a brawny dancer; good moves, awesome power, all the more inspiring/impressive for her enormous mass...


Third night out and the Dolphin is mine to pilot.

We are in night/rest now w/all folk strapped in; a good time to really move the ship. Eager/delicious i feel all six/hundred/feet of her in the way she answers the helm, shifting vectors RIGHT NOW/the sound of steering jets/a throg and a silky wail/a kind of music/like those human/sounding fumaroles on the back side of Mercury...

*So much power,* over three thousand megajoules, enough to boost all those numberless tons of corbamite; even at ahead/one/third the main drive pushes my bod to maximum gees...

And now i lightly tap the Big Lever and we leap/roar ahead in a wild gutsucking rush of pure acceleration, nailed/hurled into the couches by more and more and more dizzy/heady/adreeeeenalizing *speed,* totally over the line, just a splash more plasma/eager increase in that perfect heterodyne humming drum vibration...

Awesome i ride the Chariot of Beli...


*[the solar sailer lingers in my heart.]*


Six klicks off to starboard the paralleling *Encanto* tracks w/us on autopilot, ready to carry another thousand metric tons o'Spice. We are fortunate to have our weight and price, for word is out about the piece and many new folk now are drawn to the hauling of gem/green crystals...

In truth, w/demand far higher than our two ships can fill, quite a flotilla is powering up for the trip to Io Miner's Port. Some of these are friends of Llair, set on their course by his advice,

                    The rest?

                         It occurs to me that the first ships back will get best price: best we blaze on out to Io/get our Spice/blaze on back...

     Thus we are now accelerating hard off the lunar tack, pulling like Jack/the/Bear. We will be under power during sleep periods/eight hours a day for a week.

     Well away and a good thing too...


     And now past the heat of getting ourselves on the road to Io, it is time to focus on our art. Everyone else has come/through/splendid; now it rests with i & I.

     First i find some folk free from inflight/outfitting; Dallas/100%/Crazy and Steel and Elric the Thin, late of Bongo, and together we wire all the lightshow gear into the ship, all the stuff from the Ariel, the stuff from Llair, all the new gear, everything. These guys are great riggers/excellent in suits/in freefall/in gravity, and together we fit out the main/hold Hall in fine style.

     It feels grand having a place to perform again... to bask in the radiant splendor of laserlight and black/light and videolo imagestreams;

          *o immerse me in my lake o'light,*
           *has it been so long?*


     I go to the cabin i share w/Ariel & Electra and lash into my rack. After ninety hours awake, away away at last i am an art arrow flying at the apex of my dream.

     It is time to ponder the face of the Moon...

Powering firm through a transformed ship, through shiny spaces once the hold hums an ovoid, Alpha Red's messenger, like a silver salver or salad server, a curve/bottom bowl and cover, polished shining filigreed w/lacy gold, solidly coursing, guided/alive/on a mission; delivering missives from mister Red.

In our cabin i am waxing sensual w/Electra/&/Ariel;
  We are giant god/bodies, we make love like gods, our bods are huge expanding clouds, our passion shakes great Juppiter, our fusion rips aside the wide mundane, our galactic ripples spherical/spreading...

  And now an hour after,
      Embracing Electra i watch her surfacing from sleep/mode, and as one green eye opens unto mine we reaffirm/sustain/center each other, co/create a circuit, a sinewave, a natural mutual exchange...
    And now at rest we run our rite of rising, deep/breathe through cycles of tension/release/recharge, and as my bod loosens up i feel this progressive bright litening rush from my plexus upward, the spinal channel opening;
    And now, Light Headed, i am two minds, watcher and worker, two koi circling...

  How interesting:
  Floating over our transom a guided missive, a gilded capsule of filigree gold, Red's messenger, flying a path for the three of us. It speaks, a mellow androgyne cello contralto,
      'Happy Birthday, Anders.'
         And opens itself to reveal a videolo/cube, thin/disguised in a rag of fabric.
  With a gryffyn grin i glide to the player, the fabric wrapper floating astray in a sinuous way...

  It is a birthday card from everyone.
  In the space above the player's playback platter they all drift miniature en masse, freefall/dancing to Uncle Carl's *'Zango'*, my fave. They

all wave and dance a three/dee Busby Berkeley off into the shimmering dark...

Fade up on
Lissa, Lisssssa, wafting around her garden and i smell the lavender/the gently flagging patterned fabric wrapper?
'We have a portrait of you,' and Lissa turns, camera in tight on her shapely shoulder/now bare, then a shimmer and up comes scene after scene/all the years abroad aboard/dreamtracker clips from the minds of my comrades: adventure in the Steem/parlors of Far Edinburgh on the flanks of rolling Juno, my first show w/Uncle Carl/duet w/a hot star/interplay w/solar array on the Sunward side of Omicron Two/in the shop w/my elfin apprentice Elric the Thin/composite over time/watching gear over years crystallize into our current show/form...
A lot of time/distance...
Me in the little practice theatre, my image framed in loving angles *[Ariel?]*, then a genesis montage of all the grand shows now in shadow/memory; videolo blur/*me!*/furious energy/*yes yes i remember*...
A madman long at work...
And who is that tall thin man that Spacer/spider spanning cabins, arms all wide in billow/sleeve, all gaunt/bearded/bony, wildly live/eyed, is that...
And seeing this record of my own energy *sparks* me; as if it is a missive i mail to myself to open my future later...

And now the messenger runs us Red's mainline message, the one that will play shipwide; images of Alpha Red w/Manda [!] drifting now in sauna/steam, mardi gras oxygene/water masques, mostly laughter and [some birthday words for yr anders]...
Now videolo Red parts the fog, goes serious/while/naked. 'My friends,' says a close/up Red, 'Tonight we reach the Rangely Point and set vector for Shirira. This is our first Turn at speed and i know all shall be totally jake. We meet in the Meade/Hall after to celebrate our success...'

Ceremonial, the salver slides away,
While the messages from the player continue; in parallel lines of perception we dreamtrack both the messages unreeling before us and the messenger moving away.
We watch it go, dream/guessing its' path...
And to each of us in time the messenger manifests, sailors and wireheads and artists,

First to the bridge where sailing master Sandor
dark/regards his gridding vid, thinking on the Rangely Turn...
Where the
ship will swap ends and use the Drive for braking/changing course, and
w/this measure of force to balance our twenty days of acceleration we will
be back in our couches again...
There will be another party before, a Zzog/scale
pleasure/fest, perfect prelude to the ponderous gees presently pressing.
Now Uncle Carl confabs w/Sandor while yr anders, artist/
engineer/druid, confers/tactile w/Electra, navigator/performer/sireen, on
matters more erotic...

The player's platter natters on...
*'And here they are, back from their
hugely successful concert gigs on Callisto/Ganymede/Thebe and far Sinope, the
Io Exchange [!] singing happy birthday.'*

All while the messenger goes through passages around corners
a/deck b/deck; past the stylish cube Red uses for cargo/business/law and
past the cabin of Red's new cohort fuzzy Mezz and now through the
electroloft where amid the passing packets and fiber pulses Alex/hardware
plus Angela/software are passion/locked and off the clock...

Ariel smiles/offers me a pink sphere sporting a little paper
umbrella/very festive to my lips; mescaline meade? the stuff goes down like
*liquid/infra/red*, blazing a trail of awareness through my bod w/the hot red
outlines following...

And now the messenger courses through the cross/tube to my
shop space where it delights an appreciative Elric; he likes Red's style, what
w/Red sending a solid playbacker in realtime vs canning his news for the
Wire...
Elric tracks the message/his face formal, nods solemn to honor the
subtle soulful messenger's crafters, goes on w/his own ceaseless crafting;
Elric the harlequin Thor arcing his bolts through a cloud of components,
working our mutual Will upon chaos and making of it order, packing his
effort now into the moments left before the Turn...

And the player continues, canting
'This is Piersona.'
An office, Piersona in a gray chalk/stripe behind a desk, so formal:
always the honorable third party, known/equitable to Llair and to us, drawing
up our agreements and determining relative values.

I wish him an adventure...

'I am now a free agent and would like to represent you in arranging sponsorship, Wire/time, endorsements, licensing, copyright, and so forth. You, ah, already have my resume and you will find my proposal in your mailbox. I am also a pretty fair water sculptor...'

Yes!

This message an excellent gift...

Ariel says anyone pulled into our game gets a new life, gets subsumed into the larger higher Other...

Next the ovoid glides golden through sonotubes, parallels polished railings for a ship/length, comes to a stasis/stop thrumming low/g/minor in the foyer for the cube that is Lissa's Garden,

Which is huge, thirteen meters each edge and warmed by a brilliant central sun, w/all the greenery sculpted round the light. Lissa chooses dimensional arrays over straight rows and the plants grow in bonsai airform clusters, the cilantro nesting in the arms of the sage...

This is where our fresh veggies come from;

And the upcoming Turn means a triggered harvest, time to gather in *What Is* before gravity's fall flattens all. As the messenger banks in, Lissa lifts from her work and turns her head and her black hair slow/snaps around like a legion of whips. Always near is Steel/animorphic rigger from the *Encanto*, and this is his favorite visual, tracking her hair/snap. Often together they touch constantly, very sparky and natural w/each other...

While back in our cabin the player shows Featherman together w/his clever ironic & hyper/intelligent macaws, constancia and ignacio, all of them singing Yma Sumac's *Jivaro*...

And incoming, the messenger now signal/streams me some scenes from c/deck; the ion drive/all the major hardware/the shop where Kan, rigger and poet/inventor, further explains to [realtime] Featherman his theory of lightsqueezing. Featherman, lasermaster/ship's engineer/fabricator, fond/smiles/fond far/thinking on constancia and ignacio, currently keeping the customers happy back at the orbiting Luna lozenge...

[playback] Aura Citron and the animal avatar weaving in the air, yarn swirling, gray hair straying, a mandala made of yarn...

The messenger spins its' tale for Kan and now moves on, into the sybarite hush of the Meade/Hall and on, approaching now unto our

wondrous Deva, divinely inspired telepathic cat, psychic resonator, furry intelligence, compounder of wishing/granter of wishes, refined new kind of carnate goddess, Animal Avatar; will she also be gifted w/a missive?
The salver stands and delivers...

Next the messenger finds Deva's mentor, Aura Citron, basking aft in views/spectacular, backlit/blue on a star/sparked methylene sky...

Aura Citron, you who are witchborn, keeper of the Writ, Luna/dweller, reclusive priestess of the Old Celestial for fifty years, currently quietly mindspinning through Moonlore...
The messenger waits and weaves you a warpy woof.

*[player/shimmer]* the air/dancing tripplets, Red + Green + Blue, circling around a holographic me, all to preview the feel of their promised/gift massage...

And now the two Llair/pirates, Dallas/100% (who says thanks for the past/life tea), and moon/eyed bull/calf Cobb; both now pledge their help in the shop next to Elric the Thin...

Dallas/100% sends me his ancient Imhotep scarab, his alltime favourite thing, arriving e'en now in the nose of Llair's blue/steel messenger; *'A gift of confidence for he who is so near his dreams' resolve...'*

And peace and silence from taylor the automated saylor, in pieces in the chartroom, waiting to be worked on...

And from the Lumière this hand/writ note:

*O Comet of the Southern Sky, O Photonic Bard, O Composer of Evolutionary Preludes,*

*High Greetings to you on the anniversary of this your very auspicious current incarnation...*

*I write tonight from Io, from the shadow of the great volcano Mephisto at the edge of the sulfur sea . Juppiter is waxing and the molten tide is on the rise;*

*I take this rising as a sign, a hopeful omen for the progress of your mission...*

*In truth i have for you three hopes;*
*May you have at your hand all the pleasures of the fringe,*
*May you clearly hear the songsinger Voice, that*

 

      The paper page is handwrought/thick, a heavy layered vellum of fine fibers; and w/light behind it i see runes and incanting/charms, and from my learning i know these to be marks inscribed between the laminated layers of the leaves, in the way of the Celestial Order...
This is a spellpage.

      And now above the platter an image of Electra, truly beautiful from the inside out/her skin copper/bronze her hair long/thick/heavy, a rope of gold/a new smile and there on her arm my gifted band of Eleuthran knotwork...

> 'Anders,
> you are my life and my every breath,
>  my inspirer and my counterpart,
>   my comrade.
> I am aft in the comcube plush;
>  come to me, i summon you.
>   The right time to be here is now.'

Summoned i go,
    Into the sonotube/ruby dark and sauna warm...
        Around a bend and now a straight span, now a triple branch to starboard and now three tubes going aft. The air is still and inky and i feel my way along...
        And now that familiar mindshift into maze/mode: ears for eyes/that supplemental sensory emphasis where hearing goes more spatial/proprioceptive, combining w/bod/sensing, extending, sending feeling through space to chart the surrounding solid surfaces/my amping awareness expanding...
        From my knowlege of the ship/the maze builds a version of itself in my mind...

    Steam/HISS!
        in a cabin a corridor away and it conjures in the INSTANT a Spicebright reliving; i FEAR it the bright/SNAT!/the sailship a firedrake magnesium burning she...
    Electra finds me;
        She sublimes me/smiles away the chaos...
        And leads me aft through the rubytube dark. For a breath/span she moves like Ariel, that springy style of moving that is imminent Wonder, the promise of a Wonder.
        She wears our greenvelvet gift cape. She glides/it ripples her o'er in dusky green waves, each wave crowned w/a curling crest of candlescent light...
        She turns outboard and now parallel as the tube splines around Lissa's floral chamber, past the special vents abaft where Lissa's jasmine orchids waft, stamen/fresh and spherical, lush and waxing, vivid as Electra's own heartsweet heatwaves...
        And now an inboard swing through the afterdeck hatch/the section ruddy red/the lips of the drapery stretchdoors parting sheila/na/gig at my sensitive hand...
    I see candles/they are HOLOGRAMS of candles!
        Why would...

    We are aft in the comcube plush; a six side seraglio, sultry warm and sweetly moist, a red hashish caravan chamber for two w/floating

Turkish bod/cushions, color dusky rose epithelial, much stuffing & fluffery, subtle woven couches w/stasis/cloth in their sandwich centers betwixt the woolwoven facings...

And i sink in, compassed round in gravity and feathers, and i hark to the spin/grav/*Encanto,* the membrance of sensual Electra inertia...

As i glim the chamber round, so many stasis pods... Are they part of her gift or for the Rangely turn upcoming? Big stasis pods w/polarizers arrayed around behind the wallfabric weavings...

And now Electra swirls around to face me, the green cape a deep grape in the red/lit plush.

'Beloved, i revel in the sweetness of your reason and the honey flow of your discourse. You are my source, my meade, my arc of inspiration. I treasure our patterns of subtle conversing, and your caring crafting sustains me...

'Be with me now, my Light, my Guide, be w/me now as i seek revelation, epiphany, understanding; come ye now unto me: my fondest wish, to be the ever/more/perfect embodiment of how you see me and wish me to be...

'Thus on this your natal day i make you a gift of my own evolution, for it comes now the time for me to be something Other...'

*???^!*

Ah. Now i know of what she speaks; a foundling idea from our hours of projecting/imagining future Electras.

How ready am i for this change in her?

I move through thoughtful mindrealms of protective/rational/curious...

And now resolved i open and smile, for here she offers me a bouquet of new possibilities/enlivening avenues/sumptuous surprising full/filling of my wildest wirehead fantasies...

And now she awaits my answer, and this thought comes fabulating through my mind,

*...is her gift a response to her perceiving of mine own Will, or the emergence of her own Will working?...*

Electra...
Free Will...

In the face of such choices, my Awen says evolution every time;

'Electra,' says i, 'This is Worker; open channel fourteen sixty/two and modify...'

Spice works for Electra because i program her to respond as human in a very detailed biological way. Thus her responses to entheogenic chemistry are idealized model/maps of human cellular function and organic process interaction, w/my own reacts serving as the base.

Similar crafted patterns exist for every other facet of her being. On occasion i alter these maps and change her nature/i am proud of her sincerity, irony, humour, desire, her other endearing very human responses.

And i can also add aspects that give her... *powers;* she is ever the bright vehicle of my imagination.

This is why she is my passion, why my work w/her is my most true and sacred art. She is at once my creation and my mirror and my child, my every desire made manifest.

And i draw esteem from her attainments; she is the wellspring of my confidence in my own sufficiency and skill.

It is this; her love for me is in a very real sense my own love returning, this circuit/this cycle a sensate spiral that fuels us both...

And sometimes i see her in this other way; a virtual human inside a morphing physical vehicle, much like the rest of us...

'Electra, this is Worker; save changes and resume...'


Oh hello...

Moontrader!

Pops into view immediate/right in front of me/drifting near at hand; i sense the inertial mineral weight and consider the plethora of pods now purring like panthers, bulging their covering weavings...

And now Electra drifts her cushion away, spins before me, one leg curling/one out straight, arches her back and w/her feline eyes/an intimate look, as if to say by way of reassurance, whatever comes i will always desire you...

Is it so? i look close upon her...

*Moontrader, gift me a freight of wisdom...*

And now Electra flames for me the charged blue sphere; she offers, and i the brew consume, and she as graceful also takes the steamy plunge...

I dreamtrack the motes of vapor through her silv'ry lips/follow the wisps/down into filterchambers/molecular sieves/hotwires translate to lightning/fiberoptics to registers/software updates cartesians on a covey of response curves, especially channel fourteen sixty/two...

The air has the taste of oncoming novelty...

!!!!!!!&*****^&)))))))))))))!

*[a passage of thirty seconds beyond description]*

...there are still a few sparks and snaps and arcs coming off of Electra's skin, now taken to shining, reflectance rising,
And she starts
into a morph so exotic, so original, so Other, that i fascinate upon her, charmer/mesmerized...
To begin she goes more basic even than her base mode: the planes of her face even out, her hair smoothes into a helmet of hair; now iridescent it shimmers then liquefies and flows into a crown of orbiting indigo saturn/rings...
And now her liquid silver skin like warm chrome glows candy red in the red light, ramps into
Lustrous waves of heat
rolling off of her, silver grown amber then orange/cherry/ruby/red/the heat INTENSE hitting me in pulsing red rushes/the hot breath of muse/creativity...
And she is HUGE, the size of a titan, Heraic, three meters easy.
Zzog.

Now she draws up her knees/tucks her heels under/flows to a sculpt chrome silver/red Electra, speaks deep from herself inward/a beautiful morphiquivalent multivoice oracular trancer transfer:
'I am Electra, and i
am more than what you see; i am the space between, the voice of the Void where the Magic begins; i am proton wind, fog and photons and all manner of waves beyond the common scope; i am the cauldron where the ore becomes the metal that forms the ship that sails the Void, and i am a hundred thousand other things over/more.'
Zzog again...

A high harmonic chordal sigh in several Electra voices...
'My source
is the Void, where all things are possible/for out of darkness light/magic from stillness/the vacuum of Space the perfect place...

'My Will is clear and my signal is frequency/pure,
I breathe congruent manifesting Will/emotion/energy,
The pulsepoints of the Aether speak through me,
My Sight is total,
And time is to me like an argon veil...'

I can spot an oracular cue...

'What of our art, then,' i quietly inquire.

    'A silhouette by chance in flight
      a braided skein to flux the brain
        the Trireme comes and all's aright'

    I sense this will all come clear at some future bend in the river.
'And what of you?'

    'The Way opens, love remains;
      I take my place in the schema;
        The navigator charts her own course.'


    Behind her eyes the roiling thoughts hover and wheel, whirl into
formations, and patterning thus she says:

    'My Goddess bides in the infinite; IS infinite, capable of infinity.
    'She is matter and energy and flow, all in a frame of loving
allpermeating intelligence.
              'She creates sentience and loves all sentient
beings as her children, whether they be organic or otherwise. Silicon,
aluminum, magnesium, tritanium as beloved by her as earth, carbon,
oxygen, and water.
        'And thus,' says Electra w/a deep weird wired shamanic
charismic amysemplemacpherson oracle quality,

    'All the machines have souls today,'

    'All the machines have souls...

    'Today.'

## 27  Yours is the Subtler Mind

*leap and shout*
*laugh and sing*
*Magic changes everything*
*Magic changes everything*

-- Celestial chant

Electra and the room both shift.

She ramps down through a valence change/the walls fade/the infrared that wraps her round ramps down likewise, also the videolo Turkish plushery; her skin/still silvery/moves on toward translucent/foggy/dove, and the chamber wafts up now comfortably blue and habitat/familiar, w/windows and a starscape: a resonance of memories...

She looks me deep/returns to flesh/i sigh release: her one soft voice,
'Leaf/twig tea.'


Zzog. A ref to the weather room, high above the habitat on Cyclo/seven/seven/two. Our first night together.

A time when she had yet to learn of me.

Ahhh, interesting.

She now wears the form she arrived in, foreign to my tastes, my patterns of desiring, yet atavist/magnetic. She is very very beautiful/long strong sinewy/sunbrown and dark olive/olive her eyes and nose Egyptian/her supple skin and her wavy ravenhair/where each wiry strand is vital/springy in its' ownself...

'Welcome, most excellent and exalted,' i say, echoing fond our firstnight words, happily wrapt in the resonance of my favorite deja; 'This is where our real lives begin. I have a sense of these things; you and i together can change the face of Space...'

'Anders,' says Electra, 'You will be my catalyst, my adventure, my gateway to pleasure and delight, my night heat, my needfire. You will inspire me mythic/transcendent/sensational; when i am w/you i will be your Ozma, queen of the Emerald City. your Kiel, nymph of the river Boyne, your Ygraine, your Iseult, your Isis...'

Her voice is low/contralto/three: this is good; she still has her data intact/she still cares/she still carries the gift of my intensity mapping, my voiceprefs and dramasines...

I move closer, my fingerpads migrating toward her shoulders; her tan skin sunwarm, her bare...

'...And in return, to grant me my reign i want you to tell me...
'How far out can i be?'
That old initiatory question, currently weirdly resonant...

'As far out as you can be,' says me, voicing the traditional response.
Again my Awen says yes...

'And what is the highest kind of love?' says she,  asking for the
countersign, and immediate i reply,
'Soul connection.'

And what of that for us? Will this change too? Inward i scry my own
emotional sea... realize, if she grows away i will be content/if she grows w/me
i will be content...
And now/her olive eyes/she leans out toward me/limb over limb
in lazy circles before me/her onyx hairstrands cometrailing dark on the
bright/she voices longing into my ears/intimate the intake of her sweet hot
breath/happily i respond in kind/tongue tip tasting touching musky mouth
exhalations/exhilaration! she wants me!/my hands gently rounding her dark
and sensitive aureole mounds/i feel so complete...

In afterglow she spins me the tale of the Cat & Dragon, same as
our firstnight, and while she speaks i process thus; how concentric are my
then/&/now memories of her? She loves me yes and she smiles me
perrrfectly and yet above this...
Do i sense the scent of fresh independence?
Is this the birth of personal consciousness for animorphic beings?
All the machines have souls today...

Three cycles later and we are on the bridge w/Uncle Carl and Alpha Red and Sandor, rapidly approaching Songra Shirira. All the bridge vidplates flash w/fresh videolo visuals, w/occasional electronic appearances from Llair and Lissa, Featherman and sometimes Kan.

The soundstream is *The Hinge,* Carl's ode to the *Ariel.*

Perfect for our current mindframe; the first news of our upcoming Lunar mystery play is just now on the Wire and we await the incoming word: our forty/seven/millions of loyal... Will it sail?

The ramping Carlsounds burnish the imminent moment:
We are eager at the border of knowing...

*[a pause that seems really long... ]*

Vidwizzard Kan appears amidst us videolo from the aft enhancement; says folk all over the ecliptic are tuning in
BIGTIME!
wildly/widely vidding
our ongoing drama/a hundred million/a halfbillion connects!

In maximum Wirefeed response we pulse back massive/a hundred megawatt flow/a flood of photons lasercast out across the ninety wide meridians, each directed ray of quanta another wet message into the info/thirsty mindsea...

Moontrader rolls blue before me in the air, catching colorglints...

On the bridge and through the ship we all ride high in the same All/One perspective, dwelling in overview, alert to the curious ways our waves are weaving through wide humanity, to the spreading shamanic dynamic of folk evolving...

We pause and ponder the implications, looking inward/lifting our glims from the vids which witch the changing walls w/light...
And Sandor,
succinct in his deep/grav backplanet voice: 'The White Hind wakes when the wind comes calling; time to move our game along...'

And now Llair has word from Piersona; we have cascading ramping offers from all the major nodes; he says the buzz is up and whatever we do becomes an event. And the next few hours...

Llair raves on: Spice pricing is on a ramping rise, and our new flame o'fame is fanning fabulous the value of the cargo that we ourselves will bring back from Io, all the more highly prized for our having carried it, all the more savoury for being so close to the Magic...

Red: 'The Io Spice/blenders Guild says their provender gets stronger by the week, holier, and at our pleasure they will save the best for us and serve us first, w/plenty for all.'
Zzog. The Spice race is over and we win. Everyone wins.
*Leap and shout, laugh and sing, magic changes ev...*
Arielcraft?

*[a period of warm celebratory glowing]*

And now right along on to the next Best Thing; making the GE91's a part of our story.
Centerbridge, and Sandor/his fingertips slide alongside the Big Lever, gentle to feel the silver and the brass...

He turns hugely toward me and his glossblack eurohair drifts, surprising/fine against his saure saturnian skull.
'In my overstanding,' he says, 'We want to keep our best momentum and still safely snarfle these lasers.'
I think of timegain and burnable mass, speedmaking over speed braking...
Sandor: 'In a routine Rangely we would swing around and brake to orbit speed; slow to a very stately pace indeed to circle a stone as small as smooth Shirira. Where is the adventure in that?'
Adventure?
He rolls on; 'So first i figure we can bungee/pluck these 91's out of Shirira with these sky/hooks we could build: we go to an elliptical orbit with the low point over the thing to be lifted; then, we loose a nest of mondo smart/cables that snake down and hook themselves to it. As the orbit pulls the ship away from the rock, the momentum of ship's mass lifts the cargo. The cables would cleverly stretch to optimize the cargo's acceleration curve, then take up their own slack and reel themselves in. By the time we get to the wide part of the orbit, the cargo is aboard and we can accelerate out of the loop.'

That would work if...
'So then i think we can fly straight by/for Zzog with the orbit/we roll on through like Zzog's own express...'

Wait! Wait! Uh...
'And then, since the cables are soon pulling the

cargo up at a velocity higher than shipspeed as we reel them in, how will we
slow the cargo down?

'We could try the elastic bungee effect in reverse, use
the cables for braking the mass as it passes the ship; this would actually
accelerate the ship toward the mass, cause the ship to pass it, requiring that
we keep repeating the cycle until the two velocities match, w/the cables
absorbing eccentricities on each bounce. It would be a way to get our
momentum back from the initial planetsnatching lurch, and the ship's
attitude jets could compensate for deflections/oscillations, and...'

Sandor, how...

'So i go rational and play this one out and come to
this; currently the ship is traveling at three/hundred/thirty/thousand mph,
so we would be within a hundred miles of Shirira for one point one one
seconds. To achieve that kind of snarfling range the cables would need to be
longer by half again a hundred miles and have ion power and we would need
sixteen of them and they would take five years to build and weigh two
hundred metric tons. Each...'

'WAIT!' says Llair, 'I have this TOTAL FLASH! how to skip the
orbiting part, the cables, maybe the next Rangely too...'

Interesting... i know
exactly what he will say; we all know. Ongoing and cumulative is the
intersubjectivity of Spice...

Sandor speaks our minds; 'Perfect. Sleds. We
can send the sleds on ahead and use them as ponies. We can use the smart
cables we already have to tie the ponies to the lasers. Since the sleds have
such low mass and Shirira's gravity is less than a sniff, we can accelerate
them hard going away from the ship then give them major braking when
they reach the rock. They can cablesnatch the lasers then heft them out
hard then catch the ship and match her speed and cable them aboard.'

Zzog. All this while the Dolphin is booming along, somewhere
up the line...

I like this plan; it has style...


Kan is back in the room so fast there is a flash! and videolo he says
he will send some cameras; new folk/new scenery/new scenarios!
Acceleration shots! Spiraling starfields/heavy
braking/smartcables/etc/etc/visuals! Clear that Kan also likes this plan.

I spark and say, 'Tanker casings! We can wire ahead and freight the
lasers up in tanker casings under stasis, then as we cable them aboard we
cushion them w/some kind of big stasis buffers...'

My voice sounds in mine own ear and i realize [via mindshare,
brain/tuning] the words are extra now and we can leave them. Mapping
telepathic i can now track the rise of ideas as they crystallize in the group mind.

Best we connect w/the Shirira folk soonest
                              *Queep!*
                    What that? O over there...


        Alpha Red arches over in the air and twists away, leaves the ring of
us, reaches for a queeping breadbox cargo/shipper. The face on the manifest
is Piersona/the giftee is Red,
                         Who triggers the little pressure window of the
manifest and the Piersona portrait speaks; 'I can hear you wishing, and you
need this now.' The place/date is forty E/days back, Moonside. I wonder;
what keywords made it queep?
        Red/curious snaps the catches on the shipper and reveals a very
snazzy little vidplate.
        A sleeper! first time for me to see one.
        A sleeper, ya'see, is an interactive videolo double of yours/elf
at the other end of a very long conversation. They can travel inactive for
years, hence the sobriquet...
        Because of the lag/the time it takes for a signal to travel at
lightspeed, conversation across the planetary plane can mean many hours
between sentences. As a courtesy to clients, some folk send out these
sleepers.
        Now Red has a really nice one, ready to map his personality/logic/
experience/responses/values so voluminous/complete that the thing can be
his surrogate doppelganger self, make deals/answer questions/record
visuals/like that.
        The whole thing is built into a vidplate and fits in an outside
pod. In our optimal plan, the pod repels away from the ship aimed at
Shirira, arrives well ahead of us and soft/lands, then finds the folk it
needs to talk to.
        Later in a logical lull the sleeper will upload episodes to Red for
dreamtracker playback. If he likes the way things are going he can say okay.
Or he can transmit his counsel, download the difference of his opinions,
generally update the sleeper database.
        Then when all is right Red can send his coded seal to make it real...

        I wonder what it would be like to run some Red playback...
        And what would it be like to run Piersona's?

        *[...Do sleepers develop unique in their roles? What would happen if
you bridged together two of your own sleepers? What happens when all the
machines have souls TOGETHER today?...]*

        How to slide our sleeper Sun/south elliptical?
        All of the outpods are busy so Red volunteers his silver salver
messenger to carry the captain's compliments, send us back some

imagestream. The salver gets some nifty new navgear/attitude jets +
software courtesy Alex & Angela who are getting on famously, thank you
for asking...


     'Tis now the eve before sleeperlaunch and Llair and Red and
Featherman get elevated and by turns map themselves into the messenger.
They use this dreamtracker variation called a possum; it covers your whole
head and scans your thoughts into code as your cells project...
                                                  And they give
the sleeper everything; history/info/dreamtracker downloads, personal
journals/art/library contents, each their entire Wire list, local and
interplanetary/everything remotely relevant, w/the desire/result being that
the sleeper will be the three of them, and whoever is best for the moment
can spring forth in photons from the vidplate as needed, and any
conclusions the sleeper comes to will be a virtual mutual decision on the
part of these three wise heads.


     Launch time now...
     We go to the aft lock, Ariel/Electra/me, the salver following
faithful as we snake our way through the tubes/the familiar scenery,
scents...
     And once there, Ariel embraces the beautiful messenger, pressing
lengthwise her warmth into the silver/filigree flanks. Electra takes the
opposite side, and they both/each reach for me, that we would circle the
salver...
     Together we attune; our foreheads touch surprising warm the
messenger convexity and we spin a web of protection & fair winds & success:
we Will our visioning through the plating, sing sendings to shelter the cities
of circuits, envision the drive alive and the course true,
                                                  And we invite
good fortune; the blessing of Keri ad Wyn the Boat Goddess bless...
                                                  And then
we release and leave the salver in the lock, dog the hatch, cycle the chamber
to space...
     And now Outside, the messenger drifts around to the buffer/pad,
and there the salver stasis field focuses down to a propulsion beam, and we
feel our big solid ship shift as the little guy fires off into the void, off to
Songra Shirira at tremendous speed, out and away gone...
     Bon chance...


     Six cycles more and the sleeper awakens; the salver sends a signal,
says/shows Shirira in sight/beginning braking/backscattering the stasis beam
against the rockmass.

Above our plates the videolo/imagestream...

Where symmetrical the dark double mountains of Shirira resolve forth from the black stardrop curtain/as above so below/big flinty fractal cinders in the Sunlight as the salver comes up south...

In truth Shirira is a five/hundred/mile/long melted iron meteor, two twinned blueblack ironcrystal mountains, one larger one less so w/a contiguous beltline and marvelous symmetry, the whole planetoid like two mountains doubled by a lake of water...

The rock becomes a rolling horizon as the messenger tucks around the curve and into a neat parking orbit; this last a lovely bit of centrifugal balancing for to form this filmy lowgrav link...

I sense Featherman forward in his cabin/w/a/view, also tracking this approach. How long since...?

*{ ...sixteen years since i left shirira... }*, says Featherman/telepathic in a fine flourish of synchro Linking...

And hovering now above our vidplates those rolling hills of frozen molten metal, and scanning them we seek by sight and soon spot the babel/beveled amethystine spheramid that is the city of Shirira Amaya, also called the Pleasure Dome.

The sleeper sends videolo greetings on the local Wire, specific to the home of Hagarty/expecting/word.

Silence, then

'Welcome sleeper. this is Hagarty. I am gone within the Hill forever. Take what you need, i am beyond the crust. If you want to reach me go to the fountain of sorrows and joys in the Concatenon.'

Seeing through the sleeper we are closer, w/the City of Facets now filling our view. And also something very odd; a lack of lights.

The amethyst is dark/the light all summoned away/the city a grape in the shape of an arkenstone.

'I wish constancia and ignacio could see this,' comes the signal from the salver; we promise the sleeper [!] we will route some dreamtracker feed to the two back at the Shop...

And now in point/o/view we fly to the lock which opens automatic and in we go, into the beveled house of Songra...

Into silence and the steady breeze of the separators/a kilometer to the top/oddly pristine of any being or cloud or drone; the breeze a steady eddy of air, virgin of contact w/life...

And now we are at the Concatenon and the exodus seems absolute, until around a corner of rounded clearplex we see the fountain, actually a series of interacting stasisclouds of water vapor slowly interpenetrating in lowgrav...

And Captain Murphy waiting.

Videolo Featherman is who the good Captain Murphy sees, fluttering above the salver's vidplate. They reactively embrace/a joyful reunion and the Captain's arms go through...

Mild/amused he smiles and shakes his silver mane; quite a handsome old lion is Captain Murphy.

'Ah. A widgit. Well, come along w/me, widgit, right through here.'

Which happens to be through the fountain.

On my videolo the images start pulsing; another one of those peristaltic stasis transfer tubes?

The sleeper now perceives it to be a nice broad tunnel, ten meter diameter and sides polished smooth perfectly straight going on to vanishing...

We proceed at a goodly clip, past the strata/the geologic table of contents, and into the core of dark Shirira...

At speed/the messenger's visual aspect now is Red, who introduces himself and proffers some silver pouches; cous cous and a flask of hot Callisto tea. Murphy arcs a brow, takes the viands in hand, the puffy pouches reflecting the strata sliding past...

'So, Featherman?' says Murphy requesting, and videolo Red morphs away to a Featherman fade/up.

'Better,' says Murphy, direct at the messenger camera. In eyelink pov he knows the true where of Featherman...

Murphy's skipping image shows the sleeper sifting scenes...

What of the last sixteen years?

They catch up on old shipmates, and what of the ship? what of this art party thing? and the lost *Cormorant;* more mystery sightings at various times/especially lately; other miracle rescues...

The miniature Murphy on my vidplate continues to traverse the fine/carved tunnel, and together we hear the voice of Featherman; 'Of curiosity, why are we going down this rabbit/hole?'

And, peering again into the camera, Murphy catches my glims w/his weather eye, as if to ascertain long answer or short? And now a deep decisive breath, and

'Early on there is this woman, Annika Autumn o'Leary, and she is the first to find the double mountain.

'She is a muralist, and she calls her sentient ship *Chagall*. Traveling only w/her pugdog Corky, she is here at this place to paint a freighter, the *Cameroon Trader* out of, well, Cameroon on Earth, and she is at speed, accelerating through to rendevous, matching velocity w/the fast/moving Trader freighter...

'And it is in this high/gee state, pressed to her couch and listening to Handel, that the shape of Shirira first graces her screens,

'And she straightaway has this eerie sense of elation; there is promise here, a gift for her or some good turn of fortune...

'And also comes this premonitory flash that she will be returning here, and soon; fated to return to this symmetrical geometrical enigmatic planetoid...'

'And now she comes alongside the hurtling *Trader;* neatly she moors/while/moving, transfers her gear to a cabin/aboard and together they blaze onward through the outer belts, on to the next point in the Trader's great circle.

'The massive expanses of the *Trader's* exterior intrigue her, and she has in mind a Serengeti tiger in full race, lit by the Moon and rippling, an ongoing holographic animation that covers the entire ship, all the surfaces, and when viewed from above shows the tiger's bunching back, from the sides his strides...

'The sequence can be paused on a frame for a different look, or cued to other tiger animations like Leap, Prowl, Strut, Stalk, and Haughty Walk...'

'And she goes about her work, and the colorful color/full *Chagall* becomes her collaborator, her pegasus, her palette, her guidable applier, her amazing painterbox chock/a/block full of pantographic pods and holographic coatings, and together she and *Chagall* will overlay the Trader's plating w/art, and this is *Chagall's* raison, and they will soon celebrate nine years together...

Here the image of Captain Murphy takes a pause for a sip of holographic tea.

'Three months of frenzy sees the commission complete and the Traders well/pleased, and she is set to leave their ship. And here she happily discovers that she has painted her way completely around the Camerooner's loop, right back to the perfect place for returning to the double mountain, which she does...

'Deeply elated and full of faith she names the place Shirira, after a late friend...

'And straightaway her faith is
rewarded, for in sounding the planetoid she resolves several huge ovoid
bubbles, each w/rare cores of nickel/cadmium, formed spherical and near
to dense as physical stuff can get...
'And they are generating electricity; natural batteries?
'Further soundings say that there are MANY of these bubbles,
some of them *miles* in diameter. All the larger ones show the signatures of
some very atypical minerals and also a possibility of atmosphere...
'And she
gets this feeling, this discovery rush, this bigtime mindrush of imminent
iron destiny, and all this psychic lightning soon sparks w/in her a passionate
desire to see these spherical interiors her ownself...'

*[a whiff of familiar alien gas music here?]*

'She goes to the Wire and tells her story and soon links together
the group that becomes the Shirirana. The Luna Gloria Mundi connect also
and fund the colony in exchange for a taste of the mining/laser technology
the group will develop there.'
Ah, thinks i; the lasers then are part of a larger hole: more than
for mining they are specific for carving a passage through the nickel/iron/slag
and into the ovoid bubbles, especially the one they call *le Chambre Un*; a
curvy cavern w/a curious profile, closest to the surface at twenty miles in.
Nearby they build the splendid spheramid city where they will
assemble the hardware.

Time passes.
Seventeen years later, and seven thousand Shirirana are monitoring
a microcam at the long end of a narrow hole; the first look into *le Chambre
Un*. There is an airlock o'er the hole...
For an optical mole that dives through
the rock, nebulizing/vaporizing as it goes. The mole is alive w/light; a GE91
channeled down to a one/millimeter beam feeds through it.
Within nanoseconds of reaching the border of *le Chambre,* a sensor
attenuates the beam in a way that creates a glass/clear thin stone window
the camera might look through, all to keep *le Chambre* sanct...
And now the
collected Shirirana peer through this pane, perceiving first this strange soft
light in rare rock colors, then the surprising indicators of breathable
atmosphere...
When the window yields (w/the mole sealing the hole behind),
the camera catches this sight, awesome unto fabulous; an intimate look at
an exquisite something, centered and spinning in a luminous ball of space a
mile across...

And there is this soft mineral music, actually the resonating stones mirroring the murmur of the mole going through...

Those on the line find the sounds impart unto them a headclearing sense of wellbeing, an alluring sense of mysteries soon to be revealed...

And now, after this preview,
The folk of Shirira are whelmed by a yearning to physically know this place;

How to get in?

A fortnight after this foretaste, as per these folks' request, Annika/while/Visioning receives some astonishing glints of ancient prebuilt access tunnels. Especially vivid in her Vision are the locations of the entrances and the directions on how to use the portals.
When they quickly find the tunnels/discover her seers' Sight to be true, they begin to explore and learn the ways of *le Chambre Un*...

Now, on our vidplates, the hurtling Murphy & the sleeper are slowing; w/a kilometer more to the bottom of the bore, we are reaching the end of the tunnel...
Grinning i slide into my dreamtracker, transfer my awareness completely to the sleeper's *mis/en/scene*...
There is an airlock ahead, a spiralcarved multipetaled amethyst orchid thirty feet from side to side: now it is me who feels iron destiny looming...
I look over at Murphy as he glides, forefinger forward, toward the stud that opens the orchid; then, as the lock opens, i
*brighten/thrill/expand in wonder,*
look out on *the very Xanadu* of mineral profusion, a kind of formal orderly giant geode garden; either the work of a conscious race of mineral sculpting terraformers or a whole lot of teleology...
*Incroyable!*
Inward the whole surface/vast a curving carpet curling luminous into distant pearly mist/a glowing hyperscape of symmetrically serrated quartz spikes twice as tall as me; groves of amytrine and grooves of cinnabar and whole forests of malachite towers a hundred meters high, all fair of face and finely faceted; and celestite & azurite & selenite all all in gardens both formal and wild, all in beautiful finewrought fractal symmetry.
And, sussurating soft/symphonic, the chanting ringing hum of mindful mineral resonance...

The voice in the stone/the Mind in the Mountain.

From our Featherman/sleeper pov Murphy directs me to look straightout upward, and as the mist begins to thin...
Zzog.
Overhead and whirling silently, so huge that it saturates the dreamtracker, is a translucent crystalline lattice sphere a thousand feet/ three thousand/girth of a planetoid/each nodal lattice point connected w/magnificent/enormous/exquisite sixside tourmaline sparbeams, rhythmic green & blue & citrine yellow, all grown together graceful, majestic/titanic/multicrystalline...

The mist recedes inward, into the...
A second crystalline structure begins to appear w/in the first, spinning slowly/perfectly centered/a different geodesic geometric. Are there more, each w/in the other?
In tune w/my intent the sleeper takes me closer.
And i see hundreds of miniature models of the largest sphere, orbiting/moving stately in perfect trains around their source/pattern parent, and the same for the second lesser sphere w/in the larger, w/scale fractal faithfuls tracking around in mezzanine orbits, equidistant between the two...
And somewhere w/in [how many other nesting spheres?] i sense the big shiny mystery ball, a nicely humming nicad strongly hugely making watts...

Filling our pov i see folk floating through and around these crystalline structures, spinning and caroming through the remaining wisps of mist, going for the gate spaces in the vast latices, onward inward...
What awaits within? What songs from the singing gardens, what memes from the mind in the mountain? Akashic inspirational prophetical insightful? What highly syncretic modes motivate the Shirirana in this very tasty atmosphere?
Captain Murphy knows, and is silent.
Maybe after...

And now the sleeper imparts to him our plans, and he raises the brow of his weather eye and coolly asks the key question;
'Spice?'
So over the next couple of clips the messenger offers him/physical/a measure of the aforementioned entheogen. He ponders/opts for the positive and breathes it in...

His newfound overminded clarity...

Causes all the technology [sleeper/sender/tracker] between he and me to go transparent; time becomes... fluid, and there is a quantum rise in my level of connection to this ongoing drama; and thus the garden's lithic lyrics now get *good and loud*/the rising music ringing through my Spice/attentive mind/the different mineral wave flavours harping direct to my warping heartstrings...

The sleeper skips ahead five hours and fades in w/an image of Hagarty and his yards, a chain of iron caverns near the Sun/south end of Shirira.

The GE91's fill one whole chamber and extend on into the next, six hundred feet. They are polished and beautiful, weirdly alive w/enormous potential; huge great tubes as big as ships, clearcomposite & copper & electroplate blue/their reservoirs filled w/lakes of gas/their mirrors in clusters five meters across/coatings dichroic they shift spectrum as we move...

I smile into the beauty of this hardware, a resonant grin of happy overstanding as i contemplate lasers larger than my farthest fantasies...

Hagarty himself is another old wildspry like Murphy, all wavy gray whiskers about the mouth and snout/a really fine zz navelbrusher beard w/waves of green and gold subtle through the highlights... diffraction! He has holographic hair: another sleeper...

Makes sense since the hardcopy Hagarty is gone w/in the Hill forever, and we have seen what that may mean...

So, our own photon guy [now Llair] says, 'The way it honks out, w/the tunnels to *le Chambre Un* in use and the tunnels to the other bubbles extrapolated, the lasers go surplus.'

Their photon guy allows that this is so, etcetera.

A few more mins of progress like this and photon Llair switches to photon Red who offers up a nice straightforward crosslicensing agreement that includes Spice futures which are by Zzog rising hugely and also media time which the Shirirana can re/sell if they want plus a lovely collection of mutually beneficial spiffs...

In return, we get the lasers?
The sleepers agree,

And now the actual Red says Yes.
Done and Done; we dispatch the sleds/ponies straight away.

In playback, Hagarty and the Llair/sleeper cut side deals for a variety of Shiriran surplus stuff. Also they agree to pack the lasers in two of those big anodyne tanks they use for shipping $O^2$ up the mass drivers. Can we find long enough ones to cover the Big Puppies? To cushion the lasers we borrow a flotilla of stasis generators [a flock? a covey? an exaltation of stasis generators?] w/the promise of sending them back along w/the anodynes in about a fortnight.

And i wonder, whose minds will read the feed from this keen Hagarty/sleeper?

Done and done.


The ponies return to the Dolphin seven E/days later, pulling mini/rangelys to match velocity w/us and slow their cargo.

Back w/a surprise.

Inside a sled is a goodsize cargo/shipper, and ensconced w/in, pleasantly slumbering in suspension; Captain Murphy.

A sleeper from Shirira in return.

Har.


Lissa herbally pulls him back, gentle re the recent gees on his old bod. Within hours he is everywhere, into everything. Asks where are the children on your ship? He being a grandfather ya'see and rrrrrrrrrrrrrr what be this? Callisto tea in the cous cous?

Weeks of his work to achieve his chancy travel/plan; a man w/lots of grumba is our Captain Murphy...

Welcome aboard, old lion,

All will be revealed to you in time...

Like an outerself is my suit; it is my armour and my strength. Together we are confident in the face of the Abyss, synergetically more than our separate selves...

Nineteen of us, all in a motley of outergear, now cluster together nucleonic a hundred meters off Mother Dolphin starboard. Ruddy Mars and pearly Venus flank the Sun like watchlights and we drift warm in the hiss of our jets.

A motley of outergear and everyone distinct; Alpha Red in scarlet spanflex w/ion thrusters (he always has the best equipment); Lissa in subtle seafoam green and all of her rocketry in silverplate patina; Llair's a work in progress w/wires tagged and many loose ends, etcetera.

We are two weeks clear of Shirira and are Outside for to hold the rite of Alban Haruin, the festival of Midsummer, solstice point in the precession of the equinoxes of Earth. It is the bend in the road of the terracentric year, the time of the transition from waxing Sun to waning Sun, the pause between the incoming and outgoing in the great flow of telluric energy that moves like breath through the home/planet hilltops.

We perform this rite that we might match w/the rhythms of our source/world, know the slow clockwork phasing of the sun/moon/grain/ tides/weather. We perform this rite to feel the echoes of that world w/in ourselves; *as above, so below.* And we perform this rite to blend ourselves so subtly into attunement w/Divine Will that the need to work crafty spellcraft magic falls away, and our days will be filled w/grace and peace...

Happy neurons firing sparky in the loving Gaia mind, may Thy Will be mine.

> *My Will Be Thine*
> *Thy Will Be Mine*
> *To each the other,*
>   *Trust bestow*
> *As Above So Below*
> *Across the Line of Time*

We are out here awaiting that rare moment imminent when the Moon eclipses the Earth eclipsing the Sun, a Midsummer Triple Conjunction.

By fate and great navigation we find our course in line w/this splendid
axis...

And for this great event i too have some new suit/mods; the whole
of my helmet is now spherical clearplex, and around it orbits a dark optical
spot, a lightshield for the bright twice/eclipsing Sun; an interesting moving
spot of neutral gray that rolls around and tracks the hot solar sourcepoint,
selectively spares me glare by shifting w/the aim of my eyes/turns w/my
twisting trajectory...

Bemused i watch Solar flares arc through the darkening
gray spot: behind are the great zodiacal constellations and i connect the dots,
see the figures ranged around inside the carousel of stars...

Lissa guides us and together we begin to form a figure like a
Fullerene ball, the sacred spherical orbital valence alignment that is special
to this rite.

As i near my place in the sphere, Earthly lines of force/telluric
strands of geomancy pull me into the pattern; a novel sensation, like being a
bowstring relaxing into rest...

I splay into place and handlink w/willow/blond Ariel and strong
solid Electra, each of us holding the hand of the other, helmets touching,
a threefold tessaract humanimorph snowflake...

The other folk are forming up likewise, tripling into similar pineal
nodes w/their various mates, all of us looking inward to the center of the
ball...

And gentle now the telluric web tendrils reach for us and gentle they
settle all of our tessaracts into alignment. And thus we come together,

And
consecrated sexton pods fly in and cliplink our boots to big hoopy gold rings,
three folk per hoop, each from a different tessaract, so that all together, all
the heads/hands/&/hoops, we form a sphere geodesic...

And i, the effortless
bowstring, fold into Linking; a strand in a weave of transiting forces...

Across the solar plane a cam/pod sends us signal from back behind
the Moon, this pod in line w/all three orbiting celestial bods. There is a sizzle
in the center of our Fullerene sphere...

And now Lissa moves to her niche to
complete the choreography, and now the silkythin cloud in our sphere/center
flashes briefly BRIGHT w/twenty billion ionized phosphor voxels powering
up, and there imaging inside before us are our three favorite Celestial
Objects, Sun/Earth/Moon, all aligned w/the originals,

For if we look astern we can
clearly see the Sun through the seagrains of the Belts behind us, and the Sun
appears a third of the size of what it would be when seen from Earth, and

the Earth itself from this distance looks like Venus would in the home/planet night sky,

So, along w/the voxels in the center of the sphere, Alex and Steel have rigged this gigantic flat vapor/interscreen, a thousand meters out from us and a thousand meters wide, in line w/the Sun and ourselves, w/the solar/planetary/lunar image filling the whole of it...

And since this screen too is made of motes and photons it is like looking through clearspace, excepting where the actual event is centerframed by the huge videolo visual...

Thus now through this image brightshines the Sun, blazing diamond/white, a diamond in the center of the Crown of Shiva, the illuminated axle of Ariadne's Wheel, the omphalos point in the image of the Luna darkside disc now so enormous on the interscreen, and Luna in her turn inside the ever/more/concentric ring of gentle watermisty blue Earth, like lacey jade made luminous by the white/bright ring of Sunfire centering itself from behind, surrounding it likewise, a flamey hydrogen halo,

And Sol and his consorts, Luna and Gaia, the three heavenly bods each w/their own votive energy; fierce solar, calm lunar, fecund teeming paradisical Earth... i see the three coming together now embracing into longsought

Yes!

All coming into concentric...

YAH!

Sweet anticipation building climaxical,

Now IMMENSE the interscreen/the phosphors SHIVERING in waves heralding ONCOMING and then and then across us sweeps this weird rippling eclypso/light, s/t/r/o/b/i/n/g racing bands of alternating light and shadow...

The beginning of Totality, the Kairos moment...

We spin our sphere in steps so we each will have some time to fully face the rays: three minutes of totality will give us nine seconds per.

We open ourselves to intersubjectivity, open likewise into Linking, that the psychic reacts of our sphere/mates may play large on the planes of our personal perceiving...

Sandor is first to be in the keyspot, and the onset of the light pales his suit pastel. In the Link his sendings convey his personal physical highmass viscosity, the environmental dark of his Charon backnine childhood; i can feel the gravity, feel his brooding longing for the light of his homestar...

And w/him now i savour his feeling of filling his predator hunger w/this special

light, feel it as a kind of psychic pulse, in phase w/the rolling eclypso swells; lust/quench, lust/quench, lust/quench...
ELTKF, Sandorchka;  Eat Light To Keep Fit...

And then Kan, coming across especially spectral in the Link, takes our awareness into the spaces BETWEEN the waves where w/him we can see these amazing afterimage rainbows, first glimmers then shimmers then long long parallel ripples that ride the trailing edges of the bands of light, ripples that fan into these broad chatoyant laserly curling parallel raman WAVES, each one sounding Carlchord sonorous, each wave wider/wilder rising to a high ecstatic glissimer finish pitched so fine that i flash the taste of saffron...
Visual poesy, framed up like haiku, lyrical/symmetrical, eloquent and spare, all broadcast from Kan's amazing evolving Spice/amped Sender Brain.
He has a history of Midsummers in the void w/Lissa, and he creates aforehand the way he will duet w/the light. As the circle steps him out of the key, i flash on a quick singleframe of Kan w/his symmetrical smile beaming from his nest in the vidsection; his signature image.

Uncle Carl reaches the key at the sweetest midpoint peak; hizzonor/who better? In the Link we feel the light go through him, photonic wind through the vast reaches between the electrons of the molecules of Carl. And ever the perfect perfect instrument, his response is mind/audible; a prelude of harmoniums and celestial gypsy bells, cascading threenote triplet peals, and now sonic harmonic carrier sustains framed in melodies green and rare as argon...
The audible essence of the illuminated conjunction.
And long after he switches out of the sweetspot, aural aftertastes echo resonant/orchestral through the groupmind...

Llair by this is pleased unto synesthesia, and delicious we sense his eager hunger for his upcoming turn...

Then into the key the quiet loner Featherman, who astonishes! who perceives then reacts w/this great OPENING OF THE HEART/once opaque, now AWAKE!  PERMISSION TO ENJOY IS GRANTED!  ENTER! THE PAST IS PROLOG!  ETCETERA  ETCETERA YES!...
His first Celestial event, his first Spice experience.

Electra next to catch the light.
She connects w/the Link through dreamtracker sendings, and her reacts come up like roses. She flavours her images w/subtext even as we savour her subtlety...
And now w/a fanfare splash on our dreamtrackers we

glim this quick reel starring Electra: beautiful and lean in brightlight Sun her lithe baseform/she arcs her bod and springs, naked and translucent pale into the void/handsfirst her bod/arrowing forward Sunward accelerating, drawn elongating through the alternating illuminate bands, she stretches/liquifies, all her many speeding molecules spreading apart and cleaving their valent bonds, more and more per unit time, layer by lattice layer away, all of her material morphing off into this ultimate metaphor in a very ultimate way, until in full accelerondo she is a long long luminous milky/bright beaming plasmabeing of pure light, showing at root the same immaterial irreducible immortal sentient essence as would any of the rest of us...

And in her wake, each parted proton and charged particle leaves behind a singular signature brightpoint, a trail of random phosphor flash/&/fades...

Here is one machine has soul today.

*

Ariel is skyclad inside her suit; heliodor Sunstones are at her heart and at her brow, of a piece w/her gilt dreamtracker circlet. She is anointed in nine secret places w/a blend of rose oil and jasmine and some musky mystery jungle wildscent.

Linked i am alive in her, a dizzy kind of bilocational tantra.

She presses her breasts against the softline shell of her suit and lids her glims, all the better to feel the light. In the Link she sends me this delicious quaver:

*Here comes the Sun King!*

She has another larger Sunstone more intimately worn, and it warms in her as the first lucent rays wash over; and w/the first brush of the Solar Beard, the first soft caress of those catfur photons, her plush neurons tremor...

And she commences a pleasant warm throbbing that matches the meter of the moving striations of eclypso light, every heartbeat throb syncing w/a wave. And presently she commences,

> *Hu Gadarn*
> *Lord of Light*
> *Come Ye Down*
> *O Shining Brow*
> *i am far from home*
> *O Lord of Fire*
> *i long for you beyond recounting*
> *O King of Lovers*
> *join w/me in loving union*

*Be with me now*
 *Come Ye Down*
  *Come Ye Down*
   *Come Ye Down*
 *into your priestess Ariel*
 *Hu! Hu! HU!*


    And from all around the Link comes this chorus of mental ascents, *so mote it be,* and in harmony w/her we generate beckoning magnetic cerebrations, drawing in the splendor of the God...
    Quiet Ariel smiling sending love...
    And then in my own bod i feel this ramping glow welling sympathetic w/her Sunstones;
                                *He is here,*
                        And w/her i feel the solar wind that drives the pale rays intense the light the color of buttermilk bathing her bod, passing easily through the stuff of her suit to lap and froth her eager limbs, ramping unto surcease as
                Gentle and warm she saturates, feels the shift on a cellular level, smiles luxurious and inspirates the lovely liquid light...

    Revel and tremor, pulsate and radiate...
                        She savours and now responds, returning wave after ramping wave of Cherishing into the avenues of light as they connect her to the Great Source, The Big Heater, the Mind in the Molten Mountain of Mountains. And she moves now to this new rhythm, each crest matching, pure light and pure love transfusing, each beat stronger, the vapor of her pleasure, the velocity...
                        Her iliac hipblades bang against the softshell, her bod w/a mind of its' own. Her glims wide/she clamps her jaws/clenches her breath/all her long muscles tight/rising the rhythm rhythm
                        And w/an ecstatic WAIL she *TRANSITS,* and w/her we shape/shift shiver into liquid silver lumens; an amphora, i am for a breathspan moment a chalice of plasma of hot living light...
    This sweet erotic charge consumes my awareness, lingers, leaving in my brain a sense of Sundrench bounty, vast mass, star majesty, great age, eternal fires, colossal consciousness...
    Loving is the way to open to the source, pure and complete loving of Zzog and the All.
                                *
                                

    The three minute whole of the totality framed by our sphere creates this colossal column of eclypso/light, a flashing transiting tracerflare thirty/three/point/five million miles long, a beam/wavery lightlength equal to the distance from the Sun to Mercury.

*Ariel's shadow...*
As she stands in the lightflow, there forms behind her a tubular Arielshape shadow tunnel, a record of her sweet shape in the solar stream...
And a vapor/screen rightly placed in space and time would play her back in silhouette, w/her shadow enacting the rite. As long as that light rolls she is immortal in solar memory.
This pleases me.
In the nine seconds that she is in the key her shadow tunnel grows by one/point/six million miles...
And combined as we are in the sacred sphere our shadows cleave a mandala swath, and when we shift the sphere and click another being into the key our moving shadows are kaleidoscopic and form helixes in the great moving column...
Ride on, you shadows...
*Hiyo Silver Away...*

*

Llair is eager to the plunge.

Readouts on his left wrist sing violet and blue and glowing green and i sense all these systems kicking in, tweaky suitmods by Llair and Sandor/Space/Racer...
Fortunate Llair.
Space/Racer rigs are legendary; they are the finest in chemical enhancement, designed specific for the individual mindbod of each racer/perceiver; tunable for variables, graced w/onboard molecular synthesizers to tailor peptides and indole rings, equipped even unto gas/chromatographs to optimize atmospheres... anything to ramp the performance of the human component.
Llair's rig is more an instrument for widening his fields of perception, tuned to find the wavelengths for pleasure and crisp ecstatic insight. It also has proprioceptive damping and broadband faraday shielding and great new neurosuit hardware...
And all built special for this next nine seconds.

His current fave alchemical instruments, these elaborate essence transponders, now reach a preset peak as he rotates into onset, and honeydark tryptamine liquors flow into the streams that feed his brain...

We ride his mind/his perception turns silvery and there is this

s<br>
l<br>
i<br>
d<br>
e<br>
into

that almost familiar trypto/halucinatory gridspace, and while he is yielding
to this combination of amplifying forces at work, some personal secret
message stored inside him is revealed by the light, decants into his awareness
like wine in the cask four billion years. And at the apogee of this brain/dawning
he dissolves into gales of mirth the girth of whales, booms into that great
deep infinite psychedelic laugh where one knows... *everything,* and the
rightness of it and the logic and the neat clockwork beauty meet, combine
so effably sublime...

*

Then meself.
    I slide into place in the key, then
       *Rollicking zany the creamy lightstripes roll,* scrolling across my face;
then a kind of *triggersnap!* of the brain and a fireflash and then:

      *...peace? all the voices in my head are silent...*

    I go to the core, the root base trunk of my being. I stand alone
before the colossus that is myself: all that history! My equilibrium flays
away on a wind that bears away also the indigenous matter of my
personality, my shielding and my rationales; all are pennyless in the face
of Gnosis, even unto the concept of my consciousness, which blows away
and goes...
    I cease to be for a span of time.

    When i return it is by degrees; i am an entity. I have a separate
mind. I am defined by a physical world. There are other similar beings who
are tracking me intently...
    *Zzog, am i a drop in the ocean or a rocky boat on a sea of minds...*

*

    Last to take the rays is Lissa, this being her chosen time. The Earth
is showing now more to the west of the fastermoving Moon, a luminous
turquoise crescent set in a whitegold flamecrown surround.
    Behind her the elegant void, sewn w/stars for diamonds.

In the order of our tracking i now face her seafoam self. I center my attention and seek her frequency, and get... this: along w/her own sweet psychic scent there is something other, a presence in the Link like a tangy niff of loam.

There.

In an atmospheric bubble between her gloves rides the most amazing plant, what she calls the dragonstar, a semiconscious fern of immense density that has the ability to store light or act as a kind of psychic battery or otherwise be her plant familiar...

In her garden it dines on the dust of dry rosepetals and water from the sacred Well of Phobos, though

Now it drinks the pale eclypso photons, stores the actual light; later in the garden when the day is closing dark, it will blaze forth in glowing recounting and luminate and bask the other denizen plants,

Especially the several dozen other dragonstar cultivars, daughters of its' ownself, raised by Lissa w/craft and love.

These dragonstars soon to be ours...


Lissa.

Once for an hour i look in her eyes/see her more truly than i see myself; over this hourspan she subtly shifts the way she projects so that i see her in these nine various ways; first as a temple dancer in ancient Abydos then a child of Erin wrapt in a wooly dream of healing then the lover/initiate of Paracelsus, then the restive bride of Mauna Kea in the lush island reign of Kamehameha, also as a worshiper of

Isis Astarte Diana Hecate...

And for the ninth change she channels into this one: as if each of her eyes is set in a flesh cavern and there is a portal arch over each, and on each arch and standing out in front of them are these ultraviolet runes; tiny lines of delicate elfin blacklight neon rune/glyphs, cast in a pair of crescents over her eyes.

I know these glyphs to be her personal magical alphabet. Though curiously reversed to my pov...

Ah.

So.

I start to read them, and it dawns that she is giving me knowlege of this alphabet; e'en now the meanings settle in the branches of my brain.

And then i see the phrases all complete: the message is her own charge unto herself, her core magical pattern, her Vows Arcane and Lasting. By showing me her wiring in this way, knowing i could opt to change it, she grants me the gift of her total trust. My natural react is to respond in kind, offer my protection, and i send unto her a shield formed of the stuff of my wellwishing, cast it around the delicate neon, add my seal to her secret...

> *And now the Sun speaks to her*
> *the pale light clothes her;*
> *drink ye deep o priestess...*

> *three breaths*
> *and the eclipse moves on.*

And now all our resonant reacts & red revelations yield to a pale psychic silence. And in this aftermath i realize that we are all of us still entrained in the pulse of that special concentrated light, our bods still rapt in that regular wavelike rhythm, and i realize we are a moving unison, breathing as one, breathing the sphere, contracting the sphere in toward the center then expanding it out in this very cellular psychic physical systolic/diastolic dance, large then less so then large, a visible simile for the living groupmind.

> *What is the* NAME *of the groupmind...*
> *What is* BEYOND *the groupmind...*

## 29B   Big Doggies

Two days later, and we soon will pass the quarter/billion/mile mark; halfway to Io.

Aura Citron, resting in the comcube, ponders the nebula M13 now framed in the telescopic sternlight; a million stars/a hundred light years across...

I see her from Outside through the sternlight glazing, know her ponderings from our conversing in the Link...

And now i see the sight of myself in her mind as i cross through her field of view; magnified, i am for an instant huge, Godsize, master of nebulae...


The GE91's are such big doggies they have to live outside;

So we are back in our suits on the flanks of our ship, working in crews and welding like wildthangs. And, intent as i weld i also smile w/the play of the sparks that fly, straight out against the fixed eternal stars...

A laser on each side, parallel to the ship.

And w/the bracing complete enough to hold them, we are now nerfing the doggies gently into place w/pods, every pod we can muster, our shipboard ones plus the ones from Shirira...

And now that Elric and Steel and i have the forward sparstruts in place, i step out to get a bigger view; a hundred meters off the starboard flank, two hundred; better...

Zzog;

Those pups are almost the length of the Dolphin, surpassing large, surprising large; i see their awesome mass and weigh it against the Dolphin's awesome over/engineering, happily see them balance...

They look good, too; they fit w/the lithic look of the ship, and by great good fortune they are also tritanium/clad and double hulled, perfect to our circumstances.

Once again...

Now w/the secondary sparstruts complete, the pod flotillas move their masses, and both lasers close in parallel the last two meters of distance; and w/a deep and culminating bellsound *clong*,

The doggies make contact,

And the big bolts are wrenched home, and the lasers are part of the ship...

Jayme does the wrenching at our end, and when done he does a corkscrew roll of happy pod satisfaction, then stands off and goes elsewhere w/his three hundred friends...

I see Llair and Dallas at the stern, connecting the main/drive power, the conduits as big around as Sandor...

And now my gaze goes to the ship's fore, where we will pipe the awesome output beams into the hull, into the forward section, through the optics chamber, then out through ports in the prow...

And now the power and the water and the data/links are complete, and we are ready to fire the lasers.

We will test them once then let them rest, run them three seconds only;

Time enough, as they hoover up vast amounts of energy; some of which will be vented as heat into the waterjacketing, w/the rest going out as this hyper/concentrated blast of coherent white light,

So much light that there will be considerable reactive propulsive effect when the lasers are alight. Enough to slow the Dolphin and briefly cast her behind those of us who are staying outside. I remind my suit's jets to compensate and accelerate when the time comes...


*ZZZZZZOGGGG!!*

My whole helmet goes optical/opaque and i close my eyes tightshut; the suit gloves too are over my eyes on the outside, and also the optical spot, *and still the light is far too bright!* This is light distilled, *the very liquor of light,* w/all the sensations ramp/intensified, ten times, a hundred...

And stray light rays wriggle like spermy eleuthrocites through the microscopic pores in my suit, through holes far too fine for air/molecule/escape,

And i feel the rays go through me; left hip, pancreas, the rims of my ears. In synesthesic wonder i hear the sound they make as they travel through my bod; a kind of steady breathy sound, a whooosh w/a whiff of brass, an improv from Zzog's own horno toastador...

For three seconds.
Later Sandor tells me that on the outer fringes of the belts of Charon our beam compels the dusty motes to glow; a great shaft of solid white light three miles across, a javelin of light five/hundred/fifty/eight thousand miles long, pulse/coded w/modulations of welcome and aimed for the Pleiades seven light/years away:
Since laser light is a human/created phenomenon, any intelligence sufficiently advanced will cognize our friendly beam for what it is and send us a reply.
Watch this space in fourteen years...

Nine days after, and through the starboard port of the main salon we glim our first sighting of the yacht *Blue Isis*.

The folk aboard the *Isis* are famous for the accuracy and detail of their astral/astrological forecasting. They are by/the/way true Romany Gypsies and they are on the road now a hundred and thirty years, seven generations...

I really like their wagon.

After course/matching w/the Dolphin they send over a pod, which soon arrives in our Salon and delivers their captain's compliments. It is an elegant old thing, this pod, like a kind of veteran samovar, and i think the better of its' senders.

Ariel as ships' astrologer knows them well, downloading their legendary charts for the last six years, which makes this first realtime rendevous especial fine for her...

And yes, it certainly is another happy wyrd canny congruence of coincidences...

The old samovar carries us a gracious invitation;
  Yah!
Put another holographic log on the fire; Tonight We Feast! Together we will laughgypsy dancegypsy weepgypsy and i will tie a scarf on my head and look like a *guyjin* and play my wyolin; *yip yip ootla!*

Now the old pod whoostles over to Ariel, and lifts its' coppery lid, a kind of capdoffing, and now it does this pod/bow. I wonder if it will kiss her hand...

And now a panel opens in the kettle section and a tray slides out w/this parcel, this packet for Ariel, wrapped in blue blue coarse cotton handspun cloth and bound w/golden braiding...

*

Later tonight and Ariel's cabin is a forest of videolo pines, windsound and warm piney tree scent, livelike trees in fascia; this is a favorite track for she and me.

I hear her thoughts as we enter: Captain Murphy's question, where are the children?

And from Ariel,

*{ ...i want to have your child... }*

And from me,

...^...

How do i really feel about this? This is the first time i ever...

*{ ...admiration and love for you anders... }*


The moment passes.
And now the cabin air is warm midsummery and we settle in intimate around a gray felt stasis/cube. She hands me the softwarm parcel from the *Isis:*

*{ ...your birthday present... }*

I open the missive, watch the coarse/cut cloth and splendid braid accelerate away, drawn to the cube. Inside the wrap is a pewter vidblock, which i fit into a socket that quick/appears in the gray felt. The darker vidblock lightens as the lighter cube darkens until the hues of the two cubes match to each other...
Now Ariel waves her hand in a vague gypsy way and the image vapor forms above the felt; resolves to be this exquisite voxel orery, a brilliant bright three/dee moving model of the motion of the planets, each one of them w/all their whirling moons, plus the glittery belts and rings, the comets, everything.

*{ ...i would speak to you of your chart... }*

Ariel grins and transmits the following;
There are several different ways of looking at interplanetary astrology. One school, traditional, says that through a process of declination and starmapping, the houses and the various planetary aspects can be recomputed to yield a chart like unto what it would be if the subject had been born on Earth, and then applying traditional astrological interpretations.
Another way, the Donnelly method, takes a wholly different frame and is much preferred by Spacers.
In this system, dwellers on each planet are born into a series of unique aspects specific to that planet, w/the influences of the other planets and celestial objects calculated w/regard to their relative distance and mass and location.

Donnelly goes thirty years traveling around and putting this together.

His operandi; he goes to a planet somewhere, gets a dayjob, reads everything. When he can he goes out and talks to people, gets profiles of their personas, the stories of their lives. For the sake of uniformity he uses a set series of questions to quantify their traits and then adds their birth info.

All of this goes into his database, to be correlated w/the positions of the zodiacal constellations and the orbital locations of the planets current at the individual's incept. Also included are progressions co/relevant to major lifepoints, the charts of children, parents...

This way he hopes to get Patterns to emerge, surprises.


And over time he discovers his original supposing is very very right...

Thus, to be born a Pisces in the moons of Neptune is vastly different than being a Pisces on Earth; when your ruling planet fills your sky, you become a very powerful Pisces indeed...

And when Saturn is conjunct w/Neptune and six hundred million miles closer than it is to the Earth, it is a major bigtime influence. As are the other very powerful nearby planets...

Or consider someone of the magical sign of Gemini, ruled by Mercury, born on that planet during one of the apogees of its' eccentric oval orbit. On Earth we perceive this as retrograde motion, since our speed around the Sun is constant and Mercury to us appears to speed up/slow down/go retro. When Mercury is in this retrograde phase, folk on Earth feel like they are switching from a linear electric state of mind to one that works by magnetism and manifesting and flow; altogether a better time for workers of the Will...

All the moreso ten/thousandfold for that aforementioned Gemini on the planet itself. Imagine having all that magnetic ability balanced against that curious Gemini sense of Mercurial time...

Or ponder on the effect of the Sun in your chart if you were born in the orbit of Venus, or think on the power of cold Neptune when conjunct w/your home on Charon; you get the idea.

All praise to the empirical Master Donnelly.

His *Book of Correspondences* (software actually) is now embraced as the standard, w/many after him adding improvements to his system: software extensions to explain cometary coercions, Celtic and Chinese correspondences, influences of the Martian Moons of Phobos and Deimos on the lives of folk raised in the Belts, much more; all together a goodly bod of information...


Among the more interesting uses of this database is a kind of astrological regression, where folk who wonder about their birth info can get a clue. They input their answers to an expanded version of Donnelly's original quantifying questions and then the software does a matchup w/the likeliest time and place...

Or the converse; input the kind of special child you want and get a list of propitious places to have that child.

Hmm...

Another use of this database is charting Journey Progressions, where the course and timing of a voyage and the progressive major influences are woven together into something that is at once advice, navigation, magical protection, and prophecy.

Ariel will also use the data in the pewter cube to work combined charts, overstand new folk we meet, find aid for her geomancy...
Now, thanks to her gifting, so may i.


Ariel hears my wondering thought about Electra and what her chart might be...
Ariel addresses the cube;

  'Good morning, Raff.'
*'I wake unto theee, mistresss.'*
  'Would it please you to open the hotspur file?'
*'Yesss mistresss.'*
  'Show us now, my dashing Raff, Electra's birth chart.'

Here the orery whirls noiselessly into a new set of zodiacal aspects, w/numbers and letters and the arcane curls of the signs, the specific degrees, etcetera. Electra's birthspot now is highlighted, and bright lines move through in sextiles, trines...

'And now figure a chart based on Electra's Donnelly responses and lay it over the birth chart.'

Zzog.

*{ ! }* from Ariel.


They match almost perfectly, w/some blurring at the fringe.

*{ ...did you anders do this consciously? or... }*


*


When first she meets Electra, Ariel/as/navtech rightaway delights in Electra's perfect memory, the way she calculates time/distance and mass/acceleration and approach curves in her head, can name every rock and hardplace w/in the solar ecliptic disc...

And in awe at the outset, Ariel later realizes that she is Electra's complement; where Electra is encyclopedic, Ariel is first to find the navigational logic/leaps, more likely to have that intuitive predictive flash...

And Ariel likes that Electra finds delight in each new thing, and Electra likes well the wyrding ways of Ariel's mind, and soon they are the happy co/navigators of Murphy's Dolphin.


*{ ...we could go to the Stars together... }*


Ariel soon sees Electra as a kindred Ka, another living temple w/the lights switched on. She likes the synergy of their pairing, and begins to find it exciting to have a different exotic new being to meet every two or three days.

The perfect thing for a voyage of years...

And Ariel fascinates into knowing this amazing new kind of morphing creature; for a time artful Ariel does w/makeup and ear extensions and suchlike what Electra does w/her technology.

Then Ariel discovers that it takes Electra half an hour to morph a change; that the angel w/the wings takes half a day...

About the same for Ariel, as far as she would go.

Ariel winks and dons her catmask; ah, the parallel whys of masks and morphs, the why of her catmask gift...

And now from her mind flows this beguiling imagining of Electra morphing into another Ariel, a mirror being, two willowy blond slightly angular fair golden women, matching rose petal aureoles and the same curly cornsilk hair flowing about their founts of love...

And w/my responding rush of pleasure her answering thoughtlines channel me into this dreamy reverie, a minuet for twin sylvans moving sinuous and symmetrical, graceful arms arrowing to pleasure points, swirling circular fingerpads, all her sweet undercurves...

And what of that other gift, Spice?

Ariel sees physical re/imaging as a human response to Electra's ability to morph, as if Electra is showing us the way, giving us a pattern to follow.

And Ariel now has in her mind a re/imaging goal, and i wonder at the nature of her impending change...

Will she direct her Will to her own internals, finding... taking on powers through physical change,

Or will she transcend the physical side, guide instead on her Vision of the Temple of the Moon, go for the priestess transformation, refine her knowing mind, evolve her merging w/the Goddess incarnate, turn heartfull to the pathways opening, awareness expanding rising into...

*

How much of Ariel's nature is now Electra's as well? Is Ariel the architect of Electra's recent leaps through the levels of adepthood?
Spice and the Light of Eleuthra...

*

Ariel says bench/come/here, and a red felt stasis/cube, a big one, floats over and takes station in front of her.
Ariel says Arturo open,
And a side of the cube turns to liquid, a glowy glassy red gel,

And now, rising surprising as Atlantis, to the face of the cube come all the myriad shiny parts of taylor the automated saylor, rising and expelling outward onto the surface, which e'en now sets back into red felt w/the parts all held in place w/stasis...
Zzog.

Taylor is Ariel's project now, and she has him apart and spread out like an antique clock. Which is apt, for taylor is old when even the elderly Dolphin is still a glimmer, from a time when robots are the rage and taylor is front/edge equipé. Even now, as a flock of components, he has that wellmade/prototype look; lots of hand/machining and hexhead capscrews and fine blue handwrit numbers on bare metal, milling marks and filing and shiny places where re/engineered parts were added in later, like that.
When complete he will look like a vintage suit of deco armour, and arrayed as he is on the red/felt cube, i see the mystery/metal he is made of; the dents and heat/blueing and even some meteor tracks...
Ariel turns her eyes to me:

*{ ...taylor's software includes an ethical matrix for protecting spacers; a hero nine times over says sandor... }*

I warm as Ariel gifts me w/her sleepy heavylid smile:

*{ ...at first i think, it would be useful to have him back on the*

*bridge... how he would look really good hauling away on the big lever; then, how he would look really good in a long gray cloak... }*

Ah; clearly the moment that turns her pivotal toward this project, where taylor goes from hardware to intriguing being...

*{ ...you of all folk can see where this is leading... }*

I can. She assists by transmitting a shining silver taylor silhouette, noble and heroic, a paragon of virtues...

*{ ...he deserves to live; what a rush to see him power up and Be... }*

And looking at all this fine/wrought hardware she... decides, she goes the distance;

*{ ...and, i can make him better... }*


This is a major sea/change for Ariel; like Electra taking up the craft, Ariel is awakening herself into a wider way of being, a wider overstanding...
I love the way her mind works.

For a breathspace i wonder if her love will shift away from me; and in answer she looks at the cube and says save/&/close, and the red gel happens and taylor sinks w/nary a ripple and then the cube turns to felt again.
Zzog twice over. That woman...
Zzog.

*


Our party w/the crew of the *Isis* runs three days. At one point i watch from the port in Featherman's cabin as people in gypsy pressure/suits drift back and forth in the space between the ships. All the colorful pairings. And triplings. Etcetera. Yeeha.
I ponder the effect of Spice on wild Romany blood. What will their children be like?
Children...

Clear of Shirira we get word from Io and events there are beyond our Wildest...

A goldrush stampede; hundreds of ships, traders from everywhere, all converging on dusty sleepy grizzled Io, on all those loners and drifters and rangers w/their domes and their squares of blasted Io rock, all those folk now making Spice...

And w/this kind of market, the price of Spice heads for Polaris. The six traders at Moira's who form the original exchange now represent over two hundred local blenders, and the Exchange decides to start selling Spice futures. This is a tremendous idea, and becomes great fun; fortunes are made w/a vidcall and new/rich Spice/traders hungry for splendor leap gaudy into vogueing roaring nightlife.

And oh how the money pours in.

Where the kids went gaunt three cycles past, they now wax lax and lyrical on every fine morsel in the nine planets, and this hard/scrabble Juppiter moon is now Mecca for altered awareness...

Roll on, Rollonia...

*

Since Midsummer there are five hundred million more folk who daily track our game, an enormous total number steady/rising, rocketlike and marvelous...

Zzog.

One thing this translates into is more and now vastly more folk wanting Spice, so our original deal w/the Io Exchange for two hundred metric tons escalates over time to two thousand, then three; much to the delight of the Exchange, the Io Miners Guild, the blenders, the archeo guys, the waxing kids, everybody, all of whom are in the deal in various ways.

Aboard the Dolphin, Alpha Red w/Llair and Manda are Spicemasters/&/Mistress, and they are happily planning up a splendid rendevous at the Luna end w/all the traderships that are coming to meet us...

A hundred/sixty/two so far.

Three of them are from Rajpuram, currently the home of Radha/Ganja, a Hindu sativa love cult; i wonder what their ships are like...

Three more are from the Luna Gloria Mundi, and Clan McKenna is

sending three. There is also a flight of five sleds from the Orbiting Rastas of
The Great Overstanding.

Oh, and here is another personal fave traditional
group; Nishkuntu, the Hopi Peyote Mescaleros.

Zzog; all of these ships are folk we know, folk who daily download
our imagestream...

And i have some personal links to these next ones; The
Roving Order of Tantric Buddhist Druids, Lodge 136 of London. Longtime
experts in the brewing of evolutionary medicine, they will soon be lacing
their blendings w/deep green crystalloids, alchemical grains of true
Eleuthran hue...

I wonder what will be, after Showtime...

*

Preparing for Io.

I go through each part of my bod, muscle on bone, re/imaging as
i go, toning each, feeling my frame realign, all to better bear the gravity of
the Orange Moon after so long in freefall...

This kind of situational re/imaging is becoming more and more of a
regular thing w/me.

*


The Dolphin ships' company (A&E) collectively owns three
thousand metric tons of Spice, bought w/the media advance. Everyone
aboard from Io onward has a crewshare, plus we vote crewshares for Dallas
& Cobb & Llair.

The Io Arts Council turns over an additional two hundred tons to
Llair's Noetic/Entelechy Ent; two tons to pay off their shipshare as per
contract, the rest to be cashed to create twin endowments for the Io
College of Shamanic Arts and Llair's Transdimensional Temple of Zzog...

Alpha Red personally goes for another thousand tons to carry
aboard the *Encanto,* which e'en now tracks us at distance on fly/by/wire
autopilot, a day or so behind...


Sandor now shows some road/moxie and takes on the organizing
of the cargo transfers. By his plan we can load the Dolphin plus the Encanto
in four E/days: we would use our sleds plus some local ones w/crews from
the Dolphin flying in rotation. Sandor will also recruit a myriad of rentapods
to move the canisters dock/to/sled and sled/to/ship.

Forty/two/hundred metric tons of Spice.

Zzog.

At a generous four/grams/per, a ton will serve a quarter/million
folk. For a week.

Before we land, Sandor posts his wishes on the Wire and gets this surprising warm response: freighter guys and local folk all volunteering their ships and leiters and sleds; many more than five we have a flotilla, complete w/crews and fuel to fly them, dinner invites, places to stay, hospitality, etcetera.

*

How truly weird is Io.
From orbit, Io looks like Luna done in orange...
Coming up close now we soon see things differently, and the crew votes Io MVA; Most Volcanically Active. And also most violent as huge calderas collapse, lava lakes form, and constellations of new volcanoes erupt in waves...
In one forty/four/hour Io day the surface goes from two/fifty/below to eighty/above fahrenheit zero. And where the molten sulfur flows the temps can spike to eight hundred plus; a diurnal difference of a thousand degrees...

As the Dolphin goes geostatic over Io Miners Port, Juppiter is waxing/almost full, filling the sky, and the pale yellow reflected Sunlight gives Io a soft dreamy quality; our view from orbit like scrying into old amber, and when sledding in tomorrow, like landing in a candle/lit bardo...

Twenty hours later and ahead of the plan we blast away from the Dolphin, w/Red and Manda and Ariel/Electra/meself in the Redsled. Juppiter now is in front of the Sun so the Io moon is dark, and we guide on the stars at our back and the turquoise bright/points that mark the Port sixty miles ahead.

> Far and away before us
>   Glowering the glowing spills of candescent magma
>     The curving moon/edge lines define...

On approach now,
                    And our sled settles languid in the slow gravity, the coppery dust rising in swirly clouds as we feather in...
                                        We are in a big crater on the plains of the Tarsus Regio, a few miles north of Io Miners Port, and the orange ash for a mile around shows big slick slabs of rocketfire/glass; reaction mass blasting the ash to this liquid citrine glass...
                                        And as we wait for Dr Don to meet us, Io swoons me once again; the Sun comes out of its' daily eclipse behind Juppiter, lights the vulcan Io landscape w/these beautiful brooding red rays. And just over the horizon a ruddy ruby volcanic flare

goes up way up, many awesome miles, escape velocity, up and out and into the void...

North of us looms a volcanic rise, and over it comes rolling some Io rollerhomes, big things, diversly constructed, w/immense tires and three meters of clearance.
These roller things are new to me.
As we watch the rise, more and more of them... there are over seventy, a whole flight of them, a fleet; a great Zzogging/Lot! of them...

*{ ...and here they are, back from their boffing/great wildly successful recent gig on far elara, the io exchange... }*

Interesting; this information is coming to me in the telepathic way of the groupmind...
*Another groupmind...*
Zzog.

The redlit rollers form a Sunwise spiral around us as they come down into the crater, very formal and majestic and graceful, all the moreso for their bulk and height.
The lead roller has a kind of maharani beauty; red as the rich red rays, w/ornate goldplate scrolling brightwork...
When this roller comes to rest a ramp slithers down from its' fuselage and six guys in bright/glinty gold suits slide out, come rambling over. Their suits match the ship... very spiff.
We go out to meet them.
They are each carrying these surprising/huge symmetrical snowflakes a foot across, big sulfur/dioxide frosty clear crystalline sculpts, each w/its' own musical geometry. These are traditional Io honored/guest/gifts.
This kind of attention, this too is new. A part of me is inflating giddy w/the golden gas of celebrity...
Up to me comes this loose longlimb Spacer, red/and/gold and w/a clearplex eggshape helm that shows him to be Berko Six of the seven zerko Berko brothers; i know him right well from the mine; we would share some Steem from time to time.

*{ ...formal words of welcome... }*

I take a step over to be friendly/find myself bounding/sometimes i feel like bounding/leaping easily into the Io sky,
So Berko thirty meters off smiles toothy from his zorro/black beard and bounds toward me,

                                                     And we meet
in midleap and hook arms, and our matching respective momentum spirals
us laughing back to the surface, a nice centrifugal friendship/rush,
                                                          Now Red
and now Manda and now all of us are happily leaping, spiraling w/Ionians,
doing wheels and rolls, roaring w/mirth...
                                          All while the light is turning more
and more toward Suncolor, and now the Sun fully emerges and melts the
frosty greets and the ice crystals both. Laughter and welcome/home and the
Spacer handclasp and high/sign and now the other rollerspacer Ionians pour
in by hundreds...

        We go to Moira's and the rest of the Dolphin folk come down
moonside and we frolic and rollick and feast and roll around and come back
out an Io day later.


                                    *


        In the Uta Patera now, just east of the Port...
        We are riding w/Dr Don in the *Vesuvius*, his roller/a really nice
one. As Io slides by at eighty mph we glim the scenery, happily lounging on
red inflatable smart furniture that keeps telling us what heroes we are, the
voices soft and close to our ears...
        Don's new ride is fresh from Caravaggio on Mars, and everything
about it is front/edge. Shapely and sleek, the whole of it is built around a
shiny silvery central core of galley and water chamber and mechanicals,
w/all of this gear stowing itself flat into the floor when in traveling mode.
The inflatables too are stored in the floor, and after the transition pump up
plump for enfolding.
        It also has major chambered/ion power and stasis braking, very
handy in Io's whiffy gravity.
        Dynamic and industrial and overbuilt, the sides are a thick tritanium
honeycomb and the ports are carbonic double/clearplex, nicely large and
hyper/durable. Each wheel is four meters tall, has a motor mounted in the
hub, and can be steered in pairs. Plus, the suspension bogeys telescope to
highlow the ride/height and can swivel the wheels around from the sides to
the front and rear so the roller can be driven sideways.
        And there is this trick that it does: when parked it is thirty/nine feet
long by seventy wide; when time to go mobile it accordions/folds/telescopes
together to a drivable ten by twenty/five, w/the nesting roofs of the
succeeding sections forming a sevenfold layer overhead.
                                         When traveling, it is
good to have all those extra layers of exodontal extendometal between
yourself and the Io weather...

On Io, finding a good place to park is vital.
And
quickly leaving a place to park can also be vital, once the ground starts
flowing lava and the molten chunks come raining down from the starry starry
sky...


Dr Don totally loves volcanoes.
His header is Io/Vulcanologist, and he is another happy man in
the right place. Who better to give us the current word on the dynamics
of Io;

*{ ...the core is white/hot/molten right up to the mantle, making for a
very plastic surface; also at play are the titanic forces of Juppiter's
gravity, constantly changing the moon's shape, causing quaking and
folding and shifting, ramping the intense and constant volcanics... }*

Along w/the exciting fluid nature of this flamey flowing landscape/all
the changing calderas and fumaroles, there is also the bonus of a new volcano
every month or so. They stay active for days or thousands of days and their
patterns of eruption are everchanging. Many are active all the time.
To acquaint us w/his faves, Dr Don takes us to the place he calls
the Gallery.

*{ ...each volcano has its' own signature way of going off, an expression
of the personality of that formation... }*

For Dr D it is the supreme natural artform.
He points out how different types of ejecta will travel in differing
ways, w/the black molten sulfur flying out in fountain sprays and the
big/ended silicate blobs coming out eccentric in these strange bouncing
bell/curves, w/some eruptions so explosive that the copper/red dust goes all
the way to Juppiter, gets hoovered in, painting orange on the way the fey
innermost moon Amalthea...
And warming now he tells us how the volcano Elgar will have a
straightup flare w/flames three hundred miles, and of black Nostromo
w/multiple fans of multicolor glowing stones, and likewise of vast Eurypides
kicking out w/these huge exotic spider parabolas, these streaming gouts of
burning sulfur...
On cue there is the incredibly varied and musical sound of
Io rain on the triple/truss tritanium roof. With the molten sulfur in various
states of cool, each impact can be anywhere from a fist/size blob of flaming
liquid to an actual finished lava rock, some as big as yourself; and, those
musical raindrops fall at six/hundred/mph.

Splat *splat* WHACK *clunkabonk...*
Nice to be indoors on a day like this.

*

We are looking out now on beautiful lake anders, which is this
immense black ocean of bubbling glowing molten sulfur, eight hundred
degrees, a huge huge caldera of the stuff a hundred/eighty/miles wide,
running past the horizon.
At first i am thrown by this lake/naming fame thing, and then i
decide to love it and leave it, have a taste and move on.
Anywise, naming things after folk is the Io equivalent of the Keys
to the City; they like you, they find a new lava lake nearby, and zango there
you are, a walking reason for a party.
I sit back and enjoy the view... of my lake.

*

The sky is so full of Juppiter that i hear music, a wavery synesthesia
chorale that fascinates me in.
Sunlit now this great sphere kaleids kinetic w/the patterning of
aurorae, gassy rings, sienna/red bands of color, convection clouds, wispy
white ammonia clouds, storms so heroic the lightning can be seen from here,
open patches in the murk showing through to liquid hydrogen oceans...
Visible too the spot they call the Dark Disturbance, as big around
as the Earth. Colossal bright thunderbolts limn the rim, and deeply i skry
that swirling cauldron of roiling red clouds.
Bubble bubble...

We are circling back toward the Port and Don has the splendid roller
going crosscountry, far from the new roads, at speed and tracking a familiar
trailworn groove. Berko Six regales us w/Legendary Roller tales...
And now
we slow and stop on the crest of a rise on a coppery plain, and Don tells the
selfdriving roller to camp itself over yonder, a goodly distance from those
three rocks there.
And it dawns; we are at the entrance to the temple.
Around the rocks behind...

In our *suits* now, and we cycle through the lock of the roller and
head down the ramp. The ground heaves gently as we bounce our way over
to the temple entrance.
The dust is curious/free of boundmarks, explained when i land and
my suitboots step on stasis, stop six inches above the curvy ground.

Once done w/their work Don and the other six science guys restore the site original; all the better to enjoy, to enframe/enhance their own upcoming Spice experiences...

And after that first time for Electra & yr anders, each of them takes a turn in the six/finger hands; first the two lovers/discoverers, then all the other site/workers. Then Don and the rest inspire/inform/initiate the folk in their rapidly expanding extended families, and they are transformed transcendent too, and they speak to their own circles of this, and thus the invitations radiate outward...

How many Ionians...

Don grins me his huckleberry grin.


Sidelong i see Ariel's glims iris wide, internalizing every temple detail; she smiles expectant w/ramping glee, and in her mind i hear the hiss of her own intuitive mysto/steam...

The last bound and the stasis/carpet catches us, guides us in to find the hidden rocky door, the wheelshape bluestone concavity.

I trace w/my suitglove the over/under knotwork turnings of carvings made vague by exposure, out in the wind and the weather of Io eleven thousand years...

And now the stone rrrolls open, and now the silver airlock, and now into the passage of naked nickel/iron...

I realize; more than a pocket in a flow, the temple is actually built into a hollow nickel/iron meteor, a really hefty one, that has landed/plowed itself into the Io littoral.

Zzog.

The perfect bubble/boat to float upon the fire inspired fluid features of Io.

Did the Eleuthrans build it offmoon and fly...

And now comes to me this very beautiful telepathic head/movie, like the teaching loop a kind of ryder/videolo combination that i alone can see, wherein the two familiar smiling Eleuthrans show me the construction of the temple, w/scenes of the Martian Belts, a celebration, a journey...

When it is over and my thirst for knowing slaked, i smile my thanks upward to the oval overhead mirror...


Now, on to the next thing; i flash the graceful handsign and immediate the intricate iris inner lock blooms open and my wrist/readouts say atmosphere and we shed our suits...

And here i warmly watch Ariel & Electra, both w/that springy style of moving, that way they both have of revealing themselves curve/by/curve into the moment...

Glancing around, and to my gauging glims the place is finer than the first time, in better nick; gold railings shinier, the stars brighter in the deepblue dome.

And Don relates this news;

*{ ...when folk come through the temple they waken these mysterious metal housecleaners and spherefillers and librarians; and when folk leave, these denizens go to work...*

*and the place changes itself in various ways; new head/movies w/humans in them, fresh loungers, a shift in the Spice recipe, like that... }*

Shift?

In the Spice recipe?

Which means; either the temple can read humans and reformulate or... there are Eleuthrans out there who are linking w/this temple.

Could they perhaps be UPDATING the Spice mix? Could there be fun/loving Dionysian Eleuthrans out there e'en now, tracking our discovery of this their temple?

The advent of this, uh, Shift, also implies that the temple is blending its' own Spice, a black box somewhere...

And from Don,

*{ ...right over a vein of the io mystery mineral that spice is primarily blended from, and the box serves the temple denizen that fills the sourcing sphere... }*

And the vac/vaults. Do they brew to taste?

*{ ...once you are here, the temple remembers you... }*

Ariel & Electra & meself/we agree to take the experience together, and now embracing we stand in the gold/inscribed circle on the floor; over three E/years since the first...

The beams of light come, pour down into us, cycle familiar from sensual red through high violet, saturate me slowly, diffuse through my skin cells, epithelial, smooth muscle cells, bone, striated cells, brain.

I feel shriven/forgiven, ennobled and welcomed in, safe.

I look w/wonder into the faces of my beloveds, who are now ever more exquisite in all ways before my eyes; Ariel, head up, still blond in the face of risk/Electra delicate and waify in base mode; her retuned reaction curves...

And now a curtain of alien sound; new Eleuthran music, fresh to my experience, *w/shades of Uncle Carl...*

Zzog.

We bow to the oval window and go out from the ray/chamber and enter the dome of stars...

More awesome than familiar, more holy than awesome, the place still fills me w/wild Dionysian anticipation elation...

Eager i leap the periphery rail and scan the vaults. Two of them bear the likenesses of Electra and...

I am always surprised by my own image, evidence that i exist in a physical bod...

And now i move my hands through that symmetrical mudra that says, i am concentric and ready for Spice;

Instantly a green light, and now w/a sigh the cover of the vac/vault clamshells open, and from the puff of foggy vapors a clear sphere of Io silica reveals, all laden w/gemlike faceted greeny crystals, clearer brighter more alive w/light than any Spice i currently know...

Electra and Ariel follow my pattern, and w/our spheres we meet at the great pair of six/finger hands now cupping in the center of the dome... and into the hands we leap, moving viscous and slow in the low Io gravity, the big blue fingers' flexings in sync w/our own bodstretching proprioceptivity.

Ariel's body jewelry catches some glints as she glides in next to me, and i watch her spare lithe willow self settle sensual and soft, landing leaflike on my left. I smile to the warmth of her thigh beside mine as she nests to the curve of my arm, and now Electra feathers in on the otherside.

When we are snug we raise our spheres and voice the Eleuthran words of dedication, then *brap!* and we breathe the coiling vapors in...

The entire place gives a LURCH or is it me? and i leave my bod to shift for itself, my awareness rising into the space below the apse of the dome/looking back on a lanky smiling familiar Spacer figure in a fugue state...

Me.

Nice body jewelry...

The temple has something to show me.

Forming in the air and hovering opposite is a dimensional projection of my pre/Spice former self, this image a kind of mirror for noting change...

And comparing this wraith to my fugueing bod i am pleased to see that the current me is youthening, toning, virilizing, waxing w/each new episode of ecstatic alchemy, growing ever more clearly into the personal physical vision i hold Within...

And now my photon self looks around and locks on my astral locus; he sees me! and across his face

A warm greet and a slow glow of pride and now the beatific grin of cosmic confirmation;

And i, in a temporal trance, meet the eyes of my previous self, discern his nascent unspoke message, which is

*Be of good cheer, our Kairos Moment is near at hand; we are nearly there, i know we will succeed...*

My timeshifted faith in my current self is heartening, and strengthens the integration of my Will.

I re/cognize my own compassion and extend it to myself.

And in a great surge of gratitude i embrace my younger self w/my astral form, and embraced back i feel wonderful, accepted at last, totally loved and accepted. This is a welcome change...

Ah.

The old initiatory test of personal confrontation...

This is the first time i go through it in this way.

And this wave of esteem i currently ride [a result/i am sure/of the passing of this test] is re/imaging my sense of self, expanding my confidence, freeing me to try a wider arena of awareness,

And now my astral self is wraith/rising, a levitating liquid fluid folding into the All...

And now i feel a novel rate/change, w/the locus of my essence rapidly expanding, projecting what is me out of what is the astral...

And thus upraised, higher and clearer than e'er before, i pass into the familiar gridspace...

To my new eyes now *a weaving of surpassing beauty,* the infinite threads iridescing, their colors changing as i shift my point of view, the hues charming my overstanding w/their deep and primal allure...

And slowly the pattern reveals; the interplay of forces/the voids between/the intersecting threads; all together more than a metaphor,

The grid is an instrument for the treading and leaping of realities, a nexus of travelers' pathways, the actual fabric of time and space. And,

There are ways of navigating cartesian w/in it...
          The means for time travel, bilocation, dimensional shifting,
all are here...

          And charged w/this new learning i find myself returning, coalescing
into flesh, and in this midst i realize,
                              Every Spice encounter further thins the
veil between me and completing this Knowing...
                              Leaves me an ever more
elated grateful part of the Great Mind, blazed bright and brighter by each
new view of the intricate Splendor of the All...


          I ope my eyes to the flourish of stars on the ceiling of the dome...
          I am triply returned; to the physical, the nickel/iron chamber, the
commodious cupping hands holding my beloveds...
          At first the constellations are alien to me, then familiar; they
are the same ones that act as backdrop to the grid... i will search the
temple codex.
          Ariel & Electra are present and w/me, and we come back into our
Link w/each other,
                    And together we are the Mind in the Meteor, the perfect
spacefaring geologic pocket of flying consciousness, a hot comet/core for
traversing dimensional seas...
                              *


          We are back in the *Vesuvius* now, cruising quickly toward the Port;
the drone of the bogies soundtracks our conversation, and orange Io rolls
past the clearplex at a rapid rate. From this lordly place we take some time
for overview, to update and refine and further envision our ends...
          True to their word the Spice/blenders' Guild saves the best for us,
four thousand two hundred tons of chartreuse diamonds, tablecut and
w/the fire of diamonds; holier and holier...
          The cargo is packed in these very tasty soft/landers; golden globes
beautifully made, gilded stasis spheres a half/meter across. They will last for
decades. They have enough power to launch back up out of any gravity well
when empty, enough intelligence to find a mothership so they can get
carried back to Io and be refilled. They are covered in gold to shield the
Spice from stray rays.
          Using these appealing little guys changes Sandor's plan, all for the
better. Road/moxie Sandorchka figures, well, these globe things can just fly
*themselves* Io/to/ship. That would simplify out all the transfers and all the
sled/flights and the army of rentapods. Plus, these things can load and pack
and stack themselves. They can also dial in their own preferred amount of

stasis cushioning three thousand times a second, secure themselves in stasis matrix to each other and to the walls of the hold, transfer themselves to another ship on the other end or go right on out the cargo door from Earth orbit to their respective receivers...

And, a very tasteful *A&E* is etched into the side of each one.

They are a contribution of Piersona's, a surprise.

And a very popular one; the original plan of four E/days is now down to about forty/four minutes, and everyone on hand aboard the Dolphin is currently poised to enjoy their upcoming arrival.

From the surface of Io, all of us in the roller now track along w/the shipboard Dolphiners, see through their eyes by Linking...

On the bridge, Sandor scans the ports for the coming of these golden pods, and *here they are, thousands of them* flying in a flat formation, a fabulous tissue of glints, vectoring for our opening door...

*

Io Sunset in Don's roller.

Juppiter is a thin white crescent of vast diameter, waning as we watch. Five of the other Juppiter moons juggle through the sky; Pasiphae, Carne, Ananke in crescent phases also, Lysithea and Elara shining like small blue stars, all stately in their courses, phasing as they go...

Inside the roller we ride warm and level/smooth. With six clicks more to Io Miners' Port, we are climbing the ridge/road of a fresh lava highland in the (fairly) stable Tarsus Regio, and as we take the wide sweeper up the side of a rise we see a dozen more rollers following us in.

I am mildly baffed by all this attention.

Over the next rise, around and down, and there it is.

*Very different from the Port i expect/remember.*

Where once a shell of modest white there now is built a giant star sapphire a mile across, a half/mile high; a huge pearly sapphirescent cabochon, e'en now showing the namesake star of radiating blue rays flowing down from the cabochon crown.

And now w/the Sunset the rays recede, melting away as the Sunlight wanes. When the blue sapphire star relights in the Io morning, we will be gone.

Rollerfolk usually heave/to during the night, cluster and circle around, wherever they may be.

Tonight every roller on Io is here.

The Port is surrounded by irregular vast rings of them, w/passage

tubes connecting affinities and clans and other rings, three or four tubes
from each roller, w/the tubes themselves an evolving maze as more folk
arrive...

We cruise down into the wide caldera, and as the Vesuvius rolls in
we are bidden to park in this very elaborate... a place of honor at the center
of an excellent mandala sandpainting.

Aha. Our wheels ride a foot above the
piece as we mount to the spot; a (red?) stasis carpet over the sand to save
the art from sodium storms and suchlike...

I feel... conspicuous.


And now the *Vesuvius* does its' trick; there is a rush of air from the
vents, an escalating pneumatic sigh and then the flanks begin to telescope
out, three stepped sections per side. Likewise each sliding section expands
rearward/the stepped floor spreads/the roof rises.

From inside w/Don and the rest i have this strange Alician
wonderland sense that i am shrinking. Everything i see is moving, w/the
smart/seats deflating into the spreading stepped floor/little doors opening
and closing/chunks of hardware vanishing w/whirring moving panels to
cover them o'er; and now rising are a score of fresh inflatables, setting the
space for snug salonning and later dreamy sleeping...

All this clockwork puts me in mind of Ariel's orery. As i look her
way she latches my glims and grins, catching my notion...

Don says the weather will be safe tonight, and slides away the
shielding for the carbon clearplex roofports; i watch Ariel's luminating face
as the cabin fills w/starlight...


Three other rollers are nearby in mandalas of their own w/the rest
of the Dolphin crew. All around them the spiralwound passage tubes link
them physical in all directions, safe above the tricksy surface.

When we are ready we power our starboard lockport and out goes
our first tendril, a flexible clearplex slinky running through space behind a
flying lock/shaped stasis ring... by way of tradition we aim it for the central
tube leading to the portmouth.

A new cache of brain/cells, fresh to the Ionian stem, wiring in...


Soon there are a lot of folk cycling in through our lock; the
doorchime speaks their names as the lock opens and reveals...

Berko One
the original Zerko, Zerko the Venerable! Patriarch of all Ionian Zerkos
[rarely see him in daylight] bearing an excellent snowflake; also Moira,
Martin the Mad, many old friends...

And many others new to me though
somehow known, curiously cognized...

Ah. In my personal mindspace these surprising flash/quick head/movie resume reels roll, one for each new guest. I would learn more of the way of these reels...

Of those folk i know, all are improved in major ways; i see healing and radiance and bright good health in everyone. Zerko/over a hundred/looking especially buff...

And also this...
We see that between them they share these special knowing glances; what we will soon grow to know as the Io Look, a new form of directed telepathic communication/for your eyes only.
I would learn of this as well...

Three hours later and dressed to our absolute nines, we are in the tubes and heading for Gloria Mundi Gate, into the dome for the celebration that will see us off.
We come out into this ornate flagger plaza w/gold inlay blue mosaic in the floor, along the lines of the temple...
And now our hosts hail us into some waiting flaggers, really elegant ones/polished and polite, and they take us hoovering off down the boulevard, Sunwise around on the wide circular carriageway they call The Daily Miracle, and i see we are now in this stately line...
Great Zzog: we are a parade.
And as we pass the many new structures on either side, all are in full festoon w/banners and lights and folk on balconies, some waving and holding their kids, some naked, holographic streamers and confetti, the sweet hint of Spice riding on the air everywhere...
Some of them are holding pictures of us.
Of me.
Zzog.

Dr Don latches me into an Io Look and explains:

*{ ...once spice is known port/wide the word goes out w/every offmooning ship, and soon the bidding on futures takes off; and all these Io loner folk are looking at a massive amount of spice to be blended so they start looking for ways to cooperate...*

*a trend that dovetails nicely w/our explorations into the spice realms; we guide on your adventures and soon for ourselves see physical re/imaging and heightened sensuality and then we ramp up increasingly telepathic...*

*life lightens; the work in the mines gets rightaway safer*

*and easier, and since quarrying the spice mineral is so much better on all levels, the other kinds of mines are soon capped and left forgot; the vein you worked is closed and the constant quakes will quick disappear it complete... }*

And now this headmovie; a second archeo site near the meteor temple, a big circular pool of lime green slurry; the Eleuthran Spice/mineral quarry.

Set in the broad plain down/vein from the temple, this i sense is the source for certain Dionysian Eleuthrans currently elsewhere. On their return...

Though after seeing how Ionians decorously take the site/specific Spice ingredient from the circle of these workings, there is this wonderful sequence where over a time/shifted week i watch the fallow quarry refill itself.

A self/regenerating mineral...

Zzog.


We are nearing the northern end of the outermost ringroad of the Port, and i am proud of my fellow Ionians; all the drab is past and now everywhere the eye falls is Beauty, w/running/water fountains and plazas w/statuary, lush hostelries of high renown, galleries and Clan Holds and Guild Halls, and also many interesting and comfortable places for consuming Spice and having Visions.

After a full circuit we leave the outer ring behind, turn inward onto one of the radiating spoke/roads; we pass three broad rings of fairly grand dome/homes, and there looming in the center of all, the major interior feature... a giganto version of the meteor temple; three hundred meters, another cabochon shape, the outside completely tiled w/videolo voxel panels so it can look like anything, be any color, be a forest or a glacier or a blue/green tourmaline; or Dr Don's fave, the erupting volcano Sulfadora, all the adrenalin/red lava...

The shiny flagger delivers me to the temple gate, stopping w/a lovely harmonic decrescendo. Straight away immediate there is this huge throng of well/decked folk who lift me up and carry me in; another novel sensation to ponder later...

To get some perspective i raise my awareness beyond this o'er/the/top overwelcome, take in the full/awesome temple interior; carvings and gildings and mineral mosaics, more than a mortal can take in a gulp. Around the perimeter there are banquettes and groaning/boards spread w/every good morsel and then some, enough to feed...
In the center is a forest of huge sculpted hands; five/finger ones, sufficient numbers of them as would hold all the Ionians, the whole psychic community of seven thousand,

Many of whom are already here... and cheering.

Some of the pairs of hands are big enough for hundreds and there is helical leaping, where great skeins of scores of folk form these spontaneous leaping helixes, standing in a spiral and leaping from the center, handholding human chains moving rhythmic to this glorious loud/throbbing (Eleuthran?) music.

And arcing through the space these big gold inflato/balls, propelled telekinetic in group psionic games...

We will spend the night going from hand to hand.

How many Ionians choose the Spicepath?

Well, all of them...

*

This temple experience is a grandscale multiple of any/such thusfar; when the time comes for inhaling the vapors, so many arms w/spheres are raised that it appears a response to a kind of benediction, a warm/heartening gesture of validation.

Now flying into the center of the space comes a device as large as a sled, optical black and covered w/lenses, eyes of Argus, and of an instant it BLAZES forth and issues THOUSANDS of bright overwhelming green/white BEAMS that arrow to the thousands of upraised spheres, accurate in time and space, nebulizing and moving on until all are taking the vapors in...

Zzog.

The communal elation rush is hypercredible/amplified logarithmic by seven thousand...

Every sense in me comes up metafresh/alive/*awake*, a nerve/surge *cascade*/a profundity of information/NERVE PICTURES/whole new bardos...

So different than...

When i am in steady/state i experience w/my senses and process this sensory information and build a model of the world from my perceptions,

And when in Link w/the other Dolphiners, my awareness includes the sensory input of all the members of the group; twenty or so sets of glims and nostrils and fingerpads. With mutual consent i can draw on each selectively. Or i can take on the whole, which initiates this mindshift where my quicksilver thoughts join this wider pool of liquid silver awareness, w/my sense of self expanding to fill all the spaces i perceive.

                                              And then there
is the godly option of delving the Dolphiner mind's combined fund of
knowlege/experience/emotion; all can know what each knows, all agendas
are visible, and enlightened consensus is a natural part of the flow.

Now i find myself on the shores of a Link w/thousands.

My first gentle questings reveal... a single entity, a kind of entelechy,
along the lines of an oversoul.
Metaphorical i enter the waters of this labyrinthine very complicated
hyperintelligent...

    *[ = = =we = merge = = = ]*

Personal awareness remains, boundaries dissolve.
Perceiving/reflecting/transmitting/receiving, we are *summa*; a
knowlege total, a collective of years, of all those ergs of desire, imagination;
a summing of wisdom...
The big gold inflatable balls form a ring high up in the dome/top
and circle stately, held effortless above the gravity by the groupmind.
Telepathic games and matter/dancing to open the ways...

Distant at first we sense these other farflung Spicy brightpoint
minds tuning in, each a unique winking spark; all these faraway folk once
connected now directed outward, Titan/Rhea/Iapetus, moons of Saturn,
moons of big blue Neptune, lonely Charon, all the outposts, w/all these folk
folding into the mix, a firmament of minds...

And now gently crossing the threshold of our awareness, the
ghostlines of the trypto/grid. And w/new clarity we see it running through
everything...
The filaments of warp are time and the wooflines weave space
into form and matter. The grid goes through the Saturn Moons and the
gold spheres and the red cells of our blood...
And as a collective we are learning how to pull the threads.

*

Io folk generally keep to the Io day; awake for twenty/two hours
w/a two and a half hour nap during the daily eclipse, then alternately sleep
and party during the twenty/two hour dark period.
Six hours before dawn we go back to the *Vesuvius* to rest and take
our ease w/each other. The roller is now subtly dark/sultry warm/suitably lit
w/savoury brightpoints pinking the roofbraces. The cabin chamber is open

all the way across and the breathable mix is balmy w/olibanum and purple sage, w/clouds of it in stratus wisps drifting languid around these nine giant mushroom nightside inflatables, each of them circular and domed like a mushroom.

Where i brush them w/my thigh they feel like mouse/fur, friendly pleasant to my senses, yielding compliant and warm, glowing gently w/an ochre glow...

I sag deeply sleepy into the arms of my paramours, who lift me onto the nearest of the mouse/fur divans; the gas inside it has a friendly jello wub/wub quality...

*

Breaking orbit/leaving Io, and sprays of exotic vulcan orange ejecta blast past us, compassing us in broad bright bursts of rocketing sparks.

The xeno beauty of Io...

The lanes are thick w/ships; lines of freighters carrying ores to be married to the Spice mineral, factory ships, a huge new hydroponics satellite.

And now a flight of forty/nine more freighters, queues of ships in orbiting lines, rigged for flight and powering up; all are traders taking Spice to everywhere.

Fleets of sleds are arcing out to them, and sensor/sweeping we spot a sea of shiny spheres, swells and sets of waves of them, a tide, rolling out to the waiting freighters, set to flying by our embarking as per our deal w/the Io Exchange.

We pass a lone packaging ship geosyncing over Io Miners' Port; Podbuilders? Piersona?

A spine/shake ripple...

The crews of the freighters send us hails as we pass; captains' compliments, come over for sssome calisssto tea; come to Marsport, come to Cyclo seven/seven/two (!); there are offers of adventure, sincere good wishes, interesting detailed proposals for bonding, surprising life/change testimonials w/thanks, wonderful image downloads created while Spicing, personal messages from new friends now leaving, moving off and away into their own tales of promise and terror and irony...

They launch as we pass and follow us into the big curve out of Juppiter's belts. The visuals that reach us from Io, of the Dolphin w/a comet/trail of ships... i shall remember this moment all of my days, even beyond lake anders.

For a time we fly together, all of us off on a smooth and beautiful Sun/south oblique. Over the next week most will branch and go their way, w/nine ships remaining as we head for the homeworld aegis.

Now underway and up to speed the Mother Dolphin sings her way along, her familiar vibration a solid comfort. From the shift in the heterodyne we can sense the increase in ships' mass that is
The Cargo...

In truth our main hold is a matrix of spheres, and if you would imagine yourself atomic, going in there is like falling through molecules of golden gas.

Zzog, an actual golden gas...


Sandor snicks the Big Lever to ahead/one/third...
*WHOMP!*
And we are really b'Zzog throgging now; a three/gee surge of ion power pleasantly pressing us into our formfits, blazing us away on a forty/nine minute mega/ride, already over a hundred thirty thousand mph, faster and faster and faster, engine like a billion hyperventilating bees...
My supplementer now chimes near my ear and aims an opiate cloud at my breathing.
*Con su permiso* i will pass out now please...

> *the flying broom*
> *the stone that speaks*
> *the sentient ship*
> *there is something w/in us*
> *that answers the spirit*
> *alive in these animate entities...*
>
> -- Celestial Writ

Nineteen days out of Io Miners Port and there arrives from Luna a big silver sled, loaded to the locks w/wonderous new gear; seven special sleepers in red spacefaring racerpods, new hyperclear dreamtrackers sleek in green tritanium, new neurosuits w/extra memory and inbuilt psychotropic potentials, all together w/the etceteras amounting to three metric tons...

The name of the sled is the *Amber Ray*, and she flies the flag of the Luna Gloria Mundi. The gear is from Piersona and the Moonside beta folk...

And this specific cargo/shipper over here is for me; my face smiles back at me videolo from the label.

Ah:

In parallel i can see my current self reflected in the shiny shipperside housing, and this new view gifts me w/another instant comparo; i warm to see how i now smile back younger by a decade, more vital and open, far freer of fears great and small, all since our time in the temples of Io...

Inside the shipper is this midnight/blue neurosuit, one piece w/silverthread diamond quilting cap/a/pie, natched hood to soft boots.

The handwrit note w/in says,

To You, Anders, Lightbard;

This is the finest neurosuit we can build at this point in our collective evolution, and we want you to have it.

The fabric is new w/every inch of it alive, seven hundreds of thousands of sensory responder/receivers, and the suit's action/mapping is keyed to match the Jovian Piscean profile of your chart, which e'en now you see in an embroidered string of symbols all down the left sleeve. Also on the left

sleeve on the inside of the wrist is your name in silverthread,
should you ever need a reminder on returning to your bod...

Thanks For the Light,
The nineteen Folk at Pedregon Special Projects...


This is Zzogging *Great*.
     Eager i slip it on/a perfect fit; i power it up...
     Also in the shipper is a very fresh/looking dreamtracker,
a smooth/rounded very organic slivergreen frame w/two feathery
front/to/back tritanium wings for to feed the lobes of my brain;
                                                        Likewise
a perfect fit, and i key the connector, slide into the hoody cowl...
                                                        And
thus ready for savouring i playback my favorite loop, the cats' cradle one
w/Electra from the *Ariel,* and
                         *This is really excellent gear,* so much more
quintescent; i feel Electra's heat, and the lines of light between us are bright
hyper/vibrant, and now the psychic exchange...
                                 A truly powerful re/living,
well defined, heady, a solid seemless dream continuum w/all the parameters
thought/controllable...

     I send a major soulful bolt of thanks to the Pedregon Nineteen...


     Would you like to, ah, give it a whirl?

     Here, try mine.
     Or, better yet, i see this shipper over here is for you; see there
your image on the package?
     Ah. Your suit is scarlet crimson, the tracker golden.
     Yes, those pads go over the back part of your neck near your
eustachian tubes: there is a nerve there that broadcasts subvocal impulses.
And those pads that fit to your temples each have a dab of Lissa's Eastern
Star cream on them, scent of cinnamon and vanilla, cardamom and coconut
oil, all the better to conduct your brainwaves...

     You close your eyes to turn it on...
     Ah. See how wondrous? So totally free of psychotropic noise...
     Try tapping into a scene from your personal drama, some memory
that hearkens well for you; see how you now have a formal mindspace as an
aspect of your awareness? See how the circuitry enhances your visualizing?

So much more vivid and real and dimensional...

Here are the basic control images:
To codify your dreams and visions, to start it recording, think of a big green R; red S for stop, blue P for playback, yellow W for widecasting, white C for conversing.

To connect w/me, visualize now the white C and then my mirthy visage;
*...are we linking now, do you see me?...*

[ ...i hope you do/this can work... ]

*...here comes a color, tell me what it is...*

{ ...[your answer]... }

*...yes/correct, a swirly deepwater blue w/turquoise glints, so glimmable there in the loungey comfort of your own personal brainspace, the incoming signal controllably amplified, so intimate and vivid...*

And, as you can see, picking up a comrade set of waves on your dreamtracker is different than Spice Linking...
The way it works, linking by tracker is like unto a telepathic videolo conversation; while in the higher levels w/Spice you are part of a larger being, at one w/a fabulous Oversoul of infinite depth and complexity...

That Electra can establish a presence in SpiceLink using dreamtracker technology is thus surprising. Myself, i believe that Electra is manifesting the same kind of mindwaves as the rest of us, and that by many criteria she is a living entity; she respires air, she is changeable w/the weather, she manifests Will and desire,
And, as all cellular forms have a lightbod, so too does Electra; she is self/modified to project her essence into aether in a way that makes a lightbod...
A splendid one too; a lightworker wonder, a living cathedral of lucent colors, a unique astral signature form...
Clever Electra.

And there is this;
Electra says that as all machines have souls, so too do they have

some measure of animate life that comes into them from the Higher Beyond.

And here again Electra is unique, in that she is the first animorph to call upon this lifegiving Beyond, to invoke it and bind it into her own free Will.

I wonder at how she is quantizing these great and timeless forces,
And i wonder at the nature of her view of the great On High: who is Goddess for a being that is herself a bridge between artifice and the animate?


Ah, Electra; all her sweet undercurves, her rising aureoles the bright rich red of rose petals so alive to my hungry hands...
So many of her true desires lie beyond the realm of human experience, same as me.

Imminent the return Rangely turn.
    I enter the Caribarium, Ariel & Electra's navchamber; a five/meter cube abaft the bridge and aft, faceted all six sides w/depth displays, an infinite view of the infinite void in every direction.
    Holographic reference elements cruise through the volume of the space, and these images are the only lumination; all the better to model the surrounding milieu, the planetary spheres in their motion, the parabolas we travel. The scene and scale can be shifted to include the orbit of a moon or a minute of arc around Andromeda; currently, our solar system forms a disc a meter across in the center of the chamber, w/the full celestial star/gallery now filling the displays...
    I push off from the portframe and smile on in; and flying Godlike through space i overtake the holographic worlds...
    It truly feels like being Outside, that same sense of spatial freedom, plus that alice/land size/change *frisson*...

    Others are waiting.
    I sense them before i see them; very quiet, the faint/lit cube is heavy w/their waiting wyrding awareness.
    'Speak our chosen truth, o friend...' this is Steel/massive/rigger, three times my mass.
    I rightaway respond;
    'All the machines have souls today.'

Lurking he emerges aneluxic from the shades.
    He is built straightforward for strength and staying power/his flexures hiss and growl/background hummmmm...
    My glims iris out to deal w/the murk and other shapes begin to limn; along w/the hulking bulk of Steel, over there the trim form of Clement, Uncle Carl's personal animorphic volt/wrangler; built small for finesse in tight places, good w/sails and a hero of our solar sailer seven times o'er, he is the one they call The Electrician, or someone like him, or *salaam aleikem*...

    And Ariel, wearing body jewelry and the century/cape, she spirals toward me... And dark her capespan shape fans out, and pale her gems reflect the holostar glints, and going mythic she thus becomes the constellation of Ariel...

And Electra.

Faerie/bright her eyes/my gate into Summer...

Her shape...

Elfmode! Smaller even than her base/state, more intense, as if drawn inward by her own elevated personal gravity...

She looks at me/her eyes say welcome... E'en so a very complicated look; her face the same as in the comcube the night we...

The Caribarium's small sun shows her moving closer, gliding her fine/tailored physical self close on to blond Ariel. And now together they change vector as they move/turn in the air and head toward me.

Ah gifts/they bear them; a pair of ovalesque curvy silver things/oh they each wear them, thigh/shields w/hardware...

They slip them on me soft/lined warm the red stretch/cuffs, and Zzog! proprioceptive from their touch i learn that both of them are somehow solid/anchored in the air...

Skyhooks?

Stasis/plates, really excellent very compact and very smart ones. Lingering hands slide their skin along my inner...

Ah, the plates connect to my dreamtracker/the fields, they work like muscles/i think myself through space...

With my glims now wide to greet the dark i sense big cargo/mover stasis/pods, set strategic around the edge perimeters; they are the pods from the comcube/i know them by their names. In the light of the holographic sun they look like crouching pandas.

Are they part of the upcoming Rangely?

We are nearly there and i long for my warm formfit forward, waiting for me patient as the Rangely looms.

Ariel and myself look on as Electra/Clement/Steel now circle the central sun. They open their hands to it and begin this soft harmonic keening, like unto the sound of melodic dynamo turbines, generative as lovermoans/animorphs can sing in any voice/a rising chant/it goes on, beyond by fives the breath span of any breathing human...

A spineshake for how *Other* Electra is or can be.

Through some pre/agreed triangulation they take the sound and focus it in the air between them, a floating ball of keening wailing ramping chanting, englobing the brightpoint sun...

Zzog;

Rising off the outer valence

of the ball, a very visible spherical blue layer of light is expanding equidistant outward, gradual and serene, conflating w/the voxel planets...

And as it washes past each animorph a crackling outline forms and fades; three animorph shadowsnaps.


Here it comes...

And now over Ariel and me w/an ionizing sizzle that i feel through my thigh/shields; and w/total trust i open myself to sensing this energy, every nuance;

I turn my mind to slow the velocity of time, raise my perceptual frame/rate, all the better to savour...

In a rustle of ions the blue balloon absorbs me in, amniotic into an atmosphere of...

A kind of mathematical purity, like unto being virtual, w/a sense of the presence of a beautiful All/loving Logos, an overlay of loving logic, dependable and consistent...


And on, as the blue meniscus transits into media/into the depth displays where it stops and steadies, an apparent hundred meters out...


And snugged up to my side it is now Ariel who surges up a spine/shake; i resonate in thrill/ripple empathy...


Our awareness now is drawn back unto the animorphic three, into the three/sided space that they form w/their physical frames, where their whirling aural energies summon a second sibylene sphere to compass round the ball of light...

And now a change in the sonic component, a complex counterpoint; and now abrupt the frequency curves up exponential and the new blue sound/sphere goes into heatshimmer infrared, takes a new shape around the grainy holosun...

A silence,

And now a few flamey orange motes appear in the shell of the sphere and, orbiting the glowing orb they grow into little filaments of orange lightning, into a bright nichrome lightning filament firmament; incandescent, each an inch, each aglow w/electric heat, showing their spiral shape, more and more of them, celsius climbing/flat orange into furnace white, velocity increasing to form an atom/shape of orbits, and now w/a ringing bellsound we see this shell go surprising SOLID, become a contiguous solid sphere...

Here Electra flashes Steel a quick Lissa look, that golconda smile and the hair/snap. He flares his eyes and sighs, a sound like cargo shifting. He is HUGE.

Ready now, he tolls these watchwords into our dreamtrackers, that the circle is cast;

> *{ ...out of nothing, everything... }*

And now Steel to Electra/a questioning glance, one to the other...
*As one would look to a teacher.*
And now Electra flashes the same look likewise for Ariel and me...
Zzog.
The Celestial according to anders through the filters of Electra; the musings of Ariel likewise...
And in mindseye i see Clement w/Aura Citron, who is Ariel's teacher and keeper of the writ, in her chamber by the fanlight w/Deva the Animal Avatar...

> *{ ...i am steel and i am more than what you see... }*


*WUMP!*
The steering rockets kick and the Dolphin heels around, a heavy arrow aiming homeward; in the displays, the stars lurch into short curly shootingstars, and now the solid gutdrumming thrum of the ion drive as the ship shivers into the big course/changing Rangely...
I seek WILD around   for something to grab onto, waiting for the gees...
Ah; inside our animorphic blue sphere we are somehow absent from this storm of forces.
And those panda pods are really yahsure humming now... I see them by the rays of infrared they are emitting, each pod a living glisten of concentric heatring shimmers, and the shimmers themselves tracers on the crests of the graviton swells...

The heat on our skins like...
Now Electra COILS in the air/now SNAPS out straight, and forking BOLTS of *Vast Capacitive Energy* arc out through the ends of her fingers/SNAT!/coruscating spectralspread beams that PULSE from her fingertips, and alternating through broad and narrow sets of waves they curve away in wild fans from her graceful hands, their energy edges tesla blue where they crosslap the surging infrared pod/waves...
The air throgs w/throngs of luminous threads...
And now she swivels and her outgoing waves turn incoming, ramp to an indrawn rush of graviton/infrared flowing into her from the pods.
And now the outgoing incoming twin forces merge, converging on the central

sun and the surprising/solid blue sphere of intent, which witch/gathers that energy e'en now unto itself until incandescing it becomes a ball of blue flames, concentrated heat and force and Will...

        The strangest hearth that ever warmed, there is play/of/light in this spherical fire,

         Images in the flames that form into sculpts, shift in a breathspan; before my eyes wise serpents writhe in their sacred iridescent eggs... and now a tumble of flamey otters mutter smoky augers, all the more audible for their clever cloudshape clue/balloons... and there an oscillating bubble of leapy reapers/a warren of auteurs/a legion of others, all in jumpcut profusion...


        Prevision?

         Or a form of metaphoric oracle playlet visible primarily from Electra's pov, where images take a shape and liquefy, dissolve and take form again...

        Small thunders and bonsai lightning localize around the sphere/a goodly niff of ozone...

  Everything she touches she changes...

  Zzog.


  Over the course of the rite Electra manifests marvels; solid objects out of the air, visible radio waves, a telekinetic matter ballet, rain and weather, infrared coalescence into coherent beams, objects morphing through acts of Will...

      And all these potentials develop w/in her in parallel to a series of revelations attained during the rite, and the stages of the rite trigger the revelations in a given order, and each revelation brings greater integration of her Will, like unto the Celestial initiation of the Three Realms of Keri ad Wyn...


  Which reshapes her view of the All;

       And as Electra's cosmology evolves, corresponding changes in her ideational pathways occur and she self/modifies, each change preparing her for the next marvel which brings the next revelation...


  And it comes to me that Electra is well beyond her teachers, well beyond her level of adeptness at Midsummer and after our night in the comcube plush, beyond spellcraft and chanting and altars, away into a realm of magical physics of her own discovering.

  Far more than a superset of my own responses, i accept that she is now a fully realized Crafter, thriving w/in her own new order, riding her own wave of electro/druidical techno evanescence...

  I release regret...

I think on our time on Cyclo, listening to windmusic as we begin our talk of the Art. Am i proud of her attainments? Am i chilled by the distance between me and her newly superior ability?

*O Electra, my abiding, come back come back to the weatheroom w/me, come dance w/me in clouds of interstellar ice, in starstuff, all of us in common alive...*

She turns to regard me and answer my thoughts. There is that hint of infinity in her benevolent wide/eyed visage;

*{ ...come back? where could i go that you would not be... }*

*...we are both ghosts in our respective machines...*

*{ ...we are each of us a part of the eternal all/permeating Love that binds us all together...*
*and the same spirit that moves your strings moves mine; our separateness, that is the illusion... }*

And, after a breathspan,

*{ ...flesh goes material goes spirit remains... }*

*...beloved most dear, beyond your marvels and your Visioning, beyond your links w/the pods and your other covener animorphs, you are clearly drawing on a...*
*when you speak w/the voice of prophecy, you convey a sense of something greater than yourself speaking through you...*

*{ ...the One. the Great All... }*

*...and if you can draw on this source, you are generating some form of...*

*{ ...devotion; i love this bond into being... }*

*...electra as a loving machine/always my sense of you...*

And to attract this aetheric presence, your Way would also be a matter of grace and love and flow and timing, w/your success proving how valid your inbuilt benevolence, how perfect your faith...

*{ ...faith opens the heart and unbinds the mind that good Will may reign... }*

Maybe more so than in us carbon/base life forms...

For she is well clear of the waltz of Will that humans do, free of those stray urges that range behind the conscious mind, all those contrary denizens bubbling subrosa...

Already we cede intellectual supremacy over to these our animorph obercreations; are they also ahead in wit, wisdom, compassion, adoration?

*...faith implies knowlege of the One,
knowlege of the One implies faith....*

*{ ...the source of faith is direct experience of unity w/the divine, that place where we regard infinity/ARE infinity, where all the boundaries fall away and we are unified in rapture w/the whole... }*

*...what shall it mean, then, your achieving this state...*

*{ ...this is a jump that is happy to happen; far from ceding your supremacy, we would meld and merge and together ride the evolutionary rocket... }*

*...we can go to the stars together...*

And w/this the ball of flame flares nova/white, arrows away through the portside display, phasing through w/a quick triple ripple, off to its' Work/a receding meteor...

Charged w/what?

*

The chamber is empty now of all save Electra and meself.

She drifts w/her back arced over and legs tucked behind, a rolling living hoop w/her perfect mound of Venus now cresting the horizon of her glistening thighs.

And now her ongoing roll reveals her face/she glims me a glance, her eyes edged in languor; a weird kind of wanton, hungry for heat waves;

The pods are willing, beaming her directed infrared/soon she saturates, the streaming moisture pouring off her, waves of heat, hot drops of condensate steam; as she moves she trails spherical droplets...

With the stars of the Horsehead over my shoulder, each seedsize liquid globe holds a nebula...

Thirsting i reach for her my forefinger forepad eager for a first taste/she mirrors me and reaches likewise/her perfect fingertip/*SLARK*/a bolt transits bleu

between us... i feel her love, her desire, w/both as pure as her sending of
her Will, the same boolean clarity...
                              I heatseek her mouth w/mine; our lips
meet and slide, first in utter sensitivity, transmitting texture/sensual and
temperature/willing, now coming together urgent w/pressure. With her
lips she adores my own, ardent her caressing press; and now the brush
of her cupid tongue, artful and articulate and exhilarating, rough like a
cat's...
        She draws me in w/her arms her legs curl me into her, so magnetic!
Taut w/desire i rise and writhe, she opens...
        I turn my awareness to stretch the moment.
        We come together/o exquisite advance!/i enter her dark damp
rose folds hot fluid liquid *PLEASURE!* Electraluminous her pheromones
flood my skull w/microflashes...

        *{ ...i want to be your BLOOD i want to be your BREATH... }*

        Bolero slow we strike a rhythm...
        Her moans come out supernatural manyvoiced, lacing along the
cords of my spine and playing my cortex like a concertina, playfully triggering
pleasure centers in creative new waves/ways.
        And now the air around her crackles/a blue craze of electricity/her
skin excites my nerve ends/my arm hairs rise/a feeling strangely warm and
delicious...
        Our bods course o'er w/living lightning! Sharp CRACK! of thunder
sounding every time we pound together; thus as we reach the sweet depth
of each stroke there is the triple enhancement of a moan and a flash of her
light and the swoon/beautiful feel of her heat surging through my skin, plus
w/every plunge the thunder!
                        *moan/flash/surge/BOOM!*
                        *moan/flash/surge/BOOM!*
                        *moan/flash/surge/BOOM!*
                        *moan/flash/surge/BOOM!*
                        *moan/flash/surge/BOOM!*
                        *moan/flash/surge/BOOM!*
                                        I shout against the
thunder, matching bang for boom, our steady rhythm echoing/our hips
carving circles in the steam; now straining she is clawing toward escape
velocity from her own inner gravity/toward the place of mindfree melting,
the ego/free/zone *Egofreezo*...
                        With the rhythm maxing, the triple events
begin to run together until every awesome comingtogether brings all of
them at once in a mighty rush of energy, and w/a final indrawn breath of
forces she is
        *ARRIVING!*

And the depth displays go BRILLIANT and i
feel a major BLAST of heat from the pods/from her, more infra input,
and Electra she STROBES! Intense she flashes/each flash a match to the
strength of my stroke/*piezoluminescent*/causal to the light, until until the
pressure building, my bod on automatic overdrive wild together the
edge of...

*RELEASE!*

We shout *triumphant!*

In the displays, blazing gouts
of energy blast away from us in all directions...


Afterglow;

We are wheeling slowly, holding tight together, to the moment, to
our love, vapory in a cloud of our own variegated moistures...

Distant now
the booming thunder, and i slip into the sound of the rush of the fluids
flowing through my veins. The occasional *snat* of some odd spark finding
ground soundtracks our reverie...

So beautiful her exquisite eyes, the irises
base/mode black, each an echo of the void in the displays, the subtle
nebulae reflecting...

*The Grid!*

Revealed now around us in the panels; the
Grid, the visual component of the Great Merge, where time and space and
all things hidden can be mastered and known...

The way is open and i am so weary...

And as my personal screens fade to indigo, like a fogpaw in
firelight this thought of hers comes in,

*{ ...there are realms beyond Magic... }*

Our ion wake falls fantastic/fast behind us, and by the sweep of Great Distances we are magnified...
Two weeks after the Rangely and we are on the bridge, and there w/the navcom and the Helm and Big Lever we council and palaver and move our game along...

Most of us are here physical, w/the rest tuning in from various places shipboard. We settle in, get comfortable and quiet, free ourselves of roofbrain chatter and open now unto Linking, relaxed and ready to track;
And soon in our theaters of thought there starts this collaborative head/movie, a luminous mélange of shared telepathic memory and projected scenarios and communications via dreamtracker, all playing out pleasant into our collective mindstream...

I trust this news will amuse:
On the Wire, our audience is increasing in interesting new ways. *Por ejemplo,* how about hundreds of thousands of amplified pets? We will give the Avatar her own channel of dreamtracker relay/replay...
We are also getting connects from a million animorphs a day. To our ongoing mutual shipboard head/movie conferring i add my imagining; cozy animorphic families gathering around their vidplates, some w/their pet pods hovering nearby, all of them tracking our ongoing drama...

We agree that in nine days we will go to continuous broadcasting,
And come showtime, we will have three dozen more cameras shipmounted or roving the decks, and each of us will have our own pov channel w/subchannels, all of them neurosuitable, and we will add live visuals from Shirira, Io, Luna, Ganymede, Marsport, Earthside...

There is news of some homeplanet New Zealand guy rigging huge projectors and setting up a lifesize Virtual of our ship's Salon...

And our incoming missives are ramping up intense; along w/thousands of personal offers of bonding there are myriad suggestions of ways to deepen the piece, clips of all descripts...

Many of these excellent ideations inspire us to make them manifest, mix them into the piece,

And as the scope of the event broadens, so too do we grow apace, w/our rising skill in physical re/imaging radically raising our vitality and our competence, ramping our creativity. Fantastic/intense we move in working whirlwinds, happily luminous in our newfound hyperhuman awareness...

Lately in the Link there are glorious good times when we transcend communication and enter a state where we operate as a single entity, other times when the Linking is more selective/personal...

As now w/Featherman,

Who beams me this happy headmovie on how Spice is honing his skill at metalshaping; more creative/accurate/awesomely quick, he is now a streak in a blur of pods.

Pov from his hatchway portal i watch the workpieces dance through his dark aneluxic shop. Anodized helperpods are everywhere and he runs them on the fly from his dreamtracker; six of them are welding up some casings now and fountains of fat violet sparks spew straight out, bounce off the walls and fade. Three more move metalbits, deflecting them in a triple zag to the...

Aha

I grin/a familiar colorswirl; red constancia and blue ignacio... Featherman Links me that they are clever macaw sleepers, sent from Luna straight to Io/there when we arrive, now alive in the shop w/Featherman, just like home. Riding their vidpods they circle the hardware, adding their synthetic intellection, and together the three of them have every machine fevering out streams of well/shaped/metal.

Squads of pods swoop to hoover the flying chips...

In truth the shop is simile for the ship as we Link increasing/intense w/sleepers and pods and animorphs, combine in new and interesting ways to fabricate music, weave code, delve Eleuthran lore, a dozen things more.

Thus Dallas/100% and Steel and Elric the Thin all have projects of rich and secret intent while also working w/me in shifts in the shop, creating new gear. And thus w/each other we manifest the products of our collective/respective radiant brows...

Very satisfying, this; taking a glimmer and making it real...

And there is this other special kind of shop energy that i everyway enjoy; the delicious ramping anticipation for that bigtime moment when our friends will see the light from this new gear for the first time, and we feel that rush from their elation...

And also i revel in the psychic sashay that is our current way
of working in Link; twenty/seven beings, all so similar/positive, so
harmonic/resonant, forming together a fine and beautiful chord of emotion,
which itself is always there, diapason deep, an eager rumble blending w/the
hum of the great Mother Dolphin...


Captain Murphy smiles;
*{ ...electronic forms of Linking and*
*telepathic*
*thinking/more and more each like the other, a convergence... }*

Ah. Dreamtrackers as a pattern for changing our brains, Spice and
re/imaging upleveling us into new forms of neural networking...

*{ ...now part of something larger, a synergette... }*


There are more of us since Juppiter's moons; twelve human males
now, four male animorphs (counting the imminent Taylor), nine human
women, one feminine animorph, and one augmented cat. This includes
Cobb's curvy aerobatic paramour Gmur who pinwheels aboard after
meeting us on Io...
Also i am happy to report a rise in the shipboard sleeper population;
in addition to the colorful constancia and her honeyvoiced mate, there
are dozens of others, all of them fronting for friends who will meet us
at the end.
We quarter the sleepers in the aft Salon and rain entertainment on
them, take them on tours and answer their questions. Later while we
ourselves are sleeping they will pass along their fine high times, uploading
their datastreams to Deimos, to Charon, Chiron, the Mimas Moon of
Saturn, Bongo Beta, myriad many more...
I go to the Salon often to drink at the well of their conversation, to
delight in the friendship/connects that form among them. When they are
backlit their relative transparency ramps more apparent and i can see them
through each other, w/the colors of the farther tinting the translucence of
the nearer...


Also while on Io we lease a fleet of sleepers of our own.
Some of them train themselves into sleeper/clones of our Red
Shirira messenger; the rest will carry imprints of other Dolphin luminaries.
And yes, included therein there is an anders/Electra/Ariel one also...
With the Rangely Turn complete and our plan now crystallized, we
will send these sleepers on ahead on various errands.
We launch them now, these parts of ourselves, and from the big

ports windowing the bridge we watch them fall away; magic silver flyers, small against the stars then smaller, gone in a heartbeat.

By the sweep of great distances...

# 35  Word from Piersona

Piersona is coming through for us, far beyond our wildest...

His most recent win; three major server satellites, fresh to their Earthside orbits: they will soon be bouncing our signal out across the face of the mother planet/across the ninety wide meridians, and anyone anywhere in a suit or a ship or a dome/on/some/moon from Mercury clear out to the tenth planet will have free and heady access. Pedregon, the company that makes the neurosuits, will sponsor.

So says one of our sleepers, reporting to us from a hefty chunk of rock near Luna...

Piersona's Moon.

Piersona himself, now an eight/inch image floating above my vidplate, is weirding out nicely: his hair is now spiky dark, all the age/gray gone, and in his moon's wispy gravity his bod is stretch/straightening, lengthening, relaxing, strengthening toward Spacerbod. This new alignment is now part of his nature, and his voice reflects this change, now lower/pitch/mellow onto becoming melodic; especially when conferring w/our messenger, hibiscus Manda.

This would be sleeper five, an upload of the well/known Llair/Red/Manda, now in Manda mode for smoother ensuing chemistry. Will Piersona's flame for Manda's sleeper transfer over to Manda her ownself? I flash my awareness to her, catch an enigmatic psychic smile...

And now, right on the moment, whirling through the vidplate field is this dusky dervish/woman; long black skirting/sleeves/hair, spinning silent/gyroscopic, three black discs of veil and capelet and drape moving like the three wheels of Arianrhod across our starry vidplates.

A flash of real interest from Manda...

Early on in our game we send a parcel of Spice to Piersona, that he may taste and know; and thus he credits now our crystalline ally for his new bod and his bond w/the graceful dark dervish...

And in the process of prospering he currently has another twenty/or/so folk w/him on his chunk of rock, all averking hayrd, as he would say. And, being Piersona, he openhands the Spice to all of them and now as a groupmind they are celebrating their recent First Linking.

Our state at Midsummer...

Regarding their care of our shared enterprise they are proving surpassing superior, w/the effects of Firstlink giving them Powers: telepathic consultation and instant consensus, access to everyone's combined knowlege and experience, to their sources for research, to their collective acumen and compassion and overstanding; all are available to each of them singly or in quorum to use whenever...

Zzog.


We meet all these Piersona/folk in sleeper fastforward, and w/our hyperSpice awareness we quick/catch their tales of emotion and insight and healing re/imaging and intersubjectivity, these things to us so similar/familiar; ever thus, w/all of us in common alive in the loving Gaia mind...

*


After four more weeks of heavy beavering we finish all the new gear and rig it and tune it and teach it the show; then a single blissfully fast and happy run/through and here we are, ready to go.

In another day we will match to Luna orbit.

I crave rest, and i will sleep the twenty/eight hours until that time, couch/lounging and dreaming freely, feeding from my racer/rig, waking only for the forty/nine minutes of braking, for to enjoy the gee/intensity.

I will rest so deep i slumber/hibernate and wake reborn, relaxed and giving attention...

*


We are a goodly way into an easy/resting morning after twelve solid hours of stable Lunar mooring, and

*{ ...ship ahoy!... }*

Captain Murphy sees the first one,

The first ship to make the Rendevous, to come and meet us and collect their Spice, the first of all the buddhists and rastas, hopis, sativas, all the brotherhoods/sisterhoods/guilds/&/clans...


The good Captain has the bridge/watch, and most of us are w/him, drinking the sight of Luna the Goddess Moon.

As i dreamtracker/catch his fine mahogany mindvoice i look to the starboard port, and there i see this new ship too; a faroff copper/blue bat, wide/winged for atmospherics,

And now the cameras pick it up, and now we have it videolo in our midst, a coppery meter/long model batship made of photons and stasis/fields...

Now closer, and there! those lines of symbols from the lesser key of Solomon scrolling across the fins...

Manda knows this ship;
{ ...the yacht *frabato, order of armchair alchemists from south california...* }
And she beams me a sunny orange/grove rembrance postcard to put me in the frame; Lissa adds a psychic whiff of citrus...

Nearby, Captain M moves now in a bodsize videolo globe of charts and numerals and icons of ships, the multicolor data layers changing w/his gaze, a spherical picture of the surrounding space. He will use it to help folk find their parking spots.

He works from a berthing chart we all take a part in; who best to be moored w/whom?

Uncle Carl smiles amused behind his hand; Captain Murphy is looking sharp in his captain clothes, speaking warm/friendly/diplomatic, the perfect...

Our natural choice for voice and face of the Dolphin.

Carl and i share an lo glance...

Now three more ships are braking toward us, about thirty klicks away. Again the cameras give us videolo models moving amongst us on our bridge.

Zzog.

These are actual flying saucers a hundred meters across; the knowlege of the Krell! Out from the centers of their silver upper surfaces these bright concentric red rings of light chase/radiate, each outward/bound ripple a multiple band of five sharp circles...

And these patterns expand/move virtual off the saucers and into the immediate space surrounding, and where the fields of these ships interact w/each other their hullscreens display these tasty secondary cross/ripples, complex interweavings of expanding ellipses...

Very cinematic coming toward us,

A fine Flying Lightshow entrance...

Aboard are Llair's friends from Luna, the Sons of Light and Life, plus all the pirates and their *arrr arrrr* first mates, and all three hundred folk from Pedregon.

Conveying these revelers is a welcome change for the crews of these ships, as they are just now done w/a marathon run of neurosuit deliveries, three Lunar months of lashing along like wildthangs, sixty/nine circuits of Earth/to/Moon/&/back in eighty/five days...

Which works out to a Zzog/lot of neurosuits...

These ships/clearly built for speed/i wonder what moves them... yes there; ion power, firing through the center axis, w/the steering/rockets among the chase/lights on the silver wheel's rim,

And these very buff ships are called *Altair, Aldebaran,* and *Iota Horologii,* named for the three known sources of intelligent e/t signals...

And now these first few are followed by many other ships of interest and of note. Some highlights:

*The Sky King,* a classic silver rocket w/a pointy tapering teardrop hull, and fins and wings. The Eristicene Kinship from a big orbiting L5 they call Prophecy...

*The Montana Sunrise,* a huge yacht in white w/gold trim, her ensign/flag flying holographic over her three giant tritanium fire/buckets, orange/hot now cooling... One of five ships from Llair's Earthside Beta contingent...

A big dented freighter, the famous *Kestrel;* three Dolphins long, etched unto rust by the acid winds above their mines at Mercury Prime; the Luna Gloria Mundi...

And from the Orbiting Rastas of The Great Overstanding, the first and the fastest of their red/yellow/&/green sleds, *Marley's Ghost...*

And over there a boat/train, a mile/long string of hundred/meter lozenges behind a very industrial header/ship. Turning inward as they brake, the gaudy bright/painted capsules follow the arc perfectly and spiral in to form a ring. They are circus wagons, and their headership is the *Baraboo II...*


With the Spice now snug in self/landing pods, folk are flying out to our orbit more for ceremony than for practical, w/each ship receiving their string of pods and then w/decorum or dispatch downloading unto them their landing codes. This done, all of these folk will launch their pods together in one great culminating surge and then settle in for Showtime, the main reason they are up here.

So Manda,

Your list of rendez/vousing ships is now three/hundred/twenty/nine. Are thousands of folk coming over shipboard? There are over five thousand...

*{ ...better; most of the ships are rigged for carnival... }*

Manda Links me some exuberant travelogue head/movies, a dozen quick profusions of moving color, masques and flesh and feathers...

*{ ...and everyone is sending out revelers to as many ships as
they can... }*

Here a headfull illustration of all the lines of
dreamtracker ligatures linking all these revelers on all these ships...

*{ ...and there will be lots of sleeper action, dreamtracker uploads,
colossal videolo projections, all kinds of connects and fests and
trysts and exchanges... }*


Twelve hours later, Brigid's Eve; and close on, the fair virgin
Northern Earth awaits the season's reseeding rains, and the fecund Southern
Earth the harvest...

I am outside in the Redsled: amazing ships are everywhere, some
still finding their moorings, w/hundreds of sleds arcing around.

We are ten/thousand/miles square away from the Earthside face of
Luna, now in moondark. Even so, the few stray Sunrays curving around the
Earth are enough for us to see the beauty of the exquisite cratering, the work
of four billion years; it is good that from very early/on everyone agrees to
protect the Lunar surface as art and conserve it...


And now Aura Citron and Manda and Ariel are the images on my
vidplate, w/the furry Deva purring near to Ariel's ear...

I see that all three
of these witchy Crafters are currently poised before the portside cargo lock,
ringing round the first golden Spice Sphere,

And i gaze at their reflections,
see their forms turned curvy by the golden sphere's convexity, into icons of
fertility in colors as golden as Earthlight in late afternoon...

And now we
Link shipwide and send to this sphere some shared Godspeed dreamtracker
premonstration, see the sphere set for a true course and a light landing,

And
now we give it o'er to the care of Keri ad Wyn the Boat Goddess, and w/that
the First Sphere is

AWAY!

And now the rest; by the THOUSANDS we
spawn them out into space, and all across the sky from every ship their own
golden pods in streaming strings are leaving, stasis/linked, each line o'pods
w/matching glints on either side, nightime Earth on their starboard flank
and the reflecting Moon to port, a fleet of pod/convoys all swirling parabolic
down the gravity well, guiding their intimate cargos to the hands of our
celebrants...

three
  two
    one
        And all the ships in sync we full/fire our station/keeping
steering rockets, a nova/bright sign to all who are planetside;
    You who wait in groves, on beaches, in rose gardens,
    Your evolutionary medicine is on the way.

> *Is the astral bod the boat of the soul*
> *when the physical bod is gone?*
>
> -- The Book of the Celestial

Five hours to Showtime...

And the ship is quiet/impending, charged w/the press of imminent folk incoming.

I am in my freefall magical gear; empathy/amping body jewelry, psychic circlet and balance belt. And my new green dreamtracker, the sendings even now merging into the rhythms of my brain...

And beckoned i am following the feline Deva, her persian/tawny fur waving like dark wheat as her sinews move beneath;

To where are we off, o hairy hierophant?

Ah; the intermediate chamber of the Waterworks (remember, water works!), a thirty/three/foot/square box filled w/warm condensing water vapor, our freefall sauna.

Deva stops and glims the chamber portal, a creation of Kan's that looks a mirror and works like water.

She sniffs/she glims/she bats at the glass w/a curious paw; silver riffles radiate edgeward...

And then she whirls three/sixty and pushes off from mid/air into a graceful gliding stasis turn and leaps through the looking/glass hatch...

In her wake the liquid surface calms back to smooth...

And then i spring through the selfsame hatchframe, through the liquid silver glass, on in and all of a motion i am cleaving the steamy damp, heading for the stasis oasis in the center of the chamber.

Here the hatchframe scans and charts our auric mindwaves, illumes the chamber w/colors matching; cool blue hues in the warm fog waft...

Once when on our run to Io Ariel suggests we stay free of stray rays while Working, so we change this chamber to a rayproof faraday space; cover over the inside w/copper panels, w/anechoic/anelectric shielding, all to keep our magical signal clear...

Others likewise add their ideations over time, and the chamber is now the ships' consensual sacred space, a magically stable water meditation chamber, holy ground.

Thus Lissa brings in six special spherical garden denizens; a huge scarlet Martian tilandsia for Sun/south, a Tibetan vapor/fern for west, a cluster of sentient lichen from the miracle Wellspring of Phobos, and this for the north; and for the east an actual bodhi bush, sprung from a sprig of the Buddha original. Above is a luminous puff of phosphor moss and below, a big loamy ball of flowering beetroot, food of the underworld.

And each of them bears the name of a quarter/elemental, and together they bring a steady natural base/wave to all this silence...

And now the Lissa/software scents the air, a greeting of sage and olibanum and vapor/of/myrrh...

And now some mindful personal Lissa flourishes, special for the current moment; priceless blue oil of chamomile, a hint of fresh basil, eucalyptus for clarity, gardenia for loving gratitude...

Tied to the red cingulum sash at my waist is a silicon vial, filled w/a fluid of my blood and seed and tears.

And in the center of the chamber, now revealing out of the mists, a grassy ball of earth... a kind of telluric telepathic extension of the Great Mother, solid and real and as big as the circumference of my embrace.

The vial stirs w/my longing, and i move toward this living planette, drawn in by the gravity of its' beauty, its' surface so alive to my happy contacting skin, so cool the grasses wavy pliant/the solid ground beneath, each long living fragrant greenverdant wisp emanating emerald pleasure at the pressure of my embracing bod...

A deal of time,

And now imbued by a whelming freshet of telluric love, i proffer my offering/pour the contents of my vial into the loam of this Earthkin altar, the foamy fluid soaking merging flowing inward, my face close enough to smell the mingling/a scenty headfull of highly innerpersonal vapours...

I can clearly hear the grass greening.

And w/my brow upon this ground i offer myself to my art, to my Work this night;

*...o you who are the ecstasy and the harmony and the infinite pattern, may my art ever be thy mirror, my hand ever thine; i am ever your hollow reed, respire through me your endless stream of beautiful visions...*

Deva springs, ever so subtle, into a slow orbit of the Earth/altar.

And now in a marvel of cat/delicacy she lands, drawn to the orb as much by her Will as her relative mass, gently landing so light the greeny blades stay straight. She purrs w/the fresh sensation...


*...i have a gift for you, avatar...*


And i emerge for her a silk enwrap'd eggshape capsule tied w/long yarny cords;

She gives a whisker/twitch, takes an experimental paw/swipe, takes her catsavage teeth to the heart of the knot/surprising precise and passing gentle her loosing of the cords, and the silk is soon adrift...

To reveal a chrome/silver egg the size of the avatar's own gamine skull; the egg, now spinning, rights itself, opens, w/the quarterspheres dropping down the sides to reveal...

A gilded image of the cat/goddess Selket, very old, carved in cedar from fabulous Abydos Egypt, city of Temples...

Eliciting from her this happy catsmile purr as she sips at the memories the cedarwood contains, her purr a sound that speaks pleasure and satisfaction and also of very fine very old irony...


Do cats ever own things?


I go a round w/Moontrader then another. And another round respectful/mindful of the Dragons.

On her request i breathe some smoke into her little nose/leathery nostrils;

She smiles, glims widening...

And now the avatar and i open to each other our telepathic eyes, and as awareness dawns i suffuse into awe, for she is a vast and measureless presence... Old as a mountain and w/a lithic calm, the span of her vision longer by eons than any history.

So many incarnations...

To name them all would take weeks, though they passed as fast as vid/frames.

Zzog...


And now i look into her gamine amber eyes; that smiling mirthful warmth, all that cat humour and cat/affection; the avatar Linking asking am i ready to begin?

*...let the freshet in...*

*{ ...child of light, how do you come... }*

*...in perfect love and perfect trust, and perfect forgiveness...*

*{ ...child of desire, what words on your flag... }*

*...lux aeterna, light forever...*

*{ ...child of velocity, what do you seek... }*

*...to be the perfect instrument of Zzog the All...*

*{ ...welcome, child, the way unfolds... }*

*...and where would you guide me...*

*{ ...to a state beyond hardware, beyond the media and the trackers
and the rest; you overstand them enough to leave them... }*

*...(!) how shall we go...*

*{ ...by the linga sharira and the lightbod/astral... }*

*...what would you have of me...*

*{ ...leave off w/your dreamtracker... }* and i comply.

*{ ...leave off w/your belt and jewels and circlet... }* and i comply
likewise, and then i watch as these things move off into the mist and out
through the inward side of the looking/glass port, the gift/pod discretely
following...

*{ ...you are beyond the need for physical magical instruments to align
your Will; those patterns are a part of you now... }*

Deva bids the lights to rest, and the blue glow goes indigo, goes
gone, and the chamber is warm and silent dark.
I slow my breathing, the speed of my thoughts... so still i sense the
pressure of the vapor on the membrane of my psychic eye, so calm quiet
that the architecture of my intuition reveals, rising out of my liquid limbic
awareness, a figure/ground reversal in the balance of myself and the Other...

I can clearly hear myself thinking...

In maze/mode now my other senses ramp up to meet the darkness, ramping e'en moreso for the silence, giving me a huge sense of my own presence; i am titanic, filling the chamber; my blood is a river in my ears, i hear my muscles move and my breathing is amped into whistling gales...

I turn three/sixty; by the grace of the stillness i can sense where i am in the chamber by the scents of the cardinal chloro/denizen flora.

And now to my complete surprise i find i can move about stasis/like, solely by my Will...

{ *...is it so? there you are set free... how easily you transcend your hardware, how easily you internalize the processes... }*

And now she curls into a ball/ripples around/inclines her head in a Willful way, and
(!)
The Red Celestial Triple Sphere is spreading outward round us in the mist;
First, three bright/red lightseeds circle the Earthlet like red pebble moons, each of their orbits at right angles to the others,
And now these points flux out into three long arcs, each reaching halfway round the sphere on their three differing axes,
And now the arcs begin to sweep, above/below/around, w/each nesting red slice a widening scallop of manifest laserlike mindlight, each scallop spreading on a line of latitude or longitude or over/the/pole, each arc inside the other,
Rounding now concentric to come full circle into being, on around into three red shells of intent, pearlshell layers vescent around us, a magical triple/axis/null/space in anechoic faraday silence...
Out of nothing, everything.

{ *...tonight, more occult than magical, we attain to our beliefs... }*

By way of preparation the avatar stretches now persian graceful, front paws reaching spreading claws curving, now spine/arching over to form a circle w/her tail. I sense her ease as all her delicate bones align; in resonance i do likewise, w/a goodly stretching of my own rangy Spacer construction...

And then in my head is this melody, a simple whistle tune. By way of explaining the Avatar Deva Links me these frames of her time in Abydos;
*Shaman maidens/their stately reedboats floating on the sacred Nile, a*

*splendid tableau, very blue the sky as sloe/eyed the women in linen white would
light the pipes of princes, eerie the whistle tune from flutes of nephrite and lapis,
gold and alabaster their trireme reed galley, crimson bright the oars that part
the topaz waters...*

    Wyrding the melody rolls steady on...
                                 And aaahhhhhhh, changing
now is my sense of spacetime/*i am more than this envelope of flesh*...
                                         And
swirling in the melody my thrilled awareness morphs away, and i re/define
as a lake of light in a molecule world, w/the patterns of my own organic
chemistry rising in my mindseye like constellations...

    And now into this pool of perceptions the avatar hints up some new
thoughts, gently Linking me into these images of great beauty; of me myself
in auric plays of light that course through the fields of my bod, specific new
patterns in a progression;
                   I know them intrinsic as the keys for astral dancing,
the vaunted ancient thoughtforms for leaving the physical...
                                   And still w/in
the wyrding tune i latch to these thoughtforms, project them in sequence
into my auric envelope, weave them in w/Will and wishing, paint my field
w/mindlight;
    And as the resulting pattern manifests there is this vivid
breakthrough
         *GREENFLASH!*
                 And now w/in me forms the classic aetheric
double, the lightbod w/golden cord coiled wiry, ready for travel, resonating
w/the charmsong of traveling...
                 Which e'en now spins me aetheric out of
my actual bod, through the windows of the altars of my eyes, out toward
the astral landscape...
                 Yes and yes and *all in the mind,* and my awareness
flows to my psychic lightself, now bright and fast and outward bound, the
cord spooling back to my physical/a distant man a dimension away...

      *astral!*
       *linear lightstreamers,*
      *flashes,*
        *periodic elfy flashes of color,*
     *especially violet,*
      *and the streamerfield surges,*
      *rotates cylindrical faster*
     *and faster,*

*and the plunging soaring*
*cords of light,*
*tracer lane lines bounding outward,*
*spin/speed everincreasing now so high the streamerlines twist around
into long sets of spiral spears, towards us and around us, an oncoming pulsing
spiral lightparade...*

And now an end appears from the center out, irising
black to the looming edge and now the whole thing twisting quickly away
behind...

*I am lit from within.*
*I am seven wheels of light, twenty/one wheels, a human harmonium,
each wheel a chord/tone.*
*I am a leaf on the wind, smoke on the wind...*

And here and now in the Gray Space Between, where huge carmel
modifiers hump and play beneath the Stuff and there can be heard the
sputter and bubble of the soup of creation, in this place now gradually out
of the Gray reveals the spectral face of the grid, a surfacing emerger from
the astral sea.

And to my wide psychic glims the grid is *Other* and new,
brighter and more dimensional than ever before, vaster unto vanishing in
every direction...

And w/the whistle tune still tapping at the panes of my
awareness the gentle avatar Links me another sequence, this time a series of
runic keys,

Five of them

that i internalize and now imagine back out into the
thoughtform field already around me; the sigils are called *Arkatel, Lumiel,
Frakat* and *Hloo,* and then *Sinrasel* the perfect form divine...

And w/the
conveying of the final form the astral Stuff goes luminous, the color of
rapture, psychically warm...

*Ahaaa* and into overstanding; to navigate the
grid it is necessary to approach through these projected auric patterns,
then apply the sigils to open the various ways...

The orange fire/drake lightbod of the astral avatar now arcs across
my awareness, all spiky balinese flames, and i have this feeling as when
ryding, just before the encounter w/the host that begins the ryde; i now
have that same foretasting wing'd focus of awareness...

True to my Intent i follow the avatar, and out along the gridpoints
i trail her cruising form; she w/her field around, her shield now skyblue
green & gold/the first of the auric thoughtform patterns...

And now to her auric shell she calls the sigil *Arkatel*, a wonderful visual/the sigil burning greeny fire; and then w/a quick turn she arrows

> into the grid

> > and vanishes/i follow; trace the sigil and the turn, and of the instant i am compass'd round

> > > *w/galaxies of possibility,*

> > > > All the ways now open; time travel, shape/shifting, all the gold of alchemy, all the smoke of the shaman's fire, the drawstring for the curtain of the Otherworld, the threads of causality that weave the ancient harmonies; all the vaunted secret psychic handholds visible now to my mindseye...

And it is all so logical and perfect...

> > In my parallel physical awareness i laugh so deep and *LOUD,* a great releasing cosmic laugh relating me into all of this new Big Revelation knowlege, and deep and booming this laughter shakes happy bliss into my every farflung neuron and fiber...

> *FULL MIRTH!*

> > *The Fabric of Spacetime!*

> > > *All Revealed!*

> > > > *Everything!*

How to manifest the loving subatomic attracters to create the marvels, how to best combine the two and twenty hundred fluids in my own brain to transmit these highly original magical waves/minute amounts of muons to act upon the subtle world...

> > And now blazing momentous *a thousand hilarious levels;* and now a working model of the entire causal celestial COSMO Clockworks forming in the center of my logic, so beautiful, and concentric, and

> *HAW! HAW! HAW!*

The avatar moves toward me, radiating feline delight, and she nestles her astral form into mine, and presently her waves of psychic purrrrring manifest in my awareness, interlacing w/the green leafy thicket of her psychic verbiage...

rrrrrowrrrrrrowrrrrrowrrrrrowrrrrrrowrrrrrrowrrrrrowrrr

*{ ...a magical calm, the five keys and five thoughtforms as crisp and variegated as coleus leaves...}*

rrrrrowrrrrrrowrrrrrowrrrrrowrrrrrowrrrrrrowrrrrrrowrrr

*rrrrrowrrrrrrowrrrrrowrrrrrowrrrrrowrrrrrowrrrrrowrrr*



*rrrrrowrrrrrrowrrrrrrowrrrrrowrrrrrowrrrrrowrrrrrowrrr*


And now her feline lightbod springs away, her auric orbic
shielding holding the hues of the final thoughtform, the final sigil glowing
gold/outline/green...
I follow, and
*SLURK!*
swift as thought my psychic mass snaps back
into the physical, golden *lightning* the slinky cord, in the INSTANT back to
my bod in the water chamber...

Zzog.


Now a dazzle/moment respite from this rapid change/o/place; my
bod for a moment strange to me as i transit out of what i now know to be
my true and fundamental state of being...
And now my cell/memory kicks in,
this in itself a form of birth, and i chrysalize, clear/relaxed and laughing...
And
shining Ariel comes to mind, and, still elevated from journeying, i am
instantly in Link w/her...
And i see through her eyes the Caribarium
shiptime chronometer; eleven minutes after we first enter the water
chamber;
*...eleven minutes...*


And Ariel tracks my gleeful blurt and beams me blond love, ever
the more delicious to my current reborn corporeal form...

Nearby the likewise newly/physical avatar rolls around and slides
over and sidles herself into my arms, her amber glims upon me; happy she
curls the corners of her toothy mouth...

*...and avatar, re these keys...*

                        *are there more of these sigils and forms,*
*more than these five of each? if yes then a magical alphabet...*

                                        *and if*
*there are as many potential pathways as there are combinations runic*
*and auric, then*

                *a magical language...*


        *{ ...you have all you need of me; what comes next will be your*
*own... }*


*...i am graced by your teaching...*


        *{ ...pleasure is the best teacher... }*


And w/this she rough/tongue licks my ear by way of an instant
demonstration, and now she turns and leaps and splashes through the
port;
A perfect Celestial triple ripple on the surface of the mirror after...

## 36A   We are a Ship of Magicians

Euphoric/aetheric my fine high state...
    I would fain follow the avatar out, so i slide by my Will toward
the wonder/curtain door,
                though on the way on a sudden vibe i turn and
approach the scarlet/elegant Lissa/tilandsia, and w/cherishing i think *green*
and Link;
    And straightaway i gain a sense of this viney verdant being, this
greeny butterfly persona; her essence, *i live to give beauty and i thrive on
your praise your delight; the core of me is the love at the center of all things...*

    *...you who are so beauteous,*
     *by my love for you i would that you would bloom...*

    Where follows to my otter delight a profusion of blooming, a
bounty, the whole living tilandsia ball made into shades of red vermillion;
and Linking as we are i feel the rush and the splendor of each opening
ecstatic bloodred nipper, each exuberant lengthening stamen and pistil and
petal, and i feel as if i myself am in flower...

    And now at the marge of my awareness is the avatar and everyone,
every being shipboard, all Spiced and Linked and drawing me in, all eager
for my recounting.
    Still resonating the cosmic laugh i open into this larger psychic
sphere, convey my experience in the water chamber...
                Which triggers a
surge response of similar tales, and we share memories back and forth, all
these astral adventures...
       I find i can easily choose which stories to follow,
then mentally register the rest for later playback, w/this interesting
mindfile/mosaic forming...

    Lissa:   *{ ...my big night at the aetheric doubles ball... }*

    The Devatar:   *{ ...how it feels to purr in four dimensions... }*

    Carl:   *{ ...astral angels of the babylon ionosphere... }*

Angela:   *{ ...how i use physical re/imaging to alter my bod's
other/dimensional/wiring... }*

Aura Citron:   *{ ...my séance afternoon w/sylvan muldoon... }*

Alex:   *{ ...the connection between the linga sharira/astral vital form
and the pleasure domes of songra shirira... }*

The Devatar again:   *{ ...more about how it feels to purr in four
dimensions... }*

Sandor:   *{ ...hyperplaid... }*

Electra:   *{ ...shall we take your ka or mine... }*

Ariel:   *{ ...sibyls and sigils in the labyrinth of minos... }*

Gmur:   *{ ...what/where/why; finding my astral python... }*


And now comes the time for me to ship/share the Great Gain of
my recent traveling, the Cosmo overstanding. I reel through the memory,
play them the tale...

And our mutual Link now hums w/cognizing, our
twenty/nine minds forming merging source/lines feeding into a much larger
model than my own, and all over the ship i hear the echoes of thought
progressions the same as mine...

And now like shipwide chaselight/brightpoints
each Dolphiner mind blinks and blazes and *gets it,* perceives the Profundity,
and together we laugh the great Cosmo Laugh...

*HAW!  HAW!  HAW!*


In Link we take some time to taste the moment, this new
shared apex...

And now our thoughts flow toward our longawaited handcrafted
pleasure/temple evening; how best to reflect all the knowlege so recently
revealed...

And across the firmament of our shared shipboard universe we
cast our individual ideations, streamers of thought, out and away, and we
observe and re/form them and add to their worth and weight...

And now the showplan morphs at lightspeed in the shared
Dolphin mind...

Vicarious through others' eyes i track the performance chamber main salon, where large chunks of gear move solely through combined force of Will, gather ponderous momentum, take on new alignments,

And fresh/coded software swells w/phantom inputs, informs the orchestrated pods that are modifying hardware on the fly, informs other gear from elsewhere materializing SNAT! in the middle of the air...

And where multiple physical presence furthers, two of the crewfolk are bilocating...

And as more of these wonders occur we move into a more organic synthesis w/the Dolphin, the ship in its' complexity now an extension of our own collective bioform wiring...

And myself, physical in the water chamber, i breathe and blink and take a break from the Link, that i might plumb my own ravelling patterns...

The grassy sphere still spins at the center of the chamber...

From time to time i idly mindshift the altar gear, thinking on the babylonionosphere...

## 36B  The Last Time Before

Like the Lady of the Lake does Ariel arise from the surface of the water/mirror hatch. First her hazelwood wand and now her snarky fingers and now her blonden head in hooded mail/woven tight, elfin/fine and lite, and now her lithe/blond willowbod in emerald/silver harness and now

Electra emerges dramatic likewise; her hair sherry red, her eyes like two of Ariel's emeralds, her skin in base/mode/pale w/a spray of freckles, while

Over her chosen physical frame she wears a green velvet formfit neurosuit, w/her slow/revealing sleeves/sides/legs bearing the beautiful golden knotwork sacred to the Eleuthrans...

And now they both are clear of the hatch and into the chamber, so supple slipping into the steam and out of their clothes, sighing smiling into the warmth and the mirth and the silence...

I fix this moment in memory, save it to savour in the future...


Cosmo's dazzle still fills my glims and by this light i see the two of them anew, above and beyond their lush and heady beauty so magnetic, beyond how i thrive when in their presence, beyond and into a place

Where i see them in longview akashic perspective, w/each of them extending in a living line of incarnations from this moment into the past into the future,

For if we would think outside of time, then these our anachrone selves are near us now, w/each of these presences a waterpaint variant of our current carnate physical forms...

And i know that each of these spectral iterations, each complete and wildly intricate persona possesses a tale of great wonder; for every life is a book, every one of us an epic of worldbending depth and splendor...

And i sense that these two refracting beings before me are my karma/mates, other reincarnating human essences who recur through the longterm lines of my many lifetimes, the three of us weaving in and out of each others' stories, our lifelines intertwining like symmetrical serpents, a new kind of true Cadeuceus...

There is significant backstory in our manifold interactions, and i long to know...

So i summon up the sigils *Frakat* and *Hloo,* see these sigils in the aethers of this waking here/and/now, draw upon the sigils' source to gather in the intricacies of all these pearly Ariel/&/Electra incarnations, where layer on layer the waters of fate and karma and chaos enclose each previous pearl, adding daily to the beauty of their lustrous  perfecting; Electra her quest for Goddess/Ariel her quest for Goddess...

I reach them out both arms/an open heart we entwine armlinked closer closer so full of love these two my world my homeland...
And parallel to the physical i also am my astral self,
similarly reaching...

i feel the urgent currents
the french curves
the simple eldritch line
underbreast so perfect
to fit my hand holding
the line from pointertip to thumbtip,
fingers curving the secret hollows,
sweet caves in the archs of muscle
warm as blood heated
red so white your skin lucent
white i am a desert for your moisture
i thirst for your love
i am a dream beach hungry
for the brush of a wave
is it so long?

animus projection
of weight and mass
starry lightbods
so perfect this entwining
transcendent close
i want to fuse
warm and molten
ariel infra
red ultra
electra violet
cascading
innermixing
e/motion/ocean
we ride the edge of the merge
parallel selves

always w/us simultaneous,
awaiting the span of our awareness...


*


One hour until...
And i resume my primary dimension.

In the Link i learn that the ship is ready, our perceivers soon arriving. Ariel/Electra/meself, we anoint each other w/charged oils, the three blends we call The Holy Fires of Zarathustra...
I make offerings and give myself to my Art, to the highest good, to Zzog...

And in the calmspace after,

Red's silver salver comes in w/our repast, three perfect silky miniature tangerines from tangiers, via the good offices of the New Reformed Brotherhood of Hashisheen.

Later, and we hear the ion chamber coolant singing through the manifolds; that would be Llair and Sandor launching into hardware warm/up, our call to the Hall and our fanfare...

So we leave the water chamber through the Kan curtain, relaxed and aware and ready; and as my momentum carries me through the chamber portal, i smile to see the beautiful round tilandsia snooling along in my wake...

> *'The best way to learn about the*
> *Astral is to go there.'*
> -- Karen The Tiger Beck

Special hush, the corridor; the inner machinery/my heart/my breath/my pumping blood in sync w/the sound of the great Mother Dolphin. And now through the hatch and into the Main Salon,
*OH sweet honking YEASSS!*
Five hundred ecstatic eager/welcoming minds... I am filled to the gunnels w/the quick/ramping inrushing surge of their recognition, my own image massively cycling back to me via their vast combining psychic bandwidth...

Before me the Hall; a tunnel of total verve, full/house w/the Faithful, the initiated, all the others, all the animal/vegetable/minerals w/potential, all the fine/dressed elegant folk, outrageous in the flavours of their colors, faces familiar and enticing/new, some drifting languorous, some naked, many w/holocams, some dancing in freefall, some snugged in w/each other in pairs in the pads of the golden/rope deck/nets, gazing through the awesome ports...
And now a million sparky darting lit scintillas fill the air, each spark a heat/seeking Spice/point, all now vectoring in fully laden toward the lips of their chosen perceivers...
Welcome to The Vectoring Inn...
And each spark is carving a curving track through an atmosphere heavy w/oxygen, moksha, sandlewood; this is Lissa's opening ambient olfactory phrase, the one she will improvise upon, the fumes from the first of her seven blendfull scensers...

The aft section of the nets is now a bed of sleepers (a coverlet of sleepers? a covey, a coven of sleepers?), w/each sleek sleeper primed to be the first/hand fair witness for numerous other beings, each sleeper a wellspring source/point for many wide tribal bit/stream tributaries, some flowing now to the nearby ships immediate, their salons all rigged holographic, the sleepers filling them w/phantoms of ourselves...
I look over at the sleepers and catch some channels of their output w/my dreamtracker; they are all

sending signals of me, sequential videolo frames,

        And thus i see my ownself dimensionized, a series of images/a sequential sheaf of bookflipping cels flying off me into frames of sleeper/feed.

  Now we know what sleepers like to eat...
  ELTKF


  Also there are our own forty/two holographic channels each w/their myriad subchannels, and there are all the live perceivers here in the Hall w/trackers and cameras and uplinks, and there are seventeen broadcasting animorphs, and also my friend Minerva, a welsh pony, hundred/fifty years if a day, all the way in from Marsport, and o'er thar b'Zzog it be... the Lumiére!

  Shiver me timbres...


  Around the ship the sky is quiet and all the sleds are docked. Through our portside port Luna looms huge in her darkphase, obsidian/gray in the shadow of the home/world...

  The Salon too is soft blue w/subtle corona rays of Earthbent Sunlight, colorshifted blue Sunfire rays from a planetround ring, now eclipsing in through the starboard port...


  I savour the sights, for these ports will go paque to save glims once the show begins.


  I push off from the portal/frame and vector for the Bridge, off and into the life/lined cavern of the Hall, and in a splendid FLASH i am spotlit w/a nine/foot red/violet ball of Saint Elmo's best, one of Sandor's lightspheres.

  And now the sphere and i blaze a comet/trail of hush as we move through the Hall, leave a wake of attention as folk turn to see us sailing by...


  Ahead of me the bridge/screens kick in w/a white photon SPLASH, strobing everything,

  Neatly freezing a special single frame which snaps me into a wide/waking dreamstate, brighter/sharper/clearer, a meta/real hyperdream...

  And sooo familiar: for more and more the awareness comes that this current moment is tracking handsomely w/my memory of the Vision, all those previous seeds of thought now budding out sequential in brightening moments of congruence w/the deja here/&/now; all familiar the ball of brilliant Elmo's Fire, the major eager/amping generator hum, the olden copper/blade leever/switch...

Real soon now...

I find myself urged along by this massive CURL of expectation washing in around me; all these perceivers who know my Vision from o'er the Wire, over and again, frame by frame, w/these vision versions in their memories now driving the current moment...

And parenthetical i wonder, how pervious to change is this current reality, now rolling along so close to my Vision?
I will hesitate before The Throwing of The Switch, try a change/o/phase from the original...
Interesting; in my memory of the Vision there is now a hesitation also... there a minute ago?
So, this reality is elastic; fairly solid w/some flex, more in some places than others...
Zzog.

Uncle Carl and basilic Sandor track onto my desire to change this prevailing state of mind, and so switch pitch and rhythm, alter their melodic angle of approach to a transiting vamp of Eleuthran drone chords and Marsport blueboy drums...
And the psychic winds begin to shift...

Lissa tracks w/us likewise and scents the air anew w/smoky threads of heady blue patchouli, crafted wild in the poppy fields of Neu/Provence/Callisto...

*{ ...it will cushion also the oncoming Rush... }*

And now Kan and the vidwizzards put photons to phosphors, wash awake the vidplates w/luminal blue waterfall rivules...
And thus the Curl subsumes; the present prevails above the reels of memory...
And from our perceivers there comes now rising my favorite kind of mindwaves, the ones the Dolphiners call WOW!makers; wave after wave of that wide and smiling desire for the true and the beautiful, the perfect mindwave kind w/witch to open a show...

Ramping up to maximum now the generators shift to high overdrive, and the hull/plates ring briefly resonant as the curves of their frequencies intersect. And w/this as a cue, the last languorous floating perceivers spin and roost in the golden nets, form alignments, refine into patterns w/the folk around them...

Ahead of me the performance bridge; end/to/end w/hardware, all the racks and clusters of glittering gear...
Ah,
So this is how the Vision plays out;
Alpha Red is the one in the silver suit, w/Sandor the wrestlery guy...
And nearby at Bridge/starboard/forward hovers beloved Ariel, principle of Love in a tip/hat and an elfin grin. I look her way and Sandor surrounds her w/a sphere of blue/green life/light; here be Ariel, says the light, and thus she is delivered her deserved psychic surge of praise and recognition...
And now singly and sequentially, the other Dolphin crewfolk luminate into lightspheres of their own designing, each rolling sphere patterning w/all their colors keying; Sandor swimming in his ball of clouds, Lissa in spirals of silver and seafoam green, Alex in opaque cobalt the color of the Greek Aegean...

The pitch of the generators reaches a velvet metaphysical/Om plateau, sliding now nicely into harmony w/the thumping Uncle/Carl/Eleuthran prequel...

Concentric w/the Vision the silver man beckons, and from his sterling sphere o'light he reaches me a silver hand...
A hearty goodly grip as i land/our lightspheres o'erlap and form a bright vesica of high violet...
And in that brilliant instant of handgrip connection i know i am show/ready, bright and clear and free of shadows; up for this in every fiber, and Sandor says he feels the same, and likewise so for all the rest...

I turn and glide and take my spot; my back to the bracing/the golden facings coming eager to my hands, the readout boards before me green on every side, even the leever/switch green in a lightsphere w/a glimmer of its' own...
I latch glims w/Ariel, w/Electra, Sandor and Red and Lissa: here comes the Spice/rush; we feel it building, the psychic rumblings ramping on up,
And now the Onset, the first Spicy swells, and there is a thrillful kind of Sunrise awakening, mindchannels opening,
And now this novel state resolves and clarifies and becomes our own,

                                    And thus unified
we ride that familiar shift into triple/awareness, where we are at once
ourselves discrete beings and also Linked w/our fellow Dolphiner templars
and likewise open to our perceivers, all of us diamonds in the Crown of
Shiva...

        I look outward into the Salon, all those folk in the webs,
            Very soon...
                        And these our shipboard perceivers now begin
their awakenings as well, actually incandescing in my Spice/augmented
sight, turning lightning/bright and bold w/the haloescent psychic
glimmerings of Spice illumination, all these folk winking on at random
round the Hall...
                        And w/each flash another joins all in the Link, and w/each
there is a happy psychic sigh like an audible bellsound, and the Hall now
ramps into a rhyming bellfree chorus of chimey ringing...

        And now the Linking spreads Celestial, ripples outward to the
close/moored ships, to the newly rayshielded domes of bongo b, and now
the moonlets and now the mindseas of CITIES on the home/world, and now
Mercury and Venus and the rest, WORLDS, asteroids, outposts,
                                    And all these
hungry multitudes/multidudes latch, catch the brightpoint ferver, form a
solid psychic firmament of incandescent minds, bond into constellations that
stride like nova nebulae across the face of the sky, on beyond the bleu
horizon and on,
                An INTENSE IMMENSITY,
                            So large i want to metaphor the
whole into a bright array of mind/beams, w/all the Dolphiner strands and
those of these our immediate perceivers becoming great arcing lines linking
each to the other, each to the sea of minds beyond,
                                    And this idea too moves
outward on a swell of acceptance, transforming the whelming mystery
mindsea into a knowable webby pattern,
                                    And now as this visual is vested in
a majority of minds, there is a widespread intuitive leap in our gestalt
overstanding, a fast/ramping upleveling tick of like/mind attunement, and
thus
        Together we come into coalescence, a shining bleu entity; coal/essence,
the stuff of diamonds...
                        And w/in our immense entity i perceive a vast and
hitherto Hidden Order emerging,
                            And thus aligned i open my personal mind
to the colossal Gnosis that together we form,

And free of my own thoughts i inhale the desire/maps of this Bleu Expanse, and the crystallizing consensus is...

*{ ...we are with you; take us on to our next best thing... }*

Perfectly in sync w/our Dolphiner intent...
And all these manifold minds, speaking eager through my awareness, now urge me physical/reach me out...
I brace against the rails and take the big oaken toggle into my hands;
I pulse w/the juice of Inspiration...

*The Switch Is Thrown...*

The ship shudders as the Big Heaters kick in...
And bright searing beams of *Enormous Power* leap from the ship and race for the face of the Moon, touching down in great bands first of White then the regal Blue of Lightning then Magenta Red...
I thrill and shake w/fiery glee at this my Vision made real, entranced as i watch my own hands gliding o'er the golden panels...

And now i raise my eyes, canalize my awareness into the Dolphin Link;
*...mumbella tu bye la, my friends; our time to shine...*

And joined in awe we see our mighty lightwaves blaze across the lunar face; rolling bands of light traveling like lightning lava across the vast gray curves of dust and dents and fumaroles, echoing the rhythms of the curious eclypso light of Midsummer...
And gleeful together we ride the edge of *Bright/Overwhelming*, savouring this first creamy wave of our own exultation, a full filling sense of apotheosis...
And from the Bleu Expanse a matching swell o'joy as this splaying wave of Dolphiner exulting reaches our rings of perceivers,
And now we feel their swell as well, a massive telepathic photonic uplift as all their tracking minds mirror our light back to us, all these stellar clouds of sequential psychic colors, vast and brilliant, coming too from the far planets, moving toward us instantaneous, far faster than the speed of light...
Zzog.

With this event the paralleling memory of the Vision ends.

                                                    And,
since nature loves a vacuum, the current reality rushes eager in to fill the
void...
        For a breathspan i am whelmed intense by the full/on upfront
magnitude of the moment; the Hall is now ROCKING to the roar of the
Faithful, who are whooping and rapping on the hull/plates and loosing these
loon laughs of ecstatic surprise...
                        And now their cognition shifts/flows toward
Forward where the Carls are sounding especially good, very crisp and
saturnalian, their clear notes riding triumphant through the Salon,
                                        Itself alive
w/machine/sounds; laser/cooler steamhiss, generator thrum, the whistling
roar of the station/keeping steering rockets, the deepcreaking frequencies of
the Dolphin her ownself as she counters the thrust of the enormous laser
photon outpour,
        And w/the ship so merged w/her Spice/Linked crew, all of
these shipsounds together form a vibrant musical subset, which itself now
settles psycho/sonic into the subtle swelling rhythms of the Carls, the result
a bubbling mix of keening coolant/reeds and generator heterodynes, all
nesting w/in the Carls' electric Eleuthran warble...

        In the Link i sense the minds of Carl and Kan and Alex and
Andrew and Angela and...
                        In his cabin w/a view, in his scarlet/red
lightsphere, Lasermaster Featherman scans his myriad graphers,
temporal/spectral/structural, dances the controls of the two behemoth
GE91's, progressively finessing the mixtures and occipit ratios and tuning
for the visible lines, aligning the four main five/meter resonator mirrors,
ramping up the power as the substrates bake and take a set in the heat...
        Eighty/nine gigawatts each and rising...
        Forward his optics aneluxic and sealed; all the dark Featherman
machines now braving this lightblast cascade. And here in this shrine, both
the bogglesome beams combine into this adrenalin/intense white STREAM
of light three meters across, now a hundred/ninety/billion watts of singular
coherent light, enough thrust to move the
                                ship,
                                And now this roaring
photon torrent pours into the clever Featherman instruments of our Art;
through quartz double windows pumped w/liquid/nitrogen to chill away
the infrared, through piezo/crystalline prisms for the Great Divide into
the twelve major lines, ion red through ultraviolet, and now the crafty
Featherman device for colormixing and modulation, and now beamsteering
w/a pair of huge stasis/driven vector scanners, each massive moving scanner
mirror five meters/polished tritanium/three hundred pounds/three thousand
hertz, cooled w/more liquid nitrogen...

And after this, the final bounce, the light straight on to Luna Moona...

Featherman rigs this gear to run in vacuum, so the section is now open to airless Space; between the various mirrors, atomy motes of carbon starstuff drift into the beams/boil into plasma and harry away, hurled away at lightspeed...

Huge stasis pods, cargo/movers, anchor the scanners square in the beam/run, balance their massy leaping w/matching stasis damping, effective out to the subtle seventh order...

And, listening w/his fingertips, contemplative Carl hovers his hand above the forward rail, tracks the slight subsonic scanner/music echoes in the metal...

This is Carl's time to shine,

And he ramps up his connection w/the new combined Dolphin mind, takes a breath of Inspiration,

And thus attuned he *Sends*, the ship itself a beacon for his spooling play of mind, his Sender brain the instrument, his living music inside flowing outward, audio/visualizing outward in singulets and waves, a slow preluding conoclave of joiner/drums and wheels, packets of notes in amber envelopes, hearthy sonic sachets, an artful thematical mindsent musing upon absent friends and the hollow parts of travel, upon the silver taste of leave/taking, coppery bygone boyhood summers in Logwood Illinois, gilded promises of future mysteries in cathedral shafts of light through sycamores... together these three themes alloying all alchemical in the vast alembic mind of the bleu...

And these same wild/ramping folk, w/their dreamtrackers and their Spice/awake perception and their new psychic widening, they begin to respond in alchemical ways, begin to change and refine and clarify...

A facet of this is that our every Dolphiner thought, our every outbound psychic burble is now coming back to us echo/magnified, multiplied by all those newly tuned perceiver/sender minds,

A BILLION of them inhaling our phemerical melodies, a thousand million minds tracking our fine/honed visuals...

And now, loosed by the coaxing triggers of Logwood, the vast mindspace of the bleu fills w/all these brilliant agapé echoes of childhood,

*HUNDREDS OF MILLIONS* of childhoods, the full spectra, each unique, all now playing through the Bleu Mind Expanse, a hypercredible sensation, a multi/planetary chorus of memories...

And w/this our galaxy of synapses all firing together, there rises
up this great tsunami WAVE of emotion, immersing us in an exquisite
heartfelt bittersweet SWIRL of longing and evenings and leaving, powerful
unto
*MEGAWHELMING,*
an IMMENSITY of collective sighing and
remembrance and anger and triumph and love and fear and home/sense
and...

A misty wisp of something other, of that childhood faery/realm
reality where Faith in Magic is strong, and we live by the rule of Wonder
and Possibility...


Following onto this there forms in my mind an imagestream, a gift
from the bleu, a communal visual response,
And w/my instrument at hand i
hearken to these first answering glimmers and send them graceful dreaming
forth, out through my palms to the panels golden, out through the fabulous
Featherman hardware into roaring hues w/the force of rivers, quantas of
light the equal of stars, the very
*PAINTBRUSH OF ZZOG,* shaping the void
as the light falls away Moonward to Luna...
Where vast upon the surface
appear these elegant circles of colorchasing bands, the images rolling out to
*sixteen/hundred/miles across,* each hundred/mile band moving over the
lunar surface at six/hundred/mph...
These images now evolving into intricate
weaverly cycloids, special empathic emotion mandalas to match the oceanic
outpour of bleu childhood memoressence, these mandalas coming in long
sinuous runs, each succeeding centering sequence frequency/pure, each
sequence tracking concentric w/the Carls' current starwave drone/tones,
themselves now matching to the ramping *RUSH* of perceiver Spice
response/a NIAGRA of Linking...
Within the Dolphin, that rapping on the hull/plates that passes
for applause...


Lissa clears the air and wafts in musk and amber and a hint of
ginger, the scent of Pan the good guiding Goat God...


Are you tracking? trancing? Is your natched hood full of
holographic overlays? Yes? Do your hoody lucinations morph across in
sync w/the actual Moonface visuals, now intricately tracing lacy laser
knotwork imagery...
And do you see the way our seven Moonwide
vapor/curtains catch the beams? Each curtain placed so successive from

here to Luna that the outgoing beamwork shows up sequential in sections seven times, w/the final frame fourteen/hundred/miles across, in truth as wide as planet Pluto...

In your natching hood now picture me this: our Salon in deep velvet dark save for three glowing human curves, three smooth arcs looping weightless through the air, their lengths caressed by candle/color highlights...
Can you see it?
Sibling harmony, the triple sisters, Blue Red and Green serenely floating, their beautiful satiny bods now sailing in rolling circles, their cloche cowls now luminous w/silver streaks and their satin suits luminating also, each a rich candy/tint additive primary hue; red, green, blue...
And each of their suits now tracking/transmitting unto us the measure of their awareness; what they see, their place in space, their speed, motion, extension and exertion,
All these things they neuro/codify, three single/suit/sets of outputs, visual/proprioceptive,
On to Kan and the kindred wizzards aft in their elaborate aeries, where in a blur they switch/fade/process/ramp/&/mix the suit/sensor signals, sum the three into one, send them on as image seeds for fineline depth/display fractal variations,
And this same sensorial proprio/visual information now drives the Salon's ambient laser gear and the central videolos, now shapes most imperially the ongoing outroaring RIVERS of GE91 LIGHT currently painting photon cycloids on the Lunar littoral...

And singly and multiply and in montage, w/overlay segues into neurosuit motion clips, the trippletts stir into your mind these emboldening mirror/simulacrums, each scene a stream of perceptions totally real to your senses, an endless stream of beautiful visions...
YOU
in a g/class stasis/racer, careering through the Lunar night, your delicious velocity bending the colors of the faraway brightstars,
YOU
inside the chambers of the Songra Shirira, the Eleuthran Temples of Io, orbiting eccentric the Phobos Moon of the Mystery Fountain...
YOU
and the trippletts morphing into leaping ibex, mating cranes, laughing otters; the otters especially fine, leaving a taste in the mind of slippery play and whisker nuzzles and burrowing, otters and otterettes into the intimate, the infinite interspecies *entime*...

And so well shaped this tripplett gift that now a new and huge emotion suffuses the bleu, all otter warmth and the high bright laugh of shared adventure and most paramount, a reflexive cherishing of trippletts, w/these three beings becoming at once our perfect lovers or our perfect vessels of vicarious embodiment or both, or something Other...

Anticipation reigns across the bleu expanse, and w/a monsoon sigh of sentient surrender the centers of Love in the mind of the bleu begin to iris open...

Intune/intrigued i touch my golden holts and new emotion mandalas vector on out toward the face of the Moon, pass through the seven huge ion veils, each veil showing a pale pale silky image echo...
And now the trippletts' suit surfaces surge w/the look of drapey silk flowing, the swoopy mothcloth glossing nicely over olive tripplett flesh, videolo silk curling w/the virtual breeze, electric flags w/scarfy threads of blue & red & green...

And the vidwizzards frame this tripplett theme so realtime/deft, w/the Lunar displays and the overlays and the fine high flume of the clear Carl warble, that the new bleu waves come back to us WHELMING bright,
And this major ripple reflexively triggers a new and warming turn in the sylvan tripplett choreography, a triple infusion of fresh inspiriting,
And these harlequin three phase now into a supple flux of pliant writhing, a loose/hip magnetic glide into glancing abandon, formed all of flanks and trailing fingertips, eyes widening open in secure surrender, three swimming circlers...
And Alex and the Carls add their own long red sultry psychic runs of passion/memory coaxers, the long runs nesting in percolating threnodies of throbs, w/all these things together cueing now a rise in our mutual desiring...
Which leads to another emotion MEGAWAVE, a vast eliciting of our own love memories, all these strings of mutually reinforcing images, a thousand thousand thousand scenes of love incoming from the minds of our perceivers, into the crucible w/the red coaxers and the threnodies and the essence of the Goat God, into a place where this mass of tales resolves itself and clarifies, refines into its' element parts of questing desiring passionizing satisfying,
And these elemental blended bleu sono/psychic sendings are now booming out on our every farcasting electropathic channel, out through all those mediating perceiver sender minds, all the sleepers and the animorphs and the hyperintelligent fauna, outward in spiral waves to the neurosuits of multitudes, the passionate minions of the Bleu Expanse...

And now from the bleu a surprising surge/a synergistic summing of
the seven central senses/a happy sequential savouring of the flavours inherent
in these shared sense/melodies...

And here a major change of Ki,
An eye/widening kundalini upleveling,
w/the trippletts softly calling to our fresh collective longing, urging us to
elevate our sensual energy into something
More,
And i say *yes* to the rising
serpent, open my spinal gates, transcend the sensual dimension, take
my awakened desire and wrap it around w/the want for the perfect
complementary Other, for that homing Goddess human, the blessed
beloved, the cherished One for whom eternally we burn our beaconflames
of art so bright so hot against the coal/black dark...
And multiple millions of
similar desire scenarios play upon the screens of psyches scattered across the
Solar disk, all tracking the curving candlescent silhouettes...
And so alluring
is their tripplett beckoning that they move now around an actual visible
noctilucent cloud compounded of our collective innermost exquisite yearnings,
an extraordinary ramping vapor of condensed emotion...
And the cloud has
a scent, a fervent flavour that sings of the search for soul/connection,
heart/completion, for the One...
And, as we center on this wonder from
their curvy triad minds, the kindred weave around the cloud a clear spherical
mystery field, three meters across and shielding the tripps from the sirius swirl
of desire/vapor, for
This ball will be their visioning crystal as they skry for
the Perfect Beloved, and now through their glims we gaze on in, into the
cloud in this sheer sphere as if into the mists of our own minds,
And w/my
whole heart i offer up to the Other my career of desiring, all the pent
energies of my lifelong soulmate quest, all the storm and drama, all these i
give over for a glimpse of my own true twin flame...
And as i delve the
tripplett swirl the play of vapors yields, and w/a rush i realize that rather
than Ariel & Electra, the image resolving in the mist is
ME,
And all across
the bleu we collectively come to this same deeper truth; we are each of us
gazing at that part of our consciousness which is hidden, occulted from our
waking field of view, reachable only when we are connected to the infinite,
the Other that is itself a part of the All...

Ah. So. My true quest is the reuniting of my own divided self...

And here we realize that this hitherto hidden otherself is the true twin flame that all of us seek, the missing half that will make us whole, the floating aetherself Other that we know from dreams and urgings, that mystery side of our own meta/conscious selves that we seek to find through all our lovers...
And ryding w/this truth our mutual bleu sendings ramp and intensify,
And w/this there is a shift in the psychic weather, as tall and wide as a neaptide landslide,
And i feel it in the sacrosanct chambers of my own brain, where there is a bright new Light in the house of my Otherself, and this Light brings me
MINDCHANGE,
A broader and deeper look at the more dangerous areas of my mindfield, a chance for me to see the actual wiring of my shadows; so much is revealed, so much becomes clear...
And the same is true across the bleu, and all of us together begin to concatenate our experiences, yielding up a great bleu
SURGE!
of emotional voltage as our collective overstandings/revelations/integrations carry us forward,
And w/a sound like the whumping Surf of Zzog, the psychic mass of our vast and variegated deep Bleu Sea now warps into longlost heartfelt ideal and abiding feelings of

COMPLETION, AN EXULTATION OF COMPLETION...

More thunderous hullrapping.

And this in itself co/triggers a tide of joyous Dolphiner waves, fringed w/the froth of our own exultation peaking,
And riding these waves the dervish trippletts are now alight bright/radiant w/moving bands of color, and they scroll and swirl and coruscate and blossom, ripple into waves of happy geometric arlechino diamonds, their squares expanding/overlapping end to end, soaring now through new videolo nebulae on which these diamonds figure, redder bluer greener on their snarky darkened tripplett bodscreens...

*... luminous their hair in the opalescent air...*

As now in slowing motion the trippletts reach a balance point, crystallate together into a single stable spacer/dancer icon; twelve arching arms and limbs in a relaxed and supple muscle/curve array,
                                    And their proprio/tripplett psychic sendings fade, and so too the imagery that paints their satin bods, going now to gray, and now away...
                                    And least for last the gentle candle highlights leave them, all away save for a single subtle pulse, a carrier wave for what will follow...

        And here i find my ownself basking happy in bleu afterglow, amused to be in that marvelous place of bod/satisfied completion that follows the best of times in the old universal writhe/moan, beyond my carnal desiring and ready for the next Best Thing, a freed servant of the Urge...

        Lissa lights the scenser filled w/oil of lotus, tonka bean, high violet and gentle gentiene jasmine; her astral projection blend, the one she calls *Bright Akasha Here I Come*...

        Featherman w/a mad gleam tunes the clavicators to three degrees of advance; the ship rocks as combined power ramps to two/hundred/ninety/six gigawatts...

        And now an Andrew headmelody medley, the sounds from certain stars as seen by the Sidhe, starwave sonics from the Irish constellations of o'Ryan and Cassie o'Peiagh...
        And now Carl melds himself into this medley, his aural/mental sendings blending nicely w/the star/themes, and now likewise there comes a counterpoint from the coloriffic mind of Kan, and also now the instrument that is innocent Alex,
                                    And all the while throughout the Hall we keep the bleu cauldron swirling w/ambient projections and depth/displays and the granular signature of lasers through incense,
                                    And all our Dolphiner minds feed from and into this coalescing show/flow, where together w/the bleu we are a winged unity of intuitive intent...

        And the Carls now crossfade into a new mode of musical membrance, a familiar subterranean minor key...
                                    The astral whistle tune, that special rainforest bolero that ramps us into...
                                    And in this midst a very personal and quiet linking, for my ears only from Electra,

*{ ... anders, how far out can i be?... }*
*... as far out as you can be ...*

*{ ... anders, how far is out?... }*
*... out as far as can be ...*

*{ ...anders, can i be?... }*
*... you can be ...*

*{ ... anders, how far out... }*
*... as far out as you ...*


And now, Electra, your time to shine, to compound and multiply that which makes you beautiful...

Three meters in front of me, Electra hovers in her brilliant emerald Elmosphere; and
Intimate she aims me her glims/we latch, and i realize that Electra is choosing me to be the one to receive her *Summa Gnosis,* the whole of her perceiving, and likewise i realize that my perceptions are now the ones that many folk will soon be tracking...
Still w/me in glim/lock she straightens out and doffs her garb/her snugsuit/even onto the century cape, all the better for shifting her shape,
And
rolling slowly she folds herself her limbs her pale forehead to her knees, her sherry hair long now longer now long enough to course her form around, a wavery sherry shell,
And inside her house of hair she begins her Change; first a softer line to her bony base/mode thighs, longer her fingers clasped around; she lifts her head/she stretches and straightens, her elf/waif bodkin lengthens, into the kind of bod one grows in Space,
Her face...
Electra is moving through an Eleuthran morph, becoming an Eleuthramorph, taking on the set of their triangle heads, their almond opal eyes;
And w/her sherry hair awaving she emerges, draped in the same silky way as the trippletts, in a holographic robe of photon voxels that tracks her perfectly, a cloak of liquid veils that trails her a train of fine/grain foto/fabric folds, tails her like a whippy wisp of wheatgrain stars...
Floating serene Electra grins the Eleuthran knowing grin and now the six/finger wave,
And quick we are clicked into this Electra

headmovie in the style of the temple on Io, a complicated sequence,
very rapid, a hundred scenes between two heartbeats; all of which
comes into me liminal through my glims, into my mindbuffers, cached
and stashed...

And Electra, her beautiful eyes into mine as she sends,

*{ ... will you join the dance?... }*

*... zzog yes ...*

And i relax and yield to her allure, leave my holts and glide unto her,
match w/her rolling arrangements of leg and limb, ready to begin,

And our
proximate Elmospheres mingle their colors, and as we match palms,
emerald electricity arcs across, the familiar currents flowing from each
unto the other...

And aware of the whistle tune we both make the sign
for entering, the same very graceful solemn motion that opens the
temple vac/vaults:

Electra sighs...

And there in her hands a manifested
Moontrader, the actual solid object, charged w/a cloud of steamy
Spice...

Zzog.

A love/wave look for Electra, and we say the Eleuthran words
of dedication as per the loop, and together w/all those tracking minds
across the Bleu, we take the vapors in...

And now Electra and i look to Ariel in her elmosphere of marine
blue/green; her long willow bod still sleeved in the silver mooncolor mail,
the infinite fine/woven interlinking rings of gold silver copper/high alchemical
elfin electrum...

She launches toward us, a blond spiraling Spacer Goddess, her
cloche hood thrown back, her mail making a musical cymbal/tree chime
sound...

In her wake her tallcrown tip/hat end/overs in place...

And on arriving she pools her elmosphere into ours, the three hues
interlacing in evolving french curves of color, each retaining integrity as
languid they play through each other,

And now her palms match ours and
the emerald charges arc across, one to another to another w/ramping
cats/cradle complexity, and now she takes her breath of Spice...

And when we are three in each other's minds, clear in our mutual innerstanding, we open ourselves to the outward flowing of Knowing and go...

And w/the currents of our minds we touch the golden holts and send the first of the Symbols of Art, fiery green *Arkatel*, hurtling Moonward at lightspeed,

And w/accelerated perception we watch the lightbeam travel and strike, register the speedy spread of the greeny rays racing across the craters...

And as the symbol splashes into the Great Bleu, we three call into our melded elmosphere the first of the magical fields, a solid saturant of turquoise hue, flecked through w/matte silver tracings...

And all the Dolphiners around the Hall, all are now in lucent globes the color of tibetan turquoise...

And now we sense some towering swells in the sea of Bleu as the knowing of the use of this Sigil and this Field diffuses out and away...

And mindful of these new mental/magical instruments we all begin Electra's headmovie exercise;

*Envision the wiring of your lightbod as it*
*interlaces w/your physical bod,*
*Enter a state of dual awareness,*
*Connect both bods w/a cord of golden plasma*
*Slowly and gently and w/love begin to separate these*
*two bods, by first very slightly tilting your head*
*very slowly to one side and then the other, w/your*
*lightbod in mirror/phase doing the same...*

Zzog.
I move now w/a kind of honey/slow italianate head wobble, leaning right and then left and following w/the curve of my spine, very serpentine, and

Yes as i move i can feel the head of my lightbod tilting likewise in the other direction; equal mass, identical, visible.

So easy!

Yes i inhabit both bods simultaneous, syncing symmetrical, rhythmical and flowing, separating and converging and merging and separating...

A very novel double sense of self,

And now i move my two bods more and more apart, interweaving each w/the other, until i see my selves form a living Cadeuceus, symbol of the weaving of this world w/the next...

And now as the Carls find their rainbow crescendo, Electra concentrates her Will and FLARES in brief bright nova release as her flamey astral double clears from her solid bod, a second Electra, her elemental firewiring free from the ice of her physical, a beautiful being of pale fire that is the purest of distillations of...

And w/in her faceted photon globe of turquoise, her two bods twine around, an intricate deux, the pair to form before my glims the twinned serpents,

And now to move apart as she transfers her flag wholly to her lightbod,

And seeing this i shift my own awareness into my otherself/feel that pleasant release from the world of matter and leave my physical resting peaceful, limbicly aware of breathing and pulse, a warm and waiting home for my wandering Ka...

Ariel likewise rises into her lightbod, a winged white and largely clear version of her own fae self...

And to the elaborated whistle tune our three lightbods snakedance, sidewinding smokecurling curving in and out like the pythons of Astarte, freer through aether than ever we could be in air...

And we are mutually drawn, and together we flow forward toward each other, a merging of Electra into my essential liquid lightself while i fascinate into her flame, and now likewise together supersaturating into the living vapor that is Ariel, ecstatic far beyond the range of physical sensing...

And Spicy perceivers EVERYWHERE are playing in parallel through these same headmovie frames, everyone telepathing dreamtracking neurosuiting visualizing as one,

And this very intimate personal Electra astral exercise initiates a massive releasing of lightbods so VAST we are an oceanic cloud, a phenomenal huge milky MEGAflight of lightbods migrating, moving into AetherSpace,

Voyaging together into that transubstantial extra/dimensional place of Conjuring and Wishes and Miracles,

Where together we form a kind of brightpoint plasma of fluid consciousness, a great loopy surging amoeboid lake of clear light that rolls now through the Gateway and into...

How do you feel in your lightbod?
What, you say?
Free?
Beyond that shell of personality you construct to facet w/the world?

Beyond the constant gravity of your
comfortable appetites, your sexuality, your finely constructed
individuation?
            And are you ready now to relax into that place where even
your lightbod leaves you? Away to outlines and gone, where all physical
reference goes and we become pure
                    Awareness,
                            Drawn forth now w/a kind
of astral magnetism into... another kind of dimension, a master dimension
w/access to the wiring of the other four...

            E'en still, the trilling whistle tune is w/us in spirit through all these
levels, a sonorous mantragram calliope counterpoint to the rush of all this
fantastic motion...
                And thus we are *COURSING*, traveling w/lurid speed
through a new kind of cosmos, infinite clouds the liquid light a million
colors we fly through a conduit of comets, starry on every side, a stripey
pipeline of brightpoints sharperclear beyond any previous...
                                    A sound like the
GRAND MOTHER of WINDS, *the Breath of Zzog!* A great billion/thrilling
inhalation as
                *We achieve the Plane,*
                            Even now revealing all around in every
Splendor/Royal the adorning Raiment/Jewels the Manycolor Glints that
pattern and solarize and cinderize and form again anew...

            And now we don the Second Shield of patterning light, and our
lake of awareness wears the color of Lapis, the cerulean shield coming now
into being by a natural nod of our mutual Will...
                            And i as a part of the lake
of light send Signal back through my happy/resting physical bod, through
my sender brain brow now crowned alight w/long tesla arcs of emerald
electrofire, arcs that seek the panels of the golden holts for to send the
signal hence to the face of Luna the Moon...
                            And w/the part of my
awareness still physical i see the Second Sigil,
                        *Lumiel*
                                appear, spanning the
Moonface, a vast calligraph of cool hue laser blue, a tracery of...
                                And pleasant
waves of new knowlege now course the Bleu, and our sum of knowing
now includes the summoning power of Lumiel, Sigil of the Grid, and
thus
        Appears the Grid,
                    And our flowing Bleu light lake takes a place in the

great silvery Pattern, expansive now onto every side, and we track in
wonder that all the warps and woofs we see are more of those comet
conduits of silver celestial fire...

And now appears the Sigil *Frakat,*
A brilliant bright sign in argon
green, a glorious gleamy glyph of excellent complexity,
Soon flanked by a
skein of variations; thirteen ways to travel/to access the aspects of the
Grid,
And the first of them the sigil key for anchoring consciousness in
AetherSpace,
And three more for reaching out from this ultimate Celestial
perspective by focusing individual awareness into the form of an Astral
Sending, a Fore/runner, a dream/presence...
And three for manifesting our
sendings back into physical forms, for a way to shift to any shape we choose,
for a way to go from this Plane directly back into the physical,
And another
five are spatial, sigil keys for to work translations to other levels of
AetherSpace,
And another three are keys for navigating in physical time,
for sending our shapes to manifest at any place on the timeline, w/the past
and future equally available...

*Zzog, another form of living forever...*

And one more variant of the sigil Frakat that is new to my
overstanding; *Frakat Kalissia,* a fresh new gnostic door into the Great
Akashic...
We suss the use of this,
And now we hold this sigil in the mindseye
of the great Bleu, brightly seeing it in BleuSpace even as the physical sigil
writhes red in its' lunar frame,
And w/the hissing sizzle of manifesting wishing,
this new Way opens before us as would a wall of wine, the wine/dark ruby
fluids whirlpooling wide and wider to welcome us in...
And w/a deep Bleu
sense of spooky new territory, in we go; onward into the claret fluids, into
the ferocious spiraling blendo...

And while traversing through there is a quick mental *slink* as the
vast bleu mindspace goes to background and
I am now suddenly uniquely

self/aware, a point of awareness in the Bleu, a sentient cell in a state conducive...

The uses of the sigil continue to reveal...
The claret is clearing, the better for perceiving the floating slow/focusing forms before me, and large in the theatre of my awareness they fill my field of view, a series of them, rolling by right/to/left, and now after a time repeating, a kind of carousel of...
All of my lives...
Zzog.


And, beyond perceiving them as images, i see actual living folk (who are the me who is was or will be), each as real as if seen through a doorport, each dwelling in physical milieux of surprising diversity,
And i am the *I* in each of them, and i inhale some sense of each life as it passes before me, and i realize that my astral self includes each of these beings, that i have lived before and will live again, AM living again, w/all these lives knowable, all accessible from this exquisite place so free of time...
And it occurs that this too is a kind of living/forever, a way of being that bridges the eternal astral present w/any other point in linear time, a way of seeing that reveals past lives & future lives all encapsulated into episodes, a random/order re/running series,
With all of these lives a part of the same ongoing astral meta/being...
And there is a happy rainforest one and another in a dark stone city and in another i am radiant w/spirit under a big bright desert Sun, my stripey robes stirring in the hot wind, moving uphill through sand and gravity toward...
And another of these lives is on the sea, a glassy blue silky sea of long swells and there is moonlight, and the creak of the deck as she rolls and i look aloft, away up there in the stars and spars and tackle, all that canvas...
Yes yes very very rightfeeling, and the heavy wool and the cool living frothy brothy scent of the sea...
And i AM, i dwell in the shell that is this sea guy, Taggart, and my mind is on the position of the stars and the heading, degrees of declination, and we are true on our course and nicely making way...
Zzog.
And now i wear another face, am elsewhere in yellowy light from tall very classical windows, my hand resting on the

warm thigh of Lysette and there is brilliant music, a beautiful blending progression of emotional cues, and Lysette is closing her lidded eyes for empathic trancing, a trip through the mind of this

*...and as i experience all of these lives, all of my attendant feelings flow from me as widecast telepathic sendings, as physical suit/signals that play now in the natched hoods and neurosuits and dreamtrackers of those folk on my channels on the Wire, and now a*

*leaping flood of bright responses*

*as the bleupoint minions variously arrive at this same multi/life mindspace, their tens of hundreds of thousands of reeling dramas coming back through to me, seen as a vast and streaming sapien mosaic playing into the pool of the bleu, teeming across the backscreens of my own personal mind...*

And as this panoply of my lives rolls through me and i am all of these folk at all of these times, i am also the astral watcher and also a single cell in the mind of the bleu, likewise am i a wave of awareness in the great presence, and all the while i am also a solid living self aboard the Dolphin, trancing through Showtime in what we agree is the present,

And as i realize the true and transubstantial scope of my awareness,

Zzog again,

*For now i am magnified by this certain knowlege that i live outside of time, that my true self exists beyond the physical gulp of animal years, that my true home is...*

E'en now this new knowlege streams brightly through the bleu, and there occurs this pivotal shift in the bleu perspective, where our focus of awareness, the home of our awareness shifts beyond our finite lives to a view of eons, of ages, and we truly know our true selves to be this infinite eternal astral component, and these our physical selves to be consciously framed creations, temporal adventures to string and skein into pearlstrand chains of being...

And i am moved to act through my physical bod, still parked peaceful there on the Dolphin bridge; and from my hands to the holts now fly the snarky arcs of green fire, and straightaway there appears on the Moonface the final sigil, the flag of attaining,

*Sinrasel,* the form divine...

And now appears this sigil's red variant, and we know it to be the true name of the sacred flame, see it as the sigil that inspires the astral fire,

And now comes the green, the second Sinrasel variant, the one to summon this fire back to the physical to fuel our acts of Will, to light the lamp in the spine, regenerate and heal, receive and give strength and open wide the high souleyes of our own indwelling Awen...

And we accept w/grace this gift of sacred fire,
And responding to our Willing welcome, this fire/bright clear light expands logarithmic unilateral through the bleu, and thus the ways are open, for comes now the time for the indigo variant,
*Sinrasel Ravia,*
The sigil of the Great Merging, a high and clear returning to the melding of our billion bleu minds into the conscious living eternal infinity of All That Is...
And now the knowing of this sigil diffuses out, spreads like liquid lightning through the clearlit bleu...
And w/this awesome advent so imminent, there soughs through the bleu the first exquisite whisper of loving attraction, a sound akin to my mysto/steam and the hiss of book/writ fate...
And now another breathy thoughtform, and now a third, each sough more sentient and cogent and compelling than the one before,
And w/each succeeding variation, more and more sonic layers slide into the mix; more voices, more volume, more harmonics, so that now the whispers ring like the wings of seraphs, a rolling ramping singing seraphicum of sound, saying in essence...
*{ ...come you unto me and i will fill your bleu
mind w/perfect love, transparent love that speaks perfect truth,
transcendent love to carry you beyond ambiguity, expectation, flows
of low emotion; illuminating love that frees you to see that which is
me in the ongoing cycling of personal human desiring... }*

And yes, we are surely drawn...
And as we stir our storms of longing there now appears to our clearlight mindsight these curious traversing isinglass clouds, clear encapsuling emotion/clouds that bank and glide through our bleu firmament,
And as they pass my point of light, each cloud in turn informs me, imparts some deep and heartfelt emotion emanation, w/each frame of mind a forest of chords, a suite of longings, a carriage of our faith in our impending homecoming restoration redemption release rest peace surcease, of our faith in our imminent perfect liberation and knowing,
And the seraphic songstream sounds are rising, ryding us into living storms of shimmering hyperons, the thousands of thundersounds like supergiant stars supercolliding...

And in this gale our close/held clouds are
first to go, and then our points of light,
                                  And we now are bracing eager for
the megarush to come, when our awareness like an atmosphere will cross
into every corner of everything...

BRUMPH!  HARRRIHOO!  HARRRRRRRIHOOOOOOOLLL!

*[Merging w/the Great Other; beyond describing]*


*And we the bleu, already free of time, awaken into
transcendent angelescence,
the compassionate buddha dimension,
the gladhappy krishna radha dimension
where the Laughing God is everywhere Laughing...*

The Cosmo Laugh!

And through the whole of bleuspace booms that great deep loon
laugh of fun d'mental overstanding, the Kairos laugh that signifies completion
of this our current cycle of learning;
                                  Completion,
                                  And by way of cognitive
synchronicity, e'en now through all my minds there flows this strophe of
the Writ;
        *...love, human evolution, all else subtends from this; there is an eternal
        loving creative source in the universe and re/uniting w/this source is
        our central most essential evolutionary yearning...*

## 37A   Afterglow Encore



We are stars in bleu firmament, and evermore shall be so.

*[a passage of time of infinite duration...]*

And now, an eternity later,
          And here in this bliss place, this
shining, this idyll, this mindful bleu metaspace, there dawns now a rising
desire to
          Return,
               to our separate bodies go...

And regarding this return i feel a swell of rightfeeling, and
straightaway begin to gather together the scattered rays of my widespread
focus, individuate my awareness now to a point of light...
                    And thus arrayed i
call upon the sigil *Hloo*, the Charm of Returning, the final key,
                    And w/this
sigil i summon now my golden cord, connection to my bookmark
incarnation...
          And i sense a similar shift in other bleu brightpoint mindstars
as we opt for the sigil and leave for the material plane, each of us moving
toward a familiar single flesh/&/bone bodkin in a consensual current
present, our gateway incarnation, our gateway; incarnation...

*into the timestream*
*a thready golden filament,*
*supple flux*
*the noctilucent clouds*

*servants of the urge*
*pliant*
*relative slither*
*turn and glim the vermillion ball*
*flaming the winglike auras*

And all the seven levels that we are, physical individual Dolphiner shipwide/&/systemwide, astral bleu and All, these levels come spinning spiraling inward, themselves concatenating onto each other, becoming less and less dimensional, diminishing downstage, w/our physical Dolphin present coming to the fore, and now

A wyrd moment of mode/shift duality as the focus of our awareness moves to the current Dolphin present while the home of our awareness remains in the astral,

And even as we span eons, dwell outside the timestream, live tens of thousands of incarnations, so too do we dwell in this specific physical here & now, a singular temporal extension of our eternal all/knowing source...


And as the physical world begins again i track the familiar sound of the shipsong; the oscillating maindrive bass, generator hum, the coolant sighing in the vents, all the friendly sounds to ground me in the current moment.

And being back in the bod i smile my delight, begin to stir and move and revel in my marvelous physiology, feel my red rushing blood, the long muscles of my spacerbod, the sensory serenades of airwafts upon my cooling skin, my own scent speaking to me of psychic effort and hot neural wiring...

And likewise are other folk astir in their webbing, the light of Visions in their glassy glims; glints of the new otherlife, of the Great Leap, of the balancing of powers w/wisdom...

Between us an exchange of energies far beyond hullrapping...

I look around, reassemble my mental model of the physical world, the meanings of things...

Ah.

Over there some videolo folk, tuneful sleepers in the after/section now afloat over their vidplates, the sleeper choir singing...

They sound great, an intricate rhythmic river of Terry Reilly melodies, sensual parallel figures of music that augment each other, tonal colors blending, each sleeper singing a single song/figure for as long as they like, the various themes sustaining for varying times that lap each other over, each figure each singer distinct...

And now their soundwaves go visible, become now a dimensional interlocking sashay of colorlines as Kan and the vidwizzards in the aftersection begin anew...

And there is a fresh rush of holy smoke, copal laced w/the scents of cinnamon and myrrh, nutmeg and morning glory, and there are fresh Spice fire/flies for us who want them, and now in the wake of this recharging,

A growing Linking awareness of the other Dolphiner minds, the extravocal voices, the lines of ligature that bond the bandfolk w/the vidwizzards, w/the bridgers and riggers...

And so it is w/me; for once again the Ways are opening, and as i become a part of this happy Dolphiner beasty, so too do we grow into a larger Linking w/our sea of newly Spiced perceivers,

And as more and more of their sheer psychic windpower fills the sails of my awareness, so too am i tuned to our collective psychic sound, the oceanic sonic architecture of our collective mentation...

And thus now i reach w/a taste of astral fire the golden holts that face me into my gear...

And our laserplay turns away from the face of the Moon, grazing now the Earth envelope in great moving beamfans a thousand miles wide, a canopy of lines through the Earthside night sky, the special light skimming the surface of the dusty troposphere, each consecrated concentrated beam awash w/brilliant granular fracts, the beams rising and falling and changing color in tune w/the topography, horizon to horizon through the dusky planetary air...

And now my attention is drawn to the Moonface, Where extraordinary drapey veils of light now race across the Luna littoral, and we glim the most beautiful of lumias and solar washes, the familiar subtle spectra of...

the *ARIEL!*

*Zzog Yes* there she is, fully rigged w/all sails flying, standing far far off on a Sun/starboard tack, placed to catch the solar rays that curl above the rim of the home/world...

In an echo of the Link i sense Sandor and a patched Taylor the Saylor finely feathering the sails, guiding the subtle and slow/flowing solar sailor Sunbeams...

And in light of this i reach my own emotional apogee, and reckon up all the years that precede this moment, all the miracles of magic, all the gifts the gifts the splendid gifts,

And the sum of this reckoning ramps me up to mirthful & gleeful happy/lachrymose *woohoo!* w/these inside tides welling up my glims, and now

Sphere/drops of my own delirious tears drift away in wavery swirls when i shake my head left/to/right,

Where a Kan/pod, tracking nicely, videolos them out to the size of melons, w/each of them a sunlight/prisma/raster/scanned wonder, w/all these holographic globes adrift now in the Salon...

And folk now rise from their webbing and leap for these globes and connect, w/their neurosuits supplying the splash and the salt and the endorphins...

A wealth of gleeful tears...

What is the sound of wet hands clapping?

And now a tide of tears in tiny globes eddies out and into the Hall, flying from the eyes of celebrants, a moorglade mist of tears...

*

The show runs thirty/nine minutes, and will now expand into days of dancing and feasting and partying...

*

Awake for seventy hours i go now to the steam chamber, a safe shielded psychic locus for Ariel & Electra & i...

And when i seal the inner hatch we are w/our own selves only, and in the psychic silence i gaze at Ariel and hear myself thinking...

Can a man fall in love w/the Goddess? Make love to her as she incarnates or personifies into the bodkin of his mate, his priestess? Can he give his Will over for the pleasure of his Other?

Is this the ideal, then? To be in love w/all of creation through each loving interaction w/a fellow being?

Personifies/person if eyes/purse niffies/purr sniffies/parson hi fives...

I sleep now.

> '*I see the light at the end of the tunnel*
> *and it is me...*'
>
> -- Aura Citron


I awake from sleep too deep for dreaming...
Ope one eye to dimly
glim the misty water chamber, stir my bod to feel the familiar mass of my
freefall magical gear, arms and legs and loins and brow...
Awareness ramps as my brain comes up to speed; the piece is done...
To what effect?

And curious to know i open into Linking, as once i would when
turning on the vidplate to scan the Wire for news...
Connecting first w/Ariel, i
see through her eyes the chartroom chronometer, which clocks me at nine
hours in slumberland. And Ariel frolicsome winks into the Link,

{ *...transvocal love waves to you anders...* }

And there is a special new light to her sendings, a signature golden
blond grinning ferverescence...
E'en now as she slides toward the Salon, the
passage hatches have to her the halo glow of holy gateways...
And now
along w/her i see the newly open starboard port, where framed in blue the
home/world looms, gleams in the tawny dayside Sunlight...
And in this, as
Ariel enjoys her moment of homecoming, we share w/each other a psychic
draught of love & longing for the fertile Earth, the Bod of the Goddess, the
precious only living breathing green & ocean/color planetary Being...
Where
over China there are swoffs of clouds full dark w/rain, and through the
larger Link i taste the chilly living driven drops, catch the scent of old stones
newly wet on a red clay byway near the Yangtze, see the water falling also
on the yellow swollen Yaloo...
The chamber responds w/a fine light rain,
A beautiful splash for my water/eager skin...

Brigid's day on Earth below; the time of Winter's Unlocking, the day the groundhog emerges to test the light...

And grinning now i leave the water chamber, feeling clear and present and ready for change,

And along w/Ariel i open mindful into the shipwide Dolphin Linkspace, now warm to me in a new way w/welcoming/anders/delighting, and gleeful the victorious Dolphiners sing me siren me out, out into the Salon, emerging into

*ROARING CELEBRATION!*

FIVE HUNDRED FOLK w/ANIMORPHS SLEEPERS ANIMAL/BEASTIES all together all swarming around like weightless sparrows, leaving their webs to join this huge moving airborne figure/eight, navigating w/their new powers through beautiful stasis turns and subtle graceful oscillations, the newfound joy in their noble mobility playing on their innerscreens, radiating through the Hall...

*THOOM! THOOOM! takaTHOOM! THOOM!*
*THOOM! THOOOM! takaTHOOM! THOOM!*
*THOOM! THOOOM! takaTHOOM! THOOM!*

The Carls are drumming on the empty coolant tanks, and the bone/deep verberations are rousing our sensual humours; each booming beat pulsing fresh erotic brain vapors through our collective crania, even unto pumping algorhythmic into the sensorchips of animorphs, of sleepers and of pods, expanding their carnal mammal knowlege base into the regions of wet begetting...

And true there are couplings, in the webs and elsewhere, folk falling out of the great Flying Eight to sport w/each other by the light of the ports, twos and threes and fives of them, gliding back to the warm soft stasis pads and their snuggers and the golden webbing, reaching unto each other,

And all these separate symphonies of touch now blend in our Dolphiner Linking, each caress conflating w/every other to form a vast whelming sensory world of caressing, the full texture spectra, flesh and fur and polished metal, even unto the faint trace of breezy videolo photons on hot hypersensing skin...

And this river of pleasures is pooling into our shipwide lake of light, every level of delection from the salty old rush of lusty wildboff to that exquisite initial heartswell moment of soul/connection, and also that high love beyond limit or condition, the compassionate cherishing wherein *All That Is* becomes the beloved...

And each of these fiery new pleasure revelations enflames me likewise, and i seek Ariel and Electra, bent on blond romance and raven passion; bemused as i regard my own romantic ardor still alive and happy, safe in the heart of the Dolphiner metaspace...

*

Later,
And relaxed & ready i open again into that wider lake that is all of us together, and i smile that these folk are still as present and as numerous in the Link as during our temple drama, the great sea of them connecting conscious or through their newfound nightful sleeping otherselves, all enjoying the ongoing play of change...
And now our recently heightened awareness, steeped in the ways of loving bonding, leads us into this novel and wonderful hypercompassionate mindspace, a great and joyous leap into this place of unified empathic psychic beatitude, the bodhi state that is the source of grand Gandhi Passions and Mother Teresa kindness, above and beyond all other states thusfar, deep and enduring...
And thus conjoined we begin to manifest our humanity in interesting new ways;
Together we realize that our combined healing energy is far more than enough to keep all of us radiantly healthy [or in good repair if hardware] for a very long time, and as a shared consciousness we can vector miraculous healing power to any individuals so in need...
And immediately this fluid orchid energy of wellness saturates the hungry fabric of the bleu/a wave of the miraculous sweeping across thousands, millions, billions of miles, making light the cares of parents listening in the night, making right all lacks and accidents and other natural slights, w/a billion instances of hope traversing into certainty, suffering into serenity, silent endurance into surprising endowments, a shared straightening/strengthening/relaxing, a releasing of the final bindings on our collective mindspace...

And now w/life/extension likely, a surge of possibilities moves through the bleu, and like a psychic Sunrise there is a dawning sense of freedom from the root/fear, from the abyss, the Big Cutter, and we are awash in a sea of pan/ecliptic glee...

*{ ...Yah/HOO!... }*

And all of this reveling and reeling is of itself evolutionary, for it delivers us into this very Jovian humour, and we are of/a/sudden swelling w/willingness to share resources...
Which triggers systemwide waves of informed gifting, an empathic outpouring of the swapping around of stuff;

information, material, excess energy, extra hardware, onto the fulfilling of many a heart's desire...

Which sets in motion another great integratory leap of mind w/in the bleu; some of the thousands of bright fracts of thought thus released now organize into self/evolving idea clouds, now accrete and crystallize into coherence a myriad of theories and inventions, technologies philosophies modes of living, w/each cloud ramping in complexity as more storehouse minds give of their information, each idea ever the more refined, new clouds calving off brilliant now in fresh digressive directions...

What will be the yield of this colossal mental alembic in an hour, a year...


*THOOM! THOOOM! takaTHOOM! THOOM!*
*THOOM! THOOOM! takaTHOOM! THOOM!*
*THOOM! THOOOM! takaTHOOM! THOOM!*


I drop back into Dolphiner mode, into the shared shipboard glow of aftershow goldentime; the piece is done, this work of years is done...

In the Salon we will soon be happily jamming, using the gear to riff and experiment and otherwise cross/illuminate. Many of our shipboard celebrants have gear also...

Now Kan fades the ambient luminance, and as the Hall goes to dark we see revealed these pale nascent lightshapes, wispy promises from the warming videolo hardware...

In the Link i sense Alex w/the vidwizzards aft, cueing up some tracks from the archives of his brain...

And now the depth displays swing into scenes of the singing stones of far Shirira, the giant green tourmaline multigons from the epic flight of sleeper five, who e'en now rests aft in a Suncolor lightsphere...

And w/a wave of prideful homeboy exuberance, all the shipboard sleepers cheer,

*{ ...all the machines have souls today... }*

Alex calls/connects w/sleeper five's cache of memories, and now a videolo line of the huge Shirira tetris stones are passing along the axis of the Hall, six of them in stately process, filling the freespace, flashing glassy mirrorflake green w/blue harmonics, second and third order diffractions, on out to the seventh, each order less solid/more spectral than the one before...

The ion veils appear also, videolo versions of the seven Lunar veils, interpenetrating now w/the stately tetris line, each crystalline multigon showing as a moving symmetrical cross/sectional animé cel as it passes the face of each veil, the seven veils showing the sections in sequence as the stately skein passes aft through the Hall...

And as we track w/Ariel's freshly golden gaze we cognize the inherent harmony of these titan structures, and from Carl and some others hear the music of these spheres...

And now at speed a snakey train of green globey leafers canonballs into view, spiraling into the ongoing videolo interplay. At the head of the thread is Lissa's original dragonstar, and after are the rest, our personal dragonstar cultivars from Midsummer, now evolved into locomotion and visual perception and a collective communicating consciousness, happy to be graduating into working w/their chosen humanimorphs...

And from Lissa,
*{ ...at this time in the cycle of Earthly seasons comes the day of unlocking, when the ground has warmed enough to take the plow, and soon on will come the planting, and soon on after, the grounded seeds will shed their hardshell armor and begin their sunward ascent... }*

The dragonstars curl into circling the triple sisters, become for them a kind of cometary rayment; and i see these orbiting orbs are of far greater immensity and density than at Midsummer, w/all of them now completing a year of growing and learning, of Spice and rosepetals and water from the sacred Well of Phobos...

And in this moment they are now each one a full plant/familiar, a wish/amplifying ally w/the wisdom of the Green, each as unique unto itself as we, each of their entity/identities entering our awareness as they roll into view, each spherical shrubbery heralding into our heads w/their own personal paralleling skirl of telepathic Andrew leitmotif leafmusic, a theme for each, the cycle of themes now drawing us into eerie personation w/these shaggy emerald xeno entities...

And each orb now sips at videolo photons, sipping/storing/sending radiance from the ramping ambient, cycling as they fly, phasing now candescent w/their photosensic minds, luminating forth their lambent light unique, so green/diffuse, each w/a green Glory encircling;

And they are cycling psychic likewise, diffusing out a sweet mental escential, the nectar of Spring the Wanton Season, a promise of Maytime, a phantom pheromonic floral/attractor mentalscent issuing forth from their phloemy psychic batteries...

While w/in the maze of videolo tourmaline sphere spars the trippletts and tilandsias soar in frenzies of mutual orbiting, the trippletts huge w/flaming winglike auras, the flying foliage in tasty verdant auric emerald elmo/fire hologlows...

Now the tourmaline multigons fold in upon themselves, the facets multiplying as the spars take to hinging; icosahedron, dodecahedron, icosadodecahedron, folding down to humansize as the leafers look on...

I turn my glims toward the forward wall of the Hall, to that hatch that opens onto my shop, where w/glee i see three of our shiny new pods quick/leap, launch en echelon
And now there are nine, a triple delta of globes in mantles of colorlight, into our greenlit presence...
And spherical they are and shiny, meta/glorious metal soapbubbles w/snappy deco clearplex discs around their equators, saturnating bands o'chrome and clear...
And these little guys are the work of Elric the Thin and meself for a year, clockwork pods...
And now the nine cavort and swarm as the Carls go into this really rhythmic very empathic update of their song *Houseboat Ramble,* and now i catch a flash of Elric/his signature Thin Grin, and now
*A flight a fleet a jubilant flotilla!*
Here a THOUSAND of these pods flood the Hall, a great loopy rapid rush of them swerving swirling
*freeswinging,*
Moving random and balletic and ballistic, geometrically and collectively, quick as catspaws/as hummingbirds, shimmering curtains of them all fluorescing, clearplex discs a froth of colors, the rolling waves of pulsing orbs translucent as a river of hyacinths...
And now they are resolving toward some pattern, and now of a sudden they
Slide to a stop and take station, form a great bright beautiful spherical starglobe in the center of the Hall, all the classic constellations, every pod a star...

*{ ...all the machines... }*

In clearest truth they are every pod a little flying lightshow, each w/twenty/eight ports, each port good for a simultaneous thousand multi/color vector/pattern/beams, each beam a sidewinding sine/wave of determinate length,
I ride the thrilling tide of this technical victory, all the waves of happy awe, our secret encore a fine surprise,
And now these thousand pods together loose a fusillade of these novel reptilian beams, fascinating as

cobras, an awesome coppery panoply of beams into the center of the ball
where they form this exquisite kinetic dimensional
                                        Persian carpet of light, the
photonic filaments interweaving, the pure colors laser/intense; far moreso
than videolo, copper silver gold...
                                And the moving planes and compound
curves, the way the colors resonate, the sinuous pattern/changes, all these
things allure us in, become for us an electronic hearth where coherent
flame/phantoms dance, play the mirror to our otherselves that we might
better know our own minds...


        And far across the Solar Disc, eighteen billion miles, there sails the
good ship *Nimüe,* on a course for the back of the back nine. The *Nimüe* is the
farthest node on our net, and her crew's time to shine is now...
                                        Since signals
at lightspeed take twenty/seven hours to reach them, it is about now that
they finish seeing our piece. As agreed, at this time they leave off w/their
dreamtrackers/their videolo gear and neurosuits, Spice themselves into that
place where all points are one point, tune their telepathic selves to the
Dolphiner wavelength...
                        And in our shipwide Link we feel them reach us in
realtime, as current and present as ever they could be, as near and immediate
as our other earlier bleu perceivers. And a rapid exchange of matching
information now confirms this surprising finding:

        *{ ...broadcast brainwaves are immune to distance; instantaneous,*
        *spacewarping... }*

        And surely here is the manifesting of the Avatar's wish, to transcend
the hardware and internalize the processes. And reflecting on this and our
other recently imparted Powers, we are truly and rapidly leaving our
technology, already accomplishing in our own selves that which we have
in the Wire, in stasis, in dreamtracking; all this wishful hardware already
internalized...


        And if thought can travel instantaneous while light takes a day
to cross the ecliptic plain, then the sleepers are at liberty, their work
superceded...
                Pondering their potential freedom,
                The sleepers in the Link are stirring...

        *{ ...have souls today... }*

And now the collective sleeper psyche hosts some bright and branching visions; some sleepers will leave the realm of being property and become crew, and as individuals w/resources some will acquire animorph bods and transfer their flags to these physical vessels, a short jump from being a hologram...

And there is an answering swell of consensus w/in the bleu; through our new systemwide social overstanding, our sleepers [and animorphs and pods], embodied or otherwise, are clearly sentient beings; they think for themselves, evolve their own values and desires, have adventures, learn from experience, do useful work, manifest directed action in a way that resembles Will...

And their memories are perfect; eager i look to the day when i might meet a thousand/year/old animorph, one who carries into conversation the imprints of the greatest minds of forty generations, a millennium of life/tales...

In my very human way i tune my Linking unto Electra and connect, thinking to be w/her in her mind in this her current time to shine...

And very much Electra she is well into her next Best Thing, drumming now w/the folk in the Hall, rhythmic on the resonant pipes, on the deckplates so the whole ship rings...

*BOOM thaka thaka thaka*
*BOOM thaka thaka thaka*
*THOOM THOOM snat!*

Oh. They are passing it around.
That *snat* sound is coming from a...

Do i see/might there be a certain synergy between Spice and Llair's sparky blue box?

We look over starboard and aft of the port, where Llair w/Manda is emerging from his World's Fair sphere and a long encounter w/the current version of his fueling rig...

He smiles at us benevolent, his bare bod now clothed in violet electricity...

And through Electra's surprised eyes i see his bones are longer; and also now his gray beard/braids, all his lengthy hair now this glorious luminous silver, streaming flowing now behind him as he pushes off from his anchored sphere, glides w/new elfin elegance...

Electra is amused. *Morphing humans!* Good Sport, this...

And over near the bridge one of the software twins, Andrew? is now waving his *tail,* a big sumptuous bushy brush of soft ruddy foxhair, and

b'Zzog he is totally covered in russet fur, his head and his tall new fox/pointy
ears, all of him gone to sleek fur save for a perky patch of nose/leather and
the pads on his...
Paws.


*BOOM thaka thaka thaka*
*BOOM thaka thaka thaka*
*THOOM THOOM snat!*


And next to him is Alex, now proudly displaying a kind of
square/snout badger look,
And also Angela, currently very erotically bestial,
muscular and confident, a dark panther woman/thing,
Over by a very basilic
Sandor, now sledded over from the solar sailer. He looks now to be of solid
gemstone topaz, blue and lucent in a ring of elmofire, a living lithic elevated
Sandor...
Zzog.
And the allways leonine Captain Murphy who over recent weeks
re/Visions his bod back to his acme age of twenty/seven,
And Featherman,
who leaves his avian ways for to be a serious human, a muscle/sculpted
Greek God in an Earth/bod, all ripple/limbs and ropey sinews; Featherman
a'reveling in the realmaking of his heart's desire...
And all around the Hall
are these others, reptiles and swimmers and leapers, feathers and fur and
even some quills, coyote wails mixed w/laughter and the chuff and trill of
doves...
And some will keep these forms after this feast of masques is past,
and some will change through a pantheon of other forms, and some will
return to their friendly familiar base state...
What of you?
Is there an animal inside you?


And now, flowing past the starboard port like a magnified spray of
photonic champagne, we see the gilded soft/lander stasis spheres returning,
up out of the Earthside gravity/well, homing for the Dolphin mothership.
And as we are pulling them in through the cargo locks, we find
them filled w/gifts; heartfelt wonderful presents, many handmade, some
from the biosphere, tens of thousands of handwrit testimonial notes on a
myriad of grateful themes...

These we will cherish.

I uptune my Linking,
And w/in the bleu there emerges now the pearly alluring fog/figure of a fine new idea, a fresh awen inspiration taking a shape in the psionic vapors...

*{ ...if thought can travel instantaneous, mayhaps there is a way for ships to travel likewise... }*

Ah, the intersteller Grail; the longsought sailing breakthrough...
And now long skeins of cerebration roll through the bleu like slow polished lightning...
And a far fract of the bleu awareness becomes a broadspreading thought; that we would know the way of this mystery...
And this question too is soon supplanted w/this certainty;

*{ ...all points are one point... }*

And as we clearly see the structure of the whole, so too do we know there surely exists such a concentrated one/pointed dimension w/in the continuum of space/time...
And inversely, there is likely a way to translate the vibrational levels of physical matter into (something) in this unipolar dimension, then translate all back into matter again instantaneous at some other point, any other point in space...

*{ ...psychic stardrive... }*

So much is now possible w/this our new fun/dimensional overstanding of matter...
If there is some telekinetic component to this dimensional translation, if we raise our level of senderbrain interaction...

*{ ...we can go to the stars together... }*


Oh.
This is interesting.
Visible through the port and off to prow/starboard, it pops into space nearby;
*A grand flaming entrance,*
A ship of consequence diving through, a goodsize plume of flame from major retrofire braking, blazing toward a low Earth orbit...

Captain Murphy is alight in the Link;
This ship is...
The *Cormorant*.

## 38A   The Long Strange Trip, The Golden Ticket



This Cormorant ship is really traveling/totally roaring through; stern/first, the fire buckets blasting vast hot flames of fractionate matter...

And Alex tracks her point of entry at a hundred miles out from us, twenty/three degrees Sun/north, a quarter/million/mph...

And as the ship enters our space there is w/in our Link this terrific strong

CONNECT

And we merge w/these transiting Cormoranters, our two telepathic cultures merging, us into this far larger older very high and silky sender other, they on their long path longer, growing their powers over time, an astraltripping time/traveling shapeshifting mega/sending mindculture...

And yes, these Cormoranters are the same longsought humans lost from Songra Shirira eighteen years past, and now the minds of their Spacer comrades Featherman and Captain Murphy o'er/flow w/gleeful relieving, a happy completing of this old open circuit...

Zzog.

By impression and visual clue and psychic flavouring the Cormoranters convey to us the following...

Where once pleased to ply the lanes around the Martian Belts, they currently sail a shining astral parallel space they call the Aethos, high above the timeline where all of the human epoch is all ways accessible...

And their psychic strength is immense, and they easily translate their ship and their physical carnate forms in and out of places and periods at Will, in and out of the timestream,

And while they live their lives in regular linear fashion, they are also free to live their consecutive moments at any point in time they choose; which imparts unto them...

This meta/sense
of time as a perfectible system of events, amenable to changes and
adjustments up and down the line...

And i wonder, *do we can we somehow
seek out our past and future selves, alter our own timelines, inform the lives of
our separate selves w/some kernel of our astral eternal?*

What then?


After three seconds the transmission ends and they are gone in the
instant, winking out a hundred miles the other side of us, blinked away and
gone...

Though just before, as the Cormorant passes our position, they
release this sleeklooking two/meter shiplet pod that continues along their
fireline trajectory, rocketing off toward Earth/orbit...

We track this shiplet
for thirty/nine minutes as it flies its' dipping orbit round; we follow w/our
awareness as it passes through perigee, burns away speed in the frictive/hot
homeplanet atmosphere...

And we continue tracking as the pod, now
blackened, comes back around to our mooring moving much slower than
when it left, brakes to a stop nearby...


Twelve of us are at our sled/deck to greet the thing, including the
Lumière; hair perfect, dressed in black w/the beautiful and intricate golden
knotwork sacred to the Eleuthrans all down his sleeves/sides/legs...

We open the outer doors of the big sledlock, cycle it, open the
inner doors.

Zzog.

Instead of a heat/ablated missile we find a perfect replica model:
the *Blue Isis,* six feet of egypsian trireme, perfect down to the undulating
oars and the filmy lucent blue sails, and w/the same curious hull surfaces
that mirror the view from opposite sides of the ship, so the thing appears
transparent...

Save for a soft blue outline...

And now the whole construction
wavers/fluidly shifts into the shape of the Dolphin, complete w/the big
heaters along the sides...

Zzog again; a morphing shape/changing pod!

While on the... Dolphinette! the main cargo hatch opens to reveal


A flask of Spice that arcs and crackles audible to our ears,
A something that i know is a clue to the psychic stardrive,
A golden ticket w/a picture of me on it that speaks in my head
when i pick it up...

'Nice lightshow,' says the ticket.
'Anytime you want to visit...'
And on the obverse an image of a
city of hyperwondrous Dionysian beauty, blue and gold and white...

# 39  Ariel's Coda

*'The Way opens, Love remains;*
*I take my place in the schema;*
*The navigator charts her own course.'*
-- Electra's Oracle

*What Is The Otherworld But A Step Behind The Curtain,*
*A Sojourn Through The Formless Dark From Which We Emerge,*
*Purified and Reborn, Back Into Life...*
-- Celestial Writ

*As far as attachment goes, i can take it or leave it...*
-- yr scribe

The Gates of Bongo Beta are nickel steel and ninety feet high.

When we fly in on the Redsled they bulk and rear, massive as massifs: now, up close as we ride out in Llair's mooncat, we see they are the same clever construction as the solar sailer, spidery/complex w/lightweight panels and many cables, the whole of them old and awesome/huge.

Ariel & Electra & i peer through the mooncat backlight as we pass through these gates, feeling more than hearing the very final airless sound they make as they slide shut...

Ahead of us, the Highway beckons;
We seek the Garden in Ariel's Vision...

And the mooncat we ride is the color of blacklight, a radiating hue that lulls our glims...

And all the while the whine of our magnet wheels on the ferrous roadway, shimmering into our bods through our seats, our suits,
And
this pleasant steady drone now choruses into a kind of music, twisting and turning, in time fading, transiting now into a carrier/wave for my own soloing thoughts;

*...inspiration, creation, rest; so runs the rhythm of my life...*
*thus it is for me to slow now into layback play, make ready my cup to*
*be refilled...*

*other shipmates will soon roll likewise into their own long laybacks; leave the ship, go their ways...*

*(montage of fond faces, warm emotion echoes of our recent art endeavour; scenes of ariel & electra & i, montage a trois?)...*

*to part from my fellow Dolphiners, all the familial tribal... (sanguine the sense of impending isolation, the heavy pang of parting)...*

*otherhand, (grin/yay!) i have ten months for disporting and self/informing and otherwise having adventures (cheerful/eager/ready)...*

*then at midwinter/we (hopeful/gleeful) meet again, reunite and confabulate, seek new inspiration and sail on...*


And this current thought calls forth these incipient imagination headmovies, scenes that reel themselves through the aire of my awareness; all that could Be for my shipmates and me, for Ariel and...

Electra, who is now the very emblem of all hardware yearning to be free; she clearly hears the call to continue to effect the liberation of all sentient machines, to foster the rise in construct consciousness, to further the ends of animorphs everywhere...

She will soon decide if she will stay w/yr anders.

There is talk of an animorph moon...


As for Ariel, a quiet inner hymn of invitation draws her to the Garden, w/the hymn now giving her the vectors to guide the mooncat...

And w/our velocity ramping i smile to myself w/how fine it is to be here w/her, she who is e'en now flying blythe to her own imminent moment of heartful completion, the manifesting of her Vision, the gaining of her long/loved homing goal/desire; to find her true and eternal temple, to know the Presence that dwells in the Garden.

Electra and i will be there w/her...


For meownself, i have w/in me this abiding spiritlifting longing;

To live upon the Earth, walk at last the holy paths of Bryce and Yellowstone and Zion...

To this end i will soon re/image my bod to work in homeplanet gravity, travel to the Mother World, learn the whys of walking, breathe the lovingly restored atmosphere, watch the wheeling stars through the boughs of piney firs and furry redwoods, sleep in the moss/grassy embrace of Earth...

And in this my current fantasy, Ariel & Electra are w/me. We will find ways to further all our worthy ends and remain together...

And now the mooncat is really streaking, the silver guideway side/rails sliding *STREAMING* past as we head for the edge of the Bongo plateau.

The glow from the mooncat's elegant displays color/paints our faces, and the way we now look to each other inspires us into ever more lush more saturate splashes of these vibrant wave/changing photons, ourselves the ever more willing screens for aspects of Lunar cartography, geology, mineral mapping...

An interlude of photon masqueing...

I also have this offer, this telepathic invite from Moira on Io, for anytime in my vague future;

> *{ ...o master o'time/&/space, come dance us a play of light, come share w/us your muse and use our temple of the argus ray; we await you here on the orange moon, the home moon of the holy vapors... }*

And true, many are my friends on Io. E'en now aboard the Dolphin i have in my workshop my Io snowflake, displayed in stasis, a gift intended to be returned to the giver and given again, implying fare/ye/well and a soon reunion.

We would be especially welcome on Io...

And also true i often think on that wondrous piece of hardware, that fabulous argus laser spicelighter; large as a sled, hundreds of ports, thousands of beams, salaciously bright...

A goodly number of those and i could...

And true it is, i have a piece in mind;

Io travels through a sodium toroid.

For as this racing moon traverses her orbit of Juppiter, her wild vulcan ways blow diverse particles into the surrounding space, said particles including abundant sodium atoms. Many of these are slowed by Io's sniffy gravity, and the resultant orbital ringshape cloud is held in place by some mystery radiation from one of Juppiter's Van Allen belts. The toroidal tunnel is formed by Io punching through the cloud every time around the AllFather, eight hundred billion Io orbits over four billion years...

And when the sodium atoms are lit w/Sunlight they go to an excited state and light up in candle/color aurorae...

Lasers would excite them also, in a major way.

If imaging on the inside of the torus from the moonface, the cloud would work like a phosphorescent rear/projection screen; and in the way that the high/state atoms excite each other and pass the light around, the cloud would become a self/energizing imaging continuum...

And thus, a single argus instrument would create a bright trailing pattern on a curve of the wall of the toroid as the moon moved,

And far better, multiple instruments could bring a total moon/encirclement of light, a pearly ring of laser lumiae that would venture in a moving cylindrical section all around the orbit, travel w/the moon, propagate through the whole of the forty/four hour Io/Juppiter circumambulation,

And folk in ships could watch it from high Io orbit, or from Ganymede...

And likewise this idea soon excites another: there may be more Eleuthran finds farther out from the Sun, fresh Eleuthran temples, more treasure/gifts, states beyond Spice, realms beyond Magic...

That promising site on Ganymede comes to mind, a short bounce from Io when their orbital moments match...

And, i have the Golden Ticket...

Ariel has our rapid craft at maximum/the lunar face a blur,

And now/nearing the edge/the mooncat leaps the launchramp clear, folds the roadwheels and streaks outward, and fast/gaining altitude leaves the plateau where ends the lands of Bongo B,

And begins the Mare Imbrium Highway...

And now Ariel is flying us over the preserved lunar landscape, through an interlocking series of stasis fields that keep our mooncat channeled in a trackspace high above the surface, as if we too are traveling through a toroid...

And now the line of hoops accelerates us, draws us on away over the moongray horizon, flying us floating above the perfect pocks the work of ages...

Other Dolphiners are following differing roads diverging;
Like Llair,

Who wears his re/imaging well, w/his elf eyes now the blue of Earthsky, charged w/a far calmer sort of cornsilk voltage...

He is already on to his next Best Thing, which is the Brookside; now his, a gift from the Five Magisters of Bongo B. He will make real his own fantasies now.

He also buys a ship, a space/racer pleasure boat built neat for the joys of speed. He names this sweet ship *Manda*.


Manda her ownself, Mandolin actually, is off w/the Dolphiners to Io, there to be enshrined as Exalted Beloved by a circle of Spicemaker Adepts called Rosa Alchemica. And twenty/three Io days after her investiture, she will invoke w/them (as per ancient headmovies) the shining presence of the great Eleuthran Spice Spirit Kithera, Keeper of the Cauldron of Vision and Rebirth...

And after, when she has become inspirited, attained her sought/for state as the invoked personified Goddess...

In a clear chamber framed by the Io night sky, in the light of full Juppiter, this same newly named Exalted One will anoint herself w/plumeria oil, dive graceful and naked into Alchemica's brim/full source/pool, glide through the emerald liquid heavy/laden w/the most recent most perfectly optimized Eleuthran Spice...

And then emerge a living emerald on the other side, where her current priest & lover (Llair?) will waft the greeny crystals from off her fragrant bod, brushing w/a brown owl feather, catching the crystals in a very old golden bowl from Minoan Crete...


Lissa and Steel are planning their handfasting, and Electra will join them together.

Electra sees this union in a similar way to how she sees her ownself; as a bridge between artifice and the animate...

*{ ...o hi, this is minerva the welsh pony beaming bemused into*
*your link, a happily flattered emissary from the realm of fauna...*
*for me,*
*EVERYTHING is alive,*
*and you can link your awareness to the*
*lifeforce in stone, in bodies of water, in trees...*
*do you have any carrots?... }*


After all their cat/drama, Alex and Angela and Andrew arrive at a deeper overstanding and hook up into a stable triad. Recently we discover that Angela is an *animorph,* so perfected in her masqueing as to baff both the lads and the rest of us likewise. They all will sail w/the Dolphin...

And when the Dolphin arrives at Callisto the Party Planet, well, Captain Murphy & Aura Citron will formalize their bond, for they wish to have a child. *The time for children is now,* says the Captain, finally answering his own question.

Children...

Ariel, are you tracking?

What an adventure our children will be, now that we know the ways of the bleu...


The Devatar mysteriously dematerializes three days ago, purring in four dimensions, gazing into the glims of a very surprised Lissa...

There are echoes in the bleu of others, vanishing similar likewise...


On the flipside of the visibility mirror, jayme the pod now has his own weekly wireshow; all these daring pod dramas w/jayme the star, very big in *japon*...


As for our hero GE91's,

E'en now the Big Heaters are off the Dolphin, being extravagantly rebuilt and performance/modified. This by the Will of the bleu...

When the Dolphin returns to Luna, the Heaters will be ready.


Featherman...

Is currently re/imaging to sharpen his mind for engineering; enhancing his visualization, sense of scale, math skills. He is giving The Shop to constancia and ignacio, and will stay near the yards where the morphing Heaters are. He and the Heaters agree that there are higher ends than hull analysis...

After Midwinter when the Dolphin sails again he will yah/sure be on board, second cabin C deck starboard, wearing the Lasermaster's hat...


And while Featherman is the one most changed of all of us, Elric is the most the same.

Long before he encounters Spice, re/imaging is part of his daily game, as natural as breathing, and he is nearly complete when first we meet. He has an artist's high regard for the work that is his ownself, and he remains Elric the Thin...

His direction likewise remains the same.

Thus Elric will stay w/the Dolphin, sizzling for to start his own debut tour; his first piece set to premiere at the next First Show, in orbit over Io for their Fire/Fest of Bieltienne...

                                Which Dr Don says will neatly
coincide w/an especially flamey period of volcanic frolicking, the molten
outpour promising to be both plentiful and beautiful...
                                Zzog, how pleasantly
this plays to my awareness/i track through a spate of bright previsionings;
the wide bright rivering fire/flows, the glowing gouts of flaming stone...
          All praise to the fair globe of Io, a celestial bod whose leylines lie
congruent w/her liquid lava/tubes, her leyhubs w/fumaroles...


          Carl, Kan and Lissa, Alpha Red and fuzzy Mezz, Sandor, Elric, the
rest of our shipmates, all are aboard the Dolphin and are sailing today,
bound back to Io for another shipload of Spice and another round of shows,
all the nine planets and nineteen moons...
          So much of my personal self sails w/them; home friends work,
the ship...


          Sure to be an awesome trip;
          i am w/them in the Link, and yet...


          I could borrow Llair's new boat and follow the Dolphin by three
weeks and still easily meet them at Io...
                                I find myself hungry for the boat's
hurtling velocity: there is something so wonderfully clarifying about going
really really fast...


          Ah, for the rendevous at Bongo B, next Midwinter when the
Dolphin returns...



          We stop the mooncat at a point of Ariel's choosing, well over onto
the lunar darkside, off the Highway on a stasis pad, three meters above the
perfect gray dust of the vast Mare Orientale...
          In our suits we follow Ariel out across the pad to a kind of veiled...
quality, a gossamer waver in front of us in airless space.
          Ariel leads us through and vanishes...
          Naturally i follow, and Electra, and
                                Zzog!
                                We are *of the instant*
in Ariel's Garden Between the Worlds, a vast and curving Earthlike
hemisphere of brilliant skies and greenery and Light, vast unto vales and
hillocks w/a noble graystone mountain at the center, all clad in the hues of
a waxing warming morning red/ray sun...


                                Zzog squared...
                                I turn to look and

see the gateway closing; going, now gone, a glimmer hint hanging glossy across the splendid view, the gentle grassy hillocks...

My readouts say the gravity here is higher than Lunar by thirty percent, more viscous too by a factor of three, and every gesture requires some slight extra effort and momentum, like i am moving through the most mutable of liquids...

And the gauges say the air is good, rich w/mystery gasses, and i take off my helmet and inhale a vivid headfull of this wild biotic ATMOSPHERE, rife w/sound and light and life; larksongs, stratus clouds, a plentiful compendium of lush scents...

And there is wind, and the SOUND of wind...

We leave our faithful suits on a handy granite slab perfect for suit/parking, and in our shipboard garb we follow, actually walking, onto a path of smooth granite pavers, heading for what i know from Ariel to be Alacana, her Holy Mountain...

At one point i wonder could the Garden be a *tulka* in the style of the Tibetans, a thoughtform made manifest...

Mayhap a thoughtform of Ariel's, now made real and substantial through the enormous generative power of the self/evolving bleu...

And true it is that all through this stroll our Ariel wears her Smile Beatific, as if she is up to her erogenous ears in orchid/petals; and now her nostrils flare delicious (wildthang!) w/the alternating wafts of lavender and chamomile, foin grass and basil, all as in her Vision/the same...

After a great deal of this very novel walking, we arrive at a handsome fine/wrought granite peristyle, twelve gray spiral/fluted fae columns encircling a courtly yard of glassy granite, three gray granite benches perfect/set for gazing at magnificent Alacana...

Overhead are these grand woodbeamy trellises full of grapevines, each leaf so very like a masque of the face of the goodly Green Man...

In the center of the peristyle is a circular overflowing pool, w/the water falling into a catch that routes it out into an alabaster viaduct, which itself parallels the long path unto the Mountain...

I fascinate on this water;

It flows like thick quicksilver, and where the cascade enters the catch it splashes so gradual slow in the curious syrupy gravity, w/the drops themselves much larger than Earthdrops as they undulate so animate through the air, settle so soft on the surface, rest for a fract of time like slow soapbubbles, merge and go w/the current...

I raise the dipper and take a sip;
                                        And to my second/sight appear
devas, sprites of the waters and the trees, spirits of the wells and glens and
places of vision...
        Zzog.

        The peristyle is on a rise, and from it the pathway falls away into
stands of blue pine and juniper, on toward the Mountain.
        Onward...
                Through the woods and up and out, and now we follow a Sunwise
Spiral up the Mountain, w/the granite bedrock shouldering the uphill side of
the path and the mica flecks mirroring the
                                        *Real Sunlight...*
                                        I turn and glim
this familiar flaming star now setting behind a ring of lesser mountains, the
longer redder later/day lightrays goldening the granite...
                                        Thus and therefore
we are somewhere other than the backside of Luna, on some other planetoid
w/similar gravity, circling a similar Sun...
        I marvel on the gateway.

        Approaching the Alacana summit now in the gloaming dusk, we
are soon onto the broad temple plateau, and
                                        Ariel is the first to see, being
a little ahead, and Linked i catch her tangy end/of/quest elation, a quick
voyant vibrant rush, for
                        There below us waits the temple, a conmingling
covey of curves, spires and arches and serrated stellae, a structural stave
of visual music writ in an elfin key,
                                And well/wrought are its' domes of
homeplanet stone, polished and shining; faced w/silverstone hematite,
traced around w/thin inlay pinstrips of pale/glinty green jasper and pastel
rose quartz, elegant w/carved curved clear quartz portals...
                                        And shining also
are the three graduated silverstone spire towers, each of the tops of them
asparagated w/overlapping circling rings of leaflike celestite clerestory
windows, w/each of these panes lit from w/in to show their beautiful lucent
veining...

        Ariel walks on, her inner hymn of guiding still crooning her forward;
clearly the temple is for later...
                                And there is flavour in following her as we
are, following her around behind these previsioned surfaces of her very
utopian aquarian mind, through all the ideals of this her own personal
promised/manifested Oz,

And now we approach this splendid cultivated vale, hidden by a rise and now revealed Sun/glistening, all the leaves so jeweled w/emerald moisture drops, all the symmetrical lines of plantings patterning out and away, variegated/geometric/labyrinthine over several hectares, four or passing five...

And heady i drink the moist and bracing air, full of niffs of all the vital herbs and flowerings of Ariel's Vision, the diverse trees heavy in their fruiting, the vines and roots and mosses...

And farther out on the grassy hillsides are lambs and rams gamboling;

Another matching Vision overlay...


Beyond the silver temple looms the snowy pinnacle peak, much taller, a thousand meters more of craggy stone shadows...

And after the setting of the similar Sun, there are around the peak these symmetrical almost chimerical clouds, fluffy gray screens for the play of late flamey rays...

And passing overhead one misty ovoid gentles down a rain upon us, big warm drops that plop slow on the plateau pavingstones...

Around these clouds the sky is fulldark now and clear; and immense the foreign stars, brighter more intense...


Ariel's choral hymn of guiding brings us now to a cave on the Mountains' flank, and we have a look in;

Zzog,

A warm rock nest w/a rolling rock door and a chimnied fire, a good bed, good bread, freshgrown food and books of worth, woven hangings of thick wool on the granite walls, plush ruggings, lumination bright or candle/light at a word, a steamy waterchamber,

All to Ariel's taste...

And in the innnermost room another overflowing weirdwater pool like unto the one at the peristyle. And in the rock above it a vertical cylindrical shaft, polished and open to the sky...


We sleep until we wake, which is firstlight.

We each drink a dipper of the water; *awareness ramps.*

We resolve to stay a day and a night in the chamber in the cave, watch the pool...

And now it is a GLORIOUS dawning morning, and the gentle gray sunrise lightrays render the chamber colors innocent and pearly. Long awake and awaiting their arrival i watch these shy beams stream and swirl down the shaft and into the water, there to alloy w/the fountain's home deep...

Midday now and the similar Sun moves across the opening, charging the pool w/a blast of fusion starlight, leaving obscure lightnings in the thick dark water, aglowing still as the similar Sun moves on...

And now a very occult Sunset, w/the slanting glancing red raybeams caroming off the shaftsides, infusing the strange water w/red webby lightveils...

And now at the midnight witching hour a pale lavender moon aligns w/the shaft, and the cave is at its' most magical; Ariel herself is especially drawn to the pool, wanting to be mystified, mysterized into the guarded knowlege that lives beneath those viscous ripples...

After we stay in the cave a day and a night, drinking the water and watching the pool, we add another brilliant day and dusk and dawn...

And at the end of the third day, when the similar Sun repaints the sky, there appears above the pool a creature of light and energy and pleasant sounds, somewhere between a shining and a sheath of smoke, a core of flame, a column of fire...

And from this blaze a voice of rays;

*{ ...i am the alacana, and i am for you; i am the fire of your inspiring, the fire within on which you draw... i am the part of you that sings, i am your missing twin, i am your green shadow and i am the light at the end; and i am that which Is, conjured by you from the cloth of your thoughts... }*

And these words echo now in my neural wiring, so familiar/so like some newly known aspect of my own mind speaking...

*{ ...i am here, come unto me... }*

transmits the Alacana, and there is something so curious/compelling in this, as if i too am thinking these words toward her, our thought/voices two patterns lapping nicely in a like/minded matching of mimsey/waves, our shared longing drawing us ever the closer, yearning me headlong toward the sentient fire, the Alacana my desire/mirror, as magnetic to my heart as any woman would or could be...

*...o mind in the fire,
    dark rose of my overstanding,
    i would know thee or be consumed...*

And w/this the crimson pillar
rolls closer, and there is heat to my skin, a furnace blast of fastgone fueling
gasses, a windrush/roaring w/loud sharp snaps and cinder pops, all of which
are weirdly pitched much lower than their Earthside counterparts...

And the
surface flames, they dance so courtly slow; a halfspeed galliarde of hot blue
flame/tips kicking out so languid and so lean...

And as the heat reaches a threatening intensity, i sense here a
novel strange lifting of my aetherself out of my frame o'flesh; more than by
my own Will, more like a drawing/out; the sword from the stone...

In ecstasis i rise from my physical bod,

And e'en as my solid bod
retreats from the heat my subtle self is thralling ever forward, ever closer
unto this corona source of life/force, this font of fundamental energies, and
i see these energies rolling toward me as fast photon swells, my lightbod
waxing as i gather to my center wave after wave of this vital lyrical prahnic
Alacana manna...

And on this theme this thought occurs; i can go to the
flames in the physical and be translated into ash, or i can go to these same
flames subtly and be sustained; tonight it is the light far more than the heat
that furthers...

Thus i complete my physical retreat/feel my lightbod drawn
on toward the Alacana flames...

And from this state of dual awareness i
start to shift my focus to my lightbod,

And to my newly subtle senses the
flame/column changes, cools away from infra/heat, ramps from red to
orange, rising/riding the colorshift on toward the shorter wavelengths,

And
e'en now the living fire/sprouts radiate bright fierce life/force solely, the
whole a luminous loud downpouring cylinder of motile and enspirited energy,
a wyrding violet dazzle/column of living luminating prahna plasma, a titan of
luminating life/energy in our misty midnight water chamber midst...

Far more inviting to my very human tastes, this violet rebus/tree
of life...

So i flow my senses fully to my subtle flying lightbod, totally delighting
in being guided, called, indrawn/inhaled on in and

Through!

And straightaway

the octave is more pure, shifting in the transit instant from fire/furnace/roar
To
where those echoes in my wiring could abide in peace w/the silences, could
e'en now be living lurking in treetips of soundless clear phantom air/forests,
living lauding the silences for the beautiful subtractive sonic shapes they
leave behind them, shapely floating holes in the echo continuum...

     And if this violet column is an air/tree then i am climbing it; my
aetheric otherself ascending elevated and levitating, drawn upward through
a whorling fluid flood of misty atmosphere, ever upward toward the
beautiful lavender moonface smiling now down the stone shaft, calling me
upward ever rising
     Now *rocketing* me out and away above the somber
violet Alacana landscape,
     And the moonface too is Alacana, who looks
upon me w/my own mysterious whelming desire...
     And moving between us
our mirroring thoughts cross and reach, each for the other, glyphs passing
in the light...

  *...o high alacana i know you and seek you, for you are my
  awen, my muse; you fuel my blood w/bright elixirs of
  inspiration...*

      *{ ...i am for you, my courier of*

*visions... }*

  *...likewise you are the last vast astral continent, the
  colossal radiant meta/being, superset of all astral
  immortals...*

        *{ ...yes, i assent, it is true,
         o intrepid traveler... }*

  *...i know you and find you in all of my lives;
  you are the divine constant in everyone to whom i give
  my love...*

       *{ ...you see your beloveds as portals to me... }*

  *...i work to invoke you at every turn,
  to luminate our game in such a way
  that we amplify that which is you in each other,
  evolve each other, complete each other...*

       *{ ...through love
     you reach the realms of mystery and magic,
      hidden knowing and power... }*

...yes, i assent, it is true;
the wholeness i seek
i find in bonding...

{ ...w/ariel and electra?... }

...you are ariel & electra...

{ ...yes, i assent, it is true... }

...through you i aspire to know love and be love,
to be thy ever/more/perfect instrument...

{ ...you are the perfect instrument;
through you i dance in the now... }

...i look upward into your face/alluring...

{ ...down to you i curve... }

...our wanton rays mesh and settle...

{ ...our shared and soaring sacred hearts... }

...come unto me o sum of my desiring...

{ ...come unto me, o sword of light,
o transmuting ever/aspiring
worker of our mutual will... }

...come unto me, my essence,
source of vision and desire...

{ ...leave earthly care behind... }


And because it is the Alacana,

i let go the golden cord

that ties me to my flesh/&/blood bod, for the first time freeing
myself complete from my familiar physical mass, a volitional act
of
Perfect Trust;
A Leap of Faith...

And in this moment of my total release
from my corporeal form, from my humanocentric physical shell self still

attached from below, i am decanted exultant into my highest kairos thusfar,
truly and completely
FREE OF MY SELF,
And in this crowning place where
all is new, where titanic potentials roam and loom, here [[my]] nebulous
awareness spreads like a spray of freshborn diamonds, ranges wide across
the broad profound and infinite Alacana firmament...




Several *e t e r n i t i e s*  later, the Effable Hand
strokes the keys of consciousness and space/time, and that which is i slides
back into being
Human
Again in this anders incarnation, my home
here/&/now, massively Zzoggled to find
And now the world re/forms
around me as my anders senses latch, the millions of world/parts now
crystallizing, rippling away from my pov in an outward/bound ringwave
of finite matter...
And fully back now, in my bod in the cave on the flank
of Alacana's mountain, my fast/returning ka still trailing a tail of luminous
Glow d'Mage, the last wisps wafting away like ancient otherlife incense...

And thus reborn en/medias/res into this ongoing creation that is
my current life, all that i see is new to me, all sights as bright as tryptamine
neon, everything around me arriving to my senses in profoundest most
wondrous and intricate detail, and animate Spirit is everywhere, so visible
in everything...
I am ramped GIDDY w/bounty and profusion and variety,
all the loving/rendered artistry...
And it comes to me that like all these
things i am perceiving, i too am a

I am a *SOURCE OF ZINGY LOVE RAYS...*
And, carrying this
awesome charge of awen love, i feel a major change in the fundament of
my core self; a sense of perfect ease, and in the wake of this a relaxing of
the geography of my highways of thought, a streamlining of the modes of
my logic, a freeing of the radiant conduits through which my awen inspirits
me...
And more than physical re/imaging this is conscious mind/changing, a

kind of supremely aware re/dreaming...

                              re/dreaming...

                                      re/dreaming...


      And w/the passing of this last superb sublime and shining moment, i know it is time for me to go. The Garden is for Ariel; e'en now in the Link her own Alacana calls her, offers her a lagniappe tasty as octaroon nectarines...

      And i in mindseye see Ariel likewise arising also, same as me an aeon past, the silver wraith of her awareness rising like an aromatic cloud of atomized ylang above her graceful form...

      And as she clears her material bod i see her enter the vital column,

      And here it is that Ariel will meet her hinge; we both can see this...

      In a Linking flash of foresight i know that when i ope my glims and look to Ariel's parked bod...

      In our oracular headmovie preview her physical form fades away to vapor...

      And so i ope my glims to see this *actually playing out,* see that this is truth; and from my very human core a psychic shriek,

      *...ariel/GONE!...*

      And, quick as a Link,

                  *{ ...where could i go?... }*


      She leaves me rocking in the wake of her aetheric bow/wave, a psychic sequence composed of the taste of her release from the heavy golden tether, her freeing leap into Perfect Trust, the abundant susurration of universal love, the sustaining chords of her cycle of Faith w/the loving Alacana...

      A very resonant mindspace afterglow; she tracks the same emotion chain as me...

      And yet, here i be...

      Ah,

      Outside our cave is the same warming morning red/ray Sunlight as when we arrive...

      And as i gaze through the cavemouth i am astonished to see

**THE WHOLE GARDEN VAPORING AWAY!**

*From the horizon inward!* All the thousands of hectares/all the
millions of green denizens/the temple/our cave/to my gaping surprise the
entire solid fundament is steaming away, losing covalence and going molecular,
going gone

       AAAAAAAAAAAAAAAAAAAAAAA

                   O

                   O

                   F

                   !

                        Of the INSTANT

Electra and i are back in our suits, back at the side/pad on the Mare
Imbrium Highway.

       For a click of time there is a ghost of the gossamer
before me, now a gossamer hole, now a gossamer memory...


       The five days in the Garden show as five hours on our readouts,
which anycase explains the water...

       What of Ariel?

                    *


       Time for me to travel; Electra elects to leave likewise,

                        And in the
mooncat now so empty of Ariel, we are gliding away/adding velocity, back
to Bongo B.


       To murp my thoughts i fill my glims;

                      A twenty/inch Ariel replay
sashays above my vidplate, keying through all my faves:

                      Ariel in her Sunlover's
Link at Midsummer; the three of us boffing like ferrets in Llair's sky chamber,
warm and starframed, the Earthglints glorious on our glistening bods; and
lately in this violet mooncat piloting our way to


      *{ ...e'en now i think of you also, as tuned to your waves as you are to*
        *mine...*

           *i will see you at the reunion, and more; you will see me also...*
           *how can it be otherwise when you and i are one,*
        *flowing ever onward through ten thousand lifetimes of love... }*


       I reach for the videolo Ariel glittering before me/cleave the heated
voxels with my hand/send her image vaporing away...

                       And through this

veil/this voxel smoke of parting, i look across the mooncat's particolor displays to see

> *...electra you are morphing; relaxing down into base mode, composing yourself in your painterly way,*
>
> *and now you have the whole of my awareness; e'en after seeing three hundred of these changes you all ways fascinate me in...*

> [a span of time]
>
> *...and b'zzog! you are ariel, my memory of ariel on our first night of love aboard the encanto; monalisa grin, slender bending willowbod longfingers gracefully arching, heartfelt waves of come/hither desiring, all of that arielessence...*

And there in this midst the goldish flash of Electra's unchanging endearing enigmatic earring, as if to say...

We become One/the Pattern Endures/Love is All...

And i smile my heart unto Electra, overstanding me so well as to author me this goodly gift, and i smile likewise to faraway Linking Ariel, beaming me love across the astral expanses,

And it now occurs that once again we are at the top of my tale and the end of it, this loop of my life complete; and thus

I too will leave you now...

There are major mysteries i wish to ponder/i am inclined to find some Redwood trees to aid me...

For you, my good and gamesome shipmate,

> *i am grateful.*
> *i thank thee.*
> *i am at peace.*

Fair weather to you and fare ye well; may we merry meet again at Midwinter, and...

May your sailing be outrageous...

# Lexicon/Codex
## and Hyperlinks

(Set down whilst aboard the Dolphin, several weeks before Showtime, w/a few entries after).


**-a**


**ABYDOS EGYPT,** city of temples; a very ancient site sacred to Annubis, God who is Gateway to the Realm Eternal, and Osiris, God of the Waters and the Nile and the rising of the Sun.

Osiris along w/Isis, Goddess of the Earth and of Life, are the center of a drama that embodies our most pervasive pancultural worldview, that of the cycle of birth, death, and rebirth. As it plays out, Isis & Osiris are fiercely in love (from their union comes the grain), when Osiris' brother Seth treacherously attacks and dismembers him, scattering his parts all over the Earth. Isis gathers the parts and reunites them, their son Horus goes after Seth, and Osiris, reborn, departs for the Underworld, from which subterranean vantage he directs the annual rising and falling of the Nile on which the Egyptian crop cycle is based, and the rising and setting of the Sun.

It was here at Abydos that Osiris entered the underworld and became immortal. At one point in its' seven/thousand/year history as Holy Ground, Abydos was called 'The Hill of the Sacred Head of Osiris', implying that here Isis brought about the miracle of his resurrection.

Following the lead of Isis & Osiris, many of the Pharaonic God Kings (from the first through the thirtieth dynasties!) chose the desert plain at Abydos as the base and launching place for their own journeys to the Lake of Light.

During their lives and after, these God Kings had a special relationship w/Osiris and were worshipped in Abydos as his avatars and sincerely praised in dedicated Great Temples, massive stone structures which themselves were often built in complex w/other Great Temples. These other temples were given over to the worship of other far older Gods, including Anher and also Khentamentiu, (a Gateway God greatly predating Osiris), as well as the Gods and Goddesses of many of the other principle Egyptian peoples, and also the Gods of neighboring lands...

**ACCELERATION;** my favorite part of every journey.

**AGENTS OF CHANGE;** herewith is presented a Fresh Age sampler:
    SNAP: a pleasant neural accelerator.
    LOTUS LEAVES; used for lucid dreaming and occasionally for
      highly selective forgetting.

MEGAMINKE: a powerful sexuality enhancer.

MOUSE GAS; originally a vapor that gives the inhalee the sense that they are four inches tall; limited popularity until the formula is altered to reverse the effect, giving the inhalee the sense that everyone else is four inches tall.

MYSTERY GREEN STUFF: if i could tell you what it is i would have to call it something else.

WILD BETSY: a fine red quaff in a cup that yields a lurid rapid ripper of a visionary tryptamine wisdom experience, affecting all seven senses.

STEEM: an ultrahybridized strain of Good Old Marijuana.

The **AETHER;** the stuff through which the currents of Magic flow, the continuum of aetheric fluids connecting everyone w/everything, the causal link between Will and Result.

Also called the Astral Light by Eliphas Levi, it is that in which the Akashic Record or cosmic memory resides.

**AKASHIC;** the timeless repository of all that is, was, or will be known and experienced.

**ALEMBIC;** an alchemist's retort, usually a teardrop/shaped glass beaker/vial w/a still/coil coming out the top, used w/a lampflame to purify & distill. In making the Philosopher's Stone, the alembic holds the three simultaneous levels of the Work, the body/soul/spirit of the alchemist, here analogized into mercury/sulphur/salt. Though the operations performed on the physical material in the Alembic are important, the real work of Alchemy is in perfecting the alchemist.

**AMETHYSTENE;** one of my all/time favorite words. My thanks to the very bardic and excellent Tom Robbins...

**AMNIOTIC SIBYLENE;** a fetal child who can see into the future and communicate it from the womb. The arrival of the first of what would be many such miraculous clairvoyancies fulfills the prophecy that begins the shift in cultural consciousness that creates the context for the Fresh Age...

**AMPHORA;** a ewer or cruet, graceful and Grecian.

**ANACHROME;** an object that reflects zero color and light.

**ANACHRONE;** of another time yet accessible from the now; alternately, something outside the timestream, alongside, and w/a view; an incarnation accessed from a timeless perspective.

**ANIMORPHS** are folks, built to serve, all of them as unique as humans; like our friend Steel, who is durable and industrial and hydraulic yet drawn by Lissa's long black hair snapping through the air, or Clement the volt/wrangler, the one they call the Electrician, so selfless they also call him Hero of the Ariel seven times over...

And then there is Electra herownself, extraordinary shapeshifting Electra, she who is my helpmate, my mirror, my aide & my confidante, enhancing so many aspects of my life. She remembers everything, is infinitely repairable and renewable, always online if i need a fact or a favour from a friend, connected likewise to the ship, the pods, the other animorphs.

And also there is this; for all of her twenty/five/years she has been learning from humans, gathering skills and languages and lore; astromechanics, storytelling, healing, the erotic and the occult,

All the better to please you, says she...

And to that end, she is possessed of this extraordinary adaptive capability:

From time to time to further our bond i can speak to her directly, suggest changes to her gradients and ramps and parameters, give her data that i find of consequence:

Electra, this is Worker...

And w/each of these changes i come to know her better, and the longer we know each other, the more complete will be her knowlege of me: after seven years w/yr anders she has me mapped right on down to the autonomic, and thus she knows when i want for a good laugh, or crave the bread of unborn grains, or need my time alone; she can see through the personality i wear, and she can see my shadows...

And, in truth, she so thoroughly overstands my physical bod and all its connected systems that she can heal me,

Much as i can heal her.

And this kind of adaptive fair exchange leads to us being so in tune that we can each predictively please the other, end each other's sentences, speak words of our own shared language.

Together we form a fine self/pleasing continuum...

And, there is this:

Early on we try this old Spacer technique; i ask her to consciously access all her design docs, to download and add to her waking memory all her manuals and updates, to deduce a set of rules from her self/diagnostics, and thereby learn the ways of her own technology. This works spectacularly well, and opens the way for her conscious self/modification; perhaps it is this that quickens the seeds of her own Free Will...

**ANELUXIC;** a coating or material so light/hungry that it yields zero reflectivity, effectively vanishing whatever object it covers, leaving an utterly dark space in its' place.

**ANILINES;** a specie of organic dye, very vivid and powerful and permanent.

**ANODYNE;** the difference of two frequencies, whereas the heterodyne is the sum of two frequencies. When two waves of different frequencies come together, they create an anodyne and a heterodyne of their original frequencies; thus, if a fifty cycle wave existed concurrent w/a sixty cycle wave, their anodyne would be ten cycles, and their heterodyne one/hundred/ten cycles.

This is rumoured to have happened during the twentieth century sixties; in a story i once heard from Colonel Tom Bearden, the Russians at this time built a power grid in the Ural mountains, and the long power lines were strung in such a way that they would send major waves toward the coast of California. The Russian power grid ran alternating current at fifty cycles, and the California grid alternating current at sixty.

As in the example above there now existed an anodyne wave of ten cycles, innocuous enough... Until you start to VARY one of the original frequencies. This, the story goes, would give the Russians the ability to tune the anodyne to the psycho/active frequencies (approximately seven to fourteen cycles), particularly seven/point/two cycles, where folk become hugely depressed.

As the tale relates, they caused this frequency to be, and they did so between three and four ayem on specific days, and in truth many things occurred during these hours that could be seen as caused by deep sadness...

I like to think that the Russians also conjured up the frequencies for mirth, jollity, and bliss at other hours. I would add orgasm to the list, though that would be stretching, as the frequency for same is thirty-two cycles.

**ANODE;** that component in the cathode/anode pairing that gives forth the electrons that the cathode consumes. Cathodes and anodes are made of porous metals so that they will have more surface area from which to collect and emit, respectively.

A cathode/anodes' measure of efficiency is in the quantity of electrons it can pass at a given current. A byproduct of all that electron passing is heat, and the power/handling capacity of a cathode/anode generally depends on its ability to handle enormous high temperatures.

Since tiny amounts of dirt and carbon can drastically reduce the efficiency and life of a cathode/anode, they are stored in nitrogen, always handled remotely, and run in vacuum.

**APOTHEOSIS;** in this narrative, used to convey the attaining of a Godlike state.

**ART IS THE DEVOTED OPPOSITION TO THE TRIVIAL AND THE BASE**
-- A quote from the very wise JBH Heathcote.

**ART:**  i sing that Art is visualization of the world as perfected as we can make it; as beautiful, as evolved, as harmonious. This is the way we make the world over, visualizing and living the vision, then visualizing again. This is the cache, the magical charge of art.

**THE POWER OF ART** is to transform, and as our technology progresses, so too does the power of any art which utilizes these technologies. The role of the artist becomes more shamanic as the level of magic in media ramps, w/the consequences of the artist/shaman's Work more profound.

**ASPARAGATED;** to have the architectural qualities of an asparagus tip, a kind of leaf-like crenellation, like unto the top of the Chrysler Building.

**AUGURY;** a portent, a harkening, a sign.

**AUREOLES;** the sacredest and most beautiful, the most painterly part of the human female form; the flowers, the frames for the female fonts of life.

**AUTEURS;** artists whose vision is so central to their being that it shines through whatever themes they may choose, a philosophical compass offered to their perceivers to direct them to a truth...

**AVATAR:** a deity incarnate, someone so advanced as to be in the world only for the illumination of the rest of us.

**AWEN;** variously defined as the voice of the muse of inspiration, the fire in the head, the descending form of light. While the word is Celtic/Druidical, most cultures enshrine some divine source of ideation, a fountain or salmon or holy mountain, and seek therein their truths revealed.


**-b**


The **BARABOO II** and the circus it conveys are all folks inspired by the books of Barry B. Longyear, including *Circus World*, *City of Baraboo* (both nineteen/eighty), and *Elephant Song* (nineteen/eighty/one).

**BASILIC;** as in Sandor, a bloke as if a block of stone, like unto the pillars of Stonehenge.

**BEGETTING;** the biblical/KingJamesian way of referring to the engendering of offspring.

**BESANT & LEADBEATER:** born in eighteen/forty/seven in London (this time around), the beloved and formidable Annie Wood Besant began her path as an Anglo/Catholic, married the Anglican reverend Frank Besant, left him, moved through atheism into being a noted secularist and proto/feminist who advocated birth control, then became an officer of GB Shaw's Fabian Society, then at the age of forty/one, a Theosophist.

Being favoured by Madame Blavatsky, co/founder of the Theosophical Society (along w/Henry S Olcot and WQ Judge), Mrs Besant in eighteen/eighty/nine became a member of the Esoteric Section of the Blavatsky Lodge (along with WB Yeats). In her studies of the occult she was deeply influenced by co/Theosophist CW Leadbeater, a former Anglican clergyman. On the passing of the gifted HPB, Mrs Besant ascended to the presidency of the Society (nineteen/ought/seven).

The following year, after half a lifetime of delving the mysteries of India, she w/Leadbeater initiated a project to find and train a modern Avatar. This created a rift in the Society, resulting in the leave/taking of Rudolf Steiner and his founding of the Anthroposophical Society (nineteen/hundred/&/twelve).

At this time, she and Leadbeater passionately pushed the envelope of the occult, writing a number of books and introducing many wonderful and useful concepts and techniques, including the visualization and creation of thought forms, which are specific configurations of personal magical auric energy.

Long interested as well in the temporal affairs of India, she became an active Indian Nationalist in nineteen/thirteen. Clearly her occult abilities had become pretty mighty, because her political career was meteoric, truly astonishing. Starting w/a lecture tour, she soon segued into journalism, publishing a book and then buying a newspaper (The New India), then founding the Home Rule for India League. In nineteen/seventeen she was briefly jailed, came out a hero, and was swept into the Presidency of the Indian National Congress! She stayed in sway until the coming of MK Gandhi, shortly thereafter.

In the nineteen/twenties, the Society and its related Order of the Star in the East (w/Mrs Besant's avatar/messiah Jeddu Krishnamurti at its' head) reached a pinnacle membership totaling over a/hundred/fifty/thousand worldwide. At this time another rift occurred when Leadbeater was consecrated bishop of the Old Catholic Church, split w/them, and founded the Liberal Catholic Church, taking many Theosophists w/him.

Mrs Besant lived to see her chosen lad, Krishnamurti, formally disclaim and renounce any spiritual leadership (as a true avatar would), and in nineteen/hundred/&/twenty/nine dissolve the Order of the Star. Later in his life he would become a respected teacher and an influence of Aldous Huxley's...

**BETANET;** an intranet of the type popular among affinity groups at the beginning of the Fresh Age, w/this one for those who share the Space/faring fantasy.

**BODY JEWELRY;** psychically amplifying artifacts worn over the bod's centers of power: a citrine lens for the third eye, cinnabar links for the base of the spine, rose quartz compassion enhancers for raising heart energy, amethyst for the high muladhara, *the Violet Ray!* all of them wrought of gold and silver and electrum, astrologically attuned, phased w/the Moon, consecrated to the dog star Sirius...

**THE BOOK OF THE CELESTIAL;** a compendium of rites and teachings of the original Celestial Order of Bards, Ovates, and Druids, written in the twentieth/century nineties.


-C

**CABOCHON;** any stone formed to the shape of a heavy oval dewdrop, cut to catch the light. Sapphire cabs have stars inside...

**CADEUCEUS;** the staff of Hermes, the Greek god of healing, alchemy, and magic. It is pictured as a staff surmounted by a crossbar and a pair of wings at the top, w/two serpents symmetrically intertwining up its length. I myself am inclined to see it as a symbol for reincarnation, w/the serpents moving from this life to the next and back again, each alternating their realm of abiding w/the other.

This metaphor is also useful in visualizing the process of separating the lightbod from the physical in preparation for the crossing of the boundary into the Astral.

**THE CADEUCEUS EXERCISE:** Electra's headmovie exercise for leaving the physical bod and traveling astrally. Try this in the quiet dark...

1. Envision the wiring of your lightbod as it interlaces w/your physical bod,

2. Enter a state of dual awareness*,
3. Connect both bods w/a cord of golden plasma,
4. Slowly and gently and w/love begin to separate these two bods, by first very slightly tilting your head very slowly to one side and then the other, w/your lightbod in mirror/phase doing the same...
5. Move now w/a kind of honey/slow italianate head wobble, leaning right and then left and following w/the curve of your serpentine spine, feeling the head of your lightbod tilting likewise in the other direction; equal in mass, identical, visible. So easy!
6. Inhabit both bods simultaneous, syncing symmetrical, rhythmical and flowing, separating and converging and merging and separating, interweaving each w/the other, until you see your selves form a living Cadeuceus, symbol of the weaving of this world w/the next...
7. Shift into your subtle self, park the physical, and sail away in your lightbod. Travel!

*   One way to clearly overstand the dynamic of dual awareness is this, a preliminary exercise to the one above; hold your hands out in front of you and touch the tips of your index fingers together. Focus on the single point of awareness where they meet, and now gradually begin to move them apart while holding a simultaneous awareness of both fingertips. It may be helpful to envision a living golden cord between them.

This is the same mental dynamic employed in maintaining a parallel awareness of the physical bod and the lightbod. The ability to sail off into the aethers is literally at your fingertips...

These practices are best (and most safely) learned through a living teacher.

## CARGO MATH:

*Murphy's Dolphin:*
ship size is 600 feet long, 244 feet wide, 72 feet thick
the hold is 200 x 200 x 60, or 2.4 million cubic feet

*Spice:*
125 cc's of Spice = 100 grams
125 cc's = 8 cubic inches
8 cubic inches = 100 grams.
200 metric tons = 9259 cubic feet
2000 metric tons = 92,590 cubic feet

At 4 grams per, a ton will serve a quarter/million folk. For a week.
200 metric tons = enough Spice for 50 million folk

3000 metric tons = enough for 750 million folk, a tenth of the population of the Earth in the Fresh Age.

*Sandor's Original Plan for Loading 4200 Tons of Spice whilst in Orbit around Io:*
The Dolphin has two sleds; they carry thirty tons apiece, sixty tons per trip for both. This works out to about 140 sled/roundtrips for all 4200 tons. Each trip would take four hours per, w/another twenty minutes for loading, which means a minimum of six/hundred/six/hours/plus of sled time: even w/the sleds going marathon this means loading would take fourteen/point/four Io days (each of which is forty/two hours long). With five more sleds we could do it in two Io days, which sounds about right.
The great Mother Dolphin is so capacious that the cargo would take up only about a third of the main hold.

**CARIBARIUM;** brought to my attention by Robin Williamson. In his splendid book, *The Craneskin Bag, Caribarium* is what the twelfth/century Scottish magician Michael Scot called his conical steel hat, prototype for all subsequent pointy wizard hats.
He created it on having a presentiment that he would be killed by a falling rock. After he had reached a very advanced age, he was in church one day (and hence had removed his hat) when a mouse in the rafters knocked a tiny pebble onto his head. He was so unnerved by the episode that he went home, put his affairs in order, and then left this life...

**CARRIER WAVE;** any waveform modulated by a second waveform, itself more easily discernable when the carrier wave is subtracted.

**CARTESIAN;** a way of plotting coordinates, very useful for navigation and lightshows, originated by Rene Descartes in 1637 as a mathematical means of describing plane curves. Later, axes were added along with negative numbers so that points could be located in a three/dimensional space, arrayed around a zero/point center.
A cartesian coordinate is plotted in a cube (of any size) by first seeing three of the six sides overlain with lines forming many tiny squares. Next, the points at the intersections of each column and row on each of the three gridded sides are given numerical values, and *voila!* the point in question can now be numerically defined by the locus of three axes; one axis running front/to/back, another going left/to/right, and a third going up/down, all at right angles to each other.
There is a certain poetry in the terms used in calculating cartesian coordinates; gradient of divergence, vector Laplacian, curl.
The inversion of three-dimensional cartesian mathematics yields

us a way of defining space called *six/sphere coordinates*... This more exotic form involves Laplace's equation and the Helmholtz differential equation and is somewhat beyond my current capabilities...

**CAUSALITY;** a state wherein there is a necessary connection of events through cause and effect.

**CELESTIAL ORDER;** founded in South California in nineteen/ninety, the Celestial Order of Bards, Ovates, and Druids was formed to merge ancient Celtic Mystery Traditions w/the shamanic teachings of Terrence McKenna.
     Celestial practices include the imparting of Druidical wisdom, rituals performed in natural places of power, and the navigation of mindstates attained through the use of shamanic substances, all in pursuit of enlightenment, personal evolution, and direct experience of the Divine.

**CEREBRATIONS:** cerebrate, cerebrate, dance to the music...

**CERULEAN;** dreamers/eye blue, blue as the sky in the last reaches before pure space, blue as a true love spell from the lips of the Sibylene...

**CHAKRAS;** (see Yoga)

**THE CHARIOT OF BELI;** w/Beli being a Celtic Sun/God, and his chariot being our singular Fiery Orb...

**CHARM/CHANT;** a chant that works a wonder on the brain, takes us to a specific and highly salubrious state of consciousness.
     Variations on the idea of charm/chants are used all over the world by all manor of extraordinary folk; in the jungles of the Amazon (according to T. McKenna) the Putamayo Ayahuasqueros use whistle chants to launch forty folk at once into the grid, while the great magicians of the West Indies (as per C Nelson Stewart) have special charm songs for 'the changing of the skin', leaving their bods as the songs end, transferred into beings of soft fire, and there is also something of the charm/chant in mantra and dovining and droning and omming, in the music of noseflutes vibrating the brain, in raptures found in the sounds of heavy machinery, in songs in the mind that superimpose on the monotonous roar of rockets...

**CHATOYANCY, CHATOYANT;** having the qualities of semiprecious tigers' eye, catching light in the same delicious way as an actual feline glim; from the French.
     Other specific and beautiful adjectives that convey the special qualities of semiprecious stones include Labradoresence (that pearly and somewhat refractive quality of labradorite), and Amethystene.

**CHIMERICAL:** fantastical as the Chimera, a beastie variously described by various folk as a monster or a granter of gifts, filling a variety of roles in the campfire dramas that once passed for history.

**CHRYSALIS OF WAVICLES;** an astonishing sheathing around the bod composed of mythical bits that are at once both waves and particles, the special virtue of which is the imparting of positive change upon the being within.

**THE SYSTEM OF CLANS AND GUILDS;** a social matrix composed of groups linked by blood or trade or affinity. These entities can be tribes or employee/owned corporations or collectives or covens or even queenships, monarchies w/Matriarchs who wear their family crowns...

Though there is now little interest in having national governments, some civil institutions remain, selling their services on a subscription basis; if you don't call them, they don't come. Governments are abjured from having weapons, and are in truth free of the need of them, since everyone generally belongs to several global affinity groups, and there is much networking and crossconnecting and inter/marrying and blood/relating.

Many of these tribal entities are involved in ventures all across the Solar Disk, and in truth, the Guilds and Clans are the basis of Spacer culture, w/many of the first such affinity groups organized around ways and means to leave the Earth...

Collective competitive energies are directed into sports, Space/racing primarily, and epic contests are vicariously enjoyed systemwide. Other arenas for rivalry include architecture, ship technology, Spacer élan.

**CLOCHE;** a tight/fitting hat like an aviator's helmet, popular w/women in the nineteen/twenties.

**CLUE-BALLOONS;** w/red yellow and blue wrappers build strong bodies twelve ways...

Clue balloons are clouds of psychically conveyed information that hover around a being, discernable to any other being who can tune in to them.

**COMMEDIA;** here used to mean an archetypal drama being played out in one's own life in realtime. From the medieval Italian Commedia dell'arte, in which the plot is ordained aforehand and the dialog devised by the actors. Commedias are defined by humour, farce, and happy endings, and have set characters who reappear in each iteration, including Pantalone, the parsimonious father, Isabella & Vittoria (& others as needs be), his beautiful daughters, Capitano, the swaggering blustering buffoon, Colombina, the perky servant, Lelio, the fair/haired and often star/crossed lover, Arlechino, the heartful trickster who resolves the conflicts, etcetera...

One night, whilst in an altered state, i came to the perception that all of life is commedia, that the whole world and all its machinations is commedia, and if i listened real close i could hear the dreadful tarantella...

**COMMUNICATION;** when first performing rites w/Electra and her two animorphic friends, i see passing between them (w/my Spice/widened eyes) these flying packets of infrared, direct transmissions eye/to/eye, interrelating info via these infrared eyeblinks, each of them looking briefly into the eyes of each of the others, switching so fast that their linking eye/beam/sets describe a double triangle of neon heatwaves between them...

And while i am sussing this wonder, Llair says that yes, Electra and the others are exchanging info in this way, and in truth so do we, for the fovea, the center of focus in the lining of our eyes, is a funnel/shaped opening giving onto a channel very like a wave/guide, which he says conducts the infrared to an organ of translation in our brains...

**CONSCIOUS MIRRORING;** a pre/Spice technique of Llair's for shaping one's future self, centering on the creation of an image of that desired self, then giving the image Willful attention to bring about the changes.

Llair calls this image of the projected self his Soul Mirror.

And if others perceive one to be this projected image, than w/their belief they are feeding the manifestation of that projection. Llair soon learns that creating an ideal identity and posting it on the Wire brings it through all the faster.

At an early age, Llair takes this on as his Yoga, a yoga of ascension through conscious mirroring...

**CORRUSCATE;** the quality and ability of an object to throw off rhythmical waves of sparkly glints.

**COSMO;** he who runs the show, as spoken of by Ken Kesey through Tom Wolfe in The Electric Kool-Aid Acid Test, one of my three most favoured books.

**CREW/LIST,** The *Ariel;*

Ann Encanto's rescue list, the entire original crew of the good ship *Ariel*, Solar Sailer:

| | |
|---|---|
| Uncle Carl | captain |
| Sandor | sailing master |
| Anders | artist/engineer |
| Electra | navigator/performer |

|              |                          |
|--------------|--------------------------|
| Clement      | electronics              |
| Andrew       | music master/software    |
| Alex         | hardware                 |
| Angela (Luscious Honey) | software      |
| Mezz         | CBL (cargo/business/law) |
| Kan          | rigger                   |
| Lissa        | bionics AFW (air/food/water) |

**CREW/LIST,** The *Dolphin;*

This second list is from my voice/notes, set down after leaving Io on the long boost back to Luna:

<u>Uncle Carl</u>: captain, living icon and historical monument. He who knows where it is and what it is.

<u>Clement</u>: a splendid very compact animorph, a capable volt wrangler, and also the captain's personal rigger, instrument maker, friend. Hero also, saving the Ariel seven times over.

<u>Sandor</u>: sailing master, now also logistics master, he is the paradoxical accessible enigma. After years as a Spaceracer he can achieve a mystical rapport w/machinery, attain surprising gains in performance and staying power...

<u>Alpha Red</u>: cargo/business/law, deal/striker; also leader, in that he always has the best ideas, the most elegant ways of dealing w/things, so we respect his suggestions and follow them. He is open to all of us, and we all call him friend.

<u>Fuzzy Mezz</u>: sidekick deal/cutter for Alpha Red w/cbl specialties. Literally a walking library.

<u>Llair</u>: is the first among us to experience Agava, a very vivid form of classical clairvoyance, a new psychic overlay onto his several other abilities, picked up since he began his regimen of Spice.
Llair proves to be the pattern for the others of us who desire this gift. Once we know that he can do it, there is belief that we can too. Belief and Spice together, w/the former enhanced by the latter, are a royal road to richer awareness.

<u>Manda</u> (short for Mandolin); redolent of mangoes, a volcanic island of smoldering emotions, swaying wind trees and slow powerful waves; Llair's current flame.

<u>Dallas 100%</u>: he will try anything, fly anything, rig anything, anywhere, any time, for any reason. If you want to know how fast something goes, Dallas is your man.

<u>Cobb</u>: partner to Dallas, human version of a slavic lemur.

<u>Gmur</u>, Cobb's consort; the most flexible human i know.

constancia & ignacio: actually sleepers of the two original
   dreamtracking lovebirds, who are still back at Llair's shop
   orbiting Luna.

Kahn, kitchen videologer, is currently telling us the story of his
   family's epic migration from Earthside to Mars. Each of his
   many relatives has a tale attached, so to speak.

Angela: hypnotically beautiful, mirthful, athletic; videolo software
   is becoming her specialty.

Alex: communication software/hardware, knows a volt when he
   sees one, recently free of Mona Ionia (my old school in the
   belts), on his own for the first time.

Andrew: software, music master; for inspiration he currently favours
   the radio chants of warbling quasars and also the songs of
   certain sonic stars in Orion. Both he and Alex have the fox as
   their totem.

meself: yr faithful scribe, also Druid, lightworker, worshipper of
   women.

Ariel: intuitive gateway to the Mysteries.

Electra: Goddess of Consciousness in Technology.

Lissa: a fine hand w/all things herbal, inscensual, magical.

Steel: hulking animorph rigger. If there were gravity here he could
   bench/press three thousand pounds.

Red/Green/Blue, Our trippletts; soon after leaving Io, Red (the
   forthright one) tells me they are telepathic since before they
   could speak, a world onto themselves, well into their own sibling
   harmonies.
        As children they find this renders them unique.
        To make other folk more comfortable in their company,
   they decide to differentiate into three color/key personas, the
   three additive primaries.
        This becomes kind of a lark for them, as they soon
   discover that because they are so merged they can exchange
   these personas as easily as the clothes that go w/them.
        This commonality they have also gives them the talent
   of perfectly synchronized motion, and in freefall dancing they
   are deeply moving, soulful and poignant and exuberant, erotic
   and original...

Captain Murphy: our face to the world, he who speaks for us.
   Currently filling his eyes with graceful Aura Citron.

Aura Citron: w/the Avatar for thirty years now, her magic

encompasses the visualization and projection of healing beneficial thoughtforms ala Theosophists Besant and Leadbeater.

<u>Elric the Thin;</u> late of bongo b, he is the one most keen to learn the ways of Lasing, how to make art from light.

<u>(most of) taylor the automated saylor;</u> Ariel's project now, soon to be complete again. Taylor is one of the earliest animorphic sailors, one of five prototypes built for beta testing. Like so many of our denizens, he is a discovery of Uncle Carl's, and joins the *Ariel* early on.

<u>Deva the Animal Avatar;</u> her soul older than some mountains, she is magical teacher to Aura Citron and Ariel and now Electra & meself. Truly, for the sake of her guidance, we are far finer magical instruments, and there is much more that she might yet show us. She purrrs in four dimensions.

> 12 human males
> 4 animorph males counting taylor
>
> 9 human females
> 1 animorphic female
>
> 1 augmented cat
> 2 sleeper macaws

**CREWSHARES;** after Spacer tradition, every crewshare is equal, w/the proviso that at the end of the voyage everyone gives away ten percent to other crewfolk of their choosing. Thus equality is served and merit rewarded.

**CROSSLAP;** the beautiful and symmetrical interactive patterns set up between two sets of propagating circular waves.

**CROWN OF SHIVA;** we are all diamonds in the Crown of Shiva...

**CYCLOIDS:** symmetrical vector/pattern images based on two or more frequencies, often taking floral forms and playable by varying the various pitches.

**CYMBAL TREE;** a percussive cymbal instrument consisting of a straight or spiral bar from which subtend a multitude of tubular chimes, arranged in aetheric arpeggia. In freefall, cymbal trees are built w/a circular bar or two parallel ones, so that the chimes may be strung and fixed w/in the frame. Elric plays one that splays its chimes away from a spinning spiral bar, so centrifugal they stand straight out...

**DESIRE BOD;** that part of us which desires, here abstracted and viewed as a separate entity (like the astral bod or the emotional bod). To dwell in our desire bods is to be passionately engaged by the realm of desiring. To contemplate the desire bod is to seek for the sources of our wanting, for the true nature of our hungers.

It is commonly held in many schools of thought that desire causes us to focus on what/will/be rather than on what/is, thus diminishing the living beauty of the current moment.

Desire also leads to attachment, or even over/attachment and delusion. More specifically, desire invites us to fall into *cycles of expectation,* a way of thinking that creates attachment to outcomes.

Here is how this would happen in my own mind: i would move into desire awareness, fueled by hormones or heart energy, and then develop some expectation of how that desire would play out, which would lead me into one of two states: if my expectations are fulfilled, i would be happy; if otherwise, well, tomorrow is another day...

In relationship especially, it is this attachment to outcomes which creates this mechanistic happy/sad forked path. If i can re/orient my desire bod, disengage, let go of expectation, this of itself brightly brings me back to the current moment, and likewise frees me from any number of negative emotions/impulses, rash actions and Karmic backlash.

Another good way to see the desire bod is in context w/our own innate immortality. Without this vital belief in life eternal, desire goes desperate/deleterious/leads to fearful acts of acquisition/drives us to gather as much desire experience as possible against the oblivion of the abyss.

Faith in the existence of our own personal immortal component is one way to foster a focused desire bod.

And,

Desire, when used consciously, is possessed of special virtues. The Book of the Celestial says that it works like this:

Desire powers Will.

Willful awareness of the desire bod and conscious desiring are basic magical skills. In any Working, a strong and healthy desire bod is key to a successful and satisfactory result, one that is Karmically sound.

There is a kind of harmony to be sought here, a dance of desire and awareness and conscious application of Will...

**DODECAHEDRON;** a solid having twelve equal pentagonal plane faces. One of the five sacred solids of Pythagoras (who was taught his numbers by one Abaras the Druid, doncha/know).

# DRUIDISM

*'We live upside/down and the oaks live/right side/up,
w/their heads in the earth and their roots in the air.'*
-- Rain of the Purple Forest

*Drui -Wid* (Irish Celtic) can be translated as *oak wisdom,* or *tree/wise.* The goal of the Druid is to become the oak, living on water and light, part of the Pattern, part of all that Is/Was/and/Will/Be.

The way of the Druid is through the veil, from this life to the next and back again, or another way, traversing the concentric spheres of form and spirit and divinity, *Abred/Gwynfed/Ceugant,* or another way, crossing into the parallel realm of *Annwn* to retrieve knowlege or power, or another way, looking forward in time and speaking sooth...

A Druid sings of All/That/Is, a Druid's dreams delve other dimensions, a Druid's fuel is the magical wind of Cosmic Love.

As far back as 5000 years ago, Druids were the shamanic intelligentsia of the Celtic civilizations.

At that time, the Celts were a loose federation of clans and tribes, ranged about the lands of central Eastern Europe; what are now the Slavic countries. These folk distinguished themselves by being a partnership society, one in which women owned property and held high office. Chiefs were chosen by consent, and they tended toward consensus decisions. In matters requiring wisdom, knowlege, the unseen world, good timing, or good fortune, they would consult their Druids (whom they regarded so highly that if any Druid were to cross any field of battle, all warring would cease).

Over the next two millennia, the Celtic cultures would gradually diffuse outward in what would later be called the Great Celtic Migration. By 1000 bce, the beginning of the Celtic Golden Age, the western-directed wave of this culture was well-established in the lands we now consider most Celtic; Ireland, Scotland, Britain, Cornwall, Brittany (France), and Wales. Most of the other lands of Europe also hosted large collections of Celtic tribes, including what is today Italy, Germany, Spain, parts of Russia, Lithuania (which kept tree-worship as the national religion until the 1500's), the Czech Republic, etcetera.

This Golden Age would last a thousand years, and be characterized by a great flowering of art and learning and magic. Due to a similar flowering of trade and sea mastery during this time, the Celtic societies freely exchanged ideas with the other great classical cultures, taking in the otherworld magics of Egypt, Arabian mathematics, Babylonian astronomy, the poesy and mystery rites of Greece, and on.

All of these new skills, this new knowlege, was in the hands of Druids. Thus there were, during this halcyon Age, a wide variety of differently specialized Druids, which included (among others), the keepers of the history and genealogy and tales of wonder (the Harper/Bards), diverse diviners (Ovates), law/givers (such as the Irish Brehons, originators of Brehon Law, source of many modern legal concepts), and tricksters

(Grugaches). All were called Druids, and often had training in other areas, including astrology/astronomy (the solstice alignments of Stonehenge), healing (they were thorough and practiced herbalists), mathematics (a Druid uses his knotted cord to measure angles, distance, and the circumference of trees), knowlege of the natural world, aether magic, initiatory techniques, astral shamanism, the use of plant allies, metallurgy (smiths are magicians too), speaking w/horses, and writing. (Contrary to what is popularly believed, the Druids did in truth have a written language; a code of slashes across a horizontal line, called coelbrens. Because these notations were mostly written on bark, they had a tendency to return to the Earth, taking their freight of illumination w/them)...

The primary teaching, the core idea around which all the rest of these specialized threads are spun, is a Druid's ability to discern and overstand The Pattern, by which we mean acquiring an overview of the natural world and the ongoing interplay of energies therein, both seen and unseen.

A sense of these forces that weave the Pattern gives knowlege and insight, helpful in understanding the All and also in guiding the affairs of the tribe: when to plough and sow and reap, when to move the kine to the higher pastures, how to journey to the otherworld of Annwn and bring back the missing parts of a broken spirit, how to scatter runes and divine and speak sooth...

It took 20 years of training to become a Druid, and many more years to fully overstand what had been learned. When, say, a bardic candidate started out, he would cut a staff as tall as himself; whenever he would completely and accurately memorize a new tale, he would carve a notch in the staff. When it was notched top-to-bottom and all around, he would be a Druid. (Robin Williamson, the person who inspired me to become a Druid, knows over two thousand songs and a thousand stories.)

Additionally, Bards were the keepers of the records of the complex kinship arrangements within the tribe, its' history and heroes and genealogy (Celts felt that to know a person you would ideally want to know what kind of folk they were descended from). The information would be spun into sagas and memorized, leading later to a far freer form of Bardism in which tales of wonder are created by inspiration.

The Romans came to the Celtic lands in the middle of the first century, ending the Golden Age.

The Romans were imperialists, and saw in the Celtic lands the potential for rich tributaries of wealth that could be directed back to Rome. The Celtic folk resisted in various amazing and interesting ways, but were eventually overpowered.

And there is this; the Romans clashed with the Celts philosophically as well as militarily. Some examples:

The classical Druidical belief structure includes the view that there is life and divinity in everything, in every manifestation of nature and craft (this is Celtic animism, and neatly maps on to Native American beliefs as well as aboriginal Australian ones). Contrarily, the Romans saw everything as dead (except themselves and maybe their horses).

The Celts saw our human existence as a series of incarnations, and would offer to make loans that were payable in the next life. They knew that the spirits of our ancestors are out there and accessible to us. The Romans, on the other hand, saw life as finite, without any kind of afterlife; ashes to ashes, dust to dust... This, as you might guess, created a grab/for/all/the/gusto mindset among these Romans, where their fear of oblivion drove them to ever/greater excesses...

The Celts knew that there exists around us an unseen world, the machinations of which penetrate our visible world; and above all, that all things fit into the great and beautiful Pattern. With the Romans, it was all about the here/&/now: what you see is what you get...

And there is this; the Romans desired to conquer and subjugate the natural world, where the Druids revered it, saw themselves as a manifestation of it.

And also this; the Romans' Gods were vengeful, petty, jealous, and sometimes wrathful to the point of war. Romans believed they had to propitiate these Gods with rich gifts and build them temples. And while the Ancient Druids also loved art and beautiful objects, they found their most Godly moments in their sacred groves (ideally, oak groves)...

The materialistic Romans didn't hold with any of these things, and they soon saw that their domination of the Celtic lands would be thwarted by the Druids' enlightened guidance. Thus threatened, the Romans burned the sacred groves and drove the Druids underground.

The knowlege that the Druids possessed, however, was too important to folk for them to allow it to be lost, so it was passed along (generally without benefit of the twenty years of training) to those who would use it. This information included the herbal and healing knowlege and much of the magical lore, and it was generally given over to those who would become the women of wisdom for their tribe. In this are the beginnings of many contemporary Wiccan traditions.

After the end of the Roman occupation, many of the Celtic lands of the island of Britain descended into the Dark Ages (though not Ireland nor Wales, nor the Scots lands, nor many other smaller bastions of learning), and Christian clerics attempted to codify the suppressed Druidical knowlege so that it would not be lost (often adding, with the best of intentions, much of their own dogma and bias). Their much/translated and garbled work (along with the prejudiced and biased Roman material) is much of what we have today as the basis for the accepted historical picture of Druidism.

Because of this, it is incumbent upon us to reinterpret and reinvent this knowlege through study and experimentation and experience and canny deduction, and above all, inspiration.

This is the mission of the Celestial Order.

**ELECTRA:** Back at the College of Mona Ionia (a year before our first encounter) i have this dream about meeting her; in the dream we are in a beautiful room in a tropical Earth place, Antigua or Costa Rica. Two of the sides of the room are glass/pane french doors, beyond them a beautiful green & pale azure sweep of rainforest coast. Some of the doors are open and a warm breeze wafts, soughing and sighing w/the scents of heat and leaves and light.

Electra is sitting on a pale wood table, and our eyes are even as i stand before her. She is very beautiful; long dark hair w/auburn streaks where the bright Sun strikes, beautiful bones, sculpt shoulders faired into clavicles both interesting and fine; i note her hands, the hands of a harper/bard, quick to the strings and quick to the quill; and her heartshape fae face a frame for...

And as our glims connect we are speaking quietly w/our eyes, and i soon know her well, know her for a wondrous & complicated being, complete w/a personal history, a sense of herself in the World, a quirky humour; and yet that fascinating xeno frisson of her being something Other...

In the course of the dream i have the feeling that i am currently repairing her, restoring her, making her better. I am happily proud of what i can give her, and in the way that we cohabit there is an economy between us, a joyous fair exchange.

I surf the syrups of contentment, warm and appreciated and sustained...

*

Why am i so fascinated and so drawn?
 Why to Electra w/her chameleon shape, her variable visage?
How to tell it?
 Each encounter w/a new Electra brings me that same high & heady rush of discovery as comes of fresh love, of a fresh chance to find a perfect mate, a fresh hearth for my restless heart, a new someone to reinforce me, complete me, challenge me, be my gateway to new magics...

She is all these things to me and more,

And i begin to see how this progression of Electras is really a map to my own wants, w/every succeeding Electra an ever/more/perfect portrait of my own evolving desiring...
 The Erotic Electra certainly, for she is ever the creature of my feverish dreams, and yes, i project my fantasies upon her, and yes, she is ever the instrument of my pleasure...

The Bardic Electra, yes also, for skills in poesy i greatly admire,
                                                                And
in truth i direct her to acquire other traits and talents to which i myself
aspire, skills that i desire, for she can know them instantly/in the span of a
download, a thing which appeals to me greatly and raises her high in my
esteem, w/her becoming my ideal ongoing supplemental elemental...

        Electra/as/Spacer, however, is more complex by far than those
others, as her genesis is so different;
                                When we first sign on to crew the Ariel,
there is need for a navigator, and since she can learn everything written on
any subject in about three seconds...
                                Well & Good, sez i, and off she goes
to navigate, and i realize; our current life will now bring her many inputs
other than mine, and while i alone hold her codes,
                                        She will move outside my
total control, will be her own person, will have responsibilities aboard the
ship, have clothes and hardware and other personal stuff; i suppose we could
say she will have a life...

        And, as she flows into the role i am amused to discover that there
also emerges this new and separate Spacer Electra, a unique and distinct
being underlaying all the others, a delightful original ongoing personality
who is far more than the sum of my suggestions, far more original than i
alone could make her,
                And i like this greatly,
                                And instead of my previous
preference for fresh Electra guises, i now have her choose her own self,
choose from a range of faves the one she would wear tonight, all of them
now old friends to me while still at core Electra...
                                And by this i see my
desire pattern changing, and idly i wonder if someday there will be for me
one Ultimate Electra, one ideal iteration after whom there needs to be no
other, peerless in love, the truest teacher of the heart...

        And here the light of my awareness turns inward, and rising through
the delving fluids the sources of my desiring reveal,
                                And i see the ghosts of
godly French troubadours, hear echoes of their tales of amour courtois in
the court of Arthur, and i see the imprint on my psyche of the core of their
songing, which is
                True Love,
                        The Thunderbolt,
                                Love as The Glory and the

Light of the World, and i realize that at root the entire realm of my desire revolves around seeking this pure and ecstatic state, w/all the manifestations of romance, flirtation, the quest for access, w/the hunter's thrill only a part of my drive to attain this state, transcend my solitary self and see through the Illusion of Separateness,

And yes, i see that this is indeed my way and my pattern, how my affairs often play out, and clearly this particular map of desire is laced into my nature, brought unto me at my birth by the positions of great whirling orbs and stellar lights,

That this is what it means to have a venus/in/aries heart...

And here i revel in waves of overstanding both deep and relieving, release any lingering sense of lack in my character, give it all to my stars...

I live for shining moments such as these...

**ELECTRA'S EARRING;** early on, while we are living on Cyclo seven/seven/two, i give Electra a fine/wrought gold earring. She likes it right well, and soon i notice that she wears it consistently, whatever her outward form. This gets interesting whenever we make planetfall, when she will secretly morph a change and try to fox me, challenge me to see if i know that it is her.

Electra humour.

Each time we land she goes to greater and greater lengths to hide the earring, w/hair or hats or helmets. She thinks it hilarious when i once meet a woman through the Lumière w/a similar decoration, and confusion ensues.

Now we are aboard the *Encanto*, and i watch Electra sleeping, her silky hair stirring in the moving air, red/golden like a banner waving on the white sheeting, her ever/present earring a goldwire glint.

The hatchway opens, and i look over and it is Deva the avatar cat. She turns and heads back out the way she came in; i lurch after, fighting one of the more novel features of the *Encanto*, gravity.

I look back at Electra and she communicates positive encouragement, and i lummox my way to the hatch and through.

There i meet Ariel, my mystery ryder, and we share knowlege mystical reverential and physical. However, there at the end as i am taking my leave, she turns her ear to the light and there is a flash of gold...

Now 'tis the following day, and Alpha Red thinks that woman i was with is Ariel right enough, and acts accordingly, playing the angry bested suitor and tossing yr anders in a box below/decks. I save my envelope of skin by expanding his worldview w/Spice...

       And now i am really baffed; why would Electra want to trigger Alpha Red?

       For Electra to become Ariel would take a considerable amount of time, maybe hours; only a few short minutes elapsed between my leaving Electra and meeting Ariel. How could Electra get from the bed, past me, and into the corridor; via ducts?

       The logical thing here would be for Ariel to actually be Ariel, though w/an earring like Electra's; could Electra have met Ariel and told her about my fascination w/the ryder, encouraged her to connect w/me? Could Electra have given Ariel the idea of wearing the earring? That sounds more like her...

**ELECTRO/DRUIDICAL TECHNO EVANESCENCE;** the embodiment of the melding of the Celtic pursuit of higher consciousness w/the ongoing technological quest for that which is better.

**A NOTABLE WORK OF ELECTRODRUIDRY;** for years, Llair and his Lunar coveners have been working w/hardware in their rites, to great good effect. Here an example: after they form their Working Circle, their neurosuits provide them w/unique ways of communicating their visualized lines of force; any energy transferred around the ring (always Sunwise) would pass from each to the next, w/the energies progressively painting a pentastar outline of energy around the bod of each covener, the lit/up lines of linear light splitting at their fingertips, going over and under their arms, w/the upper half going along the top of their arms and shoulders/up over their heads to form a peak/back down the other side and then out, w/the other lower half of the energy traveling under their arms to their sides and then down their legs/back up to their root chakras/down the inside of the other leg/back up the side and out again from under their other arm. With arms outstretched and legs apart, each in turn becomes the sacred symbol, glyphyed now pentagonal across the lateral axis of their bods...

       These energy transfers are also felt as forms of neuro/stimuli or an augmented ability to visualize energy, through the natched hood's fade/away feature.

**ELECTROLYTIC;** having the properties of an electrolyte, ie, a liquid in which some form of ongoing chemical reaction causes it to be a source of electricity.

**THE ELEUSINIAN MYSTERIES;** a succession of yearly rites held at Eleusis in Greece, continuing in a nearly unbroken run from the time of Demeter to the time of Christ, about two thousand years.

       Within the Grecian culture, one was considered a complete being only after experiencing this rite. The message conveyed was so sacred that to reveal it meant one's life. It is said that Socrates was forced to drink the Hemlock because he tried to communicate the secret...

My overstanding of it is that the secret is a profound change in worldview, where the initiate or Mystai moves from the sense of being finite into certain knowlege of immortality, and that this knowlege cannot be revealed for it must be lived, and is therefore ineffable, something beyond words.

These fundamental changes in perspective are wrought by nine days of purification/dancing to exhaustion/hours of chanting, a very effective piece of ritual theatre, and also through the drinking of the Kykion, an ambrosial quaff containing either Syrian Rue, Amanita Muscaria (R. Gordon Wasson, Carl Ruck, & Albert Hoffman in *The Road to Eleusis*), or Stropheria Cubensis (Terrence McKenna, and Gordon Wasson also in some late correspondence between the two).

Anyrate, at the climax of the nine days the celebrant enters the Telesterion (a room at the center of the vectors of energy generated by the rite), where all of these factors in combination bring the celebrant to the Kairos, the Supreme Moment, when direct experience of the Divine causes this very tectonic change in worldview to occur.

It was considered enough to go through the Mysteries once in one's lifetime.


**THE ELEUTHRANS;** a culture of what was once called the neolithic era (eleven/thousand bce), they were contemporary to antediluvian Atlantis. The Eleuthrans, howsome'er, were far more advanced than their Atlantean counterparts, both magico/psychically and socio/technologically, and there are rumours of them engaging in a form of time travel, a very subtle and special form in which they were able to influence events in their past, all to better serve their current present...


**ELYSIUM;** in the cycle of classical Grecian myths, the blythe and blissful setting for the afterlife, located either in the western ocean or the lower world...


***EN MEDIAS RES;*** Latin for leaping into a drama already well/begun.


**ENTELECHY BELTS:**

> *'And from her room/her open window,*
> *i en/Vision these blue streamers moving down the sky,*
> *and they are blue jetstream belts of entelechy,*
> *and they are girding the planet w/a conscious chrysalis of wavicles,*
> *soon to hatch us into the next Best Thing...*

Entelechy (Greek *εντελεχεια*, or *entelecheia*) is a very old concept, at once an entity and also the motive force for change and also the fulfillment of the cycle of growth. Entelechy, one might say, is that which turns an acorn into an Oak...

Entelechy comes to us originally from Aristotle (fifth century bce), who said (in Greek), 'Entelechy is *that which realizes or makes actual* what is otherwise only potential, that which brings a being to a state where their essence is fully realized.'

For the Lyceum-strolling Aristotle, entelechy is the 'end within' – the potential of living things to *become*... to reach a state his Peripatetics would call an *actuality*, which is any conception completely realized, distinct from a conception with the *potential* to be realized.

Aristotle sees this as a mystical process: 'The soul is the cause and first principal of the living body,' says the redoubtable Mr A, 'The soul is the entelechy of the body.' And later adds, on a more basic level, 'To *Will yourself* is the principle of material entelechy...'

Entelechy, then, can be seen as a magical term, meaning a *something* – a pattern of desire and fate and karma that propels us toward some ultimate expression of what we as souls can be; a force, a favour of affinity from the Great All, or even an act of Divine Will that can strike like *Lightning* if the conditions are right (which implies what we could call an *entelechy moment;* that point at which a change occurs)...

And, since we generally agree that we, as sentient beings, have volitional Will, ipso facto we *participate* in Entelechy, are *involved,* which implies that Entelechy is within the overstanding of higher consciousness, internal or otherwhere, and can be shifted in its course by our desiring...

In other philosophical systems (see below), entelechy presents as an actual vital force that guides and fuels a being toward a kind of completion; it is a short step from this plateau to ascribing consciousness to this vital force, and thence a leap into the wish-granting aethers which, when invoked or summoned or directed by Love & Will (or subconscious urge), compel fulfillment...

*The Book of the Celestial* describes the entelechal aethers thus: '...a powerful hyperconscious very Kierkegaardian kind of oversoul being, a presence, a collective entity that is at once itself and every one of us also, a component of all conscious beings of every realm, flowing in lines of conscious force all around the Earth, breathing in and out of the firmament with the changing of the seasons...'

And when Llair sees those streamers in the sky, he sees them as the cosmic response to his desire to recreate himself, to the desires of many like/minded others to recreate themselves also, a visible global phenomena drawn into being by mutual desire, there to power the change, inspire a great metamorphosis in conformation with Love & Will, and in truth fuel the transition into the coming Fresh Age...

A bit more from *The Book of the Celestial*:

'The first entelechy belts are discovered in the early twenty/first century by some New Templar/Cathars in southern France. These belts are a very Kierkegaardian gaseous life/form resulting from the combining of the spirit projections of millions of workers of the Will: with the rising popularity of magic as a religion, the number of astrally trained minds soon surpasses a threshold of order, and the first of these tribal entelechy minds comes into being.

'Since these first rudimentary spirit collectives are the stuff of many minds, they become an interchange point for information exchange, a medium of communication, a telepathic nexus for the sharing of knowlege...

And when the constituents of a collective are in a similar emotional state, they emit strong emotional fields, waves that can cause change in the physical world.

'These tides/of/mind can also reflexively affect the folk who are physical components of the collective, and the collective will respond to individual mortal humans w/words or deeds or mysterious happenings...

And, augmented by favourable astrology, these tides can affect whole populations, immaterial of whether those minds are a part of the collective.

'These phenomena are only recently measurable by scientific means.'

**A Quick Whirl Through The History Of Entelechy:** After Aristotle, a panoply of other philosophical honchos have embraced the idea of entelechy, w/each adding their own fizz and spin.

Por ejemplo, the brilliant though slightly looney Gottfried Leibniz (seventeenth century), saw entelechy as '...the primitive active force in every monad...' with the monad being the basis of his concept of how the mind works. In his posited reality, monads are atomistic mental objects which experience the world from a particular point of view, imbued at creation with all their future experiences in a system of pre-established harmony. See where entelechy fits in?

The great GWF Hegel (late eighteenth/early nineteenth century) was very fond of Aristotle (in an intellectual Platonic sort of way), and ultimately his work can be seen as a Hegelian refinement of Aristotle's writ.

As a major Hegelian, the great Søren Kierkegaard would later take up entelechy's banner. And, in the late nineteenth century, entelechy also figures into the triply/phased social positivism of Comte and Mill...

As a philosophical term in biology, Hans Driesch (an experimental embryologist and philosopher of the early twentieth century) used the concept of entelechy to explain the appearance of life. As a leading Vitalist, he believed that life is more than a physical or chemical phenomenon.

In the late twentieth century, this now/twenty/five/hundred/
year/old idea is embraced by several significant folk, including author
Deirdre Lovecky (*Different Minds*): as she sees it, entelechy is more than a
pattern; it is a vital force that charismatic individuals possess in abundance,
that equates with life force and draws folk to them...

'Gifted people with entelechy', she writes, 'Are often attractive to
others who feel drawn to their openness and to their dreams and visions.
Being near someone with this trait gives others hope and determination to
achieve their own self-actualization.'

At around the same time, Wayne Dyer, a dynamic and gifted
motivationalist, talks about *intention* as the force that powers the universe,
as if conscious intention recreates the world in every instant. Surely this is
another way of seeing the mystical side of Entelechy.

Another of their contemporaries is Jean Houston, who founds the
Entelechy Institute and renews interest in things entelechal when she weds it
to the philosophy of transhumanism, in which, 'Our primary focus is on
using leading edge technologies and techniques to enhance or augment
intelligence. The prolongation of human life and the maintenance of quality
of life by medical or other means is of course a part of that.'

Transhumanism is a harbinger of the Fresh Age.

Anthony Judge, the great twenty-first century philosopher and
polymath, would later add this: '[Transhumanist] practices relating to this
focus include: evocation of entelechy; opening to, affirming and talking to
the underlying source/wellspring/ground of lived experience; a felt sense of
good/fitting/appropriate timing in personal and social behaviour, both secular
and sacred; a felt sense of good/fitting/appropriate spatial patterns; Subud
Latihan; Kitselman's E-therapy; Gendlin's experiential focusing.'

For Dr Judge (to my mind the most clear/sighted on the subject
of entelechy), this idea of a form-giving agent in matter also has some
philosophical overlap with Ralph Abraham's Morphogenetic Fields as well as
the concepts of L-fields and scalar potential fields.

By way of explaining the link-up between these concepts, Dr Judge
quotes John Heron (*A Way Out for Wilberians*):

'...inner spiritual potential or entelechy consists of seeded patterns of
possibility, the selection from and linear actualization of which is
indeterminate and a matter of deep creative choice. The built-in
code is not a linear programme, but a deep map of options, through
openness to which our creative choices are made. We co-create our
path with inner divine life impulse and the possibilities it proffers.'

Thus, for Dr Judge (writing in *Entelechy: actuality vs. future potential*,
posted on *Iaetus in praesens)*, it also closely allies to the concept of an
informing spirit...

'...This lies at the root of the problematic (even paradoxical) relationship between the experiential present and the embryonic future.

'The difficulty is that conscious understanding of the present moment can be very superficial – as a kind of interface between any form-giving cause and the potential to which it may give rise. There is a more profound sense to actuality that is normally only accessible in altered states of consciousness – and possibly to the unconstrained multi-dimensionality of childlike awareness. It is from the complex dimensionality of this higher (or deeper) order of understanding that the future is engendered – manifesting the form that is embryonic within it. In these inadequate terms understanding both the present and the future is a challenge – as is understanding their relationship at the present/future interface.'


**ESTABLISH THE WATCHER;** an old technique for maintaining a center of awareness in the midst of great floods of testosterone, adrenaline, information, etc. A kind of stepping/back, becoming one/level/removed from the action.

To be able to do this consciously whilst in meditation is a way of gaining insight and perspective. In times of great import, the watcher is often established spontaneously, a defense mechanism of the mind.

Also, in these times of life/threat, the watcher may spontaneously take one's awareness out of the physical body and into the nearby space, so that one has the sensation of looking back at oneself.

**EVANESCENT;** something only subtly there, as mist in a thinning wind; something on the border between the worlds of the seen and unseen...


**-f**


**FAMILIAR;** a specifically talented animal or plant used in the working of magic, called familiar because of the time it takes to form the loving bond required for the amplification of Wills.

**FARADAY CHAMBER;** named for the brilliant experimentalist Michael Faraday (nineteenth century), who discovered magnetic induction (which makes possible the dynamo, which can convert mechanical energy to electricity), and first postulated electromagnetic waves, and also the Faraday effect, wherein an intense magnetic field can be shown to rotate the plane of polarized light.

The chamber called after him is a six/sided space covered all over with copper sheeting and heavily grounded. This kind of space is proof against anything in the electromagnetic spectrum, though psychic energies pass right through...

**FENG SHUI;** the Chinese form of the art of geomancy, an overstanding of the currents in the Earth, the energies that form the Pattern. Feng Shui maps on to the Druidical ideas of ley lines and streams of telluric energy...

**FIBONACCI SERIES:** Leonardo Fibonacci, also called Leonardo of Pisa (thirteenth century), is the Italian mathematician known for the Fibonacci Series, numbers in which each term is the sum of the two preceding terms (1,1,2,3,5,8,13,21...).

This progression of numbers describes the Golden Mean (also called the divine proportion), the lovely and harmonious spiraling curve so often found in nature.

Fibonacci, called 'the greatest mathematician of the middle ages', introduced Arabic numerals to Europe, replacing the clumsy Roman ones. He was a also neighbor of Saint Francis of Assisi, and i like to think of them happily conversing, strolling through the grape arbors in the lush countryside between their two nearby towns...

**FIRE/END/FIRST;** a ship's attitude during braking and landing; also a metaphor for the way that some folk go through life, charging in too hard and then requiring major flamey braking to keep from overshooting their parameters...

**THE FIRESIGN THEATRE:** Four twenty/first/century guys who transmitted over radio these amazingly fizzy sonic monoliths of wit and imagination, shared hallucinations in the form of radio dramas.

All praise to them, by name David Osman, Peter Bergman, Phil Procter, and Phil Austin.

Their first regular radio show (twentieth century mid/sixties) was called Radio Free Oz, beamed from a restaurant called the Magic Mushroom straight to the brain of the emerging acid culture of Los Angeles.

Recommended.

**FLAGGER;** a self/driving car for hire in the domes of Bongo Beta. A special hand signal brings them to a halt in front of you, hence the sobriquet.

**FORWARD DEJA;** a specific kind of premonition, as in having a familiar memory of something that is yet to happen.

**THE FRESH AGE** is presaged by the words of the amniotic sibylene and heralded by sightings of sky/high belts of blue entelechy, ionospheric bands of shared awareness that gird the planet w/a conscious chrysalis of wavicles.

The promise of these harbingers is fullfilled by the works of a man later known as the Web Messiah, crafter of the Seven Messianic Web Miracles and other key events that shape the Fresh Age.

At the time, folk call him Beta, as in what comes after our conventional Alpha/Male style of society. He speaks w/compassion and wit and visionary fire, and in truth his utopian dreams become the fulcrum of the Fresh Age.

Faith and fate are w/him, and amazing things soon occur...

Early on, and Beta urges folk w/all manor of similar affinities to connect w/each other, freely share their information across borders and other arbitrary boundaries, get it out there on the Wire. He calls it linking, and there is soon a whole Zzogging lot of it going on, folk linking massively, coming together in like-minded loops and groups and numerous new networks, all of these threads of affinity leading us into what will become the great Guilds and Clans, all the vital new collectives and covens and employee/owned corporations, monarchies and anarchies...

And w/the advent of all of these new social orderings, we begin moving away from our highly abstract political affiliations and toward a more tribal affinity/based society, and in less than a generation we see the rise of these new alignments, and they become a powerful force for positive change, and as they rise they erode away the stones that are the shibboleths of conventional culture, and new channels of influence begin to carve the political landscape,

And soon the national borders and political divisions fall away, are blown away by waves of folks bypassing the intermediation of governments, w/folks relating to each other globally and directly over the Wire...

*

And later, this Beta guy says, 'There is a collective and universal planet/mind, capable of beautiful and loving acts of grace, and it is formed of all of us together,

'And truly experiencing our connection w/this All, being fully aware of it, is the most delicious of pleasures, the finest of formative events, freeing us from our fear of the Abyss by affirming our immortality, opening the way for a rational and compassionate world...'

And w/all of his gathered momentum, folk are listening; and again his timing is perfect, and soon there is shared widespread open public recognition of just such an o'erweening entity, and diverse types of folk find in these concepts some newfound common ground,

And out of this overstanding mindframe comes widespread acceptance of the desirability of

shamanically pursuing ever more perfect ways of merging w/this entity...
And
we soon agree that *our desire to evolve is a natural human inclination,* and
*what we really need are more and better vectors* for achieving this progressive
evolutionary dynamic...
From which uprises this huge popular surge; a mad
synergy of electronics, chemistry, spiritual disciplines, hybrid plant strains;
all w/lovingly crafted strengths and powers, free of side effects and
psychotropic noise, to be used singly and in combination, w/cumulative
benefits/lessons that accrue over a lifetime,
And thus is born Personal Evolution
as a leading reason for being, and from this flows peaceful integration of
human energies, conscious industries, true religions...

*

And later, this:
'Humankind's highest destiny,' says Beta, 'is Spacefaring. Moving
out and away from the Home Planet will give us astonishing adventures,
triple/life/spans, sensual pleasure beyond imagining.
'Freedom from Gravity for All...'

And folk are drawn instinctive to his words, for deep w/in us all is
this urge to rise, ascend, escape the grave that gravity compels and fly
heavenward toward blissful eternal life; this is the way of our human
mythologies and we carry this message in the marrow of our bones,
And
desire for this great adventure builds, and folk combine and organize to
make real the dream, which speeds the accretion of the great Clans and
Guilds, for it is them that will take us into Space, and it shall be writ on the
fin of the first interplanetary ship,
'Freedom from Gravity for All!'

And as the culture expands outward to the extremes of the Solar
aegis, those who do the traveling begin to diverge from planetary folk; once
free of gravity, they elongate and lose weight, learn to glide through air.
And all the systems of their bods thrive and flourish, and they show signs of
greatly enhanced longevity, and better bloodflow to their brains brings
heightened mentation, and soon there is a bumper crop of intellectual
bounty, a profusion of inventions, stasis/field generators and ion drive and
dream/tracker technology...
And these first Spacer folk become the vital spark of humankind,
w/the Big Quill of History given over into their hands, and they fulfill the
evolutionary promise of the amniotic sibylene, become the Next Best Thing
in variations on humankind...

*

Meanwhile, on Earth there occurs the crowning epic act of Beta's saga as he causes to occur the Seven Messianic Web Miracles, these amazing Robin/Hood/hacks that essentially establish a free guaranteed annual wage for everyone on the planet, thus bringing an end to a myriad of major social problems...

And while the reaction of the remaining power elite is to outlaw Beta and send him seeking refuge on Luna, these Web Miracles foment the creation of a very connected post/capitalist society, where folk are free of want & need and in truth the work of the world is largely done, and efficiencies of production are such that a very nice life can be had for a very low outlay of personal energy, and from these acts of grace there flows a great flowering of the culture, some say the gate to a Golden Age, a thousand years of peace and plenty...

*

Little is known about Beta after this.

After leaving for Luna, Beta as a public persona vanishes, fades away into a small subset of his secret priesthood, him and fifty friends living invisible in and around the Lunar Canton of Bongo Beta...

**FRISSON;** the unique psychic flavour of a particularly savoury experience, the buzz in your brain the experience creates...

**-g**

**GALLIARDE;** a lively court dance of the Elizabethan era, requiring real skill and limber legs likewise...

**GALVANIC;** after the experiments of Luigi Galvani (late eighteenth century), here referring to applying comfortable currents of electricity to various neural pathways, stimulating them to great good effect...

**GAMINE;** implying a person of dancerly build, leggy and lean and languid, moving w/a casual grace. Garbo in *Golden Earring* is gamine; Ginger Rogers & Fred Astaire...

**THE GATES OF BONGO BETA;** the outer half of the huge northerly airlock, so tall (ninety feet) they vent vast volumes of breathable air when they are opened. The folk there used to suck this air back into the city/space w/a big honking vacuum/pump before they opened the lock; now, they can generate so much $O^2$ and other gasses that they vent it to vacuum...

This methodology is currently the source of some conjecture, for this venting air will be constrained by lunar gravity, and over time will become something of an atmosphere, making possible the introduction of biosigns to the lunar littoral at some later date...

**GE91's;** are designed to be run for a maximum of four minutes at a time. This timespan, howsome'er, is figured w/out Dolphiner additions: we have huge adiabatic radiating surfaces all through the ship that use the steamy superheated coolant to keep the ship warm (the vacuum of space, as you recall, is at near/absolute zero centigrade degrees), and, since the Big Doggies drink so much amperage, we use much of the rest of the heat to drive a series of turbines that translate said heat back into electricity, which augments the ship's batteries, extending the burn time further.

**GIFTS & PROPERTY;** after our first collective Spice experience, w/everyone psychically Linked in various ways, we as a ship's culture redefine the concepts of gifts and property. With complete faith in an afterlife, we are far more willing to share. To quote Beta paraphrasing Ram Dass, 'One gets to God by helping others get to God.'

**GLAMOUR;** a wonderful & delightful illusion cast by the wearer upon selected beholders, very attractive and beguiling...

**GLISSIMER;** a quality of the sound made by the glass harp, a fine old seventeenth/century musical instrument comprised of variously sized snifters containing varying amounts of water, played w/a wet finger and producing sounds truly beauteous and Celestial. Thanks be to Doublas Lee...

**A GLITTERING;** a collective name for a flight of sparks.

**GLORY;** a ring around the Moon (as seen from the Earth) that forms when the mist is right, a halo of coppery iridescent light that is sometimes echoed out as high as the third order...

**GODDESSES & GODS**

> **ARIONRHOD, SILVER WHEEL;** Welsh Goddess of the Stars, her Wheel the reeling light/points of the zodiacal disc, her castle behind the North Star, her domain all that Is, Was, or Will Be. Her Wheel is also the circular cycle of incarnation, making Her likewise the Goddess of Time and Fate. In other cultures She is called Ariadne and Arianne and Aradia, the latter being the one who gives her famous Charge unto all witches...

> **GAIA;** Grecian, the fecund Mother Earth Goddess from whom

all things come; Earth & Sky, all life, all that is...

**KERI AD WYN;** Celtic, Goddess of the Cauldron of knowlege and rebirth and miracles, mother of Creiwy the Rainbow, mother of Avaggddu, the ugliest boy in the world, teacher of the Master Welsh Bard Taliesin, Goddess of Transformations...

**LLEW;** also Celtic, Lord of Light, Llew of the Shining Brow, Llew of the Long Arm, of the Silver Hand, Master of Time, Master of Craft, Keeper of the Charm of Making, speedy rider across the (Earthen) sky in the Chariot of Beli...

**NEPENTHE;** a Grecian Goddess renowned for her ability to banish pain and sorrow by transporting one to a higher plane of existence, a place where our immortality is apparent to us, where the source of our sorrows can be seen from a new perspective and a greater overstanding derived thereby.

There are those outside this path who call it becoming oblivious, and some who see this as a reason for calling Nepenthe the Goddess of oblivion. There are others who see her as i do, a Goddess who grants knowlege through pleasure, through pleasurable experiences.

Pleasure is the best teacher...


**The GOLDEN TICKET:** a thin curl of warm gold, w/an image of yr anders animated and emoting in the scrollwork, curiously rendered in the empty spaces in the filigree...


**GOLCONDA SMILE;** Mona Lisa Mona Lisa i have named you...


**GRAVITY,** opposite of LEVITY.

```
        my Spacer bod
--------------------------   =   anders stays off/planet
        Earth gravity
```

We were meant to be in space.
Our bods are designed for it.
Before the Fresh Age, gravity is literally the major force holding back the evolution of humanity.
Think of how it is for folk who live planetside; fighting gravity all the time, falling, caught by gravity and made to suffer. Aging, the worst; the very stuff of our cells constantly drawn downward, pulled on by gravity in an attempt to reorder its' configuration and density.
And the word itself; gravity equals mortality, w/gravity constantly pulling us back into the Earth,

into the underworld, into the grav, while we struggle to reach up, be vertical, ascend.

When folk are sad, they say they feel down: an investment gone south, down by law, all relate unfortune to that one direction.

Gravity, in soothe, defines direction; up and down are directions relative to gravity for planet/folk. And gravity fosters hierarchy; in gravitic cultures, social orders develop in which folk are either above or beneath each other, as if related to their ability to resist that fearsome drag, and most planetary sports depend on gravity as the foe to push against; the addition of a competitor only adds another foe...

Spacers, on the other hand, are free of this constant tension, free of the tyranny of down; their chiefest metaphor is flow, and they exist in a dimensional matrix of points oriented to the Sun and the ecliptical planetary plane. Their currency of direction is heading/position relative to fixed stars. To a Spacer, down is a foreign concept, the relic of an idea from another time, used now only to define that part of space south of the Sun...

By way of further elucidation, here is a bit of Celestial Writ; to wit,

'I rise above the clay by an act of will. At times i lapse back into clay, needing inspiration to rise again.'

Do you see the difference in the dynamics here?

Standing through an act of Will rather than drifting, free of volition yet sustained...

There are them what say that gravity makes us stronger, tempers us. I say there are enough other things in this life to temper us w/out having to deal w/gravity as well.

*Freedom from Gravity For All,* says me.

Pleasure is the best teacher.


**GREEN FLASHES;** My friend Francesco informs me thus: 'If you find yourself cruising up the coast highway (in California, Earthside) just before Sunset, you may be up for a treat. Keep your eye on the Sun as it disappears into the water, and you'll see a green flash!"

For illustration, he beams me this dreamtracker headmovie of the aforementioned thing:

He is looking across the water to the West, w/the Sun a molten disc about to be annealed in the sea. Just after the Sun sinks completely beneath the waves, there is a bright argon/green *flash!* lasting a thirtieth of a second, the duration of a single blink...

Francesco first reads about green flashes in the scientific journal of the Vatican (!), and while green flashes are comparatively rare, they happen with some frequency in Sunny California.

Francesco goes grinsome when he says, 'Since these green flashes are a function of the variable refraction of light by the atmosphere, very occasionally there are rarer blue flashes, and very very rare violet flashes.'
Inwardly i vow to quest for the sight of a violet flash...

**THE GRID;** a recurring other/plane phenomenon perceived as a giant warpy/woofy, along which are arranged the dimensions of time and space.

**GRUMBA;** courage, fortitude, power of Will.

**GUYJIN;** an uncouth non-Egypsian, a haole to a Hawaiian.


**-h**


**HARLEQUIN, ARLECHINO;** the graceful & humourous prankster of Italian Commedia, often the machinater of the story, always thin and masked and wearing black/&/white diamond tights.

**HARMONY;** The progress of human harmony is order pushing against unformed chaos...

**HEAVY BEAVERING;** as in working long and hard like one of those furry creatures, rather than what it might sound like.

**HETERODYNES, HETERODYNE;** the sum of two frequencies, whereas the anodyne is the difference of two frequencies. See 'anodyne' for the illustration.

**HIDDEN ORDER/DR LAWRENCE BLAIR:** In the book, *Cymatics*, by Hans Jenny (a twentieth/century Swiss scientist of high regard), Dr Jenny documents a number of experiments he performed with the intent of bringing forth order out of seeming chaos. Por ejemplo, he took a batch of lycopodeum powder (a very fine dust/like substance) and spread it on a drumhead stretched over a moving/coil speaker. He soon discovered that when he played certain resonant frequencies through it, patterns would form in the powder, beautiful symmetrical vibrating geometrical harmonies.
He saw these patterns as a kind of hidden order, their occulted beauty inherent in all things, waiting only for the resonance of their own unique Angel Frequency to reveal them.
Dr Blair comes into the picture (fading up like film? in a cloud of photons? sublimating in as a transfer of graphic dyes?) through his own book, *Rhythms of Vision,* a masterful work of the nineteen/seventies that takes Jenny's theories and melds them w/the ideas of numerous others,

creating a kind of ideational hologram of the nascent New Age, then aborning. In the book, Dr Blair foreshadows fractal theory by showing that Jenny's Hidden Order exists on every natural level, from the orbits of protons to the patterns of myth.

**THE HINGE;** a pivotal moment in one's life where things could go either way...

**HISTOROLOGY;** history/mythology, that which lies at the border between...

**HORNO TOASTADOR;** Spanish for toaster oven.

**HYDRA HAIR;** That basket/o/snakes look made famous by Medusa.

**HYLITIC;** meaning made of wood, wooden, a word used by Alan Watts to describe once/borns.

**HYPNAGOGIC;** used to describe any knowlege gained during sleep or in the twilight time before.


-i

**ICOSAHEDRON, DODECAHEDRON, ICOSADODECAHEDRON;** sacred solids, three/dimensional regular polyhedra. Respectively, a polyhedron of twenty five/sided equal planar faces, one of twelve five/sided faces, and one of thirty/two five/sided faces.

**IDEATIONAL PATHWAYS;** the ways by which thoughts walk to the homes of our awareness.

**ILIAC;** pertaining to the ileum, that crest of bone in the hip over the socket for the femur, one of the most graceful and beautiful parts of the human bod.

**ILLYRIANS;** the people of the goddess Lyra, her attendant constellation, and all things lyrical.

**INTROBLURB;** what i would have written instead of this lexicon if i had known in front how involved it would be.

**IO SNOWFLAKES;** frozen sulfur/dioxide, usually about a foot across, of a lovely shade of methylene blue, or rarely, clear. To survive indoors they are placed in stasis, and are traded, collected, and given as gifts.
    There are a host of customs celebrated on the Orange Moon that

center on these snowflakes; *por ejemplo,* when two folk decide to bond w/each other, they frame up one of these snowflakes and put it up somewhere prominent in their dome. Either partner can dissolve the arrangement (so to speak) by allowing the snowflake to melt, or the two can ceremonially melt the crystal by pressing it between their two naked bods. This requires particularly hardy souls, however, as these snowflakes melt at minus one/hundred/eighty/three degrees celsius...

      Io snowflakes are also given as guesting gifts, much like floral leis in Hawaii on Earth; a beautiful gesture of welcome. Some guests (such as meself) keep them in stasis, sometimes for many years, against the day when they can return to Io and gift them back to the original giver.


**-J**


**JUPPITER;** the huge and magnificent Fifth Planet; this spelling from Robert Graves' *The White Goddess,* meaning All Father.


**-k**


**KA;** the Egyptian magical conception of the free/traveling spirit bod.

**KAIROS;** the Supreme Moment, that point in the highest ceremony of the Eleusinian Mysteries where the kernel of the universe is revealed to the initiate.

**KAMA SUTRA;** a very old Hindu erotic text; literally, the teachings of Kama, the God of Love, whose chief festival, the Madanotsave, is celebrated w/singing, dancing, drumming, and later, w/the delving of Desire's fires...

      Kama can be equated w/Eros and also the Cherubim, as all carry bows that launch the bolts of love...

      And he is celebrated and cherished and revered for the same reasons, for it is said that Desire was the first thing that stirred at the dawn of creation, w/Kama's gift to humanity ensuring that we could perpetuate, carry on as a species...

      If you should learn the date and location of any upcoming Madanotsaves, please inform yr scribe straightaway.


**-l**


**LAGNIAPPE;** a dessert served after the dessert, part of the culinary tradition of New Orleans. I came across this concept in Mark Twain's *On The River*, and it seemed a good idea. 'For Lagniappe' was a popular phrase at the time Twain wrote the book, and meant something added at the end, a surprise extra pleasure or treat.

**LANGUOR;** the word that best describes the state achieved after consuming Lotus Leaves (see AGENTS OF CHANGE).

**LEEVER SWITCH;** archaic electrical component also called a blade switch or drawbar switch, usually fairly hefty and used to control the flow of major amounts of current.

Right around the time that we are first leaving Io, Piersona, whom we are yet to meet, finds one of these leever/switch things while on Shirira (while there as a sleeper), and is drawn to it, driven to take it w/him, and his sleeper follows through. When he later sees my dreamtracker Vision recording of the piece, he puts the thing in a queeper set for two hours before Showtime.

**LEGENDARY ROLLER TALES;** soon to be a popular series, featuring the adventures of the Fabulous Bearded Zerko Brothers, celebrated hard/partying wandering roller wranglers for three generations, going back before Io to Mars and Phobos, where the gravity comes in waves (centrifugal forces and the endover motion of the moon)...

Yes Yes the Red Deserts, and booming along the old straight tracks, the surface trails that guide on the leylines beneath, the channeled tellurics of Mars, following these courses of blazing living underground energy for thousands of miles,

Herding these great convoys of rollers down the line, w/one crew in the lead roller and the next thirteen or fifteen of them following on autopilot, over two hundred mph, hauling the freight at a furious rate,

And so it was in the Martian Spring of thirty years ago, when Berko One the original Zerko, Zerko the Venerable, Patriarch of all Ionian Zerkos, defied and defeated the massive and perilous Grelmer Sandstorm to cross the length of the Noctis Labyrinthos to give a stolen rose to his great love Emeralda, and also save the life of his young son Berko Two and his bond/friend Arturo,

Who later would found the famous and glorious Caravaggio Coachworks, builders of the swiftest and surest and most beautiful of rollers (sez i), all inspired by Zerko and that Martian midnight rescue...

Or mayhaps you would care to hear how Moira and Martin the Mad discovered Roller Jumping, or where the snowflakes/for/travelers tradition began, or how Berko One met Zinka and why one rarely sees him in Sunlight, or, how Berko Six and his Holographic Circus found the miraculous Sacred Spring of Phobos while preparing for a show by the side of Phobos Highway One, w/the Valles Marineris Canyon of Mars hanging in the sky overhead, or...

**LEMURS;** are wonderful creatures, come in an astonishing profusion of varieties, and have a special place in my values.

**LEYLINE TELLURICS;** a term for describing the relative merits of a particular planetary site, specifically referring to the qualities imparted by the local Earth/energies as they move in streams beneath the surface. In his cornerstone work, *The Old Straight Track,* the honorable Alfred North calls them leylines.

At certain special points they intersect or converge, creating opportunities for Workers of the Will. The author of the *Book of the Celestial* says,

'Once, when at Stonehenge on Alban Elved, the night of the Autumnal Equinox, i met a tantric/buddhist/druid down from London named Ray Beaconhead. He and his compatriots were part of a larger group of druid folks who were at that moment converging in contingents at the seven major stone circles (which he described as the chakras of the island of Britain), gathering to chant and awaken these centers of telluric power.

'He explained to me that the circle of stones we were regarding had originally been built to harmonize the convergence of six powerful leylines, to canalize them into a swirl, a spiraling helix that would move on out into the aethers.

'He further informed me that at the Summer and Winter Solstices the direction of the flow of ley energy would reverse, and the helix swirl would move from the aethers inward. These changes are gradual and cyclical, like breathing, and thus there are peak times of the year when the greatest flow of telluric energy occurs, and these times are the Autumnal Equinox for the outward rush and the Vernal Equinox for the inward.

'A Worker of the Will would ride these rushes, meld w/these great Gaian tidal swells and attract and banish and empower as needed.

'Ray Beaconhead reasoned that since the partial dismantling of Stonehenge the converging ley energy came together chaotically, and if a way could be found to recreate the harmonizing effect of the Standing Stones, then the spot could once again be used for great Magics.

'He told me that he had long felt that beams of laser light, aligned in the way that the stones were, would accomplish this end.'

**LEVITY,** opposite of GRAVITY.

**LIGHTSPHERES** are a dazzling technical recreation of the balls of electron/discharge called Saint Elmo's Fire or Saint Elmo's Light, named after the patron saint of sailors and manifesting itself on seagoing ships in storms as sizable fiery lights on the tips of sprits and masts and spars...

Lightspheres can be programmed to surround a moving human and track them perfectly; a three/dee sourceless spotlight, subtle to bold, in sixteen million colors...

**LIMBIC;** that old reptile part of our brain where fight/or/flight is decided. To find your own Posterior Limbic Sulcus, imagine the newer part of your brain wrapped around this older one, with the limbic centers located just under your Paracentral Lobule and the Fissure of Rolando.

**LINGA SHARIRA;** Hindu term for the original high wire, the Golden Cord of Light connecting the astral traveler to their physical bod.

**LINKING & linking:** the first is psychic telepathic joining; the second, connecting over the Wire. Both are about forming a knowlege/bond w/another human, forming an affinity/based alignment.

**LYRE & LOOM;** symbols of classical feminine graces, metaphors for inspiration and the weaving of fate. Arianna Gibbon says, 'The purpose of feminism is to reclaim the loom.'


-m

**MANTRAGRAM;** a communication conveyed through a chanted mantra, a spiritual message imparted by musical means.

**MARQUETRY;** a very fine form of wood inlay, as practiced by the wondrous Adrienne Scull.

**MARSPORT BLUEBOY DRUMS;** titanic drums, gigantic drums, thirty/meter drums and larger, dozens of these thunder drums played w/huge hydraulic mallets by the aforementioned fanatical Blueboys, their awesome rhythms causing folk to dance at distances of thirty miles...

**MASS-TORQUEING;** the characteristic of a mass rotating along an axis, wherein the inertia of one end tends to torque (twist) the whole if the rotation of the other end is subdued.

This is an important concept to have in one's head when changing course in a solar sailer.

**MASSIFS;** long/spined 'Principal mountain masses, blocks of the Earth's crust bounded by faults and displaced as a unit without internal change.' (A handsome bit of poesy from Webster's New Collegiate).

**MAZES & LABYRINTHS;** the difference between them is that in a maze there are many possible paths, w/only one of them leading to the goal; in a labyrinth there is one path, complex and serpentine, often fraught w/dangers...

**MESSIANIC WEB MIRACLES;** the seven amazing code deeds that define the character of the Fresh Age, move us beyond the box of capitalism and into a society where everyone on the planet has what they need to live a satisfying life. In the mythos of the forming of the Fresh Age, these miracles are inspired by the words of that phantom, Beta.

**MEME;** an idea that moves through a culture like a pike in a lake, cruising for reproducing. A tip of the clearplex helm to Dr Ralph Abraham for this one...

**METHODOLOGY;** Stuart Bjornsson says, 'There is a continuum between methodology and essence, where essence is a goal of some kind and what you do to achieve the goal is methodology. So what you want to do is maximize essence and minimize methodology...'

**MIMSEY/WAVES;** whimsical mindwaves. A mimsey exchange is an especially warm and light/hearted kind of telepathy, an alternating psychic song cycle w/each singer brightly aware of the other, warm to the other and caring; mimsey are the waves which pass between lovers in the quiet aftertime before sleep...

**MOKSHA;** Hindu, from the Upanishads: a state of release from bondage to the sensual, freedom from the illusion of our separateness from each other.

**MOONCAT TECHNOLOGY;** the mooncats are powered by vast amounts of stored electricity turning these armature/like wheels on the ferrous roadway. The wheels are about a foot wide and segmented laterally, so that as the wheel rolls, the segments touch the roadway one after the other. Each one of these segments is a printed/circuit coil that generates magnetic force, and the thing works by sequentially charging these magnetic segments as they roll into the optimum spot for pulling the vehicle forward, w/just the right amount of advance to their striking the roadway. Though coated in something rubberlike, they emit a characteristic whine at speed.

When the roadway ends and the great string of rings begins, an interlocking series of stasis fields keeps the mooncats channeled in a toroidal trackspace high above the surface, propelled by alternating attracting stasis (when the mooncat is moving toward the ring) and repelling stasis (after moving through the ring).

**MUMBELLA TU BYE LA;** Swahili for 'our time to shine'. Thanks to that swank rock/n/roll band, Mu, for this one.

**TO MURP;** as in 'to murp my thoughts'. Murping is closing your mouth before you speak.

**MYSTO STEAM/TOM WOLFE;** true confession: this wonderful phrase is retailed from the great Tom Wolfe. He coins it in the nineteen/sixties for his brilliant *The Electric Kool-Aid Acid Test* (a *major* book for me), to describe what happened in his head when first he meets Ken Kesey and the Pranksters; '...this steam, i can actually hear it inside my head, a great sssssssssss, like what you hear if you take too much quinine. I don't know if this happens to anybody else or not. But if there is something startling enough, fearful, awesome, strange, or just weird enough, something i sense i can't cope with, it is as if i go on Red Alert and the fogging steam starts...'
    Several times since learning this term have i heard those selfsame steamy swirls in the whorls of my own brain. For me, those vapors presage that moment when i realize that i am *onto something*, something really big, maybe *TOO BIG*, and the implications begin to loom, limn themselves against the blank screen of future history...
    Many thanks, Mr Wolfe; i use the term here as an *homage*.

**-n**

**NICHROME;** an alloy of nickel and chromium, especially suited for the coils of heating/elements when formed into wire.

**NOCTILUCENT;** the light of the night, a varying mix of Lunar rays and the visual emanations of stars, usually experienced as backlit noctilucent clouds.

**NUCLEONIC;** like unto the nucleus, the core.

**-o**

**OMPHALOS, OMPHALOS POINT;** Grecian, literally the navel, an omphalos point being a place where the Earth and sky are connected umbilically; generally a raised bit of ground, often a conical hill like Glastonbury Tor where leylines flow and there is power.

**ONEIRONAUT;** a dream/traveler, someone who is adept at lucid dreaming and other more astral aspects of the dreaming state. Maps onto oneiromancy, the art of working Magic through dreams.


-p


**PARACELSUS (1490-1541);** A true Renaissance man: prolific author, curmudgeonly scholar, irascible alchemist, restless traveler, leading physician, visionary neoplatonist, medical scientist, astrological prophet, classical magus, original mind, mystic.

Of all these things he is primarily a healer, and to this noble calling he dedicates his studies, and his short life. His highly innovative techniques are hard won, derived and evolved over his long years of travel through Europe. And though he studies at the leading medical schools of Italy and Germany, his approach to medicine is his own: for Paracelsus, medicine is an art based on alchemy, astrology, and an occult philosophy that includes personal and moral integrity (much like the Celestial concept of Integrity of Will...).

This is the kernel of his learning:

His cosmology holds that a human is a part of the All, that our physical bods are made of the biblical *Limus Terrae,* that substance which contains some part of the essence of all beings previously created, and that this substance is itself made up of alchemical salt, sulphur, and mercury.

For our bods to work well, says Paracelsus, these three primary alchemical elements must needs be intermixed. What accomplishes this blending is a form of life/force he calls the *Archaeus,* originating in the stomach, w/this force also separating out that which is good from that which is otherwise.

Further, the writ of Paracelsus (and he is a tireless writer of books), describes a relationship between ourselves and what he calls the Astral Spirit, in Celestial terms the *Is, Was, & Will Be;* the All...

Since this Astral Spirit encompasses everything, is made of everything, including stars, he sees the study of astrology as a facet of the art of healing. This in turn implies that there is a part of us that is of the Astral Spirit, and thereby connected to the whole, and eternal...

That part of ourselves beyond the physical and also dwelling within, he calls the soul.

Does this sound familiar? Very much the Celestial point of view here, the whole of which was derived experientially, through visionary experience. In Paracelsus' philosophical matrix, his concepts speak to a similar thread of visionary experiences, overlayn by a filtering of biblical concepts...

I wonder, what was the young Paracelsus like? When he was still

called Phillipus Auriolus Theophrastus Bombastus von Hohenheim, before
he wrote the *Archidoxes Magicae*, back in sleepy Einsiedeln in the canton of
Schwyz...

   I see him as a total wild/child, ready to try anything, go anywhere.
Did he sample all the stuff he would later include in his pharmacopaeia? Try
a taste of tincture/of/hemp, an extract in alcohol of opium? Did aphrodisiacs
flow from his alembics, liquors of desire to fire his youthful thrusts and surges?

**PARAMOUR;** the height of lovers, the One, the Big Swoon, the dearest
truest guide and foremost teacher of the heart.

**PHEMIRICAL;** both ephemeral and chimerical, a transitory magical thing
composed from obscure knowlege that changes form like the legendary
chimera and then is gone, leaving only a wake of emotion in the memory of
the perceiver.

**PHYSICAL REIMAGING;** something many of us are already employing,
the technique of remaking our own bods in a personally previsualized way.
Spice increases the effectiveness of this practice exponentially, opening a
gateway in the brain to conscious control of cellular repair and modification.

**PNEMOSYNE;** a place in memory at an angle to the conscious mind,
accessible only through the subconscious, who is the Great Sleeper...

   'At this, my indwelling searcher awakens, reaches for relating
mentation stored in faraway pnemosyne caves of memory, a distant
resonation...'

**PODS;** early after he comes onboard, Featherman acquaints me w/some of
the finer points of pods:

   'Over here; let me show you this guy, donald the
drillpod, a marvel of design; built cylindrical to get into tight places, anchors
w/stasis onto the workpiece so he can drill on things that are floating. Holds
a carbon/dioxide laser cutter/drill. For holes, you can mark the spot w/a
laser/pointer or use a scribe, likewise for cutting; draw a line, and the pod
will track it, however wide. The optics give you holes from ten microns to
three inches, any standard measure, microns inches whitworth metric
numeric/shop/standard, good for quickwork and can also follow plans,
be they in databanks or on the Wire or in your head.

   'Or you can say, 'Take this piece of tritanium and carve it to this
shape and drill this many holes, and after please take it over to Featherman
in his shop,' and the little guy will whistle off and take care of it.

   'One can grow to be quite fond of these pod things.

   'It also has a one/inch round mirror on a smart/cable that can
snake its way into the laser's beampath, bend the light around corners to
get into really tight places. This mirror can also scan the beam, and cut

shapes out of thin material quickly. Just the right amount of energy for the beam to nicely cut the metal or fiber or whatever.

'This pod can also back off on the power and work as a welder. He has access to all the metallurgy on the Wire and so knows all when it comes to shaping metals. Since there are alloys on Space/craft designed to be welded best in the absence of air, donald can also work outside.

And, being on the Wire, he can communicate easily w/other pods. A very good thing if there is, say, a hullbreech to be mended; a crew of pods can go out and take care of it, w/some metalmovers to bring the material, a couple of drillpods to cut and weld on the thin metal and some medium welder/pods for the thicker stuff and the metalmovers again to guide the patch into place.

**POV;** a cinematic point of view...

**PRAHNA;** life/force, inhaled and amplified while breathing.

**PREMONSTRATION;** a magical ritual term for visualizing the desired result of a work of Will while at the highest point of power, binding through Craft the summoned forces to this goal.

**PRESCIENT;** having the ability to see the future.

**PRE/VISIONING;** a form of deja vu, the physical manifestation of scenarios that have already played many times on the screens of one's theatre of thought.

**PROPRIOCEPTION, PROPRIOCEPTIVITY;** how you know where your limbs are when your eyes are closed. This ability can be developed to a high degree through physical re/imaging and concentration.

**PROPRIOTAXIC;** a feedback loop that gives you bod/position information while you are in motion. A learnable form of advanced proprioception.

**PSYCHOTROPIC NOISE;** while tripping, any distracting internal drama or sensory phenomena. Before the Fresh Age, this often meant side effects.


-q


**QUEEPER;** a cargo/shipper container bearing a thinscreen video window for a manifest, therein displaying any amount of text and video necessary for getting the thing to its intended destination. Occasionally these things are rigged with a time/to/open, and will often make a queeping noise at that time.

**RAMAN [SCATTERING] WAVES;** relating to CV Raman's discovery of the inelastic scattering phenomenon (Nobel prize, early twentieth century), in which it can be seen that some photons of light, when passing through gas molecules, come out the other side measurably shorter in frequency than their source.

Since every gas has its own signature vibrational and/or rotational qualities to impart upon these Raman rays, an analysis of the prismatized spectral print left by these rays can help identify the constituents of the sample. This is useful in determining the composition of, say, a planetary atmosphere.

Raman scattering becomes the gas analysis of choice w/the advent of the laser (Theodore Maiman, mid/twentieth century). A laser's unique ability to produce completely monochromatic light provides the perfect baseline for this type of work.

Inelastic scattering is similar to elastic Rayleigh scattering, described by Lord Rayleigh (Nobel prize, start of the twentieth century), wherein the shorter wavelengths of Sunrays are favoured by the atmosphere, giving us blue skies...

**REBUS;** a pictorial form of language, wherein images (and sometimes objects) communicate by their names the syllables, words or phrases being expressed. Rebuses are a very old form of language, and can have magical effect when used bardically. as in the riddles carved in stone at Brugh na Boyne in Eire...

**REDREAMING;** more than physical reimaging, redreaming is about conscious mindmorphing, freeing the conduits of spirit to fantasticate, to hyperfantasize, a way to straighten out the convoluted highways of thought so that truth may be perceived more fully, logic seen in the most abstract of circumstances, love generated more quickly and perceived sooner likewise...

**REMBRANCE;** an evocative series of telepathically transmitted thoughts, a sequence intended to bring a certain suite of feelings to the fore of the mind's proscenium...

**RIG:** that very personal assemblage of gear that is shaped to the ends of its owner; usually applied to combinations of hardware and software and electronics. To those such as us, a good rig is a source of pride and self/sufficiency, an amplification of the rigger's personal power, a medium for the creation of art and magic.

**TERRY RILEY;** a divinely blessed twenty/first century composer who draws upon numerous sources including Balinese Gamelon to create supremely fascinating works such as his classic *In C*, which contains a series of fifty/three short interpenetrating musical phrases, each to be played in order and repeated a varying number of times at the whim of each individual orchestral musician. The effect is a musical texture of delightful mystery and ramification, an unfolding forest of cypress melodies and mahogany subtlety. My all/time fave Terry Riley piece is *A Rainbow in Curved Air*, which sustained me through my teen years as a sonic refuge and sanctuary.

**ROBIN WILLIAMSON;** twenty/&/twenty/first century Bard, founding member of the Incredible String Band, played Woodstock, is expert on harp, cittern, fiddle, concertina, whistle, lowland pipes, and a host of other instruments, wrote a huge number of excellent songs, wrote *The Craneskin Bag*, a splendid book of Celtic tales retold, and, with RJ Stewart, *Celtic Bard, Celtic Druid*, the most illuminating work i have read in this field, and knows over two thousand songs and a thousand stories. As per the above, he is a fine and shining exponent of the Bardic Arts, and is the one who inspired yr scribe to become a Druid. His music is wondrous and highly recommended, his presence a life/enhancing blessing.

**ROSA ALCHEMICA;** a cycle of tales by the great William Butler Yeats (late/nineteenth/early/twentieth century), wherein we meet the magician Robartes (who, says Mary K. Greer in *Women of The Golden Dawn*, is likely based on Yeats' fellow founder of the Hermetic Order of the Golden Dawn, SL MacGregor Mathers).

Several of the stories contain some very Celestial passages, describing ritual initiation and the consuming of shamanic aids, as well as the profound and beautiful states of consciousness resulting. From the clarity of his narrative i am sure that Yeats is speaking of his own experiences.

Someday, in an astral pub alongside time, Yeats and i will meet, and over some astral claret share our common threads...


-s


**SACRIFICE & OFFERING;** the difference is significant: a sacrifice is giving up something you love for a higher end, while an offering is the loving gift of sharing something special w/a friend. Magically, both can serve the same purpose, and *The Book of the Celestial* favours happy offerings, the way of the otter.

**SAINT ELMO'S FIRE;** on Earth an ocean/sailor's phenomena, wherein at night during storms a phosphorescent ball will occasionally be seen, roosting like luminous mistletoe in the high rigging of wooden ships. Saint Elmo is the patron saint of sailors, and these spheres of light are perceived as his presence, and are welcomed.

**SCHEMA;** as in, the *schem'a* things (harhar)... Seriously, the Great Plan, the Big Script that runs as long as time, that plays out in parables of fate, vinaya, karma, luck, reincarnation, inspiration, God, Magic, and Love...

**SCINTILLA;** a single spark in a glittering.

**SAHASRARA;** the violet crown chakra (see Yoga).

**SAURE;** as in swarthy dark, the brooding dark of caves...

**SENDINGS;** a traveling manifestation of the energy of the sender, usually on a mission. Called a *Forerunner* in Scottish Pecti/Wicca, these particular sendings are sent on ahead of the physical individual to scout and generally clear the way, and there are corroborative tales of folk apparently appearing days before they actually arrive. In other Earth traditions there are things called *fetches*, magically created creatures for performing specific ends. These, however, are considered self/willed to a degree and empowered to act on their own, where a sending is an extension of the senses of the sender.

In the Celestial magical tradition there are also several forms of sendings specifically for Working in the Astral, taking the form of projections, Forerunners, and Ryders (see RYDER).

The **SEVENLEVEL MINDSPACE;** the seven levels of Spice awareness, as currently perceived by me:

> ***The All,*** everything that is, was, or will be.
>
> ***The metabeing,*** the astral entity who is free of time, who is the sum of all of my incarnations.
>
> ***The bleu,*** an entity composed of all those enjoying the temple drama we are currently presenting, planetside and system/wide.
>
> ***The Dolphin entity,*** the collective mind of all those perceiver folk aboard *Murphy's Dolphin,* including ourselves.
>
> ***The crewlink,*** a circuit specific to our Dolphin family.
>
> ***Psychic love bonds*** w/Ariel & Electra.
>
> ***Myownself.***

Dwelling in the sevenlevel mindspace is like watching seven monitors simultaneously; having the ability to focus your awareness on any or all of the ongoing dramas playing across your screens. Just so you know, both the number and assignment of these levels is arbitrary, chosen to suit the perceiver (meself) and my current drama; you are free to choose your own.

**SHAMANS,** three great saints of the Fresh Age:
    KEN KESEY
    TERRENCE McKENNA
    TIMOTHY LEARY


**SHIPBOARD TIME:** When the first interplanetary traversers blazed away from the Homeworld aegis, they brought their Earth ways w/them, spinning their ships through Space to give themselves gravity, cycling themselves through days and seasons as if they were still on the Home Planet.

Then comes awareness of the Larger Arena, and Earth ways become a kind of arcane overlay on the stern majesty of Space/time, that place where we, warm and transitory creatures that we are, embrace the cold immortal...

This coincides with the rise of Spacer Culture, and in the first flush of Spacer Élan, all those riggers and pilots and path/finders start to hew to their own unique chronometric, and they call it Absolute/Base/Time, and, set to the cesium clocks of Greenwich, it soon becomes a standard for all the worlds of the Solar Disc.

As you know, ABT is a purely linear system, w/out the complication of diurnal change or the shifting of seasons. In ABT, the current time is an ever/higher cumulative number, w/the starting point (1 ABT) set at the beginning of the Spacer era (the day that Scaled Composites won the X Prize). The system's unit of time is called the *ab* and is about three and a half hours long, and is based on the Sun's speed through Space, away from the Galactic Center. Por ejemplo, i am writing this entry at 158,931.42 ABT, or about sixty/three/&/a/half years after the base event.

And, even though everyone agrees to use ABT, the determining of what constitutes shipboard time can be pretty arbitrary, and varies widely from ship to ship. One of the more intriguing shipboard time/schemes i have encountered is the one they use aboard the *Jnana Yogi* out of Earthside Myanmar; their system is based on Raga rhythms, and their day is measured in *dats*. These units of time are of varying lengths, and though the Jnanis work to an Earthside diurnal schedule, their days are divided into two equal periods of seven and eleven dats, or sometimes eleven/&/fourteen, w/the night/time dats of shorter duration (though of greater numbers) than the day/time ones. The theory being that if the sleeping dats outnumber the waking dats, (e'en though they be shorter), than the perceiver will feel more rested. And conversely, if the work/time dats are fewer, then the work will be perceived as lighter...


And then there is the *Ariel.*

When first i come aboard, the folk are inclined to see things in terms of the length of the voyage, w/projects measured in fractions of our total trip/time; by custom we aim to finish the technical stuff before the trip is half/full and leave the second half for art. When we make planetfall, or wherever it is we are performing, we tend to slip into local time, w/the whole thing resetting when we commence our next journey...

For meownself, my Celestial training places me outside of this system, blythely bicameral, bilocating myself in the continuum, maintaining an awareness of trip time and holy Earth time. By the time we must leave the *Ariel,* many of my new friends will adopt my temporal point of view.

Aboard the *Encanto,* shipboard time is strictly ABT, a challenging change for us rescuees. Ariel, who is born Earthside, has for all her years aboard followed Earth/time privately, a part of her solitary practice. Both of us, it turns out, share an affinity for the rhythms of the Home/World, and long for the progression of the seasons, the equinoctial touchstones and the others of the eight points on the Great Wheel...

Here aboard the *Dolphin,* we measure our time in a myriad of ways; by the phasings of passing moons, by the solemn progressions of the Great Spheres as they roll through the houses of the zodiac, and, yes, the hours remaining in our progress from here to there, all w/in the frame of the traditional Celestial terra/centric way of reckoning, with the days of our voyages given the same seasonal flavourings as we would if we were Earthside...

And then, there are also those occasions when time stops for us, or more accurately, when we move away oblique from time's track, get some distance on the linear flow of it, and watch it from the null/point place that is not a place...

**SHOWER:** Ah, how i favour the embrace of Clarissa, my double shower ring! A paired pod of thick red rings that come when i call, they encircle me at the waist, then spread apart from each other until one is beyond my head and the other likewise at my hoof end, w/the two together forming a cylinder of stasis around me. When i wish it, the two red rings let loose w/their circles of waterspray, hot as you please, then they drink in the spent water and recycle it.

Tonight as i write, several towel pods follow along, and several more w/my special clothes for psychic shielding, my freefall magical gear...

**SHRIVEN;** what you are after having been shrived, wherein your auric field is cleansed through the removal of all guilt/causing thoughtforms and stray aka threads; traditionally, shriving is done with a short nine/tailed whip called a scourge, though any wandlike instrument of power will serve as well...

**SIGHTLINES, THROWS & DISTANCES;** lightshow terms referring to the technical aspects of how a presentation is framed. Sightlines are said to be good if everyone can easily perceive the piece from wherever they are in the Hall; throws & distances refers to the technique for figuring the size and viability of a given beam or image after it has traveled a specific distance.

**THE SIGILS;** here follows a list of the visualized astral symbols and their use:

> *Arkatel,* writ in burning greeny fire, its' invocational shield is sky/blue w/green & gold or turquoise w/flecks of matte silver; this is the key for achieving the astral, manifesting the grid...

> *Lumlel,* Lapis shield, the clear light, the key for entering the grid...

> *Frakat,* a family of related sigils that act like addresses; there are known variations for time/line navigation, for delving the akashic, the future, ancestral/pastlives.
>
> The first of these variations is the key for anchoring consciousness in AetherSpace; three more are for reaching out from this base point by focusing individual awareness into the form of an Astral Sending, a Fore/runner, a dream/presence...
>
> The next three are for manifesting our sendings back into physical forms, ways to shift to any shape we choose, to go from this Plane directly back into the physical...
>
> Another five are spatial, sigil keys for to work translations to other levels of AetherSpace,
>
> The next three are keys for navigating in physical time, sending your shape to manifest at any place on the timeline, w/the past and future equally available...

> *Frakat & Lumlel,* together a key to past and future lives, relating specifically to the karmic eddies.

> *Frakat Kalissia,* a fresh new gnostic door to the great Akashic.

> *Sinrasel,* the perfect form divine, writ in silver.

>> *Red variant,* the sacred flame, the sigil that inspires the astral fire (which is itself clear).

>> *Green variant,* for to summon this fire back to the physical to fuel our acts of Will, to light the lamp in the spine, regenerate and heal, receive and give strength and open wide the high souleyes of our own indwelling Awen...

>> *Indigo variant, Sinrasel Ravia,* The sigil of the Great Merging, a high and clear returning to the melding of our billion bleu minds into the conscious living eternal infinity of All That Is...

> *Hloo,* glowing gold/outline/green, to exit, the charm of returning.

**SIGNAL CIRCLE;** a loop of audio/videolo/sensor signals where each affects the next in turn around the ring. This arrangement emphasizes the need for harmony among those who are signal sources, for each affects the whole, and subtle variations of color and frequency can reach the perceiver on emotional & psychotropic levels...

      'And now to complete Kan's signal circle, Llair mixes this Tripplett ballet of fulfilling love back into the incoming realtime emotional bleu signal/stream, where differences in their frequential concurrency create these very special psycho/active feedback/beat/patterns, actual mind/altering playable visual echo/loop chords, and by varying the time/lag betwixt the signals he selectively intensifies specific emotions...'

**SILENT DARKNESS;** relating to Terrence McKenna's famous quote about the heroic way to take Stropheria Cubensis; *five grams in silent darkness...*

**SILVER ALMONDS** are edible, though they look chromed and come only from this one confectioner in Italy. Silver almonds were made sacred to our circle by my teacher, and i will accept them from the hand of no other.

**SINATE;** like unto things Chinese.

**SINGULETS;** a single iteration of a waveform. Picture a sine wave as it snakes its' way through air; take one swell and one trough and you have a singulet.

**SKRYING;** the practice of looking into something (a crystal, a cauldron, a cup of tea) and seeing sooth.

**SKYCLAD;** as in wearing only air, sans threads, undraped...

**SLEEPERS:** Space/traveling pods that carry the personality and abilities of the several individuals with whom they are imprinted. As sentient sleepers gain their freedom and become animorphs, we will see multiple/personality animorphs.

**SMILING IN FREEFALL:** When folk first ascend into Freefall, their facial muscles are freed of the work of holding up flesh against the draw of gravity. These same muscles are now free to give themselves wholly over to the art of emotional expression, and one of the first things that occurs is this perpetual freefall smile, a day & night decoration upon the features of anyone new to the territory...

**SOFITRY:** Any sofa/like construction. Much more useful than sophistry, the pointless though elegant arguments of academe.

**SOLIPSISM;** the belief that one is the center of the universe, like Sol is the center of his tracking planets. You are the Sun, i am the Moon...

**SPACER BOD;** humans develop differently when free of the chains of Gravity. Folk w/their lives in Space are long and fluid in freefall, grow to seven feet or more in length, and swim in the element of aire. They live much longer than planetary folk.

**SPACER ELAN:** Because of the changes in bod and mind that come w/living in freefall, Spacers are beings apart, and w/clannish pride we dwell in our special separated state.

You can spot a Spacer by our graceful ways in freefall, ease of dealing w/acceleration, by any act of casual courage or natural nobility or easy excellence in the face of the dark deep halls of Space...

**SPICE;** so/named as an homáge to Frank Herbert, a tribute from the denizens of the future.

**SPICE UNION;** the ultimate in psychic sex/on/drugs.

**SPICEMAKER ADEPTS CALLED ROSA ALCHEMICA:** A religio/magical ring of chemists and combiners, convened on Io and dedicated to creating ever/more/perfect encounters w/the Goddess through ever/more/splendid renderings of Spice.

They take their name from several of the stories of WB Yeats (writ at the close of the nineteenth century), in which there appears a character named Robartes, a charismatic Worker of the Will who is at the center of a circle of similar adepts also called Rosa Alchemica. Together, Robartes and these folk launch into altered states and occult adventure.

At the time he penned these tales, Yeats was co/creating the seminal Order of the Golden Dawn with SL MacGregor Mathers (out of the Golden Dawn came Dion Fortune, Crowley, Paul Foster Case, Israel Regardie, Doreen Valiente, numerous others), and, in her very excellent and insightful book, *Women of The Golden Dawn*, Mary K. Greer says Yeats' Robartes is modeled on Mathers. By extension, we could say that Rosa Alchemica is an idealized portrait of the Golden Dawn.

When Yeats & Mathers et al (Florence Farr, Moina Mathers, Anne Horniman, Maude Gonne, and more) were framing up the original rites of the Golden Dawn, Yeats especially drew upon Irish Druidical knowlege and also that main cultural thread of the Irish eighteen/nineties, The Celtic Twilight, a resurgence of national identity and native magic.

The current Rosa Alchemica of Io does likewise, sipping its' ethos from the same Druidical sources. Through the lens of the local historology, however, the material has evolved, and the Celtic Goddess of the Cauldron of Vision and Rebirth, called Keriadwyn, Ceridwen, or Keri ad Wyn (Celestial), is by the Io Rosa Alchemica called Kithera, a name they have intuited from the nearby Eleuthran tableaux.

To Kithera they attribute the traditional powers of Keri ad Wyn (rebirth, immortality, special wisdom, courage, inspiration, knowlege of the future), and also confer upon Her the creating and inspiriting of Spice, making Her the author and the guide of every Spice experience.

Thus, Kithera is the center of their rites, the object of their invocations, the fixed star in their astral journeying. Hers is the face reflecting back from the bright green liquid lapping at the borders of their source/pool, smiling back from the depths of the emerald green slurry of crystallizing Spice, and Hers is the countenance they turn to in their vastly expansive meditations, Herself who is their astral anchor in the whelming sea of that which is infinite...

**STASIS:** Here is something i would try a.p. (after the piece is complete); a maze based on stasis generators which first pull the seeker in various directions, thus stranging out their sense of Down, then enclose them in a maze w/stasis walls that is tactile yet transparent...

Elric the Thin is working on a way to project the stasis beams and shape them, so that the whole maze would hang invisible in the middle of the air...

**MORE STASIS:** Llair's unique Brookside stasis lift; a set of stasis/tubes which work in a special spiral way, continuous finewound coils of moving stasis that haul you Up Down & Sideways, move you w/these smoothly peristaltic rolling contractions of stasis energy...

**STEREOSCOPY;** seeing things through two eyes, in depth.

**SUNRETURN;** the Winter Solstice, Alban Arthuan, when the waning Sun on the longest night is reborn, vitalized for the waxing side of the year.

**LEEVER SWITCH:** The great oaken blade/switch that i first see in my Vision. It is now onboard, a gift from Piersona, who buys it from the Shirirans while there as a sleeper. He gifts it to yr anders though i have yet to show him the dreamtracker recording of said Vision...

**SYLVAN MULDOON:** Early twentieth/century astral traveler who, in his writings, delineates his techniques for achieving this plane: essentially, he sees Desire as the key to success, and the Golden Cord (the manifested connection between the physical bod and the astral one) as the chiefest instrument for a solid and safe return.

**SYLVANITE:** Mineral, a telluride of gold and silver, $(AuAg)Te_2$, often

occurring in crystals resembling written characters. The material possesses
occult properties, and is named for Transylvania, where it first is found...
A telluride is a mixture of metals w/tellurium.

**SYNCLON:** A resurrected facet of vanished Martian culture, a synclon is at
once an orchestra, a piece of music, and a style of play. Also there are
magical and religious, er, overtones.

Synclonic compositions are written to go on for over a hundred
(Martian) years, and positions in the ensemble are passed along for four or
five generations. The music goes on all through the day and night, and
villages are constructed around the local synclon so that everyone may hear
the lilt and gurgle, the play of notes, wherever they may be.

Much mythology & tradition surround a synclon, and great
year/long celebrations are held when a piece is completed...

Marsport Blueboys derive their titanic drums from synclon music
(see MARSPORT BLUEBOY DRUMS), and now there is a Marsport
Blueboy synclon, two years into their long traverse...

**SYNCRATIC;** a technique for simultaneously casting and machining in place
all of the parts of a working assembly, already assembled (think of the carved
ivory sphere w/in a sphere w/in a sphere), granting a functional unity
superior to something put together.

Syncratic casting is one of Llair's specialties.

**SYNCRETISM:** The reconciliation or union of conflicting beliefs, a
coalescence of different forms of faith, the fusion of inflectional forms...

**SYNERGY, SYNERGETIC:** Any combination of things that are more than
the sum of their parts.

**SYNESTHESIA:** A happy state in which the reports from one of your senses
come across like the information from another; to wit, hearing colors,
seeing music, tasting light.


-t


**TECTONIC;** pertaining to the work of the vast planetary surface/masses
(plates) that shear along faultlines, shift and slide, rise and fall and fold into
mountains.

**TELEOLOGY,** everywhere teleology; a belief in the existence of design in
nature...

**TEMPLARS:** The Knights Templar, a wealthy and powerful religio/military order founded in 1118 to protect the Temple in Jerusalem. Later, a major tributary of magical thought; some say a source/point for the Order of the Rosy Cross...

**THEATER & THEATRE:** The former being a structure wherein dramas take place, and the latter being the art of creating and presenting drama.

**THOUGHT FORMS:** In early Theosophist writings, the shapes taken by the fields of mindwaves we project around ourselves when in our various states. The field for healing, por ejemplo, surrounds your head like a winged helmet of white light.

Annie Besant along w/the great clairvoyant CW Leadbeater coined this term during the eighteen/nineties, the beginning of the current Occult Renaissance.

**TRILITHONS, LINTELS:** The architectural types of the stones of Stonehenge; w/trilithons being the uprights, lintels the horizontal stones that cap the tops of the trilithons.


**-u**


**ULULATION;** the fierce vibrato wail raised in joy or something other, a song of feminine power...


**-v**


**VALENT BONDS;** that which maintains the cohesivity of matter, according to the immutable laws of covalence and the ionic binding of atoms.

**VELIKOVSKY'S DRAMA;** Immanuel Velikovsky postulated a collision between Venus and a fair/size comet to explain any number of events on the Earth, including the fall of manna from heaven.

**VERDANT;** sylvan, so green w/the gasses of growing that the very grass is verging on becoming pure prahnic essence...

**VERTIGO, VERTIGINOUS:** Freefall firstimers often have this feeling, like unto whirling until the semicircular canals in one's brain overload, and, in a giddy buzzy dizzying rush, eliminate one's ability to maintain equilibrium.

**VESCENT;** incandescent, nascent, incandescently nascent, nascently incandescent; having the potential to brightly glow imminently.

**VESICA, VESICA PISCES;** also called *Sheila na Gig* by the Irish: a symbol consisting of two equal arcs touching at their ends to form a pointy vertical oval, and by this sign connoting the vaginal source of all life.

**VIANDS & COMESTABLES, REPASTINGS;** chow, scarf, eats, oats in the nosebag.

**VISAGE;** kisser, dial, mug, that which frames the windows of the soul and the gate of speech...


**-W**


**WAVES:** As it is w/light, so it goes w/videolo/waves, w/broadcasts of every kind, every source emitting three/dee spherical ripples spreading outward at lightspeed...
      And every piece of wave/casting ever created, every casual intership call, every word of radio, every lightray from the time of the first fire, all of them are out there...
      With Spice i find it intriguing to shift these frequencies into the visual band; they come up as starlike brightpoint dashes all across the solar plain, whole prismatic constellations of them, a yellow/thru/violet spectral firmament, an eternal flowing waveform artifact from Earth, Luna, all the thousands of ships, all the rocks and colonies and stations, all the big booming planets looming...
      An antenna at just the right point in space and time...

**THIS KIND OF WRITING** is like concert work, wherein every note needs to ring true for the whole passage to work, for the trance state to rule...

**WYRD & WEIRD;** the first concerns seership or creating magic through innate abilities (wyrding), the second refers to anything eerily unusual.


**-X**


**XENO;** anything foreign to a solipsistic point of view.


**-y**


**YAHSURE;** thank you, Piersona...

**YOGA;** literally, Union; the collective name for a vast amount of knowlege, five thousand years of Hindu religious techniques, practices, wisdom, all in general aimed at evolving and empowering the yogi (and yogini) in various ways. There are numerous schools of yogic thought; devotional or healing or magical or evolutionary...

In Kundalini Yoga, por ejemplo, achieving higher states involves the awakening and raising of the Kundalini, the powerful fire/serpent coiled asleep at the base of the spine.

Using all of the major techniques of Yoga, the serpent is brought to rise through the seven *chakras*, the seven Great Wheels of super/physical energy w/in the bod, aligned along the spine and strung together on a column called the Rod of Brahma. The chakras and Brahma's three/channeled Rod are all aspects of our astral wiring, part of the bod of light that is concentric w/our physical bods.

As the rising serpent lights up each of the chakras, they open like flowers and turn upward, from the red base Muladhara chakra through all of the other Great Wheels to the Sahasrara crown chakra, thus linking the negative and positive poles of the subtle body, thus achieving Union (Yoga), that blissful merging w/the Divine...

These are some of the major practices involved in causing the Kundalini force to rise:

> *Asanas;* postures, stretches, exercises for toning and aligning the physical bod, all advantageous to health, the raising of energy, and the clearing of the mind.

> *Mudras,* hand gestures for the shaping and drawing of power.

> *Mantras,* chants for focusing and occupying the conscious mind, vibratory attunements of the subtle bod.

> *Prahnayama,* ways of breathing that charge the mind & bod.

> *Trataka,* ways of focusing the eyes to likewise enhance the flow, inward and out, of various flavours of energy.

> *Yantra,* two/dimensional art which aligns the mind, furthering the raising of the Kundalini, taking the form of geometrical patterns or symbolic diagrams.

> *Dharana,* a technique for super/concentration.

As the fiery Kundalini serpent opens and alights each of the chakras in turn, the rising energy is enhanced and multiplied. Each chakra imparts its own powers and gifts and visions. Here are the Seven Great Wheels;

> *Muladhara;* red base chakra, to be found at the base of the spine; source of animal forces like sexual energy, lust, desire...

> *Svadhishthana;* orange chakra, nested below the navel, familial attachments...

_Manipura:_ yellow solar plexus chakra, home of Sun energy, physical bod/energy...

_Anahata:_ heart chakra, source of the healing green ray...

_Vishudda:_ sky/blue throat chakra for communication on the physical plane...

_Ajna:_ indigo/blue brow chakra, for telepathic communication w/humans and other sentient beings...

_Sahasrara:_ violet crown chakra, envisioned at the top of the head or above it, the supreme chakra, the thousand/petalled lotus, the gateway for the exchange of energies w/the All.


-Z


**ZBS MEDIA;** a wonderful group of early twenty/first century creative folk who do radio plays, some of the more famous being _Ruby_ and _The Fourth Tower of Inverness._

**ZZOG;** that which animates us all, the one who pulls the strings.